STARFIST
DOUBLE JEOPARDY

DOUBLE JEOPARDY

BOOK FOURTEEN

DAVID SHERMAN
AND
DAN CRAGG

BALLANTINE BOOKS • NEW YORK

Copyright © 2009 by David Sherman and Dan Cragg

Published in the United States by Del Rey, an imprint of The Random House Publishing Group, a division of Random House, Inc., New York.

DEL REY is a registered trademark and the Del Rey colophon is a trademark of Random House, Inc.

Library of Congress Cataloging-in-Publication Data

Sherman, David.
Double jeopardy / David Sherman and Dan Cragg.
p.   cm.—(Starfist ; bk. 14)
ISBN 978-0-345-50101-1
1. Marines—Fiction.   2. Life on other planets—Fiction.   I. Cragg, Dan.   II. Title.
PS3569.H4175D68 2010
813'.54—dc22   2009042831

Printed in the United States of America on acid-free paper

www.delreybooks.com

246897531

First Edition

Book design by Julie Schroeder

For:
Tam Cragg
First Sergeant, USMCR
Operations Desert Shield and Desert Storm, 1991–1992
Bosnia, 1996–1997
Iraq, 2002–2003

STARFIST
DOUBLE JEOPARDY

PROLOGUE

"Does the Mother bless this?" Hind Claw asked.

Mercury flicked a hand at Hind Claw's face, barely nicking the side of his snout. "You know the Naked Ones keep the men and women in separate camps," he snarled. "The Mother doesn't know about it."

"Then what does the Father say?" Hind Claw asked, not to be dissuaded in his search for proper authorization.

This time Bobtail smacked Hind Claw on the back of his head. "You know the Father is kept caged and guarded by the Naked Ones, so none can approach him."

Hind Claw slowly bobbed his head up and down on its long neck. "So," he said, "there is no authority for what you propose doing."

Mercury leaned forward with his knuckles on the ground and his head stretched out, his whiskers close enough to tickle the side of Hind Claw's face where he'd nicked it: the classic intimidation stance. "Proper authority or not," he said softly but threateningly, "it needs to be done."

"If we fail?" Hind Claw asked, unfazed by the threat.

"Then we are dead."

"And if we succeed?"

"Then we have freed the people of our clan," Ares said.

Hind Claw nodded again. "And we gain status in our clan." He looked into Mercury's eyes. "And you could challenge for the Father. I would like to be allied to the Father." He drew back far enough that Mercury's whiskers no longer tickled the side of his snout. He raised his head high, baring his neck in submission. Hind Claw had been the last of the six to be persuaded. They were ready now.

They took turns napping until the early moon set, then squeezed through the bars of the aboveground cage where they were kept at night.

"Where are you going?" a sleep-slurred voice asked, someone awakened by the sounds of their squeezing between bars that were more symbolic of imprisonment than intended to keep them in.

"We'll be back," Dewclaw whispered. "Go back to sleep." He heard a faint rustle as the questioner resettled himself next to his mates.

Hunched over, their narrow shoulders blending into long necks, the six slipped through the prison camp until they reached its edge. Mercury had scouted the way on several nights and he knew where the perimeter sentries were stationed. He also knew that the sentries would not be alert, that they weren't afraid of other, still-free clans launching a night attack. Besides, the sentries were positioned to watch out, not in.

They found the hidden armory that Mercury remembered preparing during the war against the Moon Flower Clan, a war that was interrupted by the arrival of the Naked Ones and their rapid sub-jugation of both the Moon Flowers and Mercury's own Bright Sun Clan.

The armory was well camouflaged; the Naked Ones had not found it, even though tracks on the ground made it clear that their vehicles had come by many times during the year they'd held the Bright Sun and Moon Flower clans in slavery and increased their sphere of control to include all the clans of Bright Sun's Brilliant

Coalition and Moon Flower's Starwarmth Union. For all Mercury knew, the Naked Ones had conquered part or even all of the world beyond those two nations.

The Naked Ones had come from the sky, roaring down in flaming sky vehicles such as none of the people had ever seen and only the most imaginative had ever conceived of. Their weapons were terrible, advanced far beyond the rifles and artillery of the people, and that, combined with the surprise and speed of their attack, had allowed them to conquer all the clans of two nations quickly and decisively. No one had been able to resist them for long, and none had been able yet to rise against the Naked Ones. At least not so far as Mercury had heard.

But the Naked Ones had become complacent, and Mercury believed it was time to strike at them, to begin to free his people. But to do that they needed weapons.

Getting into the hidden armory was harder than finding it. But get into it they did. They loaded themselves; each took two rifles and four hundred rounds. One carried a mortar tube and another a baseplate. The other four each took two of the canisters displaying the red skull, the mark of weapons that dispensed a lingering death. Each also carried four rounds for the mortar. They also each took four grenades. By the time they were finished, each was carrying his own weight in weapons and ammunition.

They would have liked to rest before the long run back to the prison camp, but there was too great a chance that the Naked Ones would notice they were missing in the morning. So, heavily laden, they ran until they were within half a kilometer of the camp, where they hid the weapons and ammunition in a place Mercury and Hind Claw had prepared over the previous several nights.

They only had an hour's sleep before the Naked Ones roused the camp for the day's labor in the mines.

After the night's exertions, the day was difficult for Mercury and his small team. But they took every opportunity they could to dig into the roof of the tunnel for grubs, worms, tubers, and anything else they could eat to give themselves energy; tonight would be just as difficult as last, even if they wouldn't have to run for hours carrying their own weight in weapons and ammunition. Last night they would have died if they had been caught; tonight they might die regardless.

Mercury already knew who the other eight he wanted to recruit were. Over the previous several weeks he'd listened carefully to the guarded grumblings of his fellow prisoners and sounded out those who seemed most realistic about what they'd do if the opportunity arose. The eight were also males alongside whom he'd fought the Moon Flowers or other clans with whom the Bright Sun Clan had been in conflict. During the day he and Hind Claw approached each of the eight and told them to slip from their cages after moon fall and meet at a specific location.

The two did not tell the eight why.

It was half an hour after the moon set before all fourteen were assembled. Even then, Mercury didn't tell them why—although their restrained excitement showed that they were sure of what was up.

"Follow me," Mercury whispered to his squad. "Keep your tails low until you see mine go up, then run as fast as you can to keep up with me." Mercury was well named; he was a very speedy runner.

Without another word, they followed their leader at a safe distance past a drowsy guard post, dropped to all fours to lope through the scrub, then galloped tails high when Mercury began his sprint.

It wasn't a long sprint; the weapons cache was only a half kilometer from the ill-guarded camp. Mercury whispered orders while he distributed the weapons and ammunition. The eight newcomers who joined Mercury's original half dozen grinned while they armed themselves and listened, memorizing their parts in the upcoming action.

Fourteen males. Not many to free an entire clan. But they would strike with speed and surprise, as had the Naked Ones when they first attacked. And the Naked Ones had become overly confident; they'd recently reduced the size of the force guarding the twin camps, one for the males and one for the females, in which they'd imprisoned the Bright Sun Clan.

The Naked Ones would pay dearly for that complacency.

Armed and with their instructions committed to memory, the fourteen spread out, going in pairs to their assigned attack positions, six of the positions within two hundred meters of a guard post. The mortar team remained farther out; its weapon had greater range and was to take out the camp office and the guard barracks.

None of them had a timepiece; those were among the personal items confiscated when they were interned in the camps. But everyone in the squad had put in his army time, and they were familiar with the heavens. The planet the Naked Ones called Opal was high in the night sky. When it entered the constellation of the Two-step Asp they were to listen for the mortar team to fire the shot that would launch the attack. Then they would fire on the guards in their stations and charge to kill them or drive them from their posts into the trenches the Naked Ones forced the People to dig as protection for the garrison. That was when the canisters marked with the red skull of the weapons of lingering death would come into play.

Mercury wasn't his real name. That was what he was called by the Naked Ones—at least by the Naked Ones who could tell the People apart. And Naked Ones was an ironic name, since they were not naked: They wore garments that covered all of their bodies except their heads and forearms. They were called the Naked Ones because they had no fur other than a short, thick thatch on the top of the head. Some of the Naked Ones had hair too thin to be called fur elsewhere on their bodies, as Mercury had discovered once when he saw some of them bathing. They also had a thick patch of fur at the groin, an area where the People had little or no fur. While the People wore swatches of animal skin or plant-fiber fabric for decoration or as symbols of rank, their languages and philosophies lacked the concept of modesty, so their hairy bodies had no need for clothing in the hot, arid climate in which they lived.

All the members of the squad watched the wandering star Opal as it moved through the sky nearer and nearer to the sinuous line of stars that formed the image of the deadly Two-step Asp. Mercury bared his teeth in a smile, thinking of how that night the constellation did augur death—the death of the Naked Ones who'd imprisoned his people.

Opal never moved rapidly against the starry background, and not nearly as fast as the moon. But on that night, with tension high, it seemed to move even more slowly than usual. Still, Opal did move, and eventually entered the constellation.

Karumph came the muffled sound of the distant mortar bomb being launched.

Mercury tensed and tried to imagine what the Naked Ones in their guard posts might make of the unexpected sound. Did they know it was the opening shot of an attack? Did they think it was distant thunder? Were they even awake and aware enough to recognize the sound as the launching of a mortar bomb?

Seconds later, there could no longer be any question that it was the beginning of an attack; the mortar impacted in the middle of the camp, near the Naked Ones' barracks. By the time it hit, a second mortar bomb was on its way, and then a third and a fourth and a fifth. The mortar team shifted aim slightly between rounds; a millimeter change in the angle of the mortar tube could make a change of meters in the striking point of the bomb.

Under and between the explosions in the middle of the camp, Mercury could make out the faint screams of wounded or frightened guards. A fire suddenly blazed where the mortars were striking; one had hit a fuel dump.

Now, with light to see by, Mercury made out an officer who was shouting orders and hastening the guards out of the area under bombardment, organizing them to go out of the camp in search of the mortar. Closer to him he saw, silhouetted against the flames, the two Naked Ones in the guard post directly in front of him. Instead of facing out, watching for an attack on their position, they were standing erect and looking into the camp at the bursting bombs and burning fuel.

Mercury reached out to touch the neck of Furball, with whom he was partnered, and told him what he wanted to do. Furball answered with a grin that was all teeth. The two took aim and shot at the standing guards. They were already loading fresh rounds into their rifles by the time the bullets they'd fired had hit their targets, and the standing guards dropped out of sight. The guards didn't rise again or return fire.

Mercury heard two more pairs of shots at other places around the perimeter and laughed to himself, certain that more guards had met the Two-step Asp, paying for taking the Bright Sun Clan into captivity.

By then the Naked Ones officer had his males organized and led them at a run toward the nearest gate through the fence. Mercury aimed at the officer, unsteadily seen through the flickering light of the burning fuel, led him, and fired. He rapidly reloaded and fired again. In the increasing darkness as the officer raced from the fire, Mercury couldn't judge his aim well enough; both shots missed. He stopped firing to preserve his ammunition. Besides, he had given away his position. He touched the back of Furball's neck, and the two left their position for another, from which they could better intercept the guards who were exiting the camp. Mercury had no way to be sure, but he was confident that at least two other pairs from his squad were also moving to intercept the guard force.

Mercury had been right about the wisdom of changing position; he saw half a dozen of the guards peel off and head, crouched, toward where he and Furball had been. But by the time those Naked Ones reached his former position, he and Furball would be on the other side of the guards who were heading for the mortar's position.

And they were. Mercury sniffed the air and picked up the scent of Ajax and Midnight moving in some fifty meters to his left as he faced the path of the approaching Naked Ones.

Good! Hind Claw and Junior were probably also approaching. Listening, watching, and sniffing, Mercury observed the Naked Ones as they neared his front. He hoped the other pairs would wait for him to fire first, but even if one of the others fired the first shot, his rifle would bark almost immediately. He did his best to aim at one of the guards and waited until the Naked One was almost directly to his front. He fired.

The others had obviously been waiting for him, as five more shots rang out almost simultaneously. The Naked Ones weren't far away, only seventy-five meters or so. From the cries and thuds, Mercury thought that at least three of them had been killed or wounded by the opening shots. As he reloaded he heard shots ring out in the distance as the other three pairs attacked their assigned guard posts.

Before him the Naked Ones had dropped to the ground and were manically returning fire. But they made little attempt to aim, and the shots that didn't strike the ground between Mercury and his males flew harmlessly overhead. *Flechettes,* Mercury had heard the Naked Ones' bullets called. He knew the flechettes were slender, needlelike, and that a flechette rifle seldom needed to be reloaded, unlike the rifles of the People, which had to be reloaded after every shot. Perhaps, Mercury thought, that was why the Naked Ones didn't aim as carefully as the People; if they put out enough fire, they believed that something had to hit. But only being able to fire one time before having to reload, the soldiers of the clans had to aim carefully. Besides, spending much of their lives in tunnels as the People did, they had excellent night vision, far better than the Naked Ones did. And the Naked Ones had almost no sense of smell at all.

So Mercury was confident that he and his five males could take on three times their own number in this night fight and win. Especially after the mortar team stopped firing at the middle of the camp and began dropping its bombs near the Naked Ones. Not long after that, the fire from the guards stopped.

Mercury called out for his own fighters to cease fire. He spent a long moment looking, listening, and sniffing. When the mortar stopped firing, Mercury called out instructions, and he and Furball slung their rifles across their bodies and loped, tails down, toward the end of the line of Naked Ones.

The Naked Ones were all dead or badly wounded. Mercury and Furball collected the Naked Ones' weapons and ammunition and moved them far enough away that the wounded couldn't easily reach them. He called for the rest of his men to come forward. Then he looked, listened, and sniffed for sign of the six guards who had peeled away from the main group and headed for the position he and Furball had originally held.

He smelled blood and fear. Moments later, he and Furball found two Naked Ones, one dead and the other critically wounded. They disarmed the two and returned to the other fighters.

There was still sporadic gunfire from inside the camp, but the boom of the clan's rifles outnumbered the sharper crack of flechette rifles. With all the Naked Ones' weapons and ammunition gathered, Mercury led his fighters into the camp. The fighting was over by the time they got inside. The six who had entered the camp earlier had already collected the enemy's weapons and ammunition and were opening the cages in which the People were held during the night.

The Father had been one of the first to be freed. Mercury hurried to him to report and was shocked by the condition of the clan's dominant male.

The Father didn't want all of the details, not now. He was too weak and in too much pain from the maltreatment he had suffered at the hands of the Naked Ones. After learning that all of the guards were dead or wounded, and satisfied that the wounded guards had not been executed—it was good that there were survivors to tell what had happened—the Father told Mercury to remain in command until he had freed the Mother and the rest of the females and then do as the Mother instructed as though Mercury were the Father.

Murmuring that he wasn't worthy, but not truly believing it, Mercury went to where the gate in the fence between the males' camp and the females' had been breached and sought out the Mother.

The Mother was also weak and in pain. She was even less interested in the details of how Mercury and his squad had accomplished what they did and quickly told him to continue in charge, to free all the members of the clan and lead them to safety.

It didn't take long to gather everybody; fewer than three hundred members of the Bright Sun Clan remained. The Mother and the Father weren't the only ones who had to be carried on litters, but there were enough others sound enough in body that carrying them wasn't an undue burden. They also took all of the Naked Ones' weapons and ammunition that they could find.

Before leaving, Mercury and two of his males took the eight canisters marked with the red skull of lingering death and put them in the tunnels in which the People had been harvesting stones for the Naked Ones. They put four of the canisters deep in the tunnels, set to spew their contents in a short while, after the males exited. The other four canisters they hid near entrances and other places in the tunnels, and attached hidden tripwires to them so that the next person to pass by would spew the lingering death they contained. It was a horrible weapon, but most likely Naked Ones would be the next to enter the tunnels.

Naked Ones were the next to enter the tunnels and several of them died horrible, lingering deaths before the decision was made to abandon and seal the tunnels.

In the fullness of time, individual Naked Ones completed their contracts and left the world their kind called Ishtar. And quite naturally, some of them told tales of the lingering death in bars and other gathering places elsewhere in Human Space. Once told, those tales of a killing gas eventually reached the ears of people who knew about an implacable enemy who used weapons that fired a horrible acid, and made a perhaps understandable connection between the horrible killing gas and the horrible killing acid.

CHAPTER ONE

Brigadier Sturgeon mounted the reviewing stand from the stairs at its rear. He'd briefly considered wearing chameleons for this appearance before his FIST but settled for garrison utilities rather than the dress reds that he customarily wore when he stood on the stand to address his Marines. Colonel Israel Ramadan, Thirty-fourth Fleet Initial Strike Team's chief of staff, and FIST Sergeant Major Bern Parant followed him, also in garrison utilities. The rest of the FIST's staff had remained at headquarters; they had work to do. And this was an occasion Sturgeon felt he had to face with minimal support.

Garrison utilities; this was not a ceremonial occasion. Sturgeon reached the podium and looked out over his force. The Marines stood at attention; no one moved in the thousand-plus man formation. Still, he sensed unease among his men. They were as unaccustomed as he was to appearing in formation on the FIST parade ground in garrison utilities rather than in dress reds.

They have a right, he thought, *to feel ill at ease.* They'd heard most of what he had to say after the Ravenette campaign, but he had more details now—and some changes. But they hadn't heard it right after fighting the Skinks.

"You all know," Sturgeon said without preamble, his amplified voice loud enough to carry to every man in the formation before him and beyond, to personnel working inside nearby buildings, "that the quarantine on Thirty-fourth FIST has been lifted. That was announced a few weeks ago. What everybody has been waiting for is to find out exactly what that means for us.

"The first thing it means is, nobody faces a Darkside penalty for revealing the existence of the Skinks; they are now public knowledge, thanks to President Chang-Sturdevant's announcement to the Confederation of Human Worlds." He shrugged. The Darkside penalty had been essentially meaningless so long as the Marines of Thirty-fourth FIST were restricted to Thorsfinni's World and left the unit's home world only on deployments.

"What you are all concerned with are retirements, rotations to new duty stations, and the end of active service for those of you who are not making a career of the Marines and have already served beyond your initial eight-year enlistment.

"Orders have been issued from the Heptagon. They apply to all members of every Confederation Army division, Confederation Navy air wing and starship, Confederation Marine FIST, and any other Confederation military element involved in the Skink war on Haulover. They do not necessarily apply to any planetary military forces that served on Haulover.

"Taking those concerns in order, and as they apply specifically to Thirty-fourth FIST:

"Those Marines who had put in for retirement before the quarantine went into effect are now eligible to be retired and may do so within the next six months. Anyone else who is eligible for retirement may put in an application, such retirement to take effect no sooner than four years from the date of application.

"All transfers to other duty stations are suspended for the duration." Sturgeon paused to look over his Marines again. They were still at attention, still standing stock-still; no murmurs or mutters reached his ears. But he could feel their morale melting away. All Marines in Thirty-fourth FIST, even the replacements still in Whiskey Company, were past their normal rotation dates. That wouldn't present any major problem with units stationed on more advanced worlds, but Thorsfinni's World was remote, and assignment to the Navy and Marine units and facilities on it was officially a hardship posting. Hence the normal two-year assignment, instead of the three or four or even more years at other duty stations. "There's a sound military reason for the continuing suspension of transfers," he continued, before his thoughts could affect his own morale. "Thirty-fourth FIST is the most experienced unit in dealing with aliens, hostile or otherwise. We've fought the Skinks every time we know of that they have come up against humanity. We fought the birdmen on Avionia. We fought alongside the headless hexapods on Society 419. No other human unit has fought the Skinks more than twice, and no other human unit has fought against or alongside other alien sentiences. The Confederation wants to keep its most experienced unit intact rather than dilute the experience by spreading us out by rotations to other units.

"The positive side of that is, we all have the honor of remaining with the most active, most highly decorated unit in the entire Confederation Marine Corps."

Sturgeon understood that many of his Marines would already be wondering why the Confederation didn't want other units to receive the benefit of Thirty-fourth FIST's experience by absorbing some of those "most experienced" Marines into their ranks, or how adversely their chances of surviving "the duration" were affected by remaining in the unit most likely to face the Skinks—or other potentially hostile aliens. He knew they were wondering those things because he was wondering them himself. But he didn't have an answer to that question, so he didn't give it voice.

Now Sturgeon had to give his Marines the worst news.

"You have known since we found out about the quarantine that all routine 'end of active duty' releases were suspended, that the term of service for everyone in Thirty-fourth FIST was extended for the duration. I imagine that you believe, or at least suspect, that now that the quarantine has been lifted, so has the involuntary extension for the duration of the Skink threat.

"That is not the case. Everyone in Thirty-fourth FIST, and a few other Confederation military units, is still in for the duration."

Sturgeon stopped talking and looked over his Marines again. Again, nobody moved; nobody said anything that he could hear. But he could feel morale plunge even further than it already had.

He knew that many, perhaps most of the Marines before him had joined not to start a career but to serve one enlistment. They joined the Marines to prove themselves to themselves or to someone else; they joined seeking an adventure; they joined in a quest to become "men," for the intangibles to be gained from eight years as members of a brotherhood, of an elite force; or they joined to carry on a family tradition of military service. Some from sufficiently impoverished backgrounds may have enlisted because being a Marine meant having a job that carried a certain degree of respect in the civilian community. But most didn't enlist for the money—most civilian occupations paid better than the Marines did, and with fewer risks to life and health.

While Brigadier Sturgeon himself had always intended to make a career of the Marines, by no means did he look down on those who only intended to serve one enlistment. To the contrary, he thought they formed the body and soul of the Corps. And most Marines, when they returned to civilian life after their time in the Corps, whether a full forty-year career or just one eight-year enlistment, were better, more productive citizens of the Confederation and their home worlds than they would have otherwise been.

With few exceptions, mostly in Whiskey Company, his Marines had served more than the eight-year term of the one enlistment most of them had expected to serve. He had to give them something to counter the bad news he'd just given them.

Fortunately, he had such news.

"Since Thirty-fourth FIST went into quarantine, promotions

from corporal on up have been almost totally limited to filling the billets of NCOs and officers killed or too severely injured to return to duty—which is a hell of a way to get a promotion.

"That means that many of you are still one or even two ranks below where you would have been in the normal course of events, had normal rotations been in effect.

"There aren't many Marines in Thirty-fourth FIST who are eligible for immediate retirement under the conditions I gave earlier. But everyone who does retire will open not only his own billet for someone to be promoted into, but will also open several promotion slots below his position."

Once more, there was no visible or audible reaction from within the formation, but Sturgeon hadn't expected any. After all, fewer than a platoon's worth of Marines in the FIST would be affected by the retirement-induced promotions. But most of them would be affected by what he had to say next, and the rest would be affected by it in the future.

"You will be interested to know that the Chairman of the Combined Chiefs, General Cazombi, backed up by the Commandant and the rest of the Combined Chiefs, went to President Chang-Sturdevant and Minister of War Berentus about the situation here. The President and the Minister of War then took them to the Congress to state their case.

"Congress, feeling both generous and appreciative for what Thirty-fourth FIST has done, has passed legislation moving every member of Thirty-fourth FIST who would normally have expected to be promoted by this time to be elevated to the next pay grade.

"Before you get too excited, you are not getting promoted, merely being given a pay raise.

"The pay raise is effective as of six weeks ago, the date the legislation was passed and signed. You will receive part of the six weeks of back-pay raise in your next pay, and the balance in your following pay. Following that, your pay should reflect the higher pay grades to which you are entitled by Act of Congress.

"I have one other item of good news. Most of you are beyond your normal end of enlistment. In the normal course of events, those of you who reenlisted would have received a reenlistment bonus. You will be pleased to know that the Stortinget, which you should know is Thorsfinni's World's legislature, has passed legislation granting monies equivalent to a reenlistment bonus to each individual in Thirty-fourth FIST who would have received such bonus had he reenlisted instead of being involuntarily extended. Within the next week you will each receive an envelope from the Thorsfinni's World government with that grant. The money will be paid in Thorsfinni's World Kroner, not in Confederation credits." He didn't mention that the legislature's act continued the granting of equivalent bonuses for as long as Thirty-fourth FIST's Marines were involuntarily extended—he didn't want his Marines thinking that they might be here for the rest of their lives. Instead, he said:

"That is all."

Still standing at Sturgeon's side, Colonel Ramadan bellowed, "FIST, a-ten-*tion!*"

A sharp *crack* sounded as the men of Thirty-fourth FIST snapped back to attention.

Sturgeon about-faced and as he left the reviewing stand heard Ramadan calling out the first of the series of commands that returned the individual units of the FIST to their company commanders.

"Fuck a pay raise," Lance Corporal "Wolfman" MacIlargie snarled as third platoon mounted the stairs to their quarters on the second floor of the barracks. "And a fake reenlistment bonus! I don't give a rat's ass about the money, I want *out* of this chicken outfit."

Corporal Claypoole, on the step above MacIlargie, half turned and rapped the junior man on the top of his head.

"Hey," MacIlargie objected, rubbing his head. "What's that for?"

"That's for not appreciating what General Cazombi and the

Stortinget did for you," Claypoole said, and raised his hand as though to land another hit. MacIlargie ducked out of the way.

MacIlargie wasn't the only one grumbling; there was a sussuration of complaints throughout the company, punctuated by an occasional shouted curse. Captain Conorado, the other officers, and the company's senior NCOs hung back, letting the men and junior NCOs give voice to their disappointment and displeasure. They knew the men needed to vent; they also knew that if they tried to intervene they'd take out their own frustrations on their Marines, and that would be unproductive.

"All of you, company office, now," Conorado said to the officers and senior NCOs. He rousted the company clerks and waited for First Sergeant Myer to close the door before saying anything.

"Well, that announcement shot morale all to hell," Conorado said. "We have to do something right away to keep morale from dropping any further. Suggestions?"

"We need to keep them too busy to think about it," Myer said.

"Right. But doing what? We don't have any field training scheduled."

"Inspections," Gunny Thatcher suggested.

"Close order drill," second platoon's Staff Sergeant Chway said.

"PT," Ensign Antoni offered.

"Forced marches or runs, in full gear," said Lieutenant Rokmonov.

"They're going to be trashing their quarters about now," Lieutenant Bass said. "I say we start off with a field day. Make the barracks sparkle like we're expecting the Inspector General."

"All good ideas," Conorado said before anybody else could toss out an idea of how to keep their Marines busy. "But I think Charlie's come up with the best starting point. Platoon sergeants, go bust your men's nuts about cleaning the barracks. Decide among yourselves who's responsible for the classroom, the rec room, and other common areas. Don't forget the supply shack. Officers, work with Top Myer and the Gunny to draw up plans for the other busy work.

"Do it."

There was a chorus of *aye ayes* and the platoon sergeants filed out of the company office.

"Mr. Humphrey," Conorado said to the company executive officer, "take charge of the planning team. I'll be in my office."

Conorado retired to his tiny office and closed the door before he sat at his small desk. He had everybody in his company getting too busy to dwell on the things that were hurting their morale. Now to figure out how he was going to deal with his own plummeting frame of mind.

The field day, quite naturally, was greeted with howls of protest. Nobody but *nobody* ever wanted to have a field day. At least not the Marines who had to do the work. Probably not any of the Marines who had to supervise a field day, either. There were many things a young person might expect to have to do when they enlisted in the Marines, but a house cleaning that would make the most neurotically spic-and-span of their mothers look slovenly didn't even make the list—not even the list of unpleasant things they imagined they might be called upon to do.

But the platoon sergeants were quickly joined by the squad leaders in getting everybody to work cleaning their quarters and the common areas. The squad leaders' hopes of avoiding any real work themselves in favor of supervising their men were quickly dashed when the platoon sergeants put them to work cleaning their own quarters. The platoon sergeants were then very busy making sure everybody was hard at work.

"Summers, Shoup," Corporal Doyle said to his two men, "pack everything up." Even as he gave the order, he was stowing all of his clothing into his seabag and civilian suitcase and securing everything from the top of his desk in the desk's drawers.

"Ah, everything?" PFC Summers asked.

"Everything."

"C-can I ask why, Corporal Doyle?" PFC Shoup asked.

"Because we're going to strip this room bare before we begin cleaning it."

Summers stood in the middle of the fire team's room, looking around. "Where are we going to put everything when we strip the room bare?" he asked.

Doyle looked at him; Shoup was already packing his belongings. "Outside. Where do you think?"

"Outside?"

"Outside. Now get to it."

Summers began packing, but slowly. "What's going to keep somebody from stealing stuff?"

Doyle paused in his own packing and looked at his senior man. "A company of Marine grunts, that's what." He turned back to the last of his packing. "Don't worry, there'll be a guard on the gear. Everybody's doing it."

"Really?" Summers sounded as if he didn't believe his fire team leader. As though to prove his doubt, he stopped packing and stepped into the corridor to check what other fire teams were doing. About half the other fire teams were also packing, and some of the Marines were beginning to carry their belongings down the stairs. Summers groaned and reentered the room he shared with Doyle and Summers and resumed packing. Doyle was already finished and Shoup wasn't very far behind.

"Get a move on, Summers," Doyle said. "You're never going to get your crossed blasters this way."

Summers mumbled something about being overdue for a promotion anyway but sped up his packing.

"No, you're not," Doyle muttered back.

"Shoup," Doyle ordered, "go outside, directly below our window. I'll drop our bags down to you. Keep them together, about five meters out from the wall. Stay with them until I tell you otherwise."

"Catch our bags that you're going to drop down to me. Right." Shoup left the room and headed for the stairs, shaking his head.

A minute or so later he was where Doyle had sent him and looked up.

"Catch," Doyle called down to him, and dropped his own seabag.

Shoup had to take a step to his side to catch the bag, but he was a little too close to the wall and nearly fell over backward when the seabag hit his arms. Still, he managed to maintain his feet.

"Do you see how to do it now?" Doyle asked.

"Got it, Corporal Doyle." Shoup positioned himself to catch the next one, a civilian suitcase. Instead of trying to catch it in his extended arms as he had the seabag, he clapped his hands against its sides and redirected it to his side and rear. It landed next to the seabag. Shoup grinned up at Doyle. "Got it!" he called.

Doyle dropped the next two bags. By then, Summers had his packed.

"Go down to the supply shack," Doyle told Summers. "Tell Sergeant Souavi I need a fifteen-meter length of rope. Tell him *I* need it, not you need it. Sergeant Souavi trusts me."

Summers thought for a second, not knowing why Doyle wanted a length of rope. "What if he doesn't have a fifteen-meter length?"

"Then get the shortest length he has that's more than fifteen meters."

"Fifteen meters or the shortest length longer than fifteen meters. Tell him *you* want it, because he trusts you," Summers muttered as he headed for the supply shack. *What does fifteen meters of rope have to do with a field day?* he wondered.

Other fire team leaders saw what second squad's third fire team was doing and began tossing items out the window to waiting men. Some made a game of it, the tosser seeing if he could make the catcher miss or, better yet, catch a bag off balance so that he'd fall over. The fire teams that didn't have windows facing the side where the bags were getting lined up crossed over to the rooms that did.

By the time Summers got back with a sixty-meter length of rope,

Doyle had already dropped the stripped mattresses and bundled linens and pillows down to Shoup and was lining the furniture up next to the window. Some of the other fire team leaders were organizing a fire brigade chain to pass smaller pieces of furniture down the stairs to the side yard.

"Come on, Doyle," Corporal Chan said as he passed third fire team's room. "Get with the program and join the fire brigade."

Doyle ignored the squad's senior fire team leader and took the rope from Summers.

"What are you going to do with that?"

"Do you know how to tie a timber hitch?"

"A what?"

Doyle looked disbelievingly at Summers. "You don't even know what a timber hitch is?"

Summers shook his head, wondering what had gone wrong with his fire team leader.

"It's a kind of knot that sailors on old oceangoing ships used to hoist barrels and stuff."

"I'm not *any* kind of sailor. Forget about old oceangoing ships."

"Wood ships, with canvas sails," Doyle said, managing to maintain a straight face.

Summers looked at him aghast. "Wooden ships with canvas sails? What does that have to do with anything?"

"It's how we're going to lower our furniture. Watch." Slowly at first, but more quickly as his hands remembered how to tie the knot he hadn't used since his boyhood in the Young Pioneers, he tied the knot around his desk. "Hold this tight," he said, and climbed into the open window so that he straddled the sill. "Keep the rope tight." He bent over and lifted the tiny desk over the sill and let it hang. "Okay, let go of the rope and hold on to me!" As soon as Summers had a grip on him, he leaned out so that the desk was away from the wall and began lowering it. "It's a good thing all of our books are electronic," he said. "If our desks were full of hard-copy books, they'd be too heavy to lower this way." When the desk reached the ground he gave the rope some slack and the knot fell apart. Doyle used a different knot to lower the chairs.

In minutes, all three desks were down and Shoup had them arranged with their other things. A small crowd gathered to watch.

"You know, sometimes Doyle really surprises me," Corporal Dean said to Corporal Claypoole.

Claypoole shrugged. "Before Sergeant Linsman was killed, he was in Sergeant Kerr's fire team—uh, Sergeant Kerr was a corporal then. . . ."

Dean knuckled him in the shoulder. "I know that, dumb guy."

Claypoole gave Dean a nasty look. "Sergeant Kerr said Doyle had the makings of a good Marine," he said in a questioning tone, as though he didn't really believe it.

Corporal Dornhofer, who was standing nearby watching, chimed in: "And remember how he figured out how to make the Tweed Hull Breacher work without exploding."

Dean and Claypoole looked at Dornhofer, then at each other. They shook their heads. "But it's *Doyle*," they said.

"All right people," Staff Sergeant Hyakowa called out. "Shit-can the grabassing and get back to work."

Everybody got.

Whether by fire brigade chain or by rope, it wasn't long before all the rooms—even the squad leaders' room—were emptied. Staff Sergeant Hyakowa assigned the gun squad's Lance Corporal Dickson, who still was suffering from being wounded by Skink acid on Haulover, to guard the platoon's belongings. He sent one man from each fire team, under the supervision of Corporal Dean, who was also not back up to full strength after being wounded on Haulover, to clean the company rec room.

Eventually all the interior cleaning was finished and everything from outside cleaned and restored to its proper place in the barracks rooms. The platoon sergeants held inspections, followed by the platoon commanders. Captain Conorado and First Sergeant Myer inspected last.

Everybody passed. After all, the objective of the field day wasn't to pass an IG, it was to keep the Marines too busy to dwell on their indefinite extensions, and lack of transfers and promotions.

CHAPTER TWO

The classroom was crowded with all 123 members of Company L, Thirty-fourth Fleet Initial Strike Team. No exceptions; everyone was there from Captain Conorado on down to the newest replacement who hadn't joined the company until it returned to Camp: Major Pete Ellis, who had arrived following Thirty-fourth FIST's return from combat against a Skink army on Haulover. The company's four corpsmen were in attendance. Even First Sergeant Myer and the company clerks, who just about *never* attended company formations, were jammed into the classroom.

The Marines and sailors were dressed in garrison utilities, though a few may have been wishing they were in their dress reds so they could show off the hero medals they'd been awarded for their actions on Haulover. So it was a small sea of dull green that Captain Cervera, the S3 Operations Officer of Thirty-fourth FIST's infantry battalion, looked over when he mounted the small stage to stand at the podium after Conorado introduced him. Other staff officers from FIST and battalion headquarters were meeting with other platoons and combat support elements of the FIST at the same time.

"Good morning, Marines!" Cervera said in a booming voice that identified him as having been a gunnery sergeant, or at least a senior staff sergeant, when he got his commission.

"Good morning, sir!" the Marines thundered back loudly enough to make Sergeant Souavi, Company L's supply sergeant, glad the windows were open. If the sonic shock had broken any closed windows, it would have been Souavi's responsibility to repair or replace them. But Souavi didn't let any expression show in his face. Like the other Marines in the company, he looked stony-faced back at the battalion S3.

"As you were!" Cervera boomed while the echoes of the Marines' reply were still reverberating throughout the room. An expectant silence instantly fell over the room, save for incidental sounds that drifted in from outside.

"Thirty-fourth FIST," the S3 continued with somewhat less volume, "has just returned from another successful campaign against the foe we call Skinks. Nobody knows better than Company L—and particularly the third platoon." His gaze picked out the Marines he recognized as being in third platoon. "You've faced the Skinks more often than anybody else—and you've always been victorious against them. Believe me, when I say 'you,' I mean the Marines in this room. *You* are the Confederation's best, most experienced Skink fighters.

"Thus far, every time we've fought the Skinks, it's because they attacked humanity and we had to mount a counterattack. Every time we've met the Skinks, they've had new weapons and tactics, weapons and tactics that caught us by surprise every time. And every time, we've quickly come up with tactics to counter what the Skinks were doing. I think we can be certain that in the future, when we meet the Skinks again—and we will—that they'll again have new weapons and tactics that we'll have to find a way to counter. And we *will* counter and overcome those new weapons and tactics.

"So far, we don't know who the Skinks are, where they come from, or why they attack human worlds without ever attempting to communicate with us. But every available intelligence and scientific resource, not only military but civilian, is analyzing everything we have on the Skinks. I assure you that the next time we meet the Skinks, we will know more about them.

"The Commandant wants you to know that at some date in the future, *humanity* is going to pick the time and place of a fight with the Skinks. By order of the President and resolution of the Congress of the Confederation of Human Worlds, the Confederation Navy has embarked on an intensive search for the home world of the Skinks. And when that home world is found, the Confederation military will launch a massive assault on it, to put an end to Skink depredations of human worlds."

Cervera paused to look the Marines in the eye; they looked back, hard faced. "Rest assured," he continued, "when that invasion comes, Thirty-fourth and Twenty-sixth FISTs will be the spear point. Between now and then we will be training on how to fight the Skinks on their own territory." One hundred and twenty-three hard, stony faces looked him right back in the eye.

Captain Cervera continued from there, telling the Marines everything known about the Skinks and actions against them, nearly all of which the Marines of Company L already knew. He didn't tell them about the juvenile Skink found on Kingdom, that later disappeared on Earth. Then again, he didn't know about the juvenile Skink, so it's not that he was withholding anything.

After an hour, Cervera wrapped things up and took his leave. During his entire presentation, nobody had muttered or showed any expression.

"Seats!" Captain Conorado ordered when the S3 was gone. There was a momentary clatter as the Marines resumed their seats after having stood at attention while Cervera left. He gave his men a long, hard look. Even though, sitting in the front row with his back to the company, he hadn't seen their reaction to the presentation, he was fully aware of the stony silence that met the words of the battalion operations officer.

"Marines," he said firmly, reminding them of who they were and what was expected of them, "you heard the word: We are going into training for a possible invasion of the Skink home world. FIST, battalion, and squadron headquarters have already been working on training plans. Gunny Thatcher will now brief you on what you need to know before we go into the field." He looked at Thatcher, who was sitting in the front row.

"Gunnery Sergeant."

"Sir!" Thatcher said, standing and mounting the stage.

"The company is yours."

"The company is mine, aye aye, sir." Thatcher stood at attention facing the room and barked "A-ten-*tion*!" as Conorado stepped off the stage and strode out of the classroom. The other officers, First Sergeant Myer, and the company clerks followed.

"Siddown," Thatcher snarled when first platoon's Staff Sergeant DaCosta closed the door behind the departing officers. He glared at the Marines as they resumed their seats. "I heard what you said while Captain Cervera was talking." The Marines, at least from squad leaders on down, looked at him expressionlessly. "And you're saying the same fucking thing to me. I'm telling you right now, I'm not going to stand for it. You're Marines, I expect you to behave like Marines. You've got a job to do, and you're going to do it to the best of your ability. Nobody said you have to like it. I don't give a kwangduk's ass if you don't like it. I don't either. But we're going to do our jobs, and we're going to do them better than anybody else.

"Now. Next week we're mounting out to Sumpig Island." He grinned a shark's grin. "Sumpig's a wonderful tropical paradise. You're going to love it."

"What is this happy horseshit?" Lance Corporal MacIlargie yelled as soon as third platoon reached its squadbay corridor. "First we get extended for the duration, then we get indefinitely extended on Thorsfinni's World, and now we start training for an invasion of the Skink home world. And nobody has any idea where the goddamn place is, or what it's like!"

Sergeant Tim Kerr gave Corporal Rachman Claypoole a meaningful look: *He's your man, control him.*

Claypoole didn't have to do or say anything, Lance Corporal

Dave Schultz beat him to it. Schultz didn't *do* anything, and he didn't exactly *say* anything, either. The big man merely growled something not quite intelligible.

MacIlargie shot Schultz a startled look and edged away. He also stopped complaining.

MacIlargie wasn't the only man in the platoon who was unhappy about what Captain Cervera had said; he was just the first and loudest to give voice to his unhappiness. The Marines quickly converged on their squad leaders, forming three distinct clumps of men in the corridor. Lieutenant Bass was careful to stay wherever the officers had gone, and Staff Sergeant Hyakowa studiously avoided going to the platoon's billeting area.

As the senior fire team leader in first squad, Corporal Dornhofer started off by demanding of his squad leader, "Sergeant Ratliff, what do you know about this that we don't?"

Ratliff spread his hands and shook his head. "I don't know a damn thing that you don't, Dorny. You got everything that I know at the same time I found out about it." As he spoke, he tried to edge past Dornhofer, but Corporals Pasquin and Dean, along with three other members of the squad, blocked his way.

"If you don't know, who does?" Pasquin demanded.

"And how soon are you going to find out?" Dean added.

"Yeah, who knows?" a chorus of voices called out. "And when will you find out?"

Just a couple of meters away, Kerr, the tallest man in the platoon, stared down the members of his squad who were blocking his way. By himself, he might not have been able to do it, but Schultz stood at his side and began moving forward. When Schultz moved, people tended to get out of his way. Kerr followed in his wake. Even first squad made a hole for Schultz. Ratliff took advantage of the brief opening and trailed Kerr closely enough that Kerr asked, "You trying to tell me something back there, Rabbit? You're getting awful friendly."

"Hey, wait for me!" Sergeant Kelly, the gun squad leader, cried. He managed to break through the knot of Marines surrounding him.

Schultz turned into his fire team's room, leaving the three squad leaders to fast-step to their room at the far end of the corridor. They ignored the questions and rapid footsteps coming after them and managed to reach their sanctuary before anybody caught up.

Safe behind the closed door, they dropped into the chairs in front of their tiny desks and looked at one another.

After a long moment, Kerr broke the silence. "There's going to be a lot of shot morale out there."

"Forget about out there," Ratliff said. "We've got to deal with the shot morale in here, first."

"Got that right," Kelly said. "Right now I feel even lower than I did when Barber got killed."

"Living on the point of the spear," Ratliff said, nodding.

"A *bloody* point that's in serious danger of getting blunted," Kerr said.

"Or even broken," Kelly murmured.

"Buddha's blue balls," Ratliff said softly. "Imagine, Marine squad leaders talking like this." He shuddered.

Kerr and Kelly exchanged haunted looks.

The corridor slowly emptied as the junior Marines filtered into their fire team rooms.

In his room, Corporal Dean sat at his desk, turned on his library, and pretended to look something up. He knew his men, PFCs Francisco Ymenez and John Three McGinty, had questions. He also knew that he didn't have any answers. During the years he'd been in third platoon, so many years that he was already past his initial eight-year enlistment without having ever reenlisted, he'd lost many friends and comrades to death or crippling at enemy hands. With these latest rapid-fire announcements, his being involuntarily extended "for the duration," no transfers, and preparations for an invasion of the still-unlocated Skink home world, he was almost overwhelmed with a feeling of dread that he wouldn't live long enough to make the decision whether to reenlist.

Damn, damn, and triple damn. He almost had to smile at that last. *It was Triple* John, *not triple damn. So make that "damn, damn, damn."* "Damn," he whispered.

"Did you say something, Corporal Dean?" Ymenez asked.

"What? No. No, I didn't say anything. Just thinking."

Corporal Pasquin sat straddling his chair, his arms folded across the top of its back, looking from Lance Corporal Quick to Lance Corporal Longfellow and back. He didn't take enough time to let them get too uncomfortable under his penetrating look before saying, "Now you know why they call it the Crotch. They've got Mohammet's pointy teeth clamped on our nuts and there's not a damn thing you, you, me, or anyone else can do about it."

Quick and Longfellow looked at each other, saw no help there, and turned back to Pasquin.

"So what are we going to do?" Quick asked. Longfellow just nodded.

Pasquin sat erect, filled his chest with air, blew it out in a huff. "What we're going to do is train. Train like we've never trained before. You just know that the first wave to make planetfall on the Skink home world is going to catch the worst of the shit. The best chance we have of coming through it is to be prepared for whatever the Skinks have waiting for us. So we're going to train like the Virgin's short and curlies are waiting to give us a reward if we train hard enough."

Pasquin gripped the top of his chair back, leaned against his desk, and closed his eyes. He didn't say anything about how much tougher the fighting had gotten for the U.S. Marines during the biggest war of the twentieth century as their campaigns got closer to the Japanese mainland. But he thought about it.

Corporal Claypoole wanted to say some things. He'd never intended to make a career of the Marines, but here he was, well into what would have been his second eight-year enlistment—if he'd been given the choice—and it was looking more and more like the only way he'd get out was in a flag-draped box. He could have imagined himself old, bent, and doddering, still on active duty, except that he couldn't imagine having enough luck to live that long. Not with all the deployments Thirty-fourth FIST had. Not with Thirty-fourth FIST being the designated first wave for an invasion of the Skink home world. Claypoole had thought his morale was low when Brigadier Sturgeon announced the extensions for the duration, and the no-transfer policy. But this . . . Designated first wave? He didn't think he could sink any further.

Hey! He could marry Jente! Then when the Marines found out he was married even though he was only a corporal, he'd get court-martialed, thrown in the brig for the duration, and not be in that first wave!

Nah. The way things were going, the Marines wouldn't care that he got married before he reached staff sergeant—which he probably wouldn't, unless Staff Sergeant Hyakowa, all three squad leaders, and a bunch of other corporals were killed in that invasion.

Lance Corporal MacIlargie sat at his tiny desk, facing the wall, with his library open in front of him. He wasn't reading anything or looking anything up. He was just staring at the screen, trying not to think about what had just happened. He knew that if he did, he'd explode, and if he did, Hammer Schultz would be all over him like slop on a hog. Then it would be Claypoole's turn, and anybody could see he wanted someone to take his anger out on. Then Sergeant Kerr. Then Staff Sergeant Hyakowa. Then Lieutenant Bass. Hell, he'd probably get his ass hauled up in front of the Skipper. If there was enough left of his ass to haul after Top Myer got through with him.

He folded his arms on his desk and dropped his head onto them, trying not to cry.

For his part, Lance Corporal Schultz was content. He was a member of the FIST that got deployed into harm's way more often than any other unit in the Confederation military, which meant he had more opportunity to fight than he would in any other posting.

And, once the Skink home world was found, he would be in the first wave to make planetfall. Now *that* would be a challenge for a fighting man.

He opened his library and started studying the twentieth-century campaigns of the U.S. Marines and the Royal Marines, the direct ancestors of the Confederation Marine Corps. He was sure he'd find something in those histories that would help in the invasion of the Skink home world.

In his office, Captain Conorado looked at the busywork training schedule he'd had drawn up to counter plummeting morale. What they'd done so far had staved off the worst, but today's announcement of Thirty-fourth FIST being the spear point—well, he knew morale would be dropping again, and more rapidly. It would be a couple of days yet before they headed to the field to begin training for the invasion so he had to put his Marines through more busywork.

"Gunny!"

"Yes, sir." Gunnery Sergeant Thatcher appeared in the doorway of Conorado's office.

"Assemble the company. We're going to have an hour of PT, then a fifteen-K run." He paused to consider, then added, "Sweats, not full gear."

"Aye aye, sir. How soon do you want to start?"

"Fifteen minutes." That would give him plenty of time to change into his own sweats. He needed busywork as much as his Marines did.

Two and a half hours later, the company ran back into the company area behind the barracks.

Breathing heavily, Conorado surveyed his company for a moment. Everybody was there except Corporal Palmer, who had stayed behind to answer the comm. As bad as their morale had to be, his Marines had held formation through the entire run; nobody had fallen out. They were looking a bit ragged, and some were bent over, hands on knees, lungs heaving, but they had come through fine. Maybe the exertion had raised their morale a bit. He knew he was feeling better than he had before the PT had begun. Now it was time for a break. It was only 15 hours, an hour shy of the normal time for the start of liberty, but he wanted to give something to his Marines.

"Listen up!" Conorado called out. "When I dismiss you, hit the showers. Every platoon commander is authorized to sound liberty call for his platoon as soon as everybody in his platoon is showered and in civvies."

He paused to look over the company again, then loudly and clearly called out, "Company L, dismissed!"

The Marines broke ranks and sprinted for the barracks. Yes, an early liberty call was exactly the right thing to do. Now to shower and change himself, so he could get home to Marta.

CHAPTER THREE

"Liberty call, liberty call, liberty call!" Staff Sergeant Hyakowa's voice rang out through third platoon's squadbay. Echoes rang from the squadbays of Company L's other platoons as their platoon sergeants announced liberty call.

Liberty call: free time. The chance to go to the base theater, or one of the on-base eateries instead of the mess hall. Opportunity to partake in any of the recreational facilities offered on Camp Major Pete Ellis. Or time to pull on civvies and head for the pleasures of Bronnoysund—or anyplace else on Thorsfinni's World that one could get to and then back from by the next morning formation.

Some of the Marines were on their way out of the barracks before the last "Liberty call!" sounded. But not all of them.

Corporal Joe Dean, in his fire team's room, had started stripping out of his olive drab garrison utilities as soon as the first "Liberty call!" sounded, but only got as far as shucking off his shirt and loosening his trousers before collapsing back onto his rack, with one foot on the floor and the other hanging over the side of his mattress. He reached to pull his pillow under his head, then folded his arms over his chest and lay staring at the ceiling.

PFC John Three McGinty didn't notice immediately; he was too busy changing into his civvies. When Thirty-fourth FIST returned from fighting the Skinks on Haulover, pretty Stulka, one of the serving girls at Big Barb's, had attached herself to him, and he was anxious to see if she still wanted to dally.

Lance Corporal Francisco Ymenez, on the other hand, still not quite certain about his acceptance in the platoon and without a girl to call his own, was slow enough about deciding whether to head for Bronnys or do something on base that he noticed his fire team leader's odd behavior. Normally, Dean started liberty by hustling Corporals Claypoole and Chan to the liberty bus for the short ride into town.

"Ah, what's the matter, honcho?" Ymenez hesitantly asked. "Corporal Dean?" he asked when he didn't get a response.

"Hm? What? No, nothing's the matter," Dean said in a flat voice. "Everything's five-by. You head for town and enjoy yourself." He didn't look away from the ceiling.

By this time, McGinty had noticed Dean lying half dressed on his rack. "You sure, honcho?" He was already halfway into the corridor that ran the length of the squadbay.

Dean sighed. "Yeah, I'm sure." He didn't look at either of his men.

"You don't look like nothing's the matter."

"I'm fine!" Dean snapped. "Now go away and leave me alone. Both of you."

Ymenez and McGinty looked at each other, and Ymenez quickly began changing into his civvies. Before he was finished, there was a quiet shuffling of moving bodies at the door. Ymenez grabbed a shirt and his shoes and almost ran to join McGinty in the corridor. He caromed off a large body on his way. The large body didn't seem to notice. It rumbled into third fire team's room and stopped less than a meter from Dean's rack.

"Up!" The one word cracked like the first boulder that sets off a monumental avalanche.

"Fuck you and the horse you rode in on," Dean mumbled. He lifted one arm from his chest and draped it across his eyes.

The large body reached for Dean's leg, stopped when a hand

clamped on its arm, looked at the hand, looked into the face of Corporal Claypoole.

Who looked up into those deadly eyes, swallowed, let go, and took a quick step back. After all, that *was* Hammer Schultz whose arm he'd just grabbed. "Don't hurt him," Claypoole said, taking another step back. "He's a corporal. You'll get in trouble for assaulting an NCO."

Schultz shook his head. Claypoole hoped the negative meant "I won't hurt him" and not "I don't care if I get in trouble."

"Come on, Hammer. Dean-o's still recovering from his wounds."

"He's okay," Schultz rumbled, staring down at Dean, who showed no indication that he was concerned about the threatening figure looming above him.

In the corridor, Ymenez, McGinty, and Lance Corporal MacIlargie cautiously peered around the door frame into the room. Another figure suddenly loomed behind them.

"What's going on here?" Sergeant Lupo Ratliff demanded.

Schultz turned half toward the door and hooked a thumb at Dean. "Crybaby."

Ratliff looked at Schultz, at Dean, back at Schultz. "You three," he said to the trio in the corridor, all in civvies though Ymenez's shirt was fastened awry. "Get your asses to the liberty bus. Claypoole, see to it. Keep them in town for a few hours. Hammer, go with them. Keep them out of trouble."

Schultz cocked an eyebrow and hooked a thumb at Dean again, a question this time.

"I'll deal with him." Ratliff stepped aside so Claypoole and Schultz could get by then entered the room and pulled a chair close to Dean's rack. He sat down and looked at him for a long moment, thinking about what to say; he was pretty sure he knew what the problem was. "So talk to me," he finally said.

"Leave me alone."

"Forget it, Rock. I'm *not* going to leave you alone. I know what's going on here, and I know you have to deal with it. So talk to me."

"You don't know shit about what's going on."

Ratliff blew out a breath. "I don't know shit about what's going on. Let's see. You lost a man on Haulover and got wounded yourself. I lost a man on Haulover and had another man get wounded badly enough that he was stuck in a stasis bag and left there until we returned to Camp Ellis and he could be hospitalized. A few months before that, on Ravenette, I had four men get wounded, and two old friends got killed. What part of that is it that don't I know shit about?"

Dean suddenly sat up, swung his legs over the side of his rack, and gripped its side. "*You* weren't almost killed when the Skinks killed Izzy. *You* didn't spend all that time in a stasis bag. *You* act like it doesn't mean anything to you when someone gets killed or wounded."

Ratliff flinched at the accusation but remained calm. "You're right," he said. "I didn't almost get killed by the Skinks, I didn't spend a lot of time in a stasis bag, and I *act* like it means anything to me when Marines get killed or wounded. But that *act*"—he shoved his face close to Dean's and snarled—"is just that, an *act*!

"It tears me up inside when one of my men, one of my *friends,* gets wounded or killed. But I'm a *Marine*! Marines get wounded, Marines get killed. And *Marines* learn to *live* with it." He lowered his voice. "Because if you *don't* learn to live with it, you're liable to get yourself killed. And you're a fire team leader; you can get your *men* killed if you can't live with it. What do you think would happen to this squad if I showed how I felt when my Marines got wounded, got killed? If I showed how torn up I was when an old friend got killed? Huh?

"I'll tell you what would happen. You and everybody else in the squad would start thinking I wasn't able to do my job. You'd think I was in a state that would put *your* life in jeopardy, that *you* could get killed because *I* was upset. And then Marines under me *would* get killed. Because nobody would trust me to be right when I gave them orders. *That's* what would happen if I didn't act like casualties don't bother me."

He pulled back and gave Dean a chance to say something. When Dean didn't, he said, "But that's not what's bothering you. You've been wounded before. You've lost men before, you've lost friends. So talk to me—and don't give me any of that 'you don't know shit' shit!"

Dean's face slowly changed until he looked haunted. "We're going to die, Rabbit. All of us. Every time the Skinks show up some-place, they're going to send *us* to fight them. And get killed!" He looked into Ratliff's eyes. "And we don't get time off for good behav-ior. It doesn't matter how well we do against the Skinks, they'll keep sending us after them. Again, and again, and again, until we're all *dead!*"

Ratliff slowly shook his head. "Listen to me, Rock. We're Marines, we go in harm's way. Always have, always will. It doesn't matter if it's local warlords, pirates, rebellious worlds, Skinks, other aliens, or anyone else. You know that, because you've gone against all those things. When we go in harm's way, there's always a risk of Marines getting wounded or even killed. There's a risk of me getting killed, there's a risk of you getting killed.

"*But,* and take this in and tattoo it on your heart and brain, the more we know about the enemy, and the smarter we fight, the fewer of us who become casualties.

"Third platoon has fought the Skinks three times now. They caught us by surprise the first two times. The second time, nearly half the Marines in the platoon were wounded, and some were killed. Hell"—he shook his head at the memory—"we even thought Lieu-tenant Bass got killed."

"Right, half the platoon was casualties on Kingdom. That proves my point!"

"Bullshit it does! They surprised us on Kingdom because we thought we were going up against some religious fanatics. Then the Skinks surprised us with rail guns and light armor.

"And we cleaned their clocks! We killed almost all of them, and chased the survivors out of Human Space! On Haulover, we knew who we were going up against. This time they surprised us with aircraft. The platoon only had three casualties and we wiped them out completely! We fought smarter and better, and we came out in better shape than the last time we'd fought them.

"One of the ways we fight smart is this: Our leaders, from the highest general all the way down to fire team leaders, don't show how torn up they are at losing men. And the result is, we lose fewer Marines.

"Get that through your mind, Corporal Dean. And get a grip. Your men rely on you; their lives depend on them believing in you. If you show how upset you are, they can't believe in you, and that *will* get them killed."

He sat back and folded his arms across his chest, waiting for Dean's reaction. After a long moment, Dean shook himself and sat up straight.

"Since you put it that way, yeah, that makes sense." He shuddered. "But the Skinks still scare the shit out of me."

Ratliff laughed. "Dean, when third platoon ran up against them on Waygone, we killed every last Skink on that planet. We killed most of them on Kingdom, and the survivors were lucky to get away. We killed *all* of them, hundreds of thousands of them, on Haulover. How do you think they feel about going up against us?"

Dean let out a strained laugh. "You've got a point there."

Ratliff clapped him on the shoulder and stood up. "Good. Change into your civvies. We're going into town and you're going to get drunk and get laid."

"Will that cure what ails me?" Dean asked wryly.

"Nope. But it'll take your mind off what's bothering you until you sober up and don't have a woman in your arms. Now get a move on." He checked the time. "We've got ten minutes to make the next liberty bus."

They made it with seconds to spare.

When Sergeant Ratliff opened the door to Big Barb's, the volume of sound hit him in the face and the gut at the same time. He leaned forward and muscled his way through the noise. Corporal Dean followed close behind, drafting in his wake. Unerringly, guided by voices he barely picked out from the general din, Ratliff made his way to three large tables around which most of third platoon was gathered.

Sergeant Kerr was there, with blond Frida snuggled up against one side and dark-haired Gotta on the other, one feeding him and the other giving him drink. PFC John Three McGinty looked almost giddy with pretty Stulka on his lap. Corporal Chan managed to simultaneously look embarrassed and proud, being held on the lap of statuesque Sigfreid. The other Marines were all paired off with their regular ladies. Even Lance Corporal Ymenez, hitherto with no one to call his own, was closely attended by a redhead Ratliff didn't recognize.

"Where's Claypoole?" Ratliff shouted into Kerr's ear when he'd taken stock.

"With his farm girl, I imagine," Kerr shouted back.

"The one from Brystholde?"

"Is there another one?" Kerr asked with a laugh.

Ratliff grinned. "Are they still living in sin?"

Kerr laughed and grinned in turn. "That's what they said before Haulover. So I guess so."

"Joe!" a shriek pierced the noise. Dean turned toward it and saw his lady, Carlala, working her way through the crowd.

Ratliff looked around for another face he hadn't seen, sighed when he didn't spot it, and pulled an unoccupied chair from a nearby table to sit on. He grabbed an unused mug from the center of the table and filled it with Reindeer Ale from a half-empty pitcher. He almost choked on his second swallow when a voice husked into his ear, "Buy a girl a drink, sailor?"

Corporal Pasquin, sitting next to Ratliff, pounded him on the back to help clear his airway. "Gotta stop choking up like that, boss," Pasquin yelled. He grinned at the woman who had spoken.

Ratliff plunked his mug onto the table and twisted around. "Damn it, woman," he groused, "I keep telling you, I ain't no squid!"

She smiled beatifically at him and leaned in to give him a kiss. Ratliff smiled and wrapped an arm around her to pull her onto his lap. She giggled, then threw her head back with a hearty laugh when he nuzzled his face between her breasts.

She quickly recovered, clamped her hands on the sides of his face, and pulled his head away from her chest, saying, "Not in front of the children, dear."

"Kona Statimmer, who are you calling a child?" Kerr demanded.

"No children here," Pasquin said—he and Kerr were the only Marines close enough to hear what she'd said. Then he looked at her belly and added, "Unless there's something you haven't told us about."

"My Timmy's not a child," Frida, who was between Kerr and Ratliff, said. "I can guarantee that!"

On Ratliff's other side, Erika rubbed Pasquin's chest. "Raul's all man. So there."

Kona laughed delightedly and flashed a kiss at each of the women who had insisted their men weren't children. "Even so," she told them, "there are things grown-ups don't do in public."

Erika and Frida looked at her, at each other, and around at third platoon's tables. "Are you sure of that?" Frida asked, because there was indeed a good deal of nuzzling going on in public.

"All right then. There are things *this* grown-up doesn't do in public. I'm a respectable widow! My neighbors in Hryggurandlit wouldn't understand." She lowered her face so her forehead was against Ratliff's. "Since you won't buy me a drink, how about if I buy *you* a drink—someplace not so public."

"You've got it," Ratliff said eagerly. Kona hopped off his lap and he stood, bending over to retrieve and drain his mug. As Kona began tugging him away, he leaned over to say to Kerr, "I told Dean to get drunk and get laid. See to it that he does?"

"I'll get him drunk," Kerr said, "but it looks like someone else is taking care of the getting-laid part."

Ratliff looked to where Dean was sitting at the next table; Carlala was straddling him and raining kisses on his face.

"Looks like you're right." Kona gave his arm a jerk. "Gotta go. See you at morning formation."

As it turned out, Sergeant Ratliff was right. After getting drunk, getting laid, and sleeping on what his squad leader had said, Corporal Joe Dean stopped worrying about how they were all going to get killed. He still thought about how it was possible, but he lost the all-pervasive, soul-eating conviction that it was definitely going to happen.

But the concern was still there. Concern about something he hadn't told to his squad leader. He had a son. *A son!* A son he'd never seen, a son who'd never met him. And if he got killed, he and his son would never come together; he'd never be able to help raise his son, to see him grow and become a man. Even if he didn't get killed or crippled in combat against the Skinks, his son might be all grown up by the time he was released from the Marines and able to return to Wanderjahr to meet him. And return to Hway Kuetgens, the woman he'd loved all those years ago, the mother of his son.

That ate at Corporal Joe Dean more than the loss of any Marine he led, more than the mere chance of getting killed in combat.

CHAPTER FOUR

Mining Camp No. 331 was smallish, as Sharp Edge's Ishtar operations went. Lieutenant Chumway Teeter only had twenty men to guard and oversee the Fuzzies that worked the mine. But then, there weren't quite a hundred Fuzzies in the camp, so he didn't need any more than the twenty guards and overseers he had. And the one clerk allotted to him was sufficient for the mine's needs.

Or had been enough until the past several weeks. At first Teeter had dismissed the rumors of a Fuzzy uprising as wildly exaggerated retellings of minor incidents. Until he'd been relieved for a few days' rest at Base Camp. There he learned that the rumors were true and only somewhat exaggerated. He immediately asked for more men for his command.

"No can do, Chumway," Louis Cukayla, president and CEO of Sharp Edge, LLC, had said around a plug of tobacco when Teeter barged into his office with the request. "I only have so many troops, and they're needed to reinforce the mines in the danger area."

"What's the danger area?" Teeter demanded in a low, hard voice.

"So far," Cukayla said, "the few mines that have been attacked are concentrated in one area." He waved an arm at a large digital map on the wall. "They're the red ones. As you can see, the closest one to you is nearly two hundred klicks to your northwest." He shook his head.

"I can't see the Fuzzies who're running wild going that far. Not for as small a group as you've got working." He hawked and spat tobacco juice into a can sitting on the floor at the corner of his desk.

Teeter looked at the map and saw that there were only a few red marks, and they were indeed in a small area less than a hundred kilometers on its long axis.

"How many of them have been wiped out?" he asked.

Cukayla studied his face for a moment, deciding how to answer. "You'll find out anyway. Three," he finally said.

Teeter studied the map again. Eight of the mining camps were marked in red. That meant that three out of eight had been wiped out. A pretty severe rate for trained soldiers with modern weapons being attacked by animals.

"Anyway," Cukayla said, leaning forward on his elbows and peering earnestly at Teeter to interrupt his thoughts about the severity of the situation, "there's a lot of mines between that area and Three Thirty-one. Saying, just for the sake of argument mind you, that these stampedes keep up, and the crews we've got on hand in that area aren't enough to put a stop to them, well, then, Lieutenant, it'll be months, maybe even a year or more, before the problem spreads out to where you are. By then, the reinforcements I called for will be here."

"Reinforcements?" Teeter asked.

Cukayla nodded briskly. "Reinforcements. These animals are just a bit more intelligent and a tad more rambunctious than I thought at first. So having more people here is a good idea. Even if we don't need the extra troops to bring the herds back into line, I expect to be opening more mines, so we'll be needing more bodies anyhow."

Lieutenant Chumway Teeter cut his rest short and headed back to Mining Camp No. 331 early. There he found truth in the old adage "When the cat's away, the mice will play." Instead of overseeing the Fuzzies in the mine, the overseers were joining the guards in an extended party—except for one overseer watching the Fuzzies who were dredging through the alluvial deposits, and one very drunk guard on the main gate.

Teeter glared at the drunk guard, who gave a sloppy grin and tossed him an even sloppier salute, and went in search of his sergeant, whom he'd left in command three days earlier.

"Sergeant Moringa!" Teeter roared when he found the sergeant plopped in *his* chair, with his feet on *his* desk in the camp commander's office. A three-quarters-empty bottle of contraband booze sat on the desk next to a half-empty Old-Fashioned glass. "What is the meaning of this?"

Moringa peered bleary-eyed at Teeter and his mouth fell open. "Oops," he said. He struggled to pull his feet off the desk and sit up. Then realized that he shouldn't be sitting at the lieutenant's desk, not with the lieutenant standing right there, and pulled himself up to a wobbling stance.

" 'Come back, sir," he slurred. "Yer back early?"

"Yes, I'm back early, Private Moringa," Teeter snarled. "And it's a good—"

"Ah, 'private'? I'm a sergeant, sir."

"You *were* a sergeant, Private Moringa! I've just reduced you in rank for gross dereliction of duty. Now get out of my office and assemble the men for inspection—and an ass chewing!"

"As-assemble, sir? Bu-but I'm a private, sir."

"Somebody's got to do it," Teeter spat, "and you know how. So do it!"

"Y-yes, sir." Moringa staggered around the desk and headed for the outer office but stuttered to a stop when Teeter snapped, "And take your garbage with you."

Moringa looked at the desk and picked up the bottle and glass. He started to raise the bottle to his mouth, thought better of it, and offered it to Teeter. "You want a snort, sir?" He flinched at the look Teeter shot him. "Or maybe I should pour it out, or something?"

"Get out," Teeter said harshly.

"Out. Right." Moringa looked at the bottle and stumbled away, carrying it and the glass.

Teeter waited until he heard Moringa close the outer door, then blew out the breath he'd been holding in and let his shoulders slump. He turned around and sat heavily on the edge of his desk. Fuzzies were in full revolt just a couple of hundred kilometers away. He wasn't as convinced as Louis Cukayla that the local beasts were just that; he suspected that they were much more intelligent than the Sharp Edge boss gave them credit for. It was just a matter of time before the revolt reached Mining Camp No. 331, and maybe not much time. He looked out the window at the camp. A mere five-strand fence of razor wire encircled the section of alluvial plain being worked, and not much more protected the main camp. It would be easy for a man to get over those fences, and Teeter didn't think they had a chance of holding a determined Fuzzy, either in or out. He thought for a minute about some of the details he'd picked up at Base Camp.

Where the hell had the Fuzzies come up with projectile weapons and explosives? And what was that gas they used?

He saw Moringa assembling the platoon, all except the overseer watching the Fuzzies working the mine. He wondered how many Fuzzies had taken advantage of the lone guard to get over or through the wire. He shook his head. Moringa was far from the best but was a good enough sergeant—or had been—and Teeter didn't think any of his other men were ready to take his place. But dammit, there was no way he could *not* discipline the man for his dereliction. He'd give him his stripes back in a couple of days, but he needed to make a point before he did.

Everybody drunk when they should be on duty—and at a mining camp where there wasn't supposed to be an intoxicant of any sort available. If he had someone else he could promote, Teeter would send Moringa back to Base Camp on the next supply run. But he didn't, so he'd have to do something else. The first thing would be to sweat the alcohol out of his men.

Outside, Moringa had everybody in formation. Teeter pushed himself erect, squared his shoulders, drew a harsh mask over his face, closed up his climate-controlled uniform, and stalked through the outer office to the portico, where he stood, feet at more than shoulder width, elbows cocked, left fist on his hip, right on the butt of his holstered sidearm. He raised his helmet's faceplate so his men could see his glare. He let them sweat inside their uniforms for a few moments while he looked from man to man. Not that he could look into their eyes; the faceplates of their whole-head helmets were darkened to shield their eyes from the bright glare of the day. Some of them swayed unsteadily; a few jittered or twitched with evident nervousness.

They needed a lesson, but how to start?

Suddenly, Teeter knew.

"Unseal!" he barked. "Take off your helmets!"

Hesitantly, the men obeyed, opening the closures at their necks and removing their helmets. Now Teeter could see their faces, look into their eyes. He didn't show the satisfaction he felt seeing their faces flush in the fifty-degree centigrade heat then glisten with perspiration that gushed and flowed in attempt to keep them from overheating.

"Assume the position!" Teeter ordered. The men dropped down, arms extended, hands below their shoulders, backs more or less straight. "On my count. One! Two! One! Two!" On each *one* the men lowered their bodies; on each *two* they pushed themselves back up. Teeter kept shouting through fifty *ones* and *twos*, even though most of the men had collapsed before the twenty-fifth, and none of them made it to forty.

"On your feet!" Teeter looked them over again, searching their faces to see if any had stopped sweating—a sign of impending heat exhaustion or heatstroke. All faces were still drenched.

"Right face! Forward, march! Double-time, ho!" Teeter closed his faceplate, jumped off the portico, and ran alongside the formation. He kept his climate controls on while he ran the men around the inner compound, a kilometer-and-a-half circuit, constantly looking for signs of heatstroke. He made sure nobody fell out; he had the men in better condition help those who couldn't finish the run on their own. By the time the platoon was back in front of the administration building, several of the men had stopped sweating and were turning very pale. Nobody had fallen out but they were *all* hurting badly by the end of the run.

"Hit the showers," he ordered harshly. "Cold water, the coldest you can stand! And replenish your fluids. I don't want anybody collapsing from heatstroke."

"Sir," Moringa croaked, "can we have some hangover pills, sir?"

Teeter looked disgusted for a few seconds before saying, "There aren't supposed to be any intoxicants in this camp, so hangover pills aren't part of our medical supplies." He shook his head. "Even if we had hangover pills, I wouldn't give them to you. You screwed up, you suffer the consequences. Now get into the barracks and cool off, replenish your fluids. I want you back here in one hour. Go!"

Teeter stood silently, watching, as the men staggered to the barracks. As soon as the barracks door closed behind the last of them, he headed for the mining activity.

The sole overseer didn't come to attention or salute when his commanding officer arrived. He was busy trying to keep tabs on a hundred or so Fuzzies sieving gems out of the hard-packed dirt.

"Are you drunk?" Teeter asked as soon as he reached the man.

The overseer spared him a glance. "No, sir. All I've drunk today was juice at morning chow, and water since then."

"So why didn't you get shitfaced with everybody else?"

"Sergeant Moringa said somebody had to keep the Fuzzies working, that you'd notice if we were way below quota. He asked for volunteers." The man jerked his head in the same manner that he would have if he'd spat on the ground, but if he spat, it was inside his helmet. "I was the only volunteer."

"You mean you've been out here all day, watching the Fuzzies by yourself?"

He shook his head. "Not quite. The party didn't start until after we put them to work." He made the spitting motion again.

Teeter looked at the man's shirt-front name tag. "All right, Corporal Sinvant, let's get the Fuzzies back in their cages."

"It's *Private* Sinvant, sir."

"Not anymore. You were the only man jack in the platoon with enough sense to do his duty when I was away so I just promoted you."

"Thank you! Thank you, sir!" Sinvant said, snapping to attention and lifting his hand in salute.

They counted the Fuzzies as they herded them back and locked them up. They were short eight. Sinvant stammered an apology, but Teeter waved it off.

"Not your fault, Corporal. One man can't effectively oversee a hundred Fuzzies by himself, not with the flimsy perimeter we've got."

When the rest of the platoon straggled out of the barracks in their climate-controlled uniforms, Lieutenant Teeter put them to work combing the work area for the lost Fuzzies. They only found one body. A cursory search of the landscape outside the fence showed where the missing Fuzzies had gone through or over it, but their tracks quickly disappeared on the hard ground.

It had been mid-afternoon when Lieutenant Teeter returned to Mining Camp No. 331. The shadows were lengthening now, and the sun was nearing the distant mountaintops. But the camp's defenses were thin, and Teeter wanted them strengthened as quickly as possible. Louis Cukayla might think it would be a year or more before the "stampedes" reached Mining Camp No. 331, but Teeter wasn't about to bet his life and his men's on it.

He had his men rush the Fuzzies through a small meal, their first since they'd been put to work that morning, while he made plans to reinforce the fence around the main compound. Then he arranged everybody into teams, one human and four or five Fuzzies, and put them to work. They went outside the main gate and began cutting thornbushes, and branches off thorn trees, and piling them against the fence around the main compound, making the razor-wire fence harder to penetrate. Teeter had the men in the teams direct the Fuzzies, but he also made them work alongside the Fuzzies. Corporal Sinvant helped supervise the teams. Teeter and Sinvant were the only men who carried firearms; the other men had overseer's truncheons. The Fuzzies were manacled together in teams so that no one of them could run or attack the human with them, so they'd have to work in concert. He kept everyone working until after dark. Then he had everybody return behind the fence, and the men unshackled the Fuzzies so they could be locked into their cages.

Corporal Sinvant managed to get the men into platoon formation in front of the administration building; the Fuzzies milled about listlessly between the formation and the cages they were kept in overnight. Less than half the fence had been reinforced, and that not too well. Teeter realized that he was going to have to suspend mining operations for a couple of days to get the job done properly. But it was a start.

There was grumbling in the formation and had been ever since Teeter had told his men what they were going to be doing. Now the grumbling grew louder. Private Moringa broke formation and stepped forward to stand in front of the platoon facing Teeter.

"Sir," Moringa said loudly, "you had us working like animals. You had us working *with* the animals. We demand to know why! And disciplinary action for drinking while you were away isn't a good enough reason, not for working *with* the animals it isn't."

"That's a reasonable question, *Private*," Teeter answered. "I'm sure you've heard the rumors about a Fuzzy uprising. Maybe you've dismissed them as just that, rumors. Well, they aren't. The Fuzzies have attacked at least eight mining camps and wiped out three of them." He paused to let that sink in before continuing; "Every one of those camps, including the three that were wiped out, were bigger and more strongly defended than this one. The Fuzzies that attacked those camps were armed with projectile rifles, explosives, and gas.

"That's why we just put in two hours with everybody available working to reinforce our defenses, and why we're going to put in as much time as necessary, men and Fuzzies working together, to make Mining Camp Number Three Thirty-one as defensible as possible.

"Gentlemen, when the Fuzzies attack here, I intend to beat them off." He looked from man to man in the formation. "Any more questions?"

"Yes, sir," a voice in the formation called out. "What are we going to use to make sandbags?"

"I'll come up with something."

The Fuzzies had begun chittering among themselves when they were broken into teams with the men instead of being returned to their cages after their meal, and the chittering continued despite the efforts of the men to make them shut up. The volume and intensity of the chittering increased when Teeter said that three mining camps had been wiped out. Now, abruptly, the chittering stopped.

Teeter noticed that the listless milling of the Fuzzies had drawn them closer to the formation and that some of them were now behind the platoon. Then one Fuzzy drew itself fully erect and began walking toward him. A second joined the first. Then a third dropped to all fours and scampered to join the first two.

Teeter watched them with interest. He wasn't concerned that the Fuzzies were going to attack. Sure, they had hard, strong claws evolved to grub for insectoids in the hard dirt of Ishtar, and strong, sharp teeth to crush carapaces and cut through tough tubers. But they were too weak to be a threat. A fully healthy Fuzzy was stronger than a man of equal size, maybe even a somewhat bigger man. But they were deliberately kept on short rations, generally not enough to kill them from starvation—although one did occasionally die from malnutrition and overwork—but to keep them too weak and discouraged to attack and defeat their armed overseers.

The three Fuzzies, each a full head shorter than Lieutenant Teeter, stopped an arm's length in front of the camp commander and stared at his face in such a way that he wondered if they could see his eyes through the faceplate of his helmet.

Teeter thrust an arm out, pointing at the cages. "Go!" he snapped. Just like dogs, the Fuzzies understood a few human words, and *go* was one of them.

The Fuzzies didn't turn their eyes from him for a long moment so he drew his sidearm to emphasize his order.

Then one of them screeched, a sound Teeter had never heard before.

The Fuzzy that screeched lunged forward, slashing at Lieutenant Teeter's open armpit with its claws. The one in the middle leaped at him, striking his chest with hands and feet, jamming its open muzzle up under his helmet, biting and chewing at the sealed neck of his uniform. The third Fuzzy swung around and slashed at the backs of his knees, ripping through the material and gouging into his flesh, tearing the tendons that held his legs together.

Lieutenant Teeter could barely scream as he thudded backward to the ground.

He never saw the rest of the Fuzzies fall on his men, never heard Corporal Sinvant's sidearm fire at the attacking Fuzzies, never heard the shouts and screams of his men as they tried to fight off their attackers before falling under their weight and slashing claws and biting teeth.

It was over in just a couple of minutes. The surviving Fuzzies—a dozen of them were down, dead or crippled—went from man to man, rending the remains of their uniforms from their bodies and making sure they were all dead. Then they gathered their casualties and filed out through the main gate. They stopped a short distance away to grub for the first decent meal any of them had had since they'd been taken prisoner, and then went in search of a hole in the ground where they could hide until the morning, when they would search for an empty burrow to claim for their own. Then they would send out scouts, looking for others of their kind who were rebelling against their masters.

It seemed that the Fuzzies could understand more human speech than just a few commands, like dogs.

The following afternoon, after Mining Camp No. 331 failed to make its morning report or respond to any of the calls made to it, four armed aircraft circled the camp while a MicMac C46 landed a reinforced platoon on the makeshift airstrip outside the camp. A few of the troops threw up when they saw the mutilated bodies of the guards and overseers. Later, digging equipment was brought in to dig a mass grave, and the bodies were unceremoniously deposited in the trench and covered over. The coordinates of the grave were carefully noted for later retrieval of the bodies.

CHAPTER FIVE

Chief Warrant Officer Morgan Raidly, 417th Military Intelligence Detachment, studied the Biographical Sheet that Captain Solden, his commanding officer, had just handed him. "Chief, based on the report Jenkins's source has given us, this guy would seem to have the access we need to recruit him as an agent." Solden picked his cigar out of its ashtray. It had gone out. He relit it and puffed contentedly.

The Biographical Sheet did not contain many details about Humbert Parsells. He tended bar at the Free Fire Zone bar in Worthington, a very popular hangout for mercenaries. A holograph of Parsells was attached to the Biographical Sheet. It revealed a heavyset man, probably in his late sixties, salt-and-pepper goatee, auburn hair thinning on top. He was wearing old-fashioned spectacles. The report stated that he was a frequent patron at the Four Whores casino where he enjoyed himself at the poker tables, and at a bordello called Madame Betty's.

"So he's got habits," Raidly said. He leaned forward and tapped the ash of his own cigar into the captain's ashtray. It was an Avo 25th Century, forty-two-ring size, a gift from Captain Solden, who was quite free with his cigar supply—especially when assigning one of his agents to a dangerous and difficult task.

"Yes, he does. Fifth and sixth days he's off. Set up a bump with this guy at the casino on one of those days." A "bump" was a carefully arranged casual encounter designed to allow a case officer some pretext to get the attention of a possible source, win that person's confidence with a good cover story and rapport building, and eventually recruit him to work for military intelligence. It was a delicate and prolonged process but Raidly was experienced in this type of work—and very good at it.

" 'Khayyam' fingered this guy?" Raidly asked. "Khayyam" was the cover name of a recruited source who worked as a prostitute at Madame Betty's. "Whores and barkeeps," Raidly said with a grin. "They hear more shit than the Senate Intelligence Subcommittee. We don't know what kind of poker this guy likes to play."

"They're big on Hell on the Humboldt over there. Study up on the game. Or, if you like, become a patron at Madame Betty's yourself, Chief. Meet up with him there." Captain Solden rolled his cigar in his fingers and grinned at Raidly.

"I don't know about that, sir. I could get to enjoy myself too much, let out that I'm with Confederation military intelligence." He drew deeply on his cigar and expelled the smoke slowly, grinning back at the captain through the haze. "Unless I get Jenkins's whore." Jenkins was the case officer who developed Khayyam. "Literally screw his asset." They laughed. "That goddamn Jenkins, he gets all the good assignments."

"Chief, I'm giving you this one because I think this Parsells will turn out to be one of our best sources. He hears more shit behind that bar than anyone else on Carhart's World. You get him on board and we'll have a pipeline to all kinds of stuff. I don't need to tell you, Chief, watch your back. If the corporate intel guys find out about you . . ." He drew a forefinger across his throat. CorpSec intelligence agents were everywhere on Carhart's World, especially in Worthington, spying on one another, suborning other corporations' employees, doing everything they could to get the jump on their rivals in the highly competitive business of winning contracts for professional security services.

"Okay, sir." Raidly got to his feet. "I'm on it. Well, since this op involves a bordello and a casino, I'm going to give it a code name of 'Whores, Fours, and One-eyed Jacks,'" he said with a laugh.

Captain Solden winced. "Very original, Chief, but I don't think the boys up at the Directorate of Human Intelligence would be amused. Now go, my son, and sin if you have to."

The 417th Military Intelligence Detachment operated under the direct control of the Directorate of Human Intelligence of the Ministry of War's Military Intelligence Agency (MIA). The MIA was the military equivalent of the Confederation's Central Intelligence Organization (CIO).

Under Confederation law, the CIO and the MIA were charged to cooperate with each other and exchange information of interest. This did not always happen, because each agency had a different philosophy about how to address potential threats and problems. The CIO liked to handle problems directly with cloak-and-dagger methods using its own assets, while the MIA operated under closer outside scrutiny and could not afford to overreact or try to bury its mistakes. And their respective missions were different. The CIO concentrated on developing strategic intelligence, clandestinely, among the Confederation's member worlds (and some nonmembers), while the MIA sought intelligence of use to the Confederation's military forces for actual or potential deployments.

Carhart's World, particularly the secondary spaceport at Worthington, was a rich source of information for the military services because the mercenaries who gathered in its bars, bordellos, and bedrooms between contracts had firsthand knowledge of developments in potential hot spots throughout Human Space that might require military intervention. This was known as "prebattlefield intelligence"—exactly what they were hoping to get out of Parsells.

Mercenaries: It was a dirty word. A mercenary is a privately employed soldier, a member of a probably illicit army. The corporations that provided their services preferred to be called "executive security organizations," "corporate security providers," "training contractors," or some such. Nominally, the employees of these companies weren't fighters—except in self-defense. In practice, wherever the military or other agents of the Confederation of Human Worlds weren't watching over them, they could get away with conducting offensive military actions, actions that weren't allowable in any of their charters. That was why the Military Intelligence Agency collected intelligence on these "corporate security providers" and their cousins in the mercenary business.

Recruiters for outfits such as Grummans Guards, Secure Hands, Sharp Edge, Tight Hold, and similar outfits did much of their recruiting in Worthington's bars and brothels. That made the bars and brothels places of interest to military intelligence. Intelligence on how many were being recruited and for where could alert the army to pending problem spots where troops might need to be deployed, or could let the army know where mercenaries might be gathering, with either the same aims the army had or in opposition to the army.

Raidly was an expert in tradecraft. He could devise a simple, workable communications plan in five minutes, spot a surveillance operation or run one, talk his way past a police cordon, invent defensible cover stories, pretend convincingly to be anyone he wasn't—a businessman, an artist, a chronic gambler, whatever was required to get a potential source's attention and eventual cooperation.

But Raidly's real expertise lay in his understanding of human nature. He could spot a potential source's weaknesses and strengths and play expertly on them to gain the individual's trust and eventual cooperation. Raidly had mastered the techniques of elicitation. He could get anyone to talk to him without even appearing to be asking questions. Once he succeeded in recruiting a source, he convinced that person that they were a "team," or "colleagues" working for a common good, rather than him as case worker controlling the agent every minute of their relationship. But when he made a promise, usually to protect his source or the source's family, he kept it. In some cases he had had to remove a source and his family from their native world and resettle them elsewhere to protect them from discovery. He had never lost a source.

Humbert Parsells was in his late sixties, unmarried, and lived alone. He was adept at mixing and serving beverages, from almost fatally potent drinks, such as Silvasian Toppers, to water; he could mix any kind of solution to the most fastidious standard. When on duty he was the sine qua non of the bartender, discreet, polite, always ready with a calming gesture, a sympathetic word, an understanding smile. People liked to talk to Parsells because he listened and understood their problems and often dispensed good advice. He made a good living from the tips he was given by grateful patrons.

Parsells hailed from a planet known as Cicero's, light-years from Carhart's World. While he could speak Standard English perfectly well, he often lapsed into the patois of his native world because he fancied it made him sound "exotic" and "manly." When he did that his speech came across as foul as his breath.

When off duty, Humbert Parsells enjoyed women and cards, and it was through those pastimes that Morgan Raidly planned to get at him.

Every week Parsells spent sixth night at the Four Whores casino playing a popular poker game known as Hell on the Humboldt. It was a variation of the much older game known as seven-card stud. It was played by dealing each player two cards facedown, "hole" cards, and then five more consecutively, three on the deal called the "dump," and then one each in succession known as the "screw" and "Hell on the Humboldt," which was the last card in the series. The players bet on each deal.

The name derived from the luxury starship, the *Humboldt,* which once plied the commercial routes of Human Space, affording even the lowliest laborer in the mines on a dozen worlds the opportunity of a sumptuous cruise complete with excellent entertainment, the best food known to man, comfortable accommodations, and around-the-clock high-stakes gambling. The *Humboldt* eventually collided with a piece of space junk and more than twenty thousand lives were lost, making it the greatest space-borne disaster in history. Supposedly at the time of the disaster a huge tournament was taking place involving a seven-card poker game. The pot was said to have been stupendous. The last card had been dealt and the players were placing their final bets when the ship was struck. Ever after the game was known among gamblers as "Hell on the Humboldt."

It took Raidly two weekends before he was able to contact Parsells. That night Parsells was sitting with four other players at a game of Hell. When one of the other gamblers dropped out, Raidly took his place opposite Parsells at the table. It was a conservative game with a buy-in of one hundred credits and a limit on bets of no more than that. After brief introductions, the playing resumed. Money shuffled back and forth and as the game proceeded, each player became more gregarious, all except Parsells, who sat there with a silent poker face. Raidly watched Parsells carefully. Parsells was not a very good player. Raidly won some hands and slowly his pile of chips grew.

Raidly waited patiently until he could go head-to-head with Parsells, draw him out, give them something to talk about later. He got his chance after about an hour. From the five cards displayed on the table after the Hell, Raidly felt pretty confident Parsells was betting a spade flush. In his own hand Raidly had three kings and two fives, a full house, a sure winner. Parsells raised a hundred credits. The other players dropped out. Raidly called. "Show me what you got," he said.

Parsells laid out a king-high flush. "You win," Raidly announced, feigning disgust and tossing his hand facedown into the discards. It was no one's business what was in Raidly's hand, since he had folded it. The dealer scraped up the cards and Raidly shook Parsells's hand. "Good hand, Mr. Parsells, and that's it for me, gentlemen." He picked up his remaining chips and bid good evening to the other players.

Raidly had deliberately given up the winning hand. Now he had something to talk to Parsells about. Keeping an eye on the game, Raidly took up a position at the bar and waited. In order to cash in his chips and leave the casino, Parsells would have to pass by him at the bar and that was when Raidly would accost him. Raidly nursed his drink for two hours before he got his chance.

"Hey, there, old man, have a drink with me," Raidly said, reaching out and touching Parsells on the arm as he passed by. "Least you can do after taking all my money."

Away from the poker table, relaxed and convivial, Parsells proved to be quite a talker. They had several drinks. Raidly, equipped with phony business cards and brochures, represented himself as a military hardware salesman on Carhart's World. The contact numbers on his cards and brochures were monitored at the 417th MI Detachment to maintain the cover. He was convincing. Parsells agreed to have lunch with Raidly two days later. Their next two meetings were known in the trade as "developmental" meetings, as Raidly built his rapport with Parsells and got a firm understanding of his motivations. On their third meeting Raidly announced who he really was and conducted a recruitment pitch. It was easy. For a thousand-credit sign-up bonus and a thousand credits a month (all he was authorized to offer), all Raidly wanted Parsells to do was tell him what he'd heard his patrons talking about around the bar, do nothing out of the ordinary, just keep his ears open. Parsells needed the money. Not all his poker sessions were as profitable as the one with Raidly. And whores were expensive.

Raidly patiently schooled his new source in the tradecraft, including how to spot surveillance, vehicular and foot, how to elicit information without actually appearing to be asking questions, how to execute a car pickup, follow a communications plan, and so on. "This is very important, Humbert. Never, but *never* ask direct questions of a source, you know, like 'How many men have you got on so-and-so?' That's a dead giveaway that you're probing. It'll get you in trouble if counterintelligence gets on you."

". . . Strangest-looking damn little guys you ever seen. They got some kinda weapon that burns you like hell." The speaker had a burr haircut, was wearing a sleeveless tank top cut to show off lots of hairless chest, de rigueur for mercenaries in Worthington that season. His neck, shoulders, chest, and arms bulged with the kind of muscles that only grow after hundreds of hours in a Mus-L-Max or similar bodybuilding apparatus—and possibly from ample doses of illegal substances. Parsells knew the type well. He was a couple of decades too young to be retired military. Parsells had immediately pegged him as someone who had spent an enlistment or two in a planetary army somewhere, got into special ops, then got out and went freelance because the merc companies paid better and the discipline wasn't as Mickey Mouse. And he'd have more opportunity to work out in a Mus-L-Max or indulge in illegal substances.

The guy also liked to talk.

"Weird little guys," Mr. Muscles was saying. "They don't wear no clothes and they live in tunnels. Hummer." He turned to Parsells, known to the steady customers as "Hummer," and said, "Gimme and my mates here 'nother round." The two bookending the talkative one looked to be the same type but had spent fewer hours on the Mus-L-Max. Parsells refilled their steins.

"You keep sayin' 'little guys.' What was they, midgets or sumptin'?" Parsells asked. Parsells leered at the two companions, who laughed. " 'No clothes,' eh," he leered. "Whyn't you bring one of 'em wid you, we cud gang-fuck th' little bastard right here, on th' bar. Great laughs for the guys."

Mr. Muscles winced. "Not unless midgets where you comes from have tails. They ain't no damn midgets," he replied.

"Tails?" the other bookend exclaimed, in a drunken state of awe.

"Tails and fur, too."

"You sayin' they's *aliens?*" The first bookend sounded dubious.

"Am I mumbling? What'd I say?"

"Sounds to me like you saying they're aliens." The second book-end now also sounded dubious.

Mr. Muscles audibly took a big swig from his stein before continuing. "Anyways, we had 'em mining gemstones on this gawdawful hot world they lived on, Ass-tar, or somesuch place. Kind of a twin to another world with actual civilization on it. No people live on Ass-tar, just them weird little guys. Too damn hot. Gotta wear climate-control uniforms alla time, and have some powerful climate control in the mess and quarters, or you'll roast like a side a beef, 'cause it's a desert, like, not a jungle with lots of humidity. Don't know how them little buggers stood it. But they did.

"I don't know how long the op was going on before I got there, but everything was all fine, excepting the only womens was the office workers, and only the bosses got to pork them, which made for a bunch of horny fighting men, lemme tell you! Anyhow, one night some of 'em got some rifles from someplace and killed all the guards at their camp and all the workers run off into that desert.

"Weren't long before there was fighting at more mining camps." He paused, possibly reflecting on the fighting. "Anyways, we beat their asses something fierce in most of the fights, and kept the mines working. Hell, their rifles were mostly single shot, and their mortars didn't have a lot of range, weren't like our flechette rifles and artillery. But the worst thing they had was this gas, or liquid, or something. They'd booby-trap trenches or the tunnels. Sometimes even the insides of the buildings. And that shit'd spew out and burn the hell out'n anybody close to it. Killed some good men."

At that moment the door burst open and four more muscle-bound men marched in, greeted the three at the bar, and, amid much roaring and backslapping, the seven mercenaries left the bar for one of the private rooms. Parsells smiled to himself. This stuff was worth a bonus! Quietly he cleaned glasses. *Wait'll Raidly gets an earload of this!* he told himself. He glanced at his chronometer. It was nearly midnight. No sense missing a night's sleep, but this information was *hot* so he had to set up a meeting with Raidly right now. Making sure no one was watching him, he punched the emergency contact number into his comm.

Someone answered immediately. "Is Peter there? Please tell him his laundry will be ready at nine hours this morning."

"I'm sorry, you must have the wrong number." The person on the other end hung up.

This meant that Parsells would meet Raidly at a prearranged site at noon that day, three hours after the announced pickup time.

At precisely 12:45 P.M. that day, Warrant Officer Morgan Raidly burst into Captain Solden's office exclaiming, "Sweet baby Jesus!"

"He shit in His manger again?" Captain Solden grinned.

Raidly paused to catch his breath, and then said, "Captain, I think we've got another Skink contact!"

CHAPTER SIX

If there is anything sacred to military people it's the chain of command. To jump the chain is worse to a soldier than farting in church. And jumping channels, as it's called, can ruin an officer's career. So Warrant Officer Raidly's report, as hot as it was, went up the 417th Military Intelligence Detachment's chain of command. It didn't take long for Army Intelligence on Carhart's World to identify "Ass-Tar" and its civilized twin planet as Ishtar and Opal. That and everything else CWO Raidly had overheard was put together in an intelligence report and sent on to the Heptagon on Earth, where it eventually reached the desk of Major Franklin Brown in the office of the Assistant Chief of Staff for Intelligence, Army Chief of Staff's Office.

There was an addendum to the report, further intelligence that Chief Warrant Officer Raidly and other undercover intelligence operatives on Carhart's World had gathered during the week between his initial report and the time the finished report was forwarded to Earth: A security consultancy firm called Sharp Edge, LLC, was heavily recruiting for a mission on Ishtar.

Major Brown read the report, saw small, naked, tunnel-living aliens fighting humans, put two and two together, and came up with Skinks. He made a wry face. Skinks with fur? Hardly. He shook his head. This information had been gathered in a bar, so one had to expect flights of imagination. He dismissed tails and fur as drunken embellishments and assumed that the burning gas or liquid was a misinterpretation of acid. But the bit about Sharp Edge, now *that* was military intelligence! After noodling the report and adding his analysis, he passed it up to his commander, Colonel Archie Jones.

Colonel Jones read the report and Major Brown's analysis, noodled them, added his analysis, and passed them further up the army chain of command. He also passed the material over to navy Captain Hyram Walks, his counterpart in C2, the Combined Chiefs of Staff's intelligence division. Captain Walks read the report, the attached analysis, noodled the report, added his own analysis, and passed them up, where in stages the report was further noodled and more analyses were appended.

By the time the report and its numerous analyses reached the office of General Alistair Cazombi, Chairman of the Combined Chiefs of Staff, the accumulated noodling had managed to lose all mention of tails and fur, and the "unidentified gas or liquid" had been changed to "acid."

And the addendum, while retaining the fact that a privately owned, interstellar corporation, possibly mercenary, was involved on Ishtar, Sharp Edge's name and its continued heavy recruiting for ongoing operations on Ishtar had been dropped.

Cazombi saw that the Opal-Ishtar system was independent of the Confederation of Human Worlds when he checked the location of Ishtar relative to the bases of human forces that had prior contact with the Skinks. He swore when he saw that there was only one such unit anywhere near close to the Opal-Ishtar system. He summoned his aide, Lieutenant Colonel Rebbi Piroska.

"Alert General Aguinaldo to prepare for a possible deployment," Cazombi said, handing the report to Piroska.

Piroska skimmed the report. "A desert world, sir? That doesn't really sound like Skinks."

"I know. That's why I only want the Anti-Skink Task Force alerted to a possible deployment, not to mount up." Before his aide could further comment, Cazombi said, "And inform the Commandant of the Marine Corps that I would like to conference with him at his earliest convenience." As Piroska left Cazombi's office, the chairman added, "Oh, and get me two more copies of that report and all of its addenda. Send one to the Commandant instantly, so he can review it before we talk."

I wonder if there's any significance to Skinks being on a non-Confederation world? Cazombi thought as he returned to the other work at hand, but was interrupted in two minutes by a chime. He rose from his desk and walked the few meters to the casual conference area of his office, where he settled into a comfortable chair. He pressed a button on the side of the chair and in a moment a hologram came to life on the other side of the low table that sat before him. It showed Commandant Rolf Saoli seated in furniture similar to Cazombi's. Unlike the army's Chief of Staff, who was headquartered in the Heptagon, the Marine Commandant was located at Headquarters, Marine Corps, which was on the high ground some kilometers from the Heptagon.

"Good afternoon, Rolf." Cazombi greeted his virtual visitor.

"Good afternoon to you as well, Alistair," Saoli replied. "I've had time to scan this." He lifted a sheaf of flimsiplast from the table in front of him. "It's interesting—and unexpected on more than one level."

Cazombi nodded. It was surprising that humanity would encounter the Skinks again so soon after Haulover, that they were now on a desert planet, and that they didn't start off with an offensive but appeared to have been captured by mercenaries right away—mercenaries who seemed to believe that the Skinks were indigenous to Ishtar. Not to mention the apparent lack of technological development that would allow for the aggressive, space-faring military that was one of the hallmarks of Skink operations.

"Do you want Force Recon to check it out?" Saoli asked.

"No, I want to be able to deal with a small infestation, if that's what it is—more muscle than Force Recon can apply. I hate to do it to them so soon after Haulover, but I want to deploy Thirty-fourth FIST."

Saoli let out a deep breath. "Thirty-fourth FIST does deserve a lengthy rest," he said. "But they're also our most experienced Skink fighters. And"—he glanced at the thin stack of flimsiplast—"they're by far the closest to Ishtar."

"Another consideration," Cazombi said, "is that if these aliens *aren't* Skinks, Thirty-fourth FIST has the most experience in dealing with other alien sentiences."

Saoli smiled wryly. "It sounds like you're trying to talk me into giving you permission to deploy one of my FISTs."

A corner of Cazombi's mouth twitched slightly, his version of a wry smile. "Rolf, you know as well as I do that the Chairman of the Combined Chiefs doesn't need the permission of a service chief to deploy units. But I won't send any of your Marines without your concurrence."

"I don't imagine Thirty-fourth FIST will like being deployed again so soon. Would you like for me to soften the blow?"

"Thank you, Rolf. Send your orders by me for my endorsement."

"You'll have them within the hour."

"I'll notify the Minister of War."

"It's always a pleasure to see you, Alistair," Minister of War Marcus Berentus said as he ushered the Chairman of the Combined Chiefs to a comfortable seating area in a corner of his office. A silver coffee service was already on a small table.

"Kevorian," Berentus said as he poured the coffee. He knew Cazombi well enough that he didn't offer to add cream and sugar. Cazombi smiled as he accepted the silver cup.

After brief pleasantries, Berentus said, "As much as I like seeing you, Alistair, I also know that when you request an immediate meeting, you're bringing a problem to my attention. So what do you have that's going to cost my pate some more hairs?"

Cazombi snorted a brief laugh. "You can save your hair, Marcus.

Take a look at this and I'll tell you what I'm doing about it." He drew flimsiplast sheets from his pocket, unfolded them, and handed them over.

Berentus read the Ishtar report and said, "I'm not supposed to lose any hair over another appearance of the Skinks?"

"I don't think it's necessarily Skinks."

Berentus listened attentively while Cazombi explained, and nodded reflectively when he was finished.

"You said what you *are* doing about it. Am I to understand that you are here to ask forgiveness for overstepping your authority, rather than asking permission to take an action?"

"You could put it that way, sir, yes."

"So what have you done for which you need forgiveness?"

"With the concurrence of the Commandant of the Marine Corps, I am deploying Thirty-fourth FIST to Ishtar to investigate and deal with the situation."

"Didn't Thirty-fourth FIST just return from fighting the Skinks?"

"Yes, sir, they did. And they do deserve a rest. But they're by far the closest Confederation military unit with alien experience. Time could be important here."

Berentus was thoughtful for a moment, then said, "Draw up orders for my signature and you're forgiven."

"Thank you, sir." Cazombi drew another small sheaf of flimsiplast from a pocket and handed it over.

"Pretty sure of yourself, aren't you?"

"The Chairman always has to appear to be sure of himself. Otherwise people might doubt him."

Berentus laughed as he signed the orders authorizing the deployment of Thirty-fourth FIST to Ishtar.

Commandant Saoli was right when he suggested that the Marines of Thirty-fourth FIST would be unhappy about another anti-Skink deployment so soon after the war on Haulover.

Brigadier Theodosius Sturgeon read the orders, then sat back, took in a deep breath, and let it out as a sigh.

" 'Once more, into the breach,' " he quoted. He fixed Colonel Israel Ramadan, sitting across his desk from him, with a hard look.

Ramadan slowly shook his head. "Will they be ready?"

"Oh, they'll be ready, all right," Sturgeon said, sitting up and leaning his forearms on his desk. "The question is, how hard will we be able to push them once the fighting starts?" The way he shook his head, it seemed too heavy for his neck. He pushed himself erect. "Call in the staff and component commanders so we can begin preparations to mount out. And ask Lieutenant Quaticatl to contact the *Grandar Bay*. I need to talk to Commodore Borland."

Commodore Roger Borland, commander of the Mandalay Class Amphibious Landing Ship, Force CNSS *Grandar Bay*, and any starships that might be attached to it, was planetside. As it turned out, he was en route from where he'd been taking his ease in New Oslo to Camp Ellis when the message that Brigadier Sturgeon wanted to meet caught up with him; he'd received orders from the Chief of Naval Operations to prepare to board Thirty-fourth FIST and transport the Marines to Ishtar at almost the same moment Sturgeon had gotten his orders from Commandant Saoli.

Sturgeon met Borland at the entrance to Thirty-fourth FIST's headquarters building and gave him a hearty handshake. "Thanks for getting here so quickly, Roger."

"I headed here as soon as I got my orders. How soon will you be ready to embark?" Borland asked as the two headed for Sturgeon's office.

"The entire FIST can be ready in three days. How's your ship?"

"Shipshape. I had her refueled and reprovisioned as soon as we reached orbit and the liberty rotation was announced. I need to check with Zsuz to see what progress has been made during my absence, but I'm pretty sure all necessary maintenance is done. It might take two days to round up all of the liberty shift."

"How are your sailors going to take it?"

"They'll be disappointed. Most of them had been looking forward to a lengthy period of shore leave. How are your Marines?"

They entered Sturgeon's outer office; the Brigadier guided the Commodore into his office and closed the door behind them.

"You know about the no-transfer, no-release orders for the FIST," he said as he waved Borland to a seat in his small sitting area. "Coffee? I've got some real Earth-grown coffee."

Borland grinned broadly. "I'd love some. The best I could find in New Oslo was some Dominion-grown. Good, but not as good as the original. Not Blue Mountain, by any chance?"

Sturgeon gave a brief chuckle. "A Marine brigadier doesn't have as good a supply line as a navy commodore." He touched a spot on his desk. "Have somebody bring in some coffee, please." Then he joined Borland in the sitting area.

In a moment there was a rap on the door.

"Come!" Sturgeon said in a firm voice.

The door opened and Lieutenant Quaticatl, Sturgeon's aide, entered with a tray that held a stainless-steel coffee set and two sturdy ceramic mugs. "When I heard the Commodore was arriving, I ordered coffee readied, sir," Quaticatl said when he saw Sturgeon's raised eyebrow. He placed the coffee set on the table and the mugs in front of the two flag officers. Sturgeon's mug bore the Marine Corps Eagle, Globe, and Starstream emblem. The one for Borland had the navy's Crossed Anchors and Eagle.

"Thank you, Lieutenant. That is all," Sturgeon said. Then to Borland: "Not quite the Blue Mountain in silver that you serve, but Marines aren't accustomed to the niceties the navy offers."

Borland chuckled. "That's one of the benefits of having your own starship," he said as Sturgeon poured the coffee and offered cream and sugar.

Borland doctored his coffee to his taste—Sturgeon drank his straight—and the two took a sip before Sturgeon returned to the question Borland had asked as they entered the office.

"Morale in Thirty-fourth FIST is the lowest I've ever seen in a FIST. Most of my Marines have been here for longer than the length of a regular enlistment." He looked at the other commander. "Just like your sailors. Damn that quarantine." The last sentence was said softly. "And I've got forty or fifty past their anticipated retirement dates. What's more, they've had two major engagements in the past two years—wars, actually. They're tired and need rest. And quite a few of them need a change of scenery. They've gone up against the Skinks twice, three times in the case of one platoon.

"In the end, though, they're Marines, and they'll come through. They've beaten the Skinks every time they've gone up against them. They'll do it again."

"Do you really think it's Skinks on Ishtar?"

Sturgeon shrugged. "Good question. Ishtar is too hot and dry for regular human habitation. The Skinks seem to like it hot, but they also like it wet. Ishtar seems to be a very strange place for them. Why would they be on an unoccupied planet, unless they were using it as a staging base for an assault on another planet?"

"Like they used Society 419 to stage for their attack on Kingdom."

Sturgeon nodded. "Ah, yes. Society 419, Quagmire, as the Bureau of Human Habitability Exploration and Investigation team that went there called it. A very apt name. And there's the business of these 'Skinks' being used by mercs to mine gems." He shook his head. "I have conceptual trouble with that one. The Skinks always attack without warning and always fight to the death."

"So it might well not be Skinks."

"It might well not. We have to be prepared for Skinks, or for an alien sentience about whom we know absolutely nothing."

They were silent for a moment, considering the difficulty of planning a mission when they didn't actually know whom they were going up against.

"When do you want to begin embarking?"

"I need three days to get everybody and everything ready. The first supplies and equipment can begin boarding tomorrow, with the rest following on over the next two days, and the men on the last day. Is that good for you, or would a week be better?"

"The *Grandar Bay* can be ready in three days, but a week would be better for the crew's morale."

It was the end of the month and Raidly had promptly paid Parsells his thousand-credit stipend as well as a bonus of another thousand for the information about Ishtar. So flush with the cash, Parsells was out to enjoy himself.

At their meeting earlier in the day, Raidly had warned Parsells of indications that corporate counterintelligence was very active in Worthington recently so he, Parsells, should lie low. But Parsells was beginning to like his role as an asset and once or twice he had been less than discreet when prompting a patron. That troubled Raidly but not Parsells. He knew too many people and had been around Worthington too long to feel vulnerable as he plied his customers from behind the bar.

But tonight he would celebrate month's end by engaging a very special lady at Madame Betty's. He'd first seen her there a couple of weeks ago, a new girl who went under the fetching name of Artemisia, and what a girl! He'd enjoyed her company several times since. When he had visited drunk, he remembered having had a good time with her; but sober, he was clay in her hands and wished he could stay in her cubicle forever. Artemisia was the kind of buxom, powerful, Rubens type of woman Parsells particularly liked: big breasts and hips, cream complexion, long, raven tresses. Her only defect was the size of her slightly masculine hands, but, he told himself, he didn't make love to a woman's *hands*.

"Can you afford me?" Artemisia said with a pouting smile when he greeted her that night. "You look like a potential heart attack, old man."

"Least I'd die with a smile on my face, my little coitus blossom. Can you take *this*?" Parsells leered, placing a hand over his crotch.

"I can take *any* man," Artemisia said, "but I've been waiting just for someone special like you." She unfolded herself from the couch, took Parsells by the hand, and led him upstairs.

Fifteen minutes later Parsells lay on the bed, pleasantly sweaty and drained.

"Didn't I tell you I could take any man?" Artemisia growled in her sexy, turn-on voice. Parsells disgusted her. She couldn't wait to get rid of the bum and wash up. But she had to do what she had to do. "I've got news for you, Mr. Limp Dick."

"Ummm?" Parsells's mind was still replaying the previous fifteen minutes.

"I've got a message for you, lover boy," she said, reaching behind her for something Parsells dreamily thought was an envelope. He half turned his head to look up at her. "My real name's Judith and I bring greetings from Sharp Edge, motherfucker." She expertly slipped a thin wire noose around Parsells's neck and, pinning him fast with her powerful legs in a scissors hold, used her considerable weight and leverage to slowly strangle him. The last things Parsells remembered in this life were the burning pain of the wire cutting into his throat and Judith's hot, pleasantly scented breath over the bald spot on the top of his head.

CHAPTER SEVEN

"Ah, yes," Sergeant Kerr murmured. "This is in the Grand Tradition." He lifted his screens long enough to hawk into the brackish swamp water he stood in.

"What 'Grand Tradition'?" Corporal Claypoole, Kerr's second fire team leader, asked. He'd kept his screens down, sealing his helmet to maintain climate control inside his uniform—the atmosphere of the swamp was debilitatingly hot and humid. But he had his ears turned up all the way and had heard Kerr's voice through the air.

"The Grand Tradition of training for the last war," Kerr answered, speaking this time into the squad circuit of his helmet comm.

Corporal Chan, the squad's first fire team leader, chuckled. He hadn't heard the original exchange between Kerr and Claypoole but he had been in the Marines long enough to know the reference; armies always train for the last war.

"But you heard what Gunny Thatcher said," Lance Corporal MacIlargie said. "The Skinks are supposed to be from a hot, swampy world. And we know they've got aircraft. So . . ." He paused for a couple of beats, long enough that, if Claypoole was using his infra, his fire team leader could step close and whap him upside his helmet, then added, "And we all know that Gunny Thatcher is always right."

Claypoole wished he *had* been using his infras, so he could have whapped MacIlargie upside the helmet.

Lance Corporal Schultz didn't have to crack the seal on his helmet to hawk into the swamp water; he had his screens up to begin with. Schultz didn't want anything to interfere with his ability to sense his surroundings directly. It wasn't much more than forty degrees centigrade; he could handle that heat easily enough.

"We'll get there eventually, people," Lieutenant Bass broke in—he'd been eavesdropping on second squad's circuit. "Even if not the next time. And when we do, we damn well better be able to defend ourselves against air attack in a swamp."

Kerr felt somehow vindicated by that. Claypoole tried to pull his head down between his shoulders.

"Heads up!" came Staff Sergeant Hyakowa's voice over the platoon circuit. "Fast movers, southwest, heading in our direction."

"Altitude and range?" Bass asked.

"Twelve thousand and dropping, twenty-five klicks. Closing at one K."

"Third platoon, take cover and prepare to defend," Bass ordered. Third platoon had less than a minute and a half before the aircraft were on them. Less than that to get positive ID on them and begin defensive fire if they were bad guys.

Even though many of them were carrying unfamiliar weapons and equipment, the Marines smoothly got behind anything that might have a chance of giving them cover from Skink rail guns, or at least concealing them from detection—although every one of the Marines knew that if the fast movers were descending in their direction, they'd already been spotted.

"Second fire team, tell me when you're ready," Kerr ordered.

Claypoole looked in Schultz's direction. The big man already had the scattergun set up and pointed in the general direction of the approaching aircraft. "Second fire team, ready for directions," Claypoole said to Kerr.

Hyakowa was already transmitting targeting information to the squad leaders and their antiaircraft gun teams. And Schultz was already adjusting his aim.

"Locked," the big man said as his data display showed the incoming aircraft fixed in the aiming block.

"Locked," Claypoole repeated to Kerr, who was already reporting, "Second squad locked," to Bass.

"Unidentified IFF," Hyakowa said on the squad leaders' circuit; only Bass and the squad leaders heard him—a control measure to keep the gunners from firing before the targets were within kill range.

"Wait for my order," Bass said on the all-hands circuit.

The Marines waited tensely for the command to open fire, when two scattergun antiaircraft weapons and both of the platoons' organic guns would open up on the incoming craft.

The seconds dragged, but the aircraft were finally only five klicks away. Lights strobed under their wings, simulating the fire of Skink rail guns.

"Fire!" Bass shouted.

Several of the Marines added their blaster fire to the mass of fire being put out by the bigger guns, trying to build a wall of plasma for the enemy aircraft to run into. Fire from the Marines rapidly fell off as red lights began blinking on their helmets and their weapons stopped functioning.

Seconds later, a four-aircraft division of Raptors from Thirty-fourth FIST's squadron roared overhead at treetop level, with their electronic simulated rail guns still firing. By then, most of the Marines were blinking red and their weapons had stopped working.

"Cease fire and stand by," Bass ordered into the all-hands circuit. He listened intently to the company command circuit, waiting for word from above on how his platoon had fared against the "attacking" aircraft.

He swore when Captain Conorado gave him the bad news.

"Third platoon, on me," he ordered. He removed his helmet and held up one bare arm for his men to guide on. It took a minute for everyone to assemble in a semicircle in front of their platoon commander. Sweat popped out on the Marines when they removed their helmets.

Bass's face was expressionless as he looked from man to man. He gave them enough time for a few to start fidgeting. Then he said, "Take a look at everybody's helmets."

Many of them started when they saw how many helmets had red lights blinking—even their platoon commander and platoon sergeant were casualties. Schultz was almost the only one who didn't flinch at seeing the red lights on nearly everybody in the platoon.

Of course, Schultz's helmet was one of a very few that didn't have a red light on it.

"FIST reports that one, count it, *one* of the attackers suffered damage. Not enough to take it out," Bass said conversationally.

"In other words, people, we flunked!" His voice went from mild to full-throated roar over those six words.

Most of the Marines looked chagrined. Lance Corporal Longfellow, who had fired first squad's scattergun, and the gun squad's two gunners, looked angry.

"Do you know how big a Raptor is?" Bass bellowed. "I don't give a pimple on Buddha's ass how fast they were moving, they were coming straight at us! How in Dante's nine circles could you have missed? What, have you all gone *army* on me?"

Now all of the Marines looked angry: not mad about missing the Raptors, but at their platoon commander's insult. *Gone army* indeed. They were *Marines,* the best marksmen in the known universe!

So how did they miss those big and growing targets that were coming straight at them?

And how did almost all of them get killed by the simulated rail guns?

The answer to the second question was easy—there simply wasn't anything in the swamp big enough and strong enough to stop the pellets thrown out at two-tenths of the speed of light. The only way any of them could survive a rail gun strike was to be missed.

But how in hell had they missed their own targets?

Bass suddenly lifted his helmet and tipped his head to listen to an incoming message from company headquarters. He acknowledged, then said to the platoon, "Button up, people. We've been resurrected, and more bad guys are coming after us.

"This time, bunch up a little less. If we're spread out more, they might not be able to kill as many of us."

Bass was right; not as many of them got "killed" by the next Raptor division they encountered. But they still didn't manage to kill an enemy aircraft.

Six times that day and into the night, third platoon encountered a division of enemy aircraft. Six times most of the platoon got killed. Six times third platoon failed to score a kill of its own.

"I don't consider it to be any consolation at all," Bass growled when third platoon was finally allowed to return to its bivouac, "that no other platoon in the battalion suffered less than seventy-five percent casualties on any encounter, or that nobody else scored a kill, either. All I'm concerned with is how piss-poor third platoon did!"

The exercise was called off in the morning.

The swamp was on Sumpig, a medium-size, bowl-shaped equatorial island almost twenty kilometers in diameter. The bowl was actually the caldera of an ancient volcano, and the small mountains that ringed about 80 percent of the island's periphery were what remained of the volcano's rim. When it rained, as it did frequently, the water that fell on the inside of the mountains had nowhere to flow but into the ancient caldera. Over the eons since the volcano had gone dormant, the part of the caldera that had been below mean sea level filled with the detritus of dead vegetation, erosion from the rim, and the droppings of the sea avians that nested on the mountainsides. So the excess rainwater drained away through the side of the island that didn't have a mountain wall, but it drained slowly, and the floor of the caldera was uneven. In the interior of the island, where the Marines were training, the water averaged thigh deep on a man of average height.

But that was only an average. There were places where fallen vegetation mounded up into miniature islands as much as an acre in area and up to two meters high. And there were places where if even a very tall man touched bottom, he'd be a long time coming back to the surface.

Trees grew in the swamp, mostly less than ten meters high, though there were a few giants of nearly fifty meters. All but the youngest trees were kept upright courtesy of buttress roots, and many drooped tendrils that became secondary trunks. Smaller plants, many adapted to life mostly in water, proliferated wherever sunlight penetrated to the surface between the trees.

All that vegetation provided food for insectoids that proliferated in the swamp and in turn provided food for avians that nested on the rim.

Amphibians, mostly small but some more than half a meter in length, divided their time between the water and the tussocky islands, as did water-adapted reptiloids. The amphibians and reptiloids fed mostly on the insectoids, though some fed on one another. The larger among them fed on the smaller, and sometimes on the avians. Many of the insectoids in turn fed on them, and the largest avians fed on the smaller reptiloids.

Fortunately, most of the amphibians and reptiloids knew enough to avoid humans. Equally fortunately, the insectoids were unable to penetrate the Marines' uniforms when they were sealed.

But the water depth, which could vary by meters in the space of two paces, made for difficult slogging.

The exercise may have been called off, but the Marines didn't leave Sumpig Island. Instead a range was set up to give the Marines more experience firing the scattergun, formally designated the M247 anti-aircraft gun, man-pack.

The M247 got its nickname because it looked like an oversize, slug-firing shotgun. It utilized some of the still poorly understood technology that R&D had been able to ferret out of the Skink rail gun that had been captured by the Marines on Kingdom. It put out a pattern of six thousand small pellets per minute at one-tenth the speed of light, half the speed of the Skink rail guns. It was called a "man-pack" because its weight—twenty-eight kilograms, plus ammunition case—was considered light enough to be carried by a man in the field. Still, preliminary tests at Aberdeen on Earth and on Arsenault had indicated that a strike with even two of the pellets would pulverize an armored aircraft and a hit by one pellet anywhere on a body would send fatal shock waves through the casualty. Unfortunately, it was as yet almost impossible to target properly and it frequently jammed.

The purpose of the range exercise was to give the Marines additional practice in firing the weapon under field conditions and in clearing the jams that were almost certain to happen. The targets were set up on the western rim of the caldera. The firing lines were located in various terrains ranging from three to five kilometers from the targets. To compensate for the fact that the targets were stationary rather than moving, they were pop-up; the Marine shooters had five seconds to spot a target, aim, and fire. At a tenth of a percent of light speed, they didn't need to take muzzle-to-target transit time into consideration, not at these distances. Sergeant Souavi was range master. He stood at a console that controlled which target went up and when. A display on the console told him whether the target was hit, and if so, by how many pellets.

First squad went first; Corporal Dornhofer was the best shot in his fire team, so he manned its scattergun. The first firing line was in an open area three and a half kilometers from the caldera's rim and the hidden targets.

"Miss!" Sergeant Souavi shouted.

"What?" Corporal Dornhofer twisted around to glare at the range master. "I haven't fired. How could I miss a target that wasn't even there?"

"Sorry, Dorny," Souavi replied. "Target four popped up. I guess you didn't acquire it."

Dornhofer looked at Sergeant Ratliff, who nodded. "The target came up, Dorny. Gotta look sharp."

Dornhofer was growling to himself when Lieutenant Bass knelt by his side and leaned over to say softly into his ear, "You were watching through the sights. That limits your view. Watch *over* the sights until you see a target pop up. *Then* go to the sights and shoot the fucker."

Dornhofer looked up at his platoon commander, swallowed, and nodded. "Thanks, sir," he said.

"Ready on the firing line!" Souavi called out as soon as Bass rose and stepped back.

Swearing at himself over his dumb mistake, Dornhofer looked over the scattergun's sights with both eyes open, scanning side to side along the caldera's rim, moving the aim of the weapon so it always pointed where his eyes looked.

Movement! His eyes and the scattergun's muzzle flicked to where he'd seen a target pop up, and his fingers closed on the firing lever. By the time his eyes and the muzzle were pointed at the target, he was looking through the sights. A slight adjustment had the target centered in the aiming box. He squeezed the trigger and the scattergun bucked gently against his shoulder as a hundred pellets flew downrange. He quickly brought the weapon back to bear on the target, reacquired his sight picture, and squeezed off another hundred-pellet burst just as the target started to drop.

Souavi studied the display on his console, then called out, "One ding on the second shot."

Dornhofer rolled to look at him. "What about my first shot?"

Souavi shook his head. "All pellets missed."

"Secure the firing line!" Captain Conorado called out. He strode toward Souavi; Dornhofer got up from behind his scattergun and stepped back from the firing line.

"Can we put a spotter scope on it, see where the bursts are going?" Conorado asked the range master.

"Not very well, sir," Souavi answered. "The pellets are going too fast to register visually."

"Even along the line of sight?"

Souavi hesitated, then said, "We can give it a try, sir."

"All right, try it. And while you're at it, can we hook into the sights, to verify the sight picture?"

Souavi looked at the firing line doubtfully. "I'll see what I can do."

Gunnery Sergeant Thatcher joined them. "I have an idea of how to do that," he said, only loudly enough for Conorado and Souavi to hear.

Conorado looked at him briefly, then said, "Do it, Gunnery Sergeant. I want to do some bench shooting, get that weapon properly zeroed. Range master, help him." Walking away, toward the edge of the clearing, he called out, "Company, form on me!"

In moments, Company L, minus Gunny Thatcher and Sergeant Souavi, was assembled at the side of the clearing away from the firing line.

"At ease," Conorado ordered. "Form a semicircle in front of me." He waited while the first and assault platoons shuffled around and the second and third platoons bent toward him.

"We've got a problem with the scatterguns," he said when the Marines were in position. "I don't know if it's the way they're engineered, if something was damaged in transit, or if it's something else altogether. For all we know, the pellets are burning up from atmospheric friction before they reach the target. So we're going to conduct some experiments to find exactly what is wrong. Corporal Dornhofer"—he nodded at Dornhofer—"is qualified as an Expert Blasterman. He put two hundred line-of-sight pellets downrange and only got one hit on a stationary, easily seen target. I have a hard time believing that Corporal Dornhofer's aim is suddenly that bad.

"When we return to the firing line, Lance Corporal Schultz will be on the scattergun." He looked at Schultz. "Lance Corporal, I believe you're the best shot in the company. Is that right?"

Schultz let out a soft grunt and gave a shallow nod.

"Such modesty," Conorado said drily. "I believe the last time you fired for qualification you scored one point off a possible." A possible was a perfect score on the range, a score rarely attained even by men who considered themselves the most accurate shots in all of Human Space.

A low noise rumbled deep in Schultz's chest—he didn't like being reminded that he'd missed a possible, even if it was only by one shot.

Before Conorado could go on, Gunny Thatcher called to him.

"We're ready, Skipper."

They returned to the firing line to find a scattergun set up on a stack of sandbags, braced to hold it securely in place when it was fired. A spotting scope was behind it, set where anyone looking through it would watch over the shooter's shoulder and—with projectiles traveling a mere three or four kilometers per second—watch where the projectiles went. But whether the viewer could even detect a small swarm of tiny projectiles traveling at nearly 7,500 kilometers per second was anybody's guess.

Schultz spat when he saw the setup; he didn't think he needed the bracing to hold a sight picture. He settled behind the scattergun without touching the firing lever and looked through the sights at a target that was fixed upright for the exercise. Satisfied that the weapon was aimed dead center, he looked at Sergeant Souavi and gave a shallow nod.

"Corporal Claypoole," Souavi said, looking at third platoon, "Schultz is your man, right?"

Swallowing, Claypoole nodded. "That's right, Sergeant."

"Good. You spot for him."

"Me spot for him," Claypoole muttered. "Right." He stepped behind Schultz and put his eye to the spotting scope.

"All ready on the right, all ready on the left," Souavi said in the ancient litany of the range. "All ready on the firing line. Fire when ready."

Schultz squeezed the lever almost before the words were out of Souavi's mouth. A few meters away, Captain Conorado and Gunny Thatcher watched the jury-rigged display showing the scattergun's sight picture. The lock-on didn't waver until the slight recoil.

"Corporal Claypoole?" Conorado called.

"Sir?"

"Where did his shot pattern go?"

"I don't know, sir," Claypoole said nervously.

"Didn't you see anything?"

"I—I think I saw a blur, but it was too fast for me to be sure."

"Right, left, up, down? Where?"

"High left, sir."

"Hits?" Conorado asked Souavi.

"Two pellets, upper left, sir."

"Can that thing be adjusted to fire bursts of more than one hundred pellets?"

"Yes, sir."

"Good. Adjust it for maximum burst count."

"Aye aye, sir." Souavi went to Schultz's firing position. Schultz moved out of the way while Souavi got an odd-shaped tool out of a pocket and made the adjustment. "Ready for a thousand-pellet burst, sir," he said, stepping away for Schultz to resume the firing position.

Schultz put his shoulder back into the buttstock of the scattergun and checked the sight picture. "Ready," he said, hovering his fingers over the firing lever. He waited as Souavi went through the litany again, then fired.

"I saw it!" Claypoole exclaimed. "It went to the right."

"Are you sure, Claypoole?" Thatcher demanded.

"Well, yeah, Gunny. It was just a blur, and it disappeared fast, but I *did* see it!"

"It disappeared fast? Do you mean the pellets burned out before they reached the target?"

"Gunny," Conorado said before Claypoole answered, "as fast as the pellets are going, they couldn't have registered on his eyes before they reached the target."

Thatcher peered downrange, then nodded. "I believe you're right, sir."

Conorado looked at Souavi.

"Five hits, sir. Four on the right, one top center."

"Corporal," Conorado said to Claypoole, "were the pellets spreading out, or did they stay together in a tight group?"

Claypoole looked at his company commander, wondering how he was supposed to know that when he couldn't make out the individual pellets. Then he realized how. "They spread out, sir. If they'd stayed in a tight group, the blur would have shrunk side to side, but it didn't, it just faded out."

"Did you see any flashes, like the pellets burning out in the atmosphere?"

"No, sir." Then he wondered something for the first time: "Sir, what's the absolute range on these things?"

Conorado shook his head. "I'm not certain, but they should burn up from friction with the air before they leave the atmosphere."

"So they could hit innocent aircraft?"

"If there were any in the pellets' trajectory, yes they could. But we're in a restricted flight zone; no military or civilian aircraft are allowed in line of sight of Sumpig Island without notifying us."

Claypoole didn't say anything to Conorado's assurance, but he thought that civilian aircraft might not honor the restricted flight zone. *Fuck 'em if they go where they shouldn't, and get shot down,* he thought.

While Claypoole was thinking that, Conorado did his own thinking. "I want to take a look," he said, and got behind the spotter scope as Claypoole moved out of his way. "Range master, I want another thousand-pellet burst."

"Aye aye, sir," Souavi replied. He checked with Schultz to make sure the ammo box still held enough pellets, then repeated the firing line litany. Schultz fired.

Conorado didn't need the spotter scope to see where the clot of pellets went—a cloud of dirt and dust flew up, momentarily hiding the target; the pellets had struck the ground in a tight group thirty meters in front of the target. He checked the replay of the sight picture. Just as the other times Schultz had fired, the target was centered in the image.

It was obvious that the trajectory of the scattergun pellets was unreliable. Was that because the weapon had been damaged in transit? Were the sights defective? Was it only this one weapon?

"Gunny," Conorado said to Thatcher, "I want to test every scattergun in the company. Two thousand-pellet bursts per gun. You spot, I'll watch the sight picture. Lance Corporal Schultz, you fire the weapons."

It only took ten minutes for Schultz to fire two thousand-pellet bursts from each of Company L's six scatterguns. In no case did a single weapon put both bursts of pellets in the same place, even though the sight picture for each of the weapons held tight, centered on the target.

"Corporal Escarpo, get battalion on the horn for me. I need to speak to the F4."

"Aye aye, sir."

Escarpo, Conorado's communications man, radioed the battalion logistics officer, Captain Likou, and handed the UPUD Mark II to Conorado.

"Every one of my company's scatterguns is defective. I don't know if it's the sights or—"

"I know," Likou cut in. "I've been getting reports from the other companies about scatterguns that don't shoot straight or consistently."

"So what happened, what's the problem?"

"I don't know," Likou said slowly. He didn't want to say in the open at this stage that the research and development people had sent weapons to an operational unit without fully testing them, although he knew that sometimes happened. He knew about the UPUD (Universal Positionater Up-Downlink) Mark I fiasco that had very nearly cost the lives of an entire Marine company on Fiesta de Santiago. Many Marines still didn't trust the UPUD because of that incident.

Conorado also knew about the Fiesta de Santiago incident; then-Gunnery Sergeant Charlie Bass had been with the company that almost got wiped out. "So what are we going to do about it?" he asked.

"I'm waiting for orders from Commander van Winkle to recall the battalion's scatterguns. I think he's waiting for orders from FIST to return the battalion to Camp Ellis."

"All right, we'll stand by for further orders. In the meantime, I'm not wasting any more time or energy on the scattergun. Lima Six Actual out." He handed the UPUD back to Escarpo and had the company form a semicircle around him again so he could explain what was going on.

"So that's everything I can tell you at this time," Captain Conorado said when he finished updating his Marines. He noticed a hand lifted and waving at shoulder level. "Do you have something to say, Corporal Doyle?"

"Y-yes, sir. Sir, has anybody th-thought of p-putting a choke on it?" Corporal Doyle asked.

"A choke? Explain yourself, Corporal."

Doyle reddened. "Well, s-sir, the sc-scattergun looks like a shotgun. Sort of. A choke is something on the muzzle of a shotgun that can be adjusted to m-make the pellets spread out more, or hold a tighter p-pattern." He swallowed. "Maybe if the p-pattern is t-tighter, the aim will b-be better."

Conorado looked at him speculatively for a moment before saying, "Corporal Doyle, your primary MOS is 08, administration. That's why when you joined us it was as chief clerk. I don't know if a 'choke' will work on the scattergun, but if it does—this isn't the first time you've come up with an engineering solution to a problem. Why aren't you an 04?" That was the designation for a combat engineer.

Doyle turned an even deeper red. "I—I d-don't know, s-sir."

"I'll pass the word to the S4 and suggest that the armorer give it a try."

Within hours, the entire FIST was back at Camp Major Pete Ellis. All of the M247 antiaircraft man-pack scatterguns were collected and sent to the FIST armory.

And the Marines were told to get ready for another deployment, possibly facing Skinks again. They had a week to put their affairs in order and have a final blowout.

CHAPTER EIGHT

Bass sat with his head in his hands. Before him lay a flimsiplast transcript that had just been delivered: Comfort Brattle would be arriving at Mainside on the midnight shuttle from New Oslo. She was coming to collect on Bass's promise to marry her. That promise had been made in the aftermath of the ordeal they had both endured on Kingdom. He'd made it with the full intention of honoring it, if Comfort would ever come to Thorsfinni's World. But time and events had dulled its impact and as the years passed—what was it, four now?—Bass had moved on with his life.

And now this bombshell, only a few days before another deployment!

Oh, there was the small matter of his son, Charles. If only Comfort had told him about the boy when he was born or when she'd found out she was pregnant! But she hadn't. She'd waited. *Why?* he wondered. He fingered the message and said aloud, "I guess now I'll find out. The chicken's coming back to roost."

Well, for any good Marine officer, his company commander was the first person to inform when things got out of control. He picked up his cover and stood. He'd see Captain Conorado, not to ask permission, not to seek advice (but he'd listen to any, if offered), but to keep his commander informed, let him know what was up and why things had come to this point. And let him know that his first priority, always, was to his fellow Marines; family came in second.

Lewis Conorado listened silently and patiently as Lieutenant Charlie Bass explained his predicament. Owen the Woo crouched on the edge of the Captain's desk, his bulbous eyes staring directly at Bass the whole time. It made him nervous, since Bass knew that Owen carefully evaluated everything he heard. But Bass couldn't help smiling to himself. He winked at the creature. Maybe Owen had some advice he could use.

At last Conorado leaned back and placed his hands behind his head. "You say she's coming alone, left your son back on Kingdom?"

"Yes, sir."

"Um, that's probably a good thing. Have you told Katie about any of this?"

"I told her I had a son back on Kingdom and had taken out an allotment for his support but she's a worldly girl, Skipper; she accepted that as just part of life. I never discussed Comfort with her and she never asked."

"Um, you gave her the ring?"

Bass's face reddened. "Yes, sir. But a promise is a promise—"

"Charlie, you've done nothing wrong. Hell, do you think Marta was my first girl?" Marta was Conorado's wife. "She wasn't. So what do you plan to do about this ménage?"

"Go straight at it, sir. Tell Katie, meet Comfort, marry her, if there's no other way. Find out why the hell she never told me about Charles until after he was born and weaned."

Conorado nodded. "I don't see any flanks here or any high ground. You gotta take this one head-on and deal with it as a monumental screw-up." He sighed. "Well, we all screw up, Charlie. Remember that civilian contractor back on Fiesta del Fuego or wherever? The one you put in the hospital over the UPUD he tried to sell us? That was your first screw-up. Far as I know, this is your second, and if I know Charlie Bass, it'll be your last."

"I've been to Personnel, had allotments made out, changed my will. If I don't come back from this deployment, Comfort gets two-thirds of my unpaid pay and allowances and the money I've got in the bank, and Katie gets the rest. And once I'm married, there'll be the Separation Allowance once we deploy, the Housing Allowance, and Cost of Living Allowance, so everyone'll be taken care of. My god-damn personal possessions, such as they are, I'll leave to my son if I don't come back."

"And you leave him your name, Charlie. That'll be worth a for-tune to the lad when he gets older. Go ahead, Charlie, marry this Comfort, be a good father, as good a father as you've been a good Marine. Everyone in Thirty-fourth FIST knows that. Once they un-derstand what's happened here, all the men will support you. Don't worry about your platoon. If you aren't back here in the morning, Top will handle it. Look, I know how much you love Katie and what you're giving up to do what's right. I also know you won't let this get in the way of your duty. I'd be concerned if you were a younger, less experienced Marine, but not you, Charlie. I've known you too long. I know I can count on you."

Bass was suddenly reminded of the conversation about the duties of fatherhood and military service he'd given young Corporal Dean that night, the very same night he'd found out he was a father him-self. Now he would practice what he preached.

Captain Conorado stood and extended his hand. "Better get a move on, Charlie, if you're gonna meet the midnight shuttle."

Once Bass had left, Conorado turned to Owen. "What do you think of this situation?" he asked the Woo.

"Skipper, if I had shoulders I'd shrug them. I don't understand you humans. All your gods seem to be just like yourselves. Marines are always ordering your God around, 'goddamn this, goddamn that.' When we Woos give birth, no matter which one of us does it—we're hermaphrodites, you know?—and who's responsible, we all rejoice because it's another tiny victory in the survival of our race. All your Lieutenant Bass has done is propagate."

"Yeah," Conorado replied, deep in thought, remembering his

own salad days as an enlisted Marine. "Yeah," he repeated. " 'Single men in barracks don't turn into plaster saints.' "

"Aw, what the *hell* have I gone and gotten myself into?" Bass, back in his quarters, said aloud, shaking his head. But the Captain was right. He was going to have to settle this fast. He finished the bourbon in his glass and poured himself another generous shot.

He relit his Avo DCCLXXXVII, drew in the smoke, held it a moment, and then slowly let some out through his nostrils, then more through his mouth, savoring it. He sighed and regarded the glowing tip of his cigar. Yep, that's what he'd do, make a clean breast of everything. Tell Katie about Comfort, tell her right *now*. Put Comfort up somewhere until he got back off this deployment and then marry her. That was just the way it was going to have to be.

He stood and picked up his cover. He'd catch the next shuttle to Bronnys and break the news to Katie. Then, if he was still alive, come back to Mainside and meet Comfort. "Shee-it," he grimaced. He'd rather fight a battalion of Skinks with a hot butter knife than do this. He swallowed the bourbon. " 'Once more into the breach, dear friends, once more,' " he muttered.

"You dirty bastard!" Katie screamed. "You did *what*?"

"I promised the girl I'd marry her, but Katie, it was years ago, she never showed up here, she never told me she was pregnant, I met you—" He made a helpless gesture with one hand. Things were not going according to plan. But for the first time in his life Charlie Bass had no plan except to go hi-diddle-diddle, right up the middle.

Katie twisted Bass's engagement ring off her finger and threw it at him. "Goddamn you, Bass! Take this fucking thing back! Everyone in Bronnys, everyone at Camp Ellis for God's sakes—I was at your fucking promotion ceremony!—everyone thinks I'm your fiancée but you're too fucking dumb or scared to set the date. They're all waiting for that! The girls at Big Barb's are already planning the reception for Chrissakes! Every time I go in there they ask me if we've set a date yet! But now you tell me about your squeeze from the past, from, where is it, some shithole—?"

"Kingdom, Katie. Look, everyone knows the story! Comfort nursed me back to health after I escaped from the Skinks! She saved my life. We—naturally we felt attracted to each other! We went through a lot back there!"

"Yeah. You went through a lot, you bastard," Katie snarled. "You Marines, you fly all over Human Space, screwing every skirt you can get your hands on. You sure go through a lot of us, don't you!" In Bass's eyes, consumed as she was with anger, she had never looked more beautiful.

They were sitting in Katie's apartment in Bronnoysund, the apartment Bass was renting for her, the place Katie thought would be their home once they were married. As angry as Katie was just then, Bass could not suppress the genuine love he felt for her. Her anger had infused her alabaster complexion and her dark auburn hair framed her face perfectly. She was the most beautiful woman he'd ever known. Leonardo could not have done justice to such beauty. His love for Comfort still simmered, deep inside him somewhere, but Katie was *here, now,* and he could not deny how he felt about her. But duty was duty and he was not going to leave Comfort and his son in the lurch.

"Katie, I'm committed," Bass said stubbornly. "You have to accept that. I did not plan this."

Katie dabbed at her cheeks. "What are you going to tell everybody, Charlie? What the fuck am I going to tell everyone? Everyone thinks we're engaged! Now we just tell 'em, 'Sorry, it's off. Something's come up.' How do you think that'll set with the Brigadier, all your fellow officers, men of *honor,* I presume?" Her voice broke on the word *honor,* which she uttered like a curse.

"Not very well. But Katie, I just don't have any choice. I made the promise to her and now I'm gonna have to live with it. What kinda guy would I be if I didn't keep my promises? Well, I'm an officer of Marines, and I keep my promises."

"Marine, Marine, Marine!" Katie shouted, "You're married to the goddamned Corps, *Lieutenant* Bass! What do you need a woman for? You already got your family! Fuck you! Get out of my life!" Katie began to shiver. But then, "Charlie, Charlie, Charlie," she moaned. "*I* gotta 'live' with it, too! So does Whatsername. And her boy. We all gotta 'live' with what you've done." Katie began crying, hard. Bass leaned forward and put a hand on her shoulder. *"Get away from me!"* she screamed. But suddenly she threw her arms around her man, weeping so violently she began to cough. "You've killed me, Charlie Bass, do you know that?" she gasped.

Bass held Katie tightly, his face buried in her hair. It smelled wonderful, that rich, dark, almost black, auburn hair. Sobs racked Katie's small body. He could feel her tears running down inside his shirt and her body, warm against his, full of life and promise. "Katie, you're *not* going to die and we are going to work this thing out. I promise, love, I mean it."

They sat that way, clasping each other, for a long while. Eventually Katie stopped weeping, wiped her tears, and pushed Bass away. "When does this girl arrive?"

"Midnight tonight on the New Oslo shuttle."

"Good." Katie sniffed and brushed a hand through her hair. She began to transform before Bass's astonished eyes, morphing from the raging virago, the bride jilted at the altar, into the old Katie Katanya, the strong, self-confident woman who was afraid of nothing or anybody, not even Big Barb. She was, in Bass's eyes, the ideal candidate to be the wife of a Marine infantryman. "Coffee?" she asked. "It's been on a while, Charlie, but I know you like it strong. And a steak. I have some in the cooler. We'll need our energy tonight."

" 'We'? Uh, yeah, Katie, thanks. Are you, ah, gonna—?"

"Yes. I'm going with you."

The way she said that, Bass knew there was no denying her. "Well, that's fine, Katie, that's fine," he said aloud, but to himself he said, *Fuck!*

*   *   *

The suborbital flight from New Oslo landed at midnight. Coffee cups cooling in their hands, Bass and Katie waited impatiently in the terminal for the ground shuttle to unload the passengers. As he gazed across the tarmac, watching the shuttle draw nearer, the tension in the air reminded Bass of that desperate night on Elneal, when he and his handful of Marines lost in the Martac Waste waited for the Siad horsemen to charge their position. And then the knife fight with their leader—he couldn't remember his name anymore—even that was a snap compared to what he was going through tonight. The shuttle bus pulled up to the terminal.

"What does she look like?" Katie asked.

"What?" Bass was still back on Elneal.

"I said, what does this Comfort look like, Charlie?"

"Taller than you, heavier than you, blonder than you." He shrugged, his eyes glued to the passengers entering the gate. First a gaggle of businessmen bound for Bronnoysund staggered off, laughing, talking loudly, enjoying themselves, the effects of in-flight alcohol obvious. Next some grizzled merchant seamen headed back to their ships after a trip to the capital. Then no one emerged for a few minutes. *Maybe she didn't make it,* Bass thought hopefully. Katie glanced up at him, the same conclusion evidently on her mind. *Maybe this is all for nothing. Maybe she just stayed home,* he told himself.

And then there she was. Bass couldn't believe it! Comfort looked just as he remembered her but now she stood there, a small valise in her arms, looking helplessly around the echoing terminal, and when her eyes fell at last on Charlie, her face broke into a radiant smile and she started forward. "Don't just stand here," Katie whispered.

Bass stepped forward. "Charles!" Comfort whispered and threw her arms around his neck.

Katie sized up her rival: Comfort's hair, tied neatly behind her head in a bun, was as golden as the noonday sun and she had the bluest eyes Katie'd ever seen. She stood a head taller than Katie and was heavier, with an almost muscular physique that hinted at hard, heavy work. Her fingernails were clean but clipped short, the nails of a working woman. Her clothes were practical, comfortable for traveling; she wore no makeup, no jewelry that Katie could see; she radiated freshness, cleanliness, and wholesomeness. She both threatened and fascinated Katie Katanya.

Bass held Comfort out at arm's length after a long embrace. "Comfy," he croaked. Katie felt a powerful surge of jealousy. Charlie Bass really loved the woman and, goddammit, he was *happy* to see her again! Katie had the urge to step between them and say, *"Hello there! I'm Charlie's fiancée! How the fuck you doing?"* but she couldn't, not even in jealous, righteous anger. What was going on before her was just too intimate, too genuine, too *private* to be so rudely interrupted. Katie Katanya had led a hard life, endured many hard knocks and painful disappointments, and she was well acquainted with grief, but she was instinctively sensitive to other people's feelings and could tell when emotions were genuine. What she was witnessing hurt her profoundly but there was nothing feigned about the couple's display and she respected that. And she recognized it as precisely the way she and Charlie Bass felt about each other.

"Uh, well," Bass said at last, "let's get your baggage, Comfy—and oh, this"—he gestured at Katie—"is Katie Katanya, a friend of mine. Katie, Comfort Brattle," he added quickly, snatching Comfort's baggage ticket. "Be right back," he called to them over his shoulder.

Comfort sized up the woman she already suspected was her rival for Bass's affections. Katie Katanya was the most beautiful woman Comfort Brattle had ever seen. She resembled what Comfort thought a courtesan would look like: lithe, impeccably groomed, self-confident, experienced in the ways of the world and men. To Comfort, Katie presented the perfect combination of light and dark: auburn, almost black hair, brown eyes, alabaster complexion. In short, she was Comfort's image of a woman of beauty, of a Salome or a Jezebel—Delilah!—temptresses she'd read about in the Bible all her life. And now here was one of them, right in front of her, in the flesh.

Although Katie's body was slim, not at all physically imposing, there was an aura about her that spoke of a powerful intelligence and will. Yet, strangely, Comfort felt herself attracted to the woman, instinctively aware that once the ice between them thawed, they could be friends despite their profound differences.

Katie just shook her head at Charlie's retreating back, then held a hand out to Comfort. "I'm Charlie's fiancée. Very pleased to meet you, Miss—Brattle, isn't it?"

"Yes. Likewise, Miss—Katanya, isn't it?"

Comfort's hand was cool and strong, Katie's warm and soft. Katie was surprised that Comfort showed no reaction to the announcement that she was Bass's fiancée. "I understand you left your child at home."

"Yes. Would you like to see a picture of him?" Comfort opened her valise and handed Katie a hologram of her son.

"Goddamn!" Katie couldn't help exclaiming. "That's the most perfect child I've ever seen!" She grinned. "Congratulations! He has Charlie's eyes, doesn't he?"

"Yes," Comfort said smiling, "but my father thinks the eyes are mine and the ears Charles's; the nose, too, see?" She liked the way Katie smiled.

"How old is he? Four, five?"

"Four, last September."

"Why didn't you bring him with you?"

Comfort shrugged. "Well, I think he's too young for such a long trip and besides, well, I wanted to see Charles first, alone. See, well, you know? When will you marry?" she asked, changing the subject.

Katie was taken completely by surprise by the response. Had she been in Comfort's place, she'd have flown into a towering rage. "Well, you know, the Thirty-fourth is deploying again. He doesn't know when he'll be back." She left Comfort's question unanswered.

Comfort smiled. "It's all part of God's plan," she said.

"God's—?"

"Yes, God's plan. Nothing happens by chance." Comfort smiled again, as if explaining the most elementary arithmetic problem to a dense child.

At that point Bass returned, carrying two bags. "Are these all you brought with you?"

"Yes. I—I didn't plan on a long stay, Charles." Comfort glanced guiltily at Katie and blushed.

"Let's get a move on, ladies. I've got rooms for Comfort reserved at the Uppsala—"

"No. She's staying with me," Katie said in a voice that brooked no argument. "Cancel the hotel reservations. Come on!" She put a hand on Comfort's shoulder. Eyes wide in surprise, Bass just stared at them for a moment. "Come on, *Charles*." Katie emphasized his name, speaking over her shoulder, "It's all part of God's plan."

"It's small but it's comfortable," Katie announced as they entered her apartment, "and I want you to consider this your home while you're here, Comfort. I'll fix up a bed for you and you can unpack your bags in the morning." She smiled. "Oh, it's already morning. I mean later today, after you've had a chance to get some shut-eye."

"Oh, I don't feel a bit tired," Comfort chirped.

Katie cast a penetrating glance at her and then at Bass. "Fine," she grinned. "I work mostly at night myself." She laughed. "Let's have some coffee and sit around and talk for a while."

They talked away the rest of the night. The conversation was mostly between the two women, formal at first but warmer and friendlier as the night dragged on. At one point Katie excused herself to use the toilet. Comfort leaned close to Bass and whispered, "When will you marry her, Charles? I like her. I think she deserves you."

Bass was astonished. It took him a few seconds before he could form an answer. "We won't. Not now, Comfy. I'm going to marry you. I promised. I want my son to have his father."

Tears filled Comfort's eyes. "Charles, I don't care if you marry me or not! This is all my fault! I should have told you—"

"Why in the hell *didn't* you?" Bass hissed. "Why didn't you? Oh, shit, Comfy, if *only*—"

Comfort put a finger to Bass's lips. "Don't talk like that, Charles. Father asked the same question. He'll be very disappointed if you don't become his son-in-law. I guess I've disappointed just about everybody." She smiled. "I did not tell you simply because I did not want to complicate your life—"

" *'Complicate'*—"

"Charles, I love you, with or without a ring. I did not come all this way to accuse you, to force you into marriage. I came because I wanted to see you again, touch you again. I just want to know that you still love me and will love our son and give him your name. That's enough for me. God forgives the repentant sinner, Charles. This sin is on me. I've asked Him for that forgiveness and I know He has granted it. I will have no fear standing before Him on Judgment Day. Charles, I came here to ask you to swear before God, right here, right now, that you love us and will never abandon us. That's all I ask. Will you give me your hand and swear?"

Bass gave Comfort his hand. "I swear before God and all that is holy that I will always love you and never abandon you, no matter what. And by God, when this Marine makes a promise he fucking-A keeps it!"

Katie emerged from the bathroom at that point, wiping her hands on a towel. The tableau caused a surge of jealousy that took charge of her tongue. "So, my Bible-thumping country girl, what attracted a Marine like Charlie Bass to someone like you?"

"Well," Comfort began in a small voice, "I've seen the Skinks up close and killed 'em."

"With *what*?" Katie couldn't help a smirk. "Your good looks?" It seemed ludicrous that the blue-eyed little mother was capable of any kind of violence.

"No, a Remchester 870 pump-shot rifle, the same one I used later on to kill one man and wound several others. That got me put into a concentration camp." She rolled up her sleeve and displayed the laser-engraved number on her left forearm. "Number 9639. That was me. And while a prisoner I bit off a guard's ear when she tried to put the moves on me. And then"—she shrugged—"I rammed a knife up into a guy's soft palate. It went right through his lower jaw. He bled all over the place. Didn't bother me much after that though." She shrugged again. "So, I guess Charlie was attracted to me 'cause, well, I'm *predictable.*"

Comfort delivered this little speech in a normal tone of voice, face expressionless.

"Well," Katie said, swallowing, "the bravest thing I ever did was I pissed in Charlie's beer when he wasn't looking."

Charlie Bass could only gape in silent astonishment at the two women, before replying, "Best beer I ever drank." He smiled weakly.

Comfort and Katie glared fiercely at each other for about ten seconds—and then both of them burst into laughter. Katie stepped forward and gently embraced Comfort. "I think we'll get along just fine." Still laughing, she glanced sideways up at Bass. "Bring your son out here too and he can stay with us. I love company."

Bass grinned stupidly at the two women and then said, "It's true. All those things Comfort said she did? She really did all that. She really skewered old Domic de Tomas with that knife," he said with a chuckle.

Dawn was breaking over Bronnoysund. "I better get back to base. Lots of things doing today. You know how it is when we get ready to deploy." He nodded at Katie.

"How well I do," she said sourly. She turned to Comfort. "You will stay with me. As long as you wish."

"Oh, I couldn't—I have money. I should find my own place—"

"What, go cabin crazy in some fancy hotel? Yes, you stay with me. Soon's we get rid of this big ape"—she nudged Bass in the ribs— "and the town wakes up, you and I will go shopping and then have lunch at Big Barb's, introduce you to the girls." Bass winced at that but kept quiet.

"I do need some winter clothes. Is it always this cold here on Thorsfinni's World?"

"Honey," Katie said with a grin, "it's summer weather here right now." She put an arm around Bass's waist. "Come on, I'll see you out."

"Before you go—" Comfort reached into a pocket, "I found this on the floor over there." She handed Katie her ring. "It's beautiful. It must've fallen off your finger and you didn't notice." She smiled but she knew instinctively how the ring had wound up on the floor. Certainly the way Bass's face flushed was proof positive of that.

"Why—*thank you.* I—I wonder how—?" She grinned up at Bass and blushed. He took the ring and slipped it on the right finger.

"It looks beautiful on your finger," Comfort whispered. The two women embraced warmly.

The street outside had not yet awakened. They stood in the dim sunlight. Katie kissed Bass full on the lips and held him tightly. She began to cry, not hysterically, but rather gently, the tears of departure. "Is there any way you can get out of the deployment?" She sniffled and then shook her head. "It was a dumb question, Charlie. Forgive me, you lying bastard, I know you gave the platoon to someone else this morning. Ah." She shook the tears away. Every girl at Big Barb's knew what was necessary to get ready for deployment.

"Forgive *you*?" Bass was astonished but delighted at how things were turning out.

Katie rested her head on Bass's shoulder, her breath warm against his cheek in the still, frigid air. "Charlie, promise me one thing?"

"Anything."

"Come back!" Her breath came in gasps for a moment. Then she said, "The picture of that kid of yours? If he's like that really, he's the most beautiful thing I've ever seen. If you haven't already, *give me one of those babies when you get back!*"

CHAPTER NINE

On the morning of the fifth day, the last of the supplies and equipment were trundled onto Essays and launched into orbit to load into the holds of the CNSS *Grandar Bay*. Two mornings later, the Marines of Thirty-fourth FIST boarded the buses and trucks belonging to Camp Ellis, as well as their own Dragons for the short ride to Boynton Field, Camp Ellis's landing field. There the Marines dismounted and formed up while the Dragons drove directly onto waiting Essays. More Dragons, these belonging to the *Grandar Bay*, were waiting in a line in front of the Essays. On command, the Marines moved from their formation and boarded those Dragons, which entered the remaining Essays. Beginning at one end of their line, the Essays turned to the side and launched one at a time.

There were no speeches, no pomp and ceremony. Simply arrive at the waiting Dragons and Essays, board them, and take off. That was to the disappointment of the larger than usual crowd of dependents and friends present to see the Marines off. The crowd included what looked like most of the women from Big Barb's, including the chef, Einna Orafem. A farm woman from Brystholde and a widow from Hryggurandlit stood with them. Many of those women were quietly crying. Katie Katanya wasn't there; neither was Comfort Brattle. They'd said their good-byes to Charlie Bass the night before and neither could bear to see him leave her again so soon.

The women and the visitors watched as the long line of Essays gained altitude, gradually shrinking until they were too small for the naked eye to see. Only when the last Essay had vanished from view did they disperse, some quickly, some reluctant to leave the place where they'd seen their men depart.

Within two hours of the launch of the Essays, the last of the Marines had boarded the CNSS *Grandar Bay*. Each twenty-man complement from the Dragons was met by a petty officer and a rating, who escorted them to the compartments in which they were to be billeted during the voyage to their destination—a destination whose location none of them knew, and none had even heard of before getting the deployment orders.

Opal and Ishtar? Where and what were Opal and Ishtar? The Marines, especially those in the infantry battalion, set about finding out, often even before stowing the weapons, field gear, and the few other possessions they'd brought on their persons. All of them had sailed on the *Grandar Bay* before, going to and returning from Haulover; most of them had made the voyage to and from Kingdom, with a side trip to Quagmire. So they all, or at least the infantrymen, knew how to access the starship's library from their compartments.

The compartments were long, narrow rooms, lined with three stacks of narrow racks three high. An aisle along one side was just long enough and wide enough for Marines in full combat gear to line up front to back to exit the compartment. Each stack of racks had a shared jack that anyone with a comp, comm, or personal reader could plug into and use to punch up the library's index, and through it access the library's contents. Nearly everything in the library was electronic, so storage space was of little concern; a starship's library had as much up-to-date human knowledge as possible, along with a collection of entertainment books and vids that would have been the envy of the largest library on Earth back before humanity broke the natal bonds and began colonizing other worlds.

"I found it." Corporal Doyle put up the locator code for the data the *Grandar Bay*'s library had on Opal and Ishtar.

Sergeant Kerr entered the compartment while his men were studying the data and joined them in reading it.

Even though Opal was near the outer fringes of Human Space, it had been colonized long enough for the first generation born there to have grown to maturity, aged, and died. Only its oldest current inhabitants had grandparents who were the original colonists from Earth; most were fourth and fifth generation. Because of that, there was a fair amount of data on the geology, weather, native life forms, population, culture, infrastructure, industry, and trade of Opal. Ishtar, on the other hand, was near the extreme inner limit of the liquid water zone, so it had barely been explored except for a cursory orbital survey and an even briefer land exploration.

Nobody in second squad gave the Opal data more than a quick skim, and none paid any attention to the fact that the planet had never joined the Confederation of Human Worlds, but they all dug eagerly into the scant information on Ishtar. Unlike Earth and most other human-settled worlds, more than two-thirds of Ishtar was dry land, divided into three continents separated by a meandering ocean that was not much more than a thousand kilometers wide anywhere, and in some places narrow enough that someone on the shore of one continent could see the shore of another.

Dry was the operative word to describe Ishtar. *Dry* and *hot*. Using Earth's system for comparison, Ishtar's orbit was midway between those of Earth and Venus, leaning slightly toward Venus. Similarly, Opal's orbit leaned toward the orbit of Mars. The smallness of Ishtar's oceans and the planet's closeness to its sun caused high evaporation. The resulting water vapor clouds rained heavily on the continents, but only on their edges; the rain rarely reached the interiors of the landmasses. The vastness of the lithosphere limited continental drift, so that tectonic activity rumpled the continents more than it shifted them about, resulting in lengthy ranges of volcanic mountains and numerous Valles Marineris–type rifts; many of the ranges were coastal, which caused most of the rain to fall before it could get inland. There were few permanent rivers more than a couple of hundred kilometers inland from the coasts. There were no polar ice caps. Dry winds blew constantly, ranging in strength from mild breezes to gale force. The atmosphere, while breathable, had an unhealthily high sulfur content from the volcanic activity. There were basically two worldwide seasons: hot and dry; and dryer and hotter.

Although free of ice and snow, the polar areas were cool enough for only marginal human habitation. But why bother developing dry-climate agriculture and limited manufacturing when there was a much more hospitable world right next door?

The oceans, despite a high salinity that resulted from the high evaporation, teemed with life. So did the relatively wet, steamy coastal areas. Inland, there was also considerable life well adapted to the arid environment.

Most plant life grew deep roots to find what water was available, and grew aboveground mostly as scrub, little of which even reached double the height of an average man. Animal life also went underground: burrowing insectoids, reptiloids, and some smallish creatures analogous to mammals. Some lived their lives completely underground, and many such species lost whatever ocular organs their remote ancestors may have had. The animals that hadn't completely abandoned the open air were thick-skinned or armored, to reduce or even prevent evaporation of bodily fluids. The limited study of the planet had revealed no species larger than a midsize dog. The explorers had discovered, however, that many of the insectoids and reptiloids had venom that was highly toxic to human beings and their livestock.

Some slight effort had been made to introduce Earth plants and animals at the poles, but the conditions were too harsh for edible flora, and the fauna was quickly killed off by animal venoms and the toxins ingested from both animal and plant life.

There was more in the ship's library about Ishtar, but it was mostly details of geography, geology, naming conventions, and sketchy descriptions of the flora and fauna. Much of that detail was in the form of charts, most of which the Marines didn't have the right education to fully interpret.

There was no information in the library about the situation Thirty-fourth FIST was heading into.

"Skinks?" Lance Corporal Schultz asked, once second squad's Marines had reviewed everything in the library.

Kerr looked at his other junior men. There wasn't anybody in the squad who hadn't gone up against the Skinks, and half of them had been with the platoon the first time the Skinks were encountered, on Waygone.

"What does anybody else think?" he asked. "Juniors first." He looked pointedly at PFC Summers, the most junior of his men, who had only encountered the Skinks on Haulover.

Summers hesitated, hoping that his squad leader didn't really expect him to speak first, but Kerr kept staring at him: Have the most junior speak first so he's not intimidated by what his seniors have to say.

"Ahh," Summers finally managed to say, "I don't know much about the Skinks, Sergeant Kerr. All I really know is they're tough, and they explode when they get hit by a plasma bolt." He looked to the side and added softly, "Makes me glad I'm carrying a blaster."

Kerr looked at Summers for a few seconds longer, then said, "Fisher, Shoup, what about you?" Fisher and Shoup had first encountered the Skinks on Kingdom, and Shoup had been wounded there.

PFC Shoup elbowed PFC Fisher, who cleared his throat before saying, "I think the Skinks like it wet. We've gone after them in swamps and marshes, but not in deserts. After looking at the Ishtar data, I have to ask myself, what are the Skinks doing there?" He elbowed Shoup.

"Well," Shoup said hesitantly, "we know they like caves and tunnels. It seems that all the animal life on Ishtar burrows, so I guess there are lots of caves and tunnels." He glanced at Fisher. "We've gone underground to get them, too."

Kerr nodded. "Wolfman, Little, how about you?"

Lance Corporal MacIlargie spoke up first, even though he should have let Lance Corporal Little go before him, as he was senior to the other Marine. "I'm with Fisher. What are the Skinks doing on a desert planet?"

Kerr motioned for him to keep going.

"Like the others said, the Skinks like it wet. Nearly everyplace we've fought them has been wet or underground. Even though we slaughtered a bunch of them in grasslands on Kingdom, there were plenty of little streams in those grasslands." He paused to visualize what the coastal areas might be like. "I got a feeling that the shorelines are wet enough for the Skinks, but," he said, shaking his head, "I also have a feeling that the water there's too salty for them." He looked at Little. "Sorry, I think it was your turn."

Little shrugged it off. "You said what I was going to. Now I don't have to wear out my voice saying it."

"Are you sure you don't have anything to add?" Kerr asked.

Little nodded. "I'm sure."

Kerr looked at Doyle, his most junior fire team leader; but Doyle had time in grade over the other corporals, so he decided to hold him for last. "Claypoole, what do you think?"

"I don't think it's Skinks. I think it's somebody else."

"Somebody else, as in other aliens?"

Claypoole nodded. "Look, President Chang-Sturdevant said there are at least half a dozen other alien sentiences we know about. Hell, we've met two of the other ones. I don't think it matters that the aliens we know about—except for the Skinks—are way behind us in technology. That doesn't mean there isn't another alien species that isn't developed." He looked at Corporal Chan, passing the discussion to him.

"Some of the weapons described in the intelligence briefings sound like the Skink acid shooters," Chan said. "It doesn't bother me that Ishtar is a dry world. It's got tunnels and caves, and the Skinks like them. The part that bothers me is the business about them being used as slave labor. Who the hell is tough enough to turn the Skinks into slaves?" He sat back, indicating that he was through.

"All right," Kerr said. "Corporal Doyle, I saved you for last."

Doyle nodded thoughtfully before saying, "The con-consensus seems to be that these are a-aliens other than the S-Skinks. The consensus may well be right. But whatever we do, we can't make p-planetfall thinking Skinks aren't waiting for us."

Kerr waited for Doyle to say more. When he didn't, he asked, "Does anybody have anything else they want to add?" When nobody did, he said, "Your preparation for this mission just doubled. You have to get ready to fight the Skinks again, and you have to get ready to fight some alien force that we know nothing about." He turned and left, heading for the squad leaders' compartment.

For the next two days, while the CNSS *Grandar Bay* moved far enough away from Thorsfinni's World's gravity well to jump into Beam Space, the primary topic of discussion among the Marines—particularly the infantrymen and the Raptor pilots—was just who was really waiting for them on Ishtar. Not that there was a lot of spare time for discussion. The commanders kept their Marines busy with weapons, equipment, and gear maintenance and inspections, orientation on the *Grandar Bay*'s facilities—not that any of them needed to be oriented, it wasn't all that long since they'd last sailed on her—and, of course, physical fitness training.

The jump went off without incident worth mentioning, just a few bruises caused by people or gear not being properly secured. The training regimen increased once the *Grandar Bay* transited into Beam Space; weapons and flight training in recently installed virtual reality chambers was added. That didn't, however, cut down on the speculation about who was really on Ishtar, and just what dangers might meet Thirty-fourth FIST on planetfall.

The day before the jump out of Beam Space, Captain Conorado called a company formation. The Marines didn't line up in ranks by platoon; as on the parade ground, that was impossible aboard a starship. Instead they crowded into one of the messes. The tables had been collapsed for the occasion, and enough chairs lined up in rows for everyone to be able to sit. A low platform was set up in front of one short wall of the room. Gunnery Sergeant Thatcher stood, arms akimbo, on the platform, watching as the Marines filed into the mess and took their seats, sitting together by squad and platoon. The platoon sergeants sat in the rear row, closest to the entrance. Staff Sergeant Hyakowa, the last man in, secured the door behind himself. A second entrance, near the platform, stood open. When the company was assembled, Thatcher looked to that entrance and nodded, then stepped off the platform and stood by its side.

First Sergeant Myer marched through the open door and onto the platform, faced the company, and bellowed, "*Comp*-nee, a-ten-*hut*!" There was a clatter of chairs as the Marines jumped to their feet.

Captain Conorado briskly stepped into the room and mounted the platform. The company's other officers filed in behind him and stood in front of empty chairs in the front row.

"Sir," Myer said in a booming voice, "Company L all present or accounted for!"

"Thank you, First Sergeant. Take your place."

"Aye aye, sir!" Myer joined Thatcher at the side of the platform, where the two senior noncommissioned officers stood glaring out over the company.

"Seats!" Conorado commanded. Again there was a brief clatter of chairs, and then the Marines were looking attentively at their company commander.

"I'm sure you are all aware that tomorrow we jump out of Beam Space into Space-3 in the Opal-Ishtar system," Conorado said. "You probably expect that we will make the jump as close as possible to Ishtar so we can make a quick planetfall and you can quit the training you've been undergoing since the *Grandar Bay* broke orbit around Thorsfinni's World and start doing your job, which is to fight and defeat whatever enemy we encounter planetside.

"I'm sorry to have to disappoint you." He paused to let that sink in, before continuing.

"We have entirely too little intelligence on the situation on Ishtar. Therefore, the *Grandar Bay* will return to Space-3 closer to Opal. Brigadier Sturgeon and Commodore Borland will lead a party planetside to meet with Opal's governmental heads to get everything they know about what's happening on Ishtar. Then, and *only* then, will we maneuver into orbit around Ishtar. We won't make planetfall until plans based on the latest intelligence are drawn up. In the meantime, we will continue with the same training regimen we've been under.

"One more detail, which may or may not have an impact on Company L: One platoon from the infantry battalion will be selected by lot to go planetside with the Brigadier and the Commodore as color guard.

"That is all." Conorado turned his head toward Myer. "First Sergeant, the company is yours."

"The company is mine, aye aye, sir! *Comp*-nee, a-ten-*hut*!"

Conorado strode off the platform and exited the room, with the other officers trailing behind him.

Myer mounted the platform while Thatcher moved around it and closed the door by which the officers had left.

The First Sergeant began pacing side to side across the platform, glaring out over the company for a moment before shouting, "Seats!" He stopped pacing once the Marines were seated and quiet, watching him.

"I know what you've been thinking," he said in a low growl. "You've been thinking that the intelligence we have says the Skinks aren't on Ishtar. Many of you remember the birdmen of Avionia, and you've gotten the idea that we're going to have a cakewalk when we make planetfall.

"Well, you're *wrong*!

"We're Marines, going in harm's way, and there ain't no such thing as a cakewalk when Marines go in harm's way. As soon as Marines start thinking a mission is a cakewalk, Marines start making mistakes, *stupid* mistakes. And when Marines make stupid mistakes, Marines *die*.

"You just know that if any swinging dick in this company makes a stupid mistake that gets Marines killed, I'm going to follow him all the way to hell and make him pay!" His voice started off low and reached full roar by the time he reached "make him pay!"

"We don't know that it's not Skinks on Ishtar, so we have to be ready for them. You might be right that it's not Skinks down there. But I guarantee you, whoever's there, they aren't like the birdmen. The birdmen's most advanced weapon was a pellet thrower. We know whoever's on Ishtar has much more powerful weapons. The birdmen had hollow bones, they were physically weak, as those of us who went hand to hand with them know. The creatures on Ishtar are supposed to be miners. Miners are *strong*.

"Maybe we're going to be facing Skinks. Maybe someone else, someone strong, with advanced weapons. Either way, they've been able to take on and beat mercenaries." He paused while a wave of snickers went through the company. *Mercenaries were men who couldn't make it in the military,* is what most of the Marines thought. "Don't forget, most of those mercs were special forces of one sort or another," Myer said firmly. "Some of them may have been former Confederation Marines. They weren't pushovers."

He gave the men of Company L a hard look. "And neither are we!

"So be ready for a tough fight!" He looked grim and finished: "The old U.S. Marines used to say something when people asked them why they joined the Marines. It was 'I joined the Marines to visit exotic places and meet exotic people—and kill them.'

"Now stand by to do exactly that."

He turned to leave the platform. Gunny Thatcher opened the door through which the officers had left, and followed Myer out, with one last scowl at the Marines in their seats.

Company L's third platoon won the color guard lottery.

CHAPTER TEN

An Essay with three Dragons launched from the CNSS *Grandar Bay* and dove planetward in a plunge of the kind that no one on Opal had ever seen, the standard Marine combat assault landing. One of the Dragons carried Brigadier Theodosius Sturgeon and Commodore Roger Borland, with selected members of their staffs. The other two held Company L's third platoon. Borland had selected formal whites for himself and his staff, with all the gilt they could pile onto their uniforms, and every decoration, medal, ribbon, and badge each of them could claim. Brigadier Sturgeon and his Marines were splendid in dress reds, with even more decorations, medals, ribbons, and badges than the navy officers.

Not that any of the Marines ever carried their dress reds on combat deployments. But the Commodore thought it was important to impress the locals with splendiferous uniforms, so he'd put the *Grandar Bay*'s tailor shop to work making dress reds for the Marines. The starship's store had enough copies to go around of every campaign and expedition medal the various Marines had earned, even the lower-ranking decorations for heroism. All the medals and decorations were on loan, of course. A few of the officers and enlisted personnel of the starship had earned personal decorations that they were willing to loan the Marines. At some time that he swore was in a past life, a chief petty officer had earned a Gold Nova and was cajoled into lending it to Lance Corporal Schultz for the occasion. The one thing the starship's store didn't have was Marine marksmanship badges, but the machine shop was able to knock out reasonable facsimiles.

When the plunging Essay reached the part of its descent the Marines called "high speed on a bad road," the part of the descent that felt like a road that had potholes deep enough to swallow an Essay whole, Sturgeon looked across the aisle and grinned at Borland, who was firmly secured in the web landing couch. Sturgeon had made so many combat assault landings that he'd long since lost count, but this was Borland's first. The Commodore looked distinctly "green around the gills," as a fisherman might put it. Sturgeon looked toward a retching sound forward and saw one of the navy staff officers disgorging his stomach's contents.

"You clean that mess up, sailor," Sturgeon bellowed. "And do it most ricky-tick, before it stains your uniform!" He studiously avoided looking directly at the man. He didn't want to know which navy officer couldn't control his digestive tract during a combat assault landing; if he did, he'd certainly say something later that would embarrass the man. Or was it a woman? Unlike Marine combat units, the *Grandar Bay* had a mixed-gender crew.

Whoever he—or she—was, the sick officer either didn't hear Sturgeon's order or didn't know how to clean up the mess. Fortunately, there was a petty officer third class crewman in the passenger compartment who *did* know. The third class was already unstrapping himself from his webbing before Sturgeon shouted out his order. Freed from his secured position, he swiftly but carefully pulled himself through the Dragon to the stricken officer, where he reached to the overhead and withdrew the suction tube that was installed above each position. The third class's hand on the tube wasn't as skilled as it might have been—the Essay's passengers were normally Marines, who knew how to clean up after themselves, so he didn't have much practice at cleaning up somebody else's mess. He nonetheless managed to get all of it before any splattered on the sparkling white uniform. He made it back to his own webbing and strapped in just in time for the Essay to break into the velocity-eating spiral that would ultimately land it safely in Opal's ocean.

Opal had strong similarities to its twin planet, as well as striking differences. Like Ishtar, Opal had no permanent polar ice caps. Where Ishtar was three-quarters land, Opal was 80 percent ocean. Opal's sole continent, unimaginatively called Mainland, was roughly the shape of a gnawed jelly bean, slightly more than 3,500 kilometers in its greatest length, and a bit less than 2,500 kilometers along its greatest north–south axis, and straddled the equator. For the rest of it, there were forty islands between 200,000 and 800,000 square kilometers in area, and a plethora of other islands of more than 25,000 square kilometers. There was no significant aggregation of land at either pole, nor was either polar area ringed with landmasses that restricted water movement in and out—which accounted for the lack of permanent polar ice caps despite the planet's relatively low mean temperature. There were no significant volcanic ridges such as were common on Ishtar, but the mountains and rifts on Mainland and the larger islands, along with numerous steam vents and hot springs, gave mute testimony to the planet's ongoing tectonic activity.

Again, like Ishtar, the indigenous life was primarily flora, with no fauna bigger than a medium-size dog, and a fair percentage of the insectoids, reptiloids, and mammal-analogs burrowed. However, in the case of Opal the burrowing was more to reach succulent roots than for protection from the sun and heat. Similar to Ishtar, much of Opal's fauna was venomous. As on Ishtar, Earth-evolved animals didn't survive exposure to the flora and fauna of Opal for long. That didn't create any particular dietary stress for the human colonists; most of Opal's fauna was edible, and nutritious, even if some of it required processing to remove toxins before being consumed.

The human population, some 30 million people, was concentrated on Mainland, with self-sustaining populations on most of the larger islands, and smaller populations on many of the midsize and smaller islands.

As always with Marine landings, the Essay set down on the ocean's surface, over the horizon from the selected landing beach on Mainland. The Essay rolled gently on the swells as it lowered its front ramp and opened its doors. The navy crewmen in the Dragons got out and unlatched the Dragons from their firmholds, then rapidly retreated to the Essay's cabin. The Dragons drove out to bob in the swells, their air cushion fans throwing up great sprays of water, until all three were out and in formation. On command, they raced toward the distant beach. The Essay closed its hatches and ramp and waited for the Dragons to reach a safe distance before firing its engines and heading back into orbit.

The three Dragons roared ashore on the popular recreation beach at Berrican, the capital of Mainland and of all Opal. Prime Minister Duane Foxtable and his cabinet, all looking exceptionally well fed, stood on a flagstone terrace some five meters above the beach, dressed in their finest garb, with all their sashes and badges of office and recognition—including some they'd made up for the occasion. Like Commodore Borland, the PM and his cabinet wanted to present themselves in the most impressive manner possible.

A crowd officially estimated at more than two hundred thousand but closer to forty thousand was held back from the terrace and landing beach by police guarding hastily erected barricades. Most of the people closest to the barricades evidently were at the beach for recreation at least as much as to see the offworld visitors; they were dressed for bathing or other recreation—some hearty souls were nude, or close enough that it made little difference.

Two wooden staircases with broad steps led from the sand of the beach to the flagstones of the terrace where the local dignitaries waited. The Dragons with third platoon sped ahead and came to an abrupt, sand-blowing halt to the sides of the stairs. The drivers throttled back and gently set their armored amphibious vehicles on the sand. Everybody waited for a long moment for whatever was going to happen next, the crowd expectantly, the dignitaries nervously.

The drivers gave the blown sand time to settle, then simultaneously dropped their ramps, and the Marines marched out and around the Dragons to the stairs, holding their blasters across their bodies at port arms. The ten Marines of first squad mounted the left stairs; second squad mirrored them on the right. They halted one pair at a time, the last Marine stopping on the bottom step, each man ahead halting two steps above. Lieutenant Bass, leading first squad, and Staff Sergeant Hyakowa, leading second, stood on the terrace and about-faced to look down at the Marines standing at attention on the steps.

"Squads," Bass bellowed, loudly enough for his voice to reach nearly everyone in the surrounding crowd, and loudly enough that some of the dignitaries flinched at the volume, "Face, *center!*" As one, the two squads of Marines pivoted to face the space between the staircases. Their boots thudded on the stairs.

The gun squad, meanwhile, had formed a single line between the Dragons that had brought the platoon. The gunners bore sidearms rather than the blasters carried by the others. As soon as third platoon was in position, the third Dragon eased forward and lowered its ramp.

Brigadier Sturgeon and Commodore Borland stepped out, side by side, followed by their staff officers. Sturgeon went around the Dragon's left, Borland to the right. The gun squad saluted them as they passed.

As the two flag officers approached the stairs, Bass commanded, "Squads, sa-*lute!*" The Marines on the stairs sharply shifted their blasters from port arms to rifle salute, holding their weapons vertically in front of their bodies.

Sturgeon and Borland kept pace with each other as they mounted the stairs. On the terrace they exchanged salutes with Bass and Hyakowa, then advanced to the local dignitary standing in the middle of the line of besashed and bedecked people, the one who was also wearing the broadest sash and most badges and medallions—and happened to be the fleshiest. In the background, Bass commanded, "Order, *arms!*" and each of the Marines snapped his blaster down, butt on the stair next to his right foot, aligned with the middle of his leg.

"Mr. Prime Minister, I presume?" Borland asked.

"Y-yes," the dignitary croaked. The entrance of the Marines had been rather more impressive than he'd expected.

"I'm Commodore Roger Borland, Confederation Navy, commander of the CNSS *Grandar Bay,* which is now in orbit around your planet. This"—he indicated Sturgeon—"is Brigadier Theodosius Sturgeon, Confederation Marine Corps, commander of Thirty-fourth Fleet Initial Strike Team, which is aboard my starship."

"I—I'm pleased to meet you, sir, ah, sirs. I'm Duane Foxtable, Prime Minister of the independent world Opal. And these ladies and gentlemen are my cabinet." He stumbled through introducing his companions, most of whom looked as impressed by the navy and Marine uniforms as he was.

"You said," Foxtable said when he was through with the introductions, "that your mission here has to do with Ishtar?"

"That's right, sir. May we retire to someplace where we can discuss the matter?"

"Oh, certainly! And and would you care for some refreshments? For your, ah, entourage?" Foxtable asked, nervously eyeing the Marines of third platoon.

They met in the Cabinet Room. Prime Minister Foxtable sat in the middle of one side of the conference table. The ten members of his cabinet were crowded by occupying one side of the table that they normally sat around. Far less crowded on the other side of the table were the six members of the delegation of the *Grandar Bay.* Porcelain dishware, a linen cloth, and silver setting was in place before each chair. Platters filled with what the visitors assumed were local delicacies were placed along the table's midline. Waiters moved about, filling glasses with sparkling water, and offering local caff and teas.

"Please, gentlemen," Foxtable said, waving a hand at the platters, "help yourselves. You must be hungry after your long journey to our humble world."

"Thank you, sir, but we dined before we made planetfall," Commodore Borland answered with a nod and a smile. He hoped Lieutenant Commander Gullkarl's stomach wouldn't rumble and make a liar out of him—*he* knew which of his officers had lost it on the plunge from orbit.

Foxtable blinked owlishly a couple of times, then said, "But, sirs, these are the finest delicacies Opal has to offer. They're sure to delight the most discriminating palate!" When nobody from the delegation reached for any of the food, he raised his hand to signal the waiters to remove the food. But he stopped when he saw the Minister of Exploration and the Minister of Arts and Crafts already filling their plates. He sighed.

"As you said, sir, we've come a long distance. Can we get right down to business?" Borland asked, looking pointedly along the line of ministers.

"Oh, of course, sir. Excuse my poor manners, we aren't accustomed to receiving visitors from the Confederation of Human Worlds." He haltingly made his introductions.

"To my right," Borland said after the cabinet members had been named, "is my orbital weapons officer, Lieutenant Commander Gullkarl. To his right is Lieutenant (jg) McPherson, surveillance and radar division. You've already met Brigadier Sturgeon." He looked to the Marine.

"On my left," Sturgeon said, "is Commander Daana, Thirty-fourth Fleet Initial Strike Team's intelligence officer. Beyond him is Captain Chriss, FIST operations."

Foxtable nodded and repeated the names as the officers were introduced. "I'm pleased to meet you, gentlemen," he said with a slight tremor in his voice. "But I'm sure you know that Opal is an independent world, not a member of the Confederation. No offense meant, but you have no legal standing here."

Borland's face crinkled with a wry smile. "Under normal circumstances, Mr. Prime Minister, you'd be absolutely correct. However, when the security of the Confederation of Human Worlds, or any of its members, is at issue, a Confederation Navy warship not only has legal standing, it has jurisdiction and war powers."

First squad stood at parade rest, erect, feet at shoulder width, left hand in the small of the back, blaster butt next to the right foot and held forward and out by the right hand gripping the forestock, facing the Cabinet Room from the other side of the corridor. The rise and fall of the Marines' chests with their breathing and their eyes shifting from one to another of the local guards facing them were their only movements.

The six guards, uniformed members of the Opal paramilitary, tried to look relaxed by slouching against the wall. But they were entirely too unnerved by the silent and still men facing them. Those Marines might have been dressed as gaudily as calico tanagers, but they radiated strength and threat, as though the slightest wrong move would spark them into instant, deadly violence.

Meanwhile, second squad and gun squad were enjoying an hour's liberty, restricted to Government Plaza, a largish square in front of the Stone House, the main offices of Opal's administration. The similarly named Government Square, alongside which the planetary legislature was housed, was a kilometer and a half to the west. Government Plaza was lined with intimate eateries and trendy shoppes—all of which were quite happy to accept Confederation military scrip in lieu of local currency; the restaurateurs and shoppe keepers knew they could resell the scrip as novelties for more than the official trade rate.

Lance Corporal Schultz looked around, his gaze seeming to scan the square like radar, seeking out enemy shapes or movement. On his second sweep, his eyes stopped, fixing on a lunch counter with a sign announcing "Summerville's Garden." Each letter in the name was a different color; a dozen covered the spectrum from brilliant red to pale yellow; there were two greens, dusky blue, bright blue, a blue so dark it was almost black, and a lone pink. The apostrophe was inverted, point up, looking like nothing so much as a spot of blood about to drop.

Schultz didn't say anything, or point at the sign—he didn't even grunt. He just stepped out on a beeline for Summerville's Garden.

"Hammer looks like he knows where he's going," Lance Corporal MacIlargie said. "Has he ever been here before?"

Corporal Claypoole shook his head as he got out his personal comm. He tapped a query into it and looked at the reply for a long moment before saying wonderingly, "Who'd a thunk it? Hammer Schultz is a fructivore?"

"A *what*?"

"A fructivore. An animal that subsists on fruit."

"Hammer?"

"This I gotta see." Claypoole briskly followed Schultz's rapidly receding back. MacIlargie yelped and scampered to catch up. Along the way, Claypoole explained, "Summerville's Gardens is an agricultural world that grows fruits of all kinds and exports them to the richer worlds."

"Whatever you say, honcho." MacIlargie didn't sound as if he really believed his fire team leader. "But that sign says 'Garden,' not 'Gardens.' "

Claypoole shrugged and picked up his pace.

Inside they found Schultz sitting at a table set for three, his back to the wall, facing the entrance. A waitress was just finishing taking his order as the two arrived.

"Same for them," Schultz rumbled at her.

"Three house specials, coming up," the waitress said. Her eyes twinkled as she spun about to carry the order to the kitchen window.

"What's that?" Claypoole asked suspiciously. "What's the house special?"

"Yeah, what's that?" MacIlargie echoed, but he made sure he was beyond Schultz's easy reach before he did.

"Fargo has gotten information that mining using slave labor is being conducted on Ishtar," Commodore Borland said. "We require every-thing you have on Ishtar's mining operations and the labor situation there."

"B-but," Prime Minister Foxtable sputtered, "there isn't any min-ing on Ishtar!"

A couple of places to his right, the Minister of Mines and Re-sources nearly choked when he heard Borland's words. He cleared his throat and kept his eyes on his plate so he didn't see the way Sturgeon looked at him.

"That's not what we hear, sir," Borland said. "Our mission is to in-vestigate the situation and, if we find slave labor, to put an end to it." He stared into Foxtable's bewildered face, but the Prime Minister had nothing to say. "We also have reports that the slaves are aliens and are in active rebellion. Our mission is also to put down the rebellion."

The Minister of Security paled when he heard that. Borland turned to him.

"Sir, do you have something to say on the matter?"

"Who, me? No, no—no. I've heard nothing about slaves or a re-bellion. Or mining, either," he quickly added. "No, I do-don't have anything to say."

"Rondow? Do you know something you haven't told me?" Foxtable asked the Minister of Security.

Minister of Security Rondow started at being addressed by Foxtable. Looking down at the empty plate in front of himself, he said, "Th-there's nothing I haven't t-told you, Prime Minister. You get my f-full report every morning. I n-never leave anyth-thing out."

Foxtable's nostrils flared as he studied the Minister of Security, but he didn't challenge the statement. Instead he looked from one end of the line of ministers to the other.

"Can anybody shed any light on this matter?"

The officers from the *Grandar Bay* attempted to make eye contact with the ministers. The Minister of Commerce looked baffled. The Minister of Transportation looked back at them blankly. The Minister of Space Operations blinked a few times but met the eyes that looked at him. The other ministers looked down or to the sides, anywhere but at the navy and Marine officers.

When he could see that none of his ministers had anything to offer—or anything they were willing to admit to—Foxtable looked at Borland and Sturgeon and spread his hands apologetically.

"All right, then," Borland said. "We still require all the information you have on Ishtar: geology, geography, weather, and indigenous life forms. Also, we need to interview everybody who has been there."

Foxtable swallowed. "The data is easily enough done. But the few people who have actually been there . . . I'll have to have a list made up. But some of the few who have been to Ishtar, well, some of them might have relocated to islands elsewhere on Opal."

"That's no problem. We have suborbital craft that can get us anywhere on Opal in no more than two or three hours."

The waitress returned in less than fifteen minutes with a tray on which were three covered dishes. She deftly set one in front of each of the three Marines, tucked the tray under her arm, and upended the covers from the deep dishes.

"Thank you," Lance Corporal Schultz said. He plunged his fork into his dish's contents, began eating, and sighed contentedly.

Corporal Claypoole and Lance Corporal MacIlargie looked suspiciously at their dishes. Claypoole picked up his fork and experimentally poked at the colorful contents.

"What is this mess?" he asked.

Schultz masticated, swallowed, and growled, "Eat." He forked more into his mouth.

MacIlargie timorously slid his fork into the food and took a tentative bite. He chewed, blinked a few times, and took a bigger bite. Then he dug in with almost as much gusto as Schultz.

Claypoole looked at his men, wondering if they were setting him up for some trick, and decided that MacIlargie wasn't that good an actor. He took a bite.

Summerville's Garden's house special was something Claypoole and MacIlargie had never imagined, although it was quite obvious that Schultz had eaten—and liked—it sometime in the past. The dish, not quite deep enough to properly be called a bowl, held a multicolored arrangement of fruit, not all of which Claypoole could identify, and chunks of seared meat, all in a thickened sauce of what seemed to be mixed fruit and meat juices. Claypoole couldn't identify the meat, either, but that might have been because of the mix of fruit flavors in which it was buried rather than because he hadn't had it before.

"Good," he said around mouthfuls.

"Got that right," MacIlargie said through a mouthful of food.

Schultz nodded, too busy eating to make any vocal noises.

Just as they were finishing, Claypoole got a call on his comm. "Report back to the Dragons immediately."

"What *was* that?" Claypoole asked as the three headed back to the beach.

"House special" was all Schultz said.

"How many of them do you think will wind up in prison?" Commodore Borland asked when the officers were back on the Dragon that had brought them to Berrican. They'd gotten all the data Prime Minister Foxtable admitted to having on Ishtar, and what the Prime Minister swore was a complete list of everybody who had been to Ishtar, with their current locations.

Brigadier Sturgeon snorted. "Could end up more than half of them."

Borland shook his head. "Fools. Don't they realize how much trouble they could be in for deliberately withholding information from a Confederation expeditionary mission?"

"Locals seldom do," Sturgeon answered.

Soon after, the last of the Marines on liberty reported back to the Dragons.

Borland called for two suborbitals from the *Grandar Bay*. He divided the list of persons who had been on Ishtar among the officers, including Lieutenant Bass, and had Bass assign two enlisted Marines to accompany each of them when they went to interview the people on their lists. After that, Sturgeon allowed first squad and the Dragon crews onshore liberty. Staff Sergeant Hyakowa would be in charge of the three Marines left at Berrican guarding the Dragons, and of the Marines on liberty.

By mid-morning the next day, everyone on the master list had been interviewed. They all seemed more forthcoming than Prime Minister Foxtable and his cabinet had been. But they added nothing to what the *Grandar Bay* and Thirty-fourth FIST already knew.

CHAPTER ELEVEN

Ishtar was a third of an orbit ahead of Opal, far enough to justify jumping into Beam Space. Two and a half days out from Opal, the *Grandar Bay* made its first jump—to one light-year out of the system. Beam Space navigation wasn't precise enough to allow for jumps of a few light-hours with anything close to accuracy; the generally accepted shortest distance for a reasonably accurate jump with a good navigator was three light-years. Commodore Borland was confident enough of his navigator that he was willing to go the shorter distance. His confidence was justified when the *Grandar Bay* returned to Space-3 only two days' travel from Ishtar. Total transit time was just under five days, standard.

The bad part was, anybody on Opal who wanted to alert the supposed slavers on Ishtar could have gotten a radio message to them a good four and a half days before the *Grandar Bay* reached orbit around the inner planet.

"Sir, radar reports contacts in orbit," the talker said into the hush of the bridge.

Commodore Borland reached for his comm and tapped for Surveillance and Radar. "This is the Commodore. Tell me."

"Sir, McPherson. Three ships and at least one satellite in geo. No IFF. I have my best people working on identification of ship types."

"Notify me immediately. Good work."

"Aye aye, sir. Thank you, sir." The *Grandar Bay* had only been out of Beam Space for a few minutes and already they'd spotted the ships in orbit around Ishtar. Excellent work.

Borland tapped S and R off, and tapped for communications.

"Captain Arden, sir."

"S and R reports three contacts in orbit, plus one geosync. Notify me instantly if they make contact. Do not attempt to initiate contact unless I give specific orders."

"Sir, notify you instantly if contact is attempted. Do not initiate contact without specific orders from you. Aye aye, sir."

"Borland out."

Captain Wilma Arden, running the communications division. A captain in a lieutenant commander's billet. Borland refrained from shaking his head at the thought. She and Lieutenant Commander Gullkarl had the misfortune of having been in the chain of events that brought the attention of the Chief of Naval Operations to the possibility of Skinks on Maugham's Station. A possibility that didn't pan out, as it happened. They'd understood the vague report that had been unofficially passed on to them well enough to know that it implied hostile aliens, about whom they'd heard rumors. But it was evidence of the existence of aliens, which at the time was a closely guarded military secret, so secret that the *Grandar Bay* had been reported lost in Beam Space and Thirty-fourth FIST had been quarantined to prevent word from getting out. Arden and Gullkarl had been given their choice: life on the penal world Darkover or assignment to a starship lost in Beam Space. The two civilians in that chain of events weren't given the choice. Gullkarl had been a fit into the *Grandar Bay*'s Orbital Weapons Division. But there was no proper place to assign a captain. So Borland had assigned Arden to temporarily replace the communications officer, a lieutenant commander, when the man was injured and unable to return to duty. The existence of the hostile

Skinks was now public knowledge, but Arden and Gullkarl were stuck on the *Grandar Bay* under the no-transfer, no-release-from-active-duty orders for the starship.

Still, a captain in a lieutenant commander's billet. It offended Borland's sense of propriety.

But there was nothing he could do about it. Not now. Perhaps if, in the future, an amphibious task force was assembled around the *Grandar Bay*, he could reassign Arden to the Commodore's staff. But not now. For now she was stuck in a billet two ranks below hers, one at which she wasn't totally competent. She did a good enough job, though. She knew enough to pay attention to her subordinates who knew more than she did.

Borland shoved thoughts of Arden and Gullkarl from his mind and looked at the main display. Ishtar was a small circle in its center. Too small and too distant to show the orbiting ships. All he could do was wait. Wait until the S and R division identified the ships, or until one of the orbiters attempted to contact the *Grandar Bay*.

He turned to the officer of the deck. "My compliments to Brigadier Sturgeon, and an invitation for him to join me on the bridge."

The two flag officers stared at the display, which had barely changed in the quarter hour, standard, since Borland first looked at it after learning of the orbiting ships.

"It's a whole lot of we-don't-know?" Sturgeon asked after a moment.

"A *whole* lot," Borland agreed. "And no way of knowing—yet."

They watched quietly for a while longer before a report came in from Surveillance and Radar.

"Sir," McPherson reported, "they are starships. One of them is a freighter, class unidentified, but estimated at one hundred thousand tons. One appears to be a Countess-class cruise starship." He hesitated before adding, "The third is a Bomarc, model not yet identified."

"Thank you. Keep looking. Keep me informed."

"Aye aye, sir."

Borland mused for a long moment. A Bomarc in orbit was unusual; it was the only starship designed to land on a planet's surface. So why was it in orbit? The only reason he could think of was that the conditions on the surface had deteriorated too badly to risk the starship by landing it.

After they'd watched for a few more minutes, Sturgeon asked, "We're close enough to identify the types of starships in orbit. Shouldn't they have detected us by now?"

"Yes."

"Yet they've made no attempt to make contact."

"That's right."

Sturgeon looked thoughtful for a few seconds, then said, "With the Commodore's permission, I'll prepare boarding parties."

Borland nodded. "Bear in mind that we won't be in position to launch boarding parties for approximately forty-five hours."

Sturgeon nodded in turn. "My Marines haven't practiced orbital boarding in a few years. They'll need every bit of time available to train for the mission."

"Stop complaining, people," Sergeant Ratliff growled. "I know as well as you do what it was like when we boarded the *Marquis de Rien*. I was there, remember?"

"Yeah, and we lost people," Corporal Dean muttered. Ratliff shot him a look; he had thought Dean was over his fatalistic fear.

"All right, gather round," the first squad leader ordered. He looked at his men and slowly shook his head. "As I recall, only three of you, the fire team leaders, were in this squad when we boarded the smuggler's starship. There are a couple of huge differences between that boarding and the boarding we might be making tomorrow. First, we know the Tweed Hull Breacher works—Corporal Doyle fixed that."

Lance Corporals Quick and Longfellow glanced at each other but cut their snickers short when Ratliff glared at them.

"The other major difference is, then we had to chase a starship that was slingshotting around a star, close enough that we were all in danger of taking serious doses of hard radiation. *This* time we'll be boarding a starship orbiting a planet, far enough out from the planet's primary that there isn't much radiation danger, not in the time we'll be exposed."

"Are you saying this is going to be easy, Sergeant Ratliff?" Corporal Dornhofer asked.

"A lot easier than boarding the *Marquis de Rien* was."

"Who's waiting for us?" Dean asked.

Ratliff shook his head. "We don't know yet. For all we know, that Countess-class is filled with babes visiting Ishtar to work on their tans."

"Or there could be a battalion of Skinks," Dean muttered.

"Dorny, Pasquin," Ratliff said through gritted teeth, "you done this before. Start showing the newer men what to do and how to do it. Dean, come with me." He turned and stalked to a remote corner of the bay in which the Tweed Hull Breacher was being assembled for launch. He stood, arms folded across his chest, fuming, until he heard Dean's footsteps stop behind him.

Spinning around, he thrust his face into Dean's and, barely refraining from yelling, demanded, "What the hell's the matter with you, Corporal? Are you trying to scare the shit out of everybody? Get your shit together, and stop the negative comments!"

Dean looked coldly at Ratliff, not at all abashed. "When we breach that hull, we don't have any idea what's going to be waiting for us. It's a mistake to think that boarding a starship, any starship, in orbit isn't hazardous."

"Nobody's saying different, Dean. But you're the only one saying it in a way that will unnecessarily scare people."

"People *should* be scared before a boarding."

"Scared enough to be sharp, but not scared enough to be paralyzed."

The two glared at each other for a long moment. Dean was the one who broke it. He dropped his head.

"I'm sorry, Sergeant Ratliff. I'm scared. You know that." He looked at his squad leader. "And there's a lot of danger in boarding a starship. You know that, too."

"Yes I do. Now what say you help me get the junior men ready—without scaring the shit out of them."

Dean nodded. "Aye aye. Let's do it." He stepped to the side so Ratliff could pass and followed him back to where the other fire team leaders were showing the Tweed Hull Breacher to the rest of the squad.

It was less than one day to orbit, and the starships orbiting Ishtar still hadn't opened communications with the *Grandar Bay.* Borland was beginning to wonder if they were abandoned. What could have caused the watch crews to abandon their vessels? Or what could have killed or incapacitated them? The Surveillance and Radar division hadn't detected any emissions from any of the starships that couldn't more easily be accounted for by automatic systems than by directed action.

"Get me comm," he told the officer of the deck.

"Communications, aye, sir." He spoke into the comm and signaled Borland.

"Commodore here," Borland said when he reached for his comm. "Contact the starships in orbit. Tell them to identify themselves and their business here." He signed off without waiting for acknowledgment. That was an advantage of having an officer two ranks too high in that division; he knew that his orders would be carried out exactly, even if the captain in charge wasn't all that expert at her job.

S and R had identified the three starships growing on the main display. The freighter was the SS *Tidal Surge,* leased from Interstellar Tramps, a charter freight company. The Countess-class was the SS *Lady Monika,* retired from the WeddingWays Line, also leased from Interstellar Tramps. The *Grandar Bay* had no data on who leased the two starships. The Bomarc was a model 39V, registered to one Louis Cukayla; he'd named her *Pointy End.* According to several entries in

Jane's Private Paramilitary Organizations, Cukayla was the owner of Sharp Edge, a "corporate security provider."

"Now we know," Brigadier Sturgeon said when he saw that. "The 'privately owned, interstellar corporation' in the intelligence report is mercenaries."

"Mercenaries, indeed," Commodore Borland agreed. He turned his head from the display to look at the Marine. "The Skinks fight Marines to the death, but let themselves be taken prisoner and turned into slaves by mercenaries?"

"Not likely."

"I don't think so, either." Borland looked back at the display. "If the Skinks don't attack outright, like they did on Kingdom, they do something sneaky, the way they sucked in Force Recon on Haulover."

"Or on Society 437, which was where we first encountered them."

"Mercs." Borland shook his head. "Hell of a thing to have to call in the Marines for, to rescue mercenaries who got stung while doing something illegal."

"This is the Confederation Navy Starship *Grandar Bay*. Starships orbiting Ishtar, identify yourselves and state your business. CNSS *Grandar Bay* calling unidentified starships orbiting Ishtar. Identify yourselves and state your business. Over." Radioman First Class Testor sat back, waiting for the long seconds it would take the radio signals to reach the starships around the planet, for someone on board to hear the message, then to compose and send a reply. Being a generous sort, he allowed three seconds for the radio round-trip and a dozen seconds for somebody to decide what to say and to say it.

When fifteen seconds had passed with no reply to his challenge, he again called, "Confederation Navy Starship *Grandar Bay* to unidentified starships orbiting Ishtar. Identify yourselves. Over."

After another fifteen seconds without a reply, he swiveled to Captain Wilma Arden.

"Ma'am, they aren't replying." He moved his hands to indicate his comm controls. "I'm broadcasting on all standard guard freqs. Unless they've got their comms turned off, they heard me."

Arden nodded; she fully understood the implications of the lack of response. She tapped comm for the bridge and reported, "No response from the orbiting starships. Next message?"

There was a pause before Commodore Borland's voice came to her: "Tell them to identify themselves or stand by to be boarded by Confederation Marines."

"Aye, sir. Identify themselves, or stand by to be boarded by Confederation Marines." She was looking at Testor while she repeated the order. Borland signed off, and Arden told the radioman, "You heard the order. Tell them."

"Aye aye, ma'am!" Testor again requested identification from the orbiters and issued the warning. After fifteen seconds he swiveled to face Arden again. "Now what, ma'am?"

"Now we wait."

Ten minutes later, word filtered down to third platoon that it looked like they were going to have to breach the hull of the *Pointy End*.

"Third platoon got picked to go after the Bomarc because we've gone into one before, as those of you who were with us on Avionia remember," Lieutenant Bass explained to the platoon.

Corporal Dean bit his tongue to keep from yelling out, "We lost Van Impe when we boarded that Bomarc!"

"For the rest of you, the Bomarc is very unusual; it's the only starship designed to land on a planet's surface," Bass said. "Another odd thing about the Bomarc is, it has a sharply conical shape. That shape might cause problems in securing the Tweed Hull Breacher to the *Pointy End*." He smiled wryly. "We're lucky we have Corporal Doyle in the platoon. He's the one who figured out how to keep the THB from killing the Marines using it—so if the cage doesn't hold on, Doyle might be able to figure out how to make it do its job anyway."

Several of the Marines looked at Doyle, who flushed and wished he were wearing his chameleons instead of the armored vacuum suit so he could disappear.

"All right, people, button up, we're going outside for a test boarding," Bass commanded.

He waited while the Marines donned their vacuum helmets and locked them into place, waited while the fire team leaders checked the seals on their men's helmets, and the squad leaders did so on the fire team leaders'. Then he and Staff Sergeant Hyakowa checked the squad leaders' seals, donned their own vacuum helmets, and checked each other. He gave a last look at the lines tethering the Marines together.

"Third platoon sealed and ready," he reported to the chief petty officer in charge of the airlock by which the platoon was exiting.

The airlock's inner hatch opened and third platoon crowded into it, each Marine in direct contact with the one to his front, his rear, and both sides. Even though the airlock was designed to admit bulk containers, the armored vacuum suits were so bulky that contact-crowding was the only way the Marines could all fit into the airlock. The inner hatch closed with a clunk. As the air was pumped out, the chief's voice came over the platoon circuit: "You Gyrenes had best engage your boot magnets right about now, 'cause local gravity is about to disappear."

Clicks, more felt than heard, sounded through the airlock as the Marines turned on the magnets that would hold them to the deck when the local gravity was turned off. The atmosphere in the airlock wasn't completely purged when the Marines felt themselves lifting slightly; they were happy for the magnets that held them in place. A moment later, the outer hatch opened. Pressure from behind forced the front row of Marines to lean out of the hatch so they were standing at an angle to the deck.

"Don't turn your boot magnets off until you're told to," a petty officer second class who was waiting outside said into the platoon circuit. "Don't exit by yourselves; let my deckhands guide you." The

Marines had already been drilled on the procedure, but that was in a cargo bay, with full gravity throughout the exercise.

Four sailors used brief puffs from their backpack jets to approach the front row of four Marines and took their arms. They touched helmets and said, "Release your magnets now." The words carried by induction, so only the men being told heard. The front row released and the sailors drew them out and gave them a gentle push. The sailors repeated with the second row of Marines as they shuffled to the front of the airlock. In less than two minutes, all of third platoon was outside the *Grandar Bay,* slowly drifting away from the starship.

The sailors, under the direction of the chief, jetted to the front of the four lines of Marines, grasped them by an arm, and tugged them toward the Tweed Hull Breacher, situated a kilometer distant. The THB was already attached to a large sheet of 50mm-thick plate armor, much stronger and probably thicker than the skin of the Bomarc V39. The four sailors guided the Marines at a tangent to the THB before turning directly toward it. Unlike the earlier version of the THB that third platoon had used when boarding the *Marquis de Rien,* this one didn't have an airtight chamber but rather was open to space except for a deck for the Marines and the petty officer operating the cutting controls to stand on. And the deck had been extended so that three of the four files of Marines could stand on it at the same time. The fourth file took defensive positions around the THB, simulating guarding against an attack from a hatch somewhere else on the simulated vessel. Four of the Marines in the first two rows picked up rams that were waiting for them.

The business end of the THB was a three-meter by three-meter hatch, open for the moment. The two sides of the hatch exposed a rectangle of gas jets aimed at the sheet of plate armor. When turned on, they would cut through the plate.

A petty officer second class manned the controls. He finished checking the nozzles and closed the sides of the hatch. He waited for the order to begin cutting. As soon as the first three lines of Marines were secured to the deck by their boot magnets, the chief supervising the operation told him, "Cut it," and he turned the dials that caused gases to be pumped into the mixing chamber and then shoot out of the nozzles.

Almost immediately, everybody on the THB felt the vibrations and pops of the metal heating up—but they couldn't see what was happening through the closed hatch. A harsher crack told them the plate armor was breaking loose along the cut. A few seconds later, the second class cut the gases off and opened the hatch to expose a rectangle of red, runny metal adjacent to the nozzles.

The four Marines with the rams stepped forward and slammed them into the plate. The cut section of plate armor shot away and began tumbling. The Marines released their boot magnets and bolted through the opening, where they were met by three of the same sailors who had guided them to the THB. The sailors brought the first Marines under control and began guiding the three lines away from the remainder of the plate armor and the THB.

"Is that all there is to it?" PFC John Three McGinty asked when the sailors had the Marines formed up again and headed back to the still-open airlock.

"Not hardly, Triple John," Corporal Dean said. "We weren't dealing with atmosphere gushing out of the hole in the hull, or with transition to the starship's generated gravity."

"Or not, if the gravity's turned off," Sergeant Kerr added.

When third platoon exited the airlock back into the cargo hold where they'd formed up for the exercise, they learned that they were standing down from a forced entry of the *Pointy End.*

"A message is coming in, ma'am," Radioman First Class Testor said.

"Don't reply," Captain Arden said. "Pipe it to me."

"Aye aye, ma'am." Testor did something with his controls, and Arden listened to the incoming message.

"Hello, *Grandar Bay*! This is the *Pointy End,* you know, that sharp-looking Bomarc you can probably see. Whom do I have the honor of speaking to? And what the hell is the Confederation Navy doing here? Not that we're not glad to see you, of course; we most certainly are. The *Grandar Bay,* huh? That's a surprise, I heard you were lost in Beam Space."

As soon as the caller identified where he was calling from, Arden contacted the bridge. "For the Commodore," she said. "We have a message from the *Pointy End.*"

"Let me hear it," Borland said. After listening, he said, "Pipe me in. I'll answer the call."

As soon as he was told he was patched into the ship-to-ship comm, Borland said, "*Pointy End,* this is Commodore Roger Borland, captain of the CNSS *Grandar Bay.* Who is speaking for you?"

"Well, now, Commodore. Hmm. Ain't commodore some kind of admiral? Never mind. I'm Louis Cukayla, owner and master of the *Pointy End.* Also owner, chief executive officer, and chief operations officer of Sharp Edge, LLC. Now, like I said, what brings the Confederation Navy to Ishtar? Gotta say, though, I'm sure glad you showed up."

"Perhaps the better question, Mr. Cukayla, is what are *you* doing here? And while you're at it, you can explain to me about the two leased starships you also have in orbit around Ishtar."

"I'm here doing what Sharp Edge does, providing corporate security. The two leased ships are here to transport and provision my security personnel. What else would they be doing here?"

"Mr. Cukayla, as soon as we are close enough I will send a lighter to the *Pointy End* to bring you to me—"

"That'd be kinda difficult, Commodore, seeing as how I'm planetside. You might have heard, I've got a bit of a situation here. Come to think of it, you've probably heard of my situation and that must be why you're here. Say, isn't the *Grandar Bay* part of the gator navy? Do you have Marines on board? I'll be even happier to see them than I am to see you!"

"Give me your coordinates. I'll send a platoon of Marines to secure a landing field. Then I'll come to meet with you. *Grandar Bay* out."

Only then did Borland look at Brigadier Sturgeon, who had entered the bridge during the conversation. "How much of that did you hear?" he asked.

"Enough. I'll have the infantry battalion prepare a reinforced platoon to be the point team, with the rest of its company to follow shortly. My primary staff and I will be with the company."

CHAPTER TWELVE

"Button up tight, Mo-reens," the coxswain ordered when the three Dragons his Essay was ferrying to the surface of Ishtar were locked in place. "We got us a long way to go on this here rocky road, and you just know I'm taking it at high speed."

"Great, just what we need," Corporal Claypoole grumbled. "A squid who likes the sound of his own voice driving this sucker."

"Maybe the g-forces will clamp his mouth shut," the gun squad's Corporal Kindrachuck offered.

"Nah, ain't how it works," Lance Corporal MacIlargie said. "On an assault landing, g-forces force your mouth open. He won't be *able* to shut up."

"Nobody told you you could talk, Wolfman." Corporal Chan had chimed in. "This is corporal talk; no peons allowed."

"Say what?" MacIlargie squawked.

"Corporal talk," Corporal Taylor agreed. "Right, Corporal Doyle?"

"What? Doyle gets to talk, and I don't?" MacIlargie sounded outraged.

"That's 'Corporal Doyle' to you, Wolfman," Claypoole said. He reached from his webbing to smack MacIlargie on the helmet.

"Lance Corporal MacIlargie," Doyle, glad to be included in the corporals' banter, said, "you're a senior lance corporal. It's incumbent upon you to set a good example for men junior to you. Now be quiet and respectful of your superiors."

Chan howled with laughter, then hooted, "That's telling him, Doyle!"

In the rear of the Dragon's troop compartment, Lieutenant Humphrey, the company's executive officer, listened to the high-spirited chatter with half an ear, amused by the way the enlisted men distracted themselves from the coming rough ride planetside. The rest of his attention was fixed on the sounds and movements that told him the atmosphere was being sucked from the *Grandar Bay*'s well deck, that the well deck hatch was being opened, and that the Essay bearing the Dragon was being gently pushed out of the starship.

Everybody noticed when the Essay's engines engaged and sent the shuttle along the axis of the starship to get into position to begin its rapid descent to the surface.

Most of Company L's third platoon was in one Dragon; the rest of the platoon was in the second Dragon with half of the assault section that Commander van Winkle had decided to reinforce the platoon with. The remainder of the assault section was in the third Dragon, along with the FIST's recon squad. Lieutenant Humphrey was along in overall command of the fifty Marines heading planetside. Humphrey would be the first man off the first Dragon when they reached Base Camp, Sharp Edge's primary base of operations, where Louis Cukayla awaited them.

Base Camp was far to the north, where temperatures weren't too extreme, normally in the upper thirties centigrade, in order to give Sharp Edge's operatives occasional relief from the high temperatures they worked in elsewhere. It was too far inland for the Essay to make the Marines' traditional over-the-horizon water landing. Instead it came down on what passed for a lake on Ishtar, a smallish hollow no more than four acres in area, filled with brackish water, a couple of kilometers from Base Camp. Orbital observation had shown Base Camp to be a cluster of ten buildings laid out on a grid, with clearly delineated walkways. Two of the buildings were oversize and tentatively identified as storehouses. Three were probably living quarters, and a smaller one was likely the quarters of Louis Cukayla. One, centrally located, was identified as a dining facility. Two others were garages. Another was likely the administration building, and the remaining one was tentatively identified as an energy control center. There were three watchtowers and what appeared to be a small airfield for VTOL/VSTOL aircraft.

The Essay disgorged its Dragons, which roared ashore on their air cushions, and sped inland on billowing clouds of dust and dirt.

"Calculated to impress the natives," Humphrey murmured to himself. As were the chameleon utilities the Marines all wore. Not that these natives were all that impressed.

The Dragon jolted to a stop in front of the clapboard building with the most ornate frontage, the one that had been identified as the probable administration building. The Dragon spun about so it faced away and dropped its ramp. Lieutenant Humphrey was the first man off. He marched straight at the three men standing on the building's portico. The three could see him only because he carried his helmet tucked under one arm and had his gloves off and sleeves rolled up. The exposed skin of his head and arms prickled as beads of sweat popped out and evaporated almost immediately.

The Marines who'd ridden with Humphrey sprinted out behind him and wrapped around the sides of the building to set up security to the rear of Base Camp. The other Dragons nosed in toward the first and dropped their ramps; the Marines aboard them boiled out to complete the defensive circle around Base Camp. The air rang with the shouts of NCOs moving their men into position and the clangs of heavy weapons locking onto bipods and tripods. A background hum of climate control equipment issued from the buildings.

Two of the three men on the portico were startled by the voices and noises they heard in places where there was nobody to be seen. The man in the middle ignored the voices and clangs in favor of staring at the approaching disembodied head and arms—he didn't appear to be startled.

"Can't quite put my finger on exactly what it is, but you don't look like my image of a Confederation Navy commodore," the middle man said.

"And I am not, sir," Humphrey said, stopping a pace before the stairs leading the the portico. "I'm Lieutenant Humphrey, Confederation Marine Corps. I'm the executive officer of Company L of the infantry battalion, Thirty-fourth Fleet Initial Strike Team. And you are?"

"Why, I'm Louis Cukayla," the man said, looking from one to another of the Dragons. He was thin-faced and wiry, except for bulging shoulders and arms; his shirt was tailored to accentuate those muscles. "Where's Commodore Borland? Why isn't he here yet? Or is he here in one of those invisibility suits you Marines wear?" For the first time he looked to where the shouting voices and clanging weapons had fallen silent. "And speaking of Marines, just what are you doing there?"

"Sir, Commodore Borland will be planetside once proper security is set. Which is what my Marines are doing right now."

"Setting security?" Cukayla said incredulously. "Why, this is the most secure place on this whole damn roasting world!"

"I'm sure it is, sir," Humphrey said drily, "but we Marines always take care of our own security."

Lieutenant Bass, having just completed a quick survey of the defensive positions the Marines had taken, suddenly appeared at Humphrey's side. *Suddenly* is the operative word—he didn't take off his helmet until he was standing next to the company's XO, when he whipped it off in a well-practiced motion that made his head appear to pop into existence.

"Security's in place, sir," he reported.

"Thank you, Lieutenant," Humphrey said. He turned to Cukayla and said, "Lieutenant Bass is temporarily second in command here."

" 'Temporarily'? What do you mean 'temporarily'?" Cukayla demanded. But Humphrey didn't answer; he was contacting the *Grandar Bay* to let them know that third platoon (reinforced) was on site and had secured the perimeter. He listened for a moment, acknowledged the message he received, and, signing off, returned his attention to Cukayla. "Did you say something, sir?" he asked.

"Yes—no, wait a minute. Did you say Fleet Initial Strike Team?"

"Yes, sir. Thirty-fourth FIST."

Cukayla looked thoughtful for a moment, then cocked his head and said, "Seems I've heard of that outfit. Thirty-fourth FIST is some kind of famous, isn't it?"

"We are well traveled, sir."

Bass had finished removing his gloves and rolling up his sleeves. He grinned fiercely. "We've got a reputation, yeah. More deployments and more combat than any other unit in the Confederation military."

Cukayla still looked thoughtful, but his excitement was building, visible in the slight twitching of his arms and legs. "Seems to me I've heard something else. Something about aliens." He gave the two Marines a challenging look.

"Yes, sir, we've had more contact with aliens, hostile and otherwise, than any other unit."

"Well now," Cukayla said grinning broadly, "you've come to exactly the right place. 'Cause we're fighting aliens here."

Commodore Borland, Brigadier Sturgeon, and their primary staffs, along with the rest of Company L, began boarding the Dragons on two Essays as soon as Lieutenant Humphrey notified the *Grandar Bay* that his party was planetside and had received a friendly greeting from Sharp Edge. They were all aboard and strapped into the webbing and the Essays were easing out of the well deck when Humphrey radioed that the perimeter at Base Camp was secure. Moments later, the two Essays began their planetward plunge. They landed in the same small lake in which the first Essay had made planetfall. The Dragons flowed off the Essays and roared ashore.

Louis Cukayla met them on the portico of his administration building. His second in command, Johnny Paska, stood on one side of the Sharp Edge boss, and Lieutenants Humphrey and Bass on his other. Cukayla and Paska were in shirtsleeves; Humphrey and Bass had their helmets tucked under their left arms. All four men's faces and arms glistened with sweat.

"Commodore Borland, I'm sure glad to see you!" Cukayla almost shouted as he bounded down the stairs to grasp Borland's hand and pump it with both of his. He grinned as he looked at Sturgeon, obviously wanting an introduction to the man he just as obviously thought commanded the Marines.

Borland extracted his hand from Cukayla's and introduced Sturgeon.

"Fleet Initial Strike Team, hot damn!" Cukayla crowed. "Thirty-fourth you say? Ain't that outfit some kind of famous?"

"We've had our share of deployments into harm's way," Sturgeon said modestly.

"Gentlemen, it's *hot* out here," Cukayla said, just as loudly as he'd greeted Borland. Sweat was running down his face and had darkened his shirt. "Let's get inside before we roast out here." He led the way up to the portico and inside.

"If you think this is bad," Cukayla said once the door was closed behind them, "wait till you go south. For Ishtar, this is a pretty temperate climate, bordering on cool."

The clerks' desks had been pushed to the walls, and chairs set about so everybody could have a seat. The clerks themselves were pressed into waiter duty and busied themselves serving cold drinks to the visitors. Plates of cookies were set in easy reach of everyone.

"I'm sure glad to see you gents," Cukayla said when everybody had found a place to sit. "My operations have been going to hell in recent months."

"Just what are your operations here, sir?" Borland asked.

"Mining!" Cukayla beamed. "Ishtar has some of the best rubies and sapphires ever found in Human Space, not to mention the best diamonds. So many diamonds that, if they weren't such high quality, they would drop the bottom right out of the market. We've got almost sixty mines in operation." His smile abruptly turned into a frown. "Or we did, until our workers began stampeding. I've had to shut down a quarter of the mines because the animals were killing the guards and overseers."

"Mr. Cukayla, I'll admit, we don't have full mapping of Ishtar yet, but so far we haven't found any mining pits. Where are your mines?"

Cukayla grinned at Borland. "Course you didn't see any pits, Commodore. The mines are mostly underground."

Borland looked reflective as he said, "Underground? I thought gems were mostly found in alluvial deposits, or volcanic pipes that lead from deep in the magma."

"They are, they are. But the geology of Ishtar is so active that alluvial deposits don't last long before they get covered by volcanic ash or pyroclastic flows." He grinned again. "I like to think of our mines as being dug in fossil alluvial deposits."

Borland nodded, accepting the explanation for the moment.

"Sir," Sturgeon said, "you said your workers have begun stampeding and animals are killing your people. I don't understand workers stampeding, and how is it that animals are attacking your people? Where do the animals come from?"

"Ah, yes, that's right, you don't know," Cukayla said, looking like he was about to tell a great secret. "The workers and the animals are the same. You see, the initial investigations of Ishtar didn't discover the Fuzzies—that's what we call these animals. They live in burrows, like rabbits or something, so nobody saw them I guess. They're pretty smart, like chimpanzees or something. They can be taught some basic jobs, like how to bash a rock into the sediment, and pick the gems out of it and put them into a collection bin." He shrugged. "At first it seemed a lot easier and cheaper than using human miners. Hey, no labor unions, no wage problems, we don't have to search the Fuzzies to keep them from stealing, and they can't talk, so no complaints."

Sturgeon felt disgusted, both by Cukayla's attitude toward his "workers" and about the situation.

"Marines aren't animal control, we're warriors," he said.

Cukayla looked at him levelly. "You may change your mind about 'animal control' when you learn more about the situation here. Anyways, aren't Marines supposed to protect humans?"

"Tell me about the 'stampedes,'" Sturgeon said, pushing Cukayla's question aside.

Cukayla shrugged and adopted a serious mien. "One night some of them got out of their cages at one of the mines and attacked the crew. Killed all of 'em."

"You keep them in cages?" Borland asked.

"Overnight? Course we do! We have three, four hundred of 'em at most of the mines, and only thirty or so of my people on staff." He snorted. "That's not enough to keep them from wandering off at night, not unless we restrain them somehow. Cages turned out to be the easiest way."

"Mr. Cukayla, you've raised so many questions in my mind," Borland said. "I've read the reports from the Bureau of Human Habitability Exploration and Investigation, and Opal's reports on their explorations of Ishtar. There is no mention of gemstones anywhere in those documents. How does it happen that you found these places and set up mines?"

"I didn't find them," Cukayla said with a shake of his head. "I'm not a prospector. Someone else did and contracted Sharp Edge to oversee the operations here."

"Who is that someone else?"

Cukayla shook his head. "I'm sorry, Commodore. I'm not at liberty to tell you. And even if I was, all I could tell you is the name of the intermediary who came to me."

Sturgeon raised a skeptical eyebrow. "You don't know who you're working for?"

Another head shake. "All I can tell you is their creds are good. I'm making enough on this operation to keep Sharp Edge going for a lot of years, and for me to retire early." His eyes gleamed.

Borland and Sturgeon exchanged looks, neither quite sure how much of what Cukayla said to believe—except that neither believed he had been totally truthful in what he'd said so far. Borland gave Sturgeon an almost imperceptible nod, and the Marine took over.

"These 'Fuzzies,' as you call them," Sturgeon said. "Do they have claws or fangs? Are they particularly big? How did they kill your staff, and exactly what do you mean when you say they stampeded?"

"Nah, they aren't particularly big. Not much more than a meter and a half tall on their hind feet. They've got claws, but more like what a dog has than cat's claws. They eat bugs and tubers, shit like that that they dig out of the ground. That's what their claws are for, and they don't need big fangs for that. Here, I'll show you what they look like. Johnny, if you will, please."

Johnny Paska drew a remote from his shirt pocket and aimed it at a vid screen hanging on the wall. A 2-D slide show began.

The first image was of a roughly man-shaped being thinly covered with reddish fur. There was nothing in the image to indicate his size, but he looked small, like a fifteen-year-old human. The creature was aggressively male, if the bulge on his lower abdomen was the penis sheath it appeared to be. His arms hung forward from sloping shoulders, and his legs were bowed. Both hands and feet ended in short but strong-looking claws. He had large eyes, a black button nose, and a weak chin. A tail hung down behind. The reason for the weak chin was apparent in the next image, a profile view; the lower part of the creature's face protruded in a short snout. In this view, the tail was angled back and looked to be longer than the torso. He was also shown in profile on all fours. His fingers were curled to make a platform that turned his arms into front legs. His tail stuck almost straight up.

"They drop onto all fours if they're in a real hurry to get someplace," Paska explained.

The images of the evident male were followed by two of what looked like a female. At least, this one lacked the penis sheath and had two pairs of prominent, breastlike bulges on her abdomen. A fifth showed the two side by side from the front, and the female before the male in profile. The male was a couple of centimeters taller than the female.

A last image showed the two standing to either side of Paska. They reached his shoulders. Neither creature wore any clothes but both were adorned with an array of straps and pouches of what looked like some kind of leather.

"Did they give you any problem about wearing the straps and pouches?" Sturgeon asked when the slides had run their course.

Cukayla barked out a short, high-pitched laugh. "We didn't do that. The Fuzzies come with that stuff on them."

Sturgeon and Borland looked at him.

"They make belts and pouches out of, of—what is that, leather?" Borland asked.

Cukayla smirked. "I told you they were *smart* animals. Yeah, they make that stuff. It's from the hide of this giant snakelike thing that grows in the tropics here."

"They make things," Sturgeon said slowly. "And you call them animals?"

"Sure. They run around naked and live in holes in the ground. They come out during the day and grub around in the dirt for insectoids and roots that they eat raw. And we caught them just like you catch herd animals; we put up large fences like corrals and chased them into them. That ain't too bright of them."

"How do they kill people?" Sturgeon asked. "The Fuzzies you've showed us are small and unarmed, except for the stones they use to pound on the sediment in the mines. Your people are armed."

Cukayla made a face. "When they attack, they're armed," he said hesitantly.

Sturgeon raised an eyebrow. "Armed? How?"

"Some kind of projectile thrower," Cukayla reluctantly said.

"Bows?"

"Nah. Shit, I hate to say this, but they came up with some kind of single-shot rifles. Damned if I know where they got them, or how they learned to use 'em." He looked from Sturgeon to Borland and back. "Like I said, they're smart animals."

"*Very* smart animals," Sturgeon said. He thought for a moment. During his career he'd encountered a few species of exceptionally intelligent animals, including a couple of species that could be trained to use simple firearms. He remembered that those species had trouble aiming and reloading, so they weren't very effective with the weapons. He asked, "How good is their aim with those rifles?"

" 'Bout as good as you or me."

Sturgeon looked at Borland, who asked, "Mr. Cukayla, has it occurred to you that the Fuzzies might actually be sentient, and not just 'smart animals'?"

"What? Don't be ridiculous! They live in holes in the ground and grub in the dirt for food."

"Have you or any of your people gone into their burrows?" Sturgeon asked.

"Of course not! What do you think we are, moles?"

"Then how do you know that their burrows are just 'holes in the ground'?"

"What else would they be?" Cukayla asked incredulously.

Sturgeon chuckled. "You might be surprised, sir. My Marines and I have chased many foes into 'holes in the ground' that turned out to be very elaborate tunnel systems with living and storage caverns."

Cukayla snorted. "All you have to do is look at how the Fuzzies act when they're out in the open to know that they're just animals."

"Animals who make leather belts and straps and pouches, and can accurately aim rifles," Borland said. "Tell me," he said briskly, "do you pay your workers wages? What about medical services? Do you give them days off? What about home leave?"

"Wages for animals? Days off? Home leave? Commodore, were you in the heat too long before we came inside? Now *you're* talking like a dumb animal."

Borland looked at Sturgeon, who nodded and turned back to Cukayla.

"Sir," Sturgeon said, "Thirty-fourth FIST is the Confederation's designated military first alien contact force. Everything you have told and shown me about the Fuzzies leads me to suspect that they are sentient. We must make a determination of that before we can proceed."

"Mr. Cukayla, as the senior Confederation official on or around Ishtar, I hereby instruct you to immediately cease all mining operations and let loose every Fuzzy under your control until this matter is decided one way or the other."

"You can't do that!" Cukayla exploded.

"Oh, but I most certainly can, Mr. Cukayla. And there is an entire Marine FIST aboard my starship to enforce my instructions, should you fail to abide by them."

"And I've got two thousand seasoned fighters on Ishtar, and more on their way if you want to try and stop me," Cukayla snarled.

"That would not be advisable, Mr. Cukayla," Sturgeon said softly. "Not only would you be throwing away the lives of your people, but you'd be in violation of Confederation law and make yourself subject to severe legal penalties."

"I'm no spacelanes lawyer, but I don't think you have the authority to shut down my operations here."

"But we do." Borland slipped his right hand into a pocket and brought out his personal comp. He tapped out a quick command. "Will this do?" he asked, showing the display to Cukayla.

OFFICE OF THE PRESIDENT

THE CONFEDERATION OF HUMAN WORLDS

FARGO, EARTH

PRESIDENTIAL DIRECTIVE:

TO: WHOMEVER THIS DOCUMENT IS PRESENTED

GREETINGS:

THE BEARER OF THIS DOCUMENT, COMMODORE ROGER BORLAND, COMMANDING OFFICER OF THE CNSS *GRANDAR BAY,*

CONFEDERATION NAVY, IS ACTING UNDER THE DIRECT ORDERS OF
THE PRESIDENT OF THE CONFEDERATION OF HUMAN WORLDS IN
OPERATIONS AGAINST HOSTILE ALIENS. IN SAID CAPACITY, HE IS
AUTHORIZED TO DEMAND ANY INFORMATION AND/OR ASSISTANCE
THAT HE DEEMS PERTINENT TO HIS OPERATIONS FROM ANY
INDIVIDUAL HE BELIEVES HAS ANY SUCH INFORMATION OR CAN
PROVIDE SUCH ASSISTANCE. FAILURE OF ANY INDIVIDUAL TO
COMPLY WITH THE DEMANDS FOR INFORMATION BY THE BEARER
SHALL BE CONSIDERED TO BE AN ACT OF TREASON AGAINST
HUMANITY, AND WILL BE MET WITH THE MOST SEVERE PENALTIES
ALLOWABLE BY LAW.

CYNTHIA CHANG-STURDEVANT
PRESIDENT
CONFEDERATION OF HUMAN WORLDS

Cukayla read the directive, took the comp from Sturgeon's hand, read it again, returned the comp, and looked the Marine in the eye.

"How do I know that's not a forgery?" he demanded. "Any halfway competent comp operator could cobble up a document like that."

"Are you impugning my character, Mr. Cukayla?" Borland held up a hand to forestall Cukayla's reply. "You can print it out and check the watermark, if you like. It would take someone far more than halfway competent to forge that. Or you can send a message off to Fargo and wait for a reply while you're sitting in the *Grandar Bay's* brig."

"You wouldn't, you *couldn't*!"

"I would, and I can." Borland paused to study the other's face for a moment. "If you're thinking of resisting by force, how many armed people do you have in Base Camp just now? Brigadier Sturgeon has a hundred and sixty Confederation Marines present, and the rest of his

FIST is ready to make planetfall. I strongly suggest that you comply with my legitimate requests and that you do so immediately."

Cukayla studied Borland's face right back, and concluded that, upper-body musculature aside, the officer was perfectly capable of winning any contest of arms between them. But he wasn't about to simply give in.

"I want a printout."

"Certainly. You have every right to a printout."

Cukayla reached for the comp, which still had the directive displayed. Borland let him take it.

Cukayla handed it to Paska and said, "Print this for me, Johnny." Paska attempted to network it to a printer.

"Mr. Cukayla, it doesn't want to transmit to the printer."

"Basic security," Borland said. "Captain Chriss, would you please?" he said to the FIST's acting operations officer.

"Aye aye, sir." Chriss took the comp from Paska and tapped in a few commands. In seconds the printer spat out the hard copy. He returned the comp to the Commodore while Paska handed the printout to Cukayla.

Cukayla held the printout to a light, looked at the watermark, and shook his head. "My printer isn't supposed to be able to do this," he said. "I guess your directive is for real." He looked at Borland. "Don't ask me to tell you anything that will compromise *my* mission."

"I'm afraid your operation is in suspension. Order your men to stand down."

"Look, Commodore, what we're doing here is all aboveboard. I've got copies of the permits from the appropriate agencies on Opal. I even have a couple of permits from the Confederation government."

"Then you'll have no problem with giving us copies of the permits, will you?" Borland said.

Cukayla gave him a hard stare, then snarled "Give 'em to him" at Paska.

While Cukayla's number two was getting copies of the permits,

Sturgeon resumed the questioning. "We have reports that the Fuzzies are using some sort of acid weapons. Elucidate."

Cukayla looked blankly at Sturgeon. "Acid? They don't have any kind of acid weapons." He paused, then added, "Unless you're thinking of the gas bombs they have."

Sturgeon gestured with his hand: Keep talking.

"They sometimes set booby traps. When they're set off, they spray some kind of mist into the air. It burns on contact. Horribly. If you breathe it in, it eats your lungs out."

"Where'd they get the gas?"

Cukayla shook his head. "Made it themselves? I don't know."

"The Fuzzies are sounding less and less like smart animals."

Cukayla gave Sturgeon a suspicious look. "Smart like chimpanzees," he said.

"You already said that. Maybe smarter than chimps?"

Cukayla shrugged. "Maybe a little smarter."

"They'd have to be, if they can figure out how to use firearms."

Borland raised his eyebrows at "smart like chimpanzees." But he didn't comment. "For now," he said, "you have to shut down your mining operations—as a security measure. Let the Marines deal with the raids. They're expert at that, and you won't lose any more of your employees. We'll settle matters as quickly as we can."

"I require maps showing the location of every one of your mines, including mines that are no longer active, and mines that you plan to establish. Also showing the locations of every burrow you know about," Sturgeon said.

There wasn't much more to be said after Cukayla had digital maps transmitted to Sturgeon's comp, so Sturgeon and Borland left the administration building, Borland to return to the *Grandar Bay,* Sturgeon to establish a base of operations for his FIST. Sturgeon was to name it Camp Usner, after the FIST operations officer who had been killed in action on Haulover.

Cukayla and Paska sat silently for a few moments once they were alone again, before Cukayla said, "Nothing gets shut down. As soon as our new men arrive, we'll double or triple the garrison at each mine."

"Let's hope they don't look too hard at those permits," Paska said softly.

Cukayla snorted. "The permits are good enough. They won't be able to find anything amiss."

CHAPTER THIRTEEN

A hopper dropped Thirty-fourth FIST's recon squad's second team in a small clearing fifteen kilometers from what was identified as a burrow belonging to a Fuzzy rebel force.

Brigadier Sturgeon and his staff had studied the maps provided by Sharp Edge and compared them with data gleaned by the *Grandar Bay*'s Surveillance and Radar Division.

The mining operations were easy to pick out once they knew what to look for: blocks of cages lined up behind clapboard buildings, all surrounded by aboveground bunkers. They were all in the foothills and lower slopes of mountain ranges. Active mines showed signs of current occupancy, occasional guards or Fuzzies moving about. Inactive mines betrayed no sign of anybody present, and tumbled debris lay about.

The rebel burrows were harder to spot. Unless Fuzzies were seen disappearing into the ground, the only indication of the burrows was faint trails all terminating at the same spot. Sturgeon wasn't prepared to seriously think of the Fuzzies as mere smart animals. That was a major reason for sending out the reconnaissance squad; he wanted to find out more about them. He'd never heard of an animal that decked itself with straps and pouches for carrying things. Maybe the Fuzzies weren't as intelligent as *H. sapiens,* but he strongly suspected that they qualified as sentient.

If possible, the recon teams were to penetrate the burrows. If possible, they were to capture a Fuzzy and bring it back for navy scientists to examine and test.

If.

But *only* if entering a burrow or capturing a Fuzzy wouldn't alert the Fuzzies to the presence of men they couldn't see. According to Louis Cukayla and his top people, the Fuzzies saw in the same visible spectrum that humans did. But Sturgeon wasn't any more prepared to accept the word of Sharp Edge about the Fuzzies on that than he was to accept their assessment that they were "merely" smart animals, not even animals maybe a little smarter than chimpanzees. On Earth, humans had trained animals to do a variety of jobs as far back as the Paleolithic Age, but Sturgeon had never heard of helper animals digging holes and bringing gems out of them for their human masters. Or using firearms, or explosives, or poison gas, whether they got them from humans or made the weapons themselves. The Fuzzies might be able to see into the infrared or the ultraviolet. Their snouts indicated that they had a well-developed sense of smell, more than humans did, and the size of their eyes suggested they could see better in the dark than a human with unaided vision.

The four recon men cautiously approached their assigned burrow. They spread out as they neared it until they were on a line a hundred and fifty meters wide. The particular burrow they were checking was one that Sharp Edge said was unoccupied, its Fuzzies taken to work in a mine a couple of hundred kilometers away. The *Grandar Bay's* Surveillance and Radar Division reported recent activity at the burrow so it was suspected of being a base for the rebels. Each of the Marines had a detailed map of the area that he could access in his heads-up display. A bit more than half a kilometer from the burrow, each of them encountered a trail.

"Hold," Sergeant Saber ordered. In addition to the HUD map stored on his comp, he was tied in real-time with the string-of-pearls satellite display of the area and with one of the S and R techs on board the *Grandar Bay*.

He saw no indication of people moving on the display from the string-of-pearls. Not that that meant anything; he couldn't see his own men, either—their chameleons' infra-damping effect cut their heat signatures down too far for his equipment to make out. "I'm going upstairs for more intel," he told his men. Saber was a few meters from a tree that towered above its neighbors by a good three or four meters, and looked sturdy enough to support his weight close to the height of the surrounding trees. He climbed it as high as he dared and located the position of the *Grandar Bay*.

"Sky-Eye, this is Sneaker Two," he radioed, and repeated his call.

"Sneaker Two, this is Sky-Eye," came the voice of Surface Radar Analyst 2 Hummfree. Hummfree hadn't yet gotten over being recalled to active duty and assignment to a starship that had supposedly been lost in Beam Space. But the reported Beam Space disappearance had been rescinded so he got some occasional planetside liberty, which helped. So did his almost instantaneous promotion. The main thing he had to do now was clear up with that SRA2 Auperson that he was the better analyst. After all, it had been Hummfree, not Auperson, who had figured out how to track the Skinks when the Marines had first encountered them on Waygone, Society 437. "I have you one hundred and fifty meters from your target," he said. "All four blips."

"Sky-Eye, is anybody nearby?"

"That's a negative, Sneaker Two. I've been watching for the past hour and haven't seen any man-size traces."

"They're smaller than us, Sky-Eye."

"Not that much smaller. Do you know what a dik-dik is?"

"It's a kind of miniature antelope, isn't it?"

"You got it. And that's the size of the biggest thing I've seen."

"We're going in closer."

"Go safely, Sneaker Two. I've got your back."

"Roger, Sky-Eye. Sneaker Two out." Saber climbed out of the tree and contacted his men. "Sky-Eye says nobody's near. Let's check it out. Stay ten meters off the trails until we have the burrow in sight. Acknowledge." He waited for his men to acknowledge, then said, "Move out."

Half an hour later, Saber squatted down with the entrance to the burrow in sight less than fifty meters away. It didn't look like much, just a hole scooped at an angle out of the ground, barely high enough for the Marines to enter, even crouched over. He checked with his men. They could also see the entrance and were halted, looking in different directions so that among them they could see all approaches to the burrow. He used his sniffer, but not to learn anything about the current presence or absence of Fuzzies in the area. The Marines had no data on the chemical signals of the Fuzzies for the sniffer to tell him anything from the chemicals that it collected drifting in the air. He used the sniffer to begin building a database.

After a quarter hour of observation, Saber rose to his feet and said into his comm, "Let's do it. Sonj, me, Hagen, and Soldatcu." He slid his infra into place so he could see his men as they approached the burrow's entrance. When he saw the red blur that indicated Corporal Sonj, he followed. He turned his helmet's ears all the way up so he could hear the footsteps of Lance Corporal Hagen fall in behind him, and then Corporal Soldatcu trailing. Ten meters from the entrance, he dropped what looked like a broken branch on the ground. It was a transceiver with an antenna; hopefully it would relay messages between him and Sky-Eye while the Marines were inside the burrow. The Marines slid light-gatherer screens into place as they passed into the entrance.

Saber wished he could have sent a minnie in ahead, but the Marines didn't know what kind of small animal could enter a burrow without raising an alarm, so for this mission the recon teams had to go without.

The entry tunnel was barely wide enough for the Marines to walk along without brushing its sides. Less than a meter from the surface, the ground was compacted from the weight of the looser dirt on top and from having all its water sucked out by the vegetation that grew mostly in that top layer. The tunnel's floor was hard enough that ruts had been worn into it from generations of feet moving along it. For the first twenty meters, the tunnel's downward path was straight and unadorned. Then it made an abrupt sixty-degree turn to the right, and its angle steepened, so the Marines had to be careful of how they placed their feet to keep from slipping and falling. The boots they wore, soft soled for silent stepping, aided here as well, as they more easily gripped the smooth surface of the tunnel floor.

"I can still see," Sonj said. "Much better than I expected."

Saber realized he could see better than expected as well. He raised his light-gatherer. A dull glow suffused the tunnel, which was also getting wider and higher—almost enough for them to walk with ducked heads rather than in a full crouch. He looked at the overhead and saw faint lines drawn along its length, the source of the faint light.

"Hagen, use your own eyes. Take a sample of that light-emitting stuff—a small sample."

"Aye aye," Hagen answered. Saber heard a scraping as Hagen did as he was told.

"Bioluminescence?" Soldatcu asked. He'd also raised his light-gatherer.

"Maybe. We'll let the scientists in orbit figure it out."

The slope of the tunnel leveled out to the same angle it had before the turn, and now small alcoves appeared in its sides, each just big enough to hold two of the Fuzzies. The tunnel continued to widen and grow higher to where the Marines were able to walk erect, although they still had to be careful not to bump the overhead with their helmets.

"Got a big glow ahead," Sonj said some seventy-five meters from the entrance to the burrow. "The tunnel takes another turn up ahead, and it's bright beyond that."

"Approach with caution," Saber said.

Sonj reached the next bend in the tunnel and cautiously looked around it. He gave out a low whistle. "You gotta see this, boss."

"What do you have?" Saber joined his point man at the bend. Sonj squatted to allow his team leader to look over his head.

Saber sucked in a chestful of air and blew it out. "We need to get a closer look," he said after a few minutes of watching without seeing movement.

What they saw was a spreading cavern with a level floor and an even overhead about four and a half meters above. Five meters from the bend was the beginning of what looked like a three-meter-wide street, along which sat structures that went from floor to overhead and melded into both. The structures had openings like doors and windows facing the street, and there were spaces between that might be cross streets. The overhead was run with lines like those in the tunnel, enough to give about the same light as a heavily overcast day. The temperature in the cavern was ten degrees cooler than on the surface.

"Move out," Saber said. Sonj did, and he followed. Behind him, he heard gasps from Hagen and Soldatcu as they made the turn and saw what Saber now thought of as an underground town.

Immediately before the first of the structures, another, gently curving street ran off to either side. It was difficult to judge in the confined space of the cavern, but it looked to Saber like it ran close to a quarter of a kilometer in each direction. Structures with window and door openings fronted it.

"Sonj, Soldatcu, check out the structure on the right," Saber ordered. "Don't stay inside long, and don't disturb anything. Hagen, with me." He led the other into the structure on the left.

Inside, the structure was obviously a house, even though it was dug out of and into the stonelike ground. The first level was one large room, with low benches that might have been used for sitting or sleeping. Luminous lines in the ceiling gave the room more light than there was on the street. Curtains of some gossamer material hung in the windows. Wood shelving was built along one wall. The shelves held baskets, and fired clay vases and pots. Some of the pots held water; none had food. A few rats' nests of what looked like leather might have been more of the strap and pouch arrangement the Fuzzies had worn in the 2-D images the recon Marines had examined in preparation for the mission. There was a stack of objects that looked suspiciously like books. Saber went close to examine it and picked up the top object. It was about forty sheets of thin material that could have been parchment or inner bark lining—and every sheet was covered with markings, which he could only explain as writing. So excited he was trembling, Saber took pics of the object, both the exterior and the first several pages.

"No way the Fuzzies are just clever animals, no matter what the mercs say," he murmured. Wishing to the depths of his soul that he could take one of the books, he replaced the one he had imaged and continued looking around.

In a corner away from the entrance, a stairway so steep it was almost a ladder led upward. He climbed it. The floor between the two levels was thick, almost a meter. The upper level had no luminating lines in the ceiling and was more heavily curtained than the downstairs windows, so that little light seeped in. Saber slid his light-gatherer into place to look around. The room held four padded platforms, and shelves along one wall held what looked like bed linen, though it was cloth of a kind he didn't recognize. Again, he wanted to take a sample, although not as badly as he'd wanted to take one of the Fuzzy books. He settled for taking images.

Back downstairs he took more images, then he and Hagen left the house.

"We didn't see anything that looked like a head," Sonj said after reporting what he and Soldatcu had found—the same that Saber and Hagen had.

"Maybe they've got communal heads," Saber said. "Or maybe they do their business outside. Let's look some more, I don't want to be down here much longer."

* * *

SRA2 Auperson was coming on duty. He looked over SRA2 Humm-free's shoulder at the display he was studying and examined it for a long moment.

"Your eyes getting tired, Hummfree?" he asked.

"Yeah, I guess they are." Hummfree leaned back, stretched, and yawned.

"I figured. Looks like you missed that." Auperson pointed at some faint traces.

"What?" Hummfree lurched back toward his display and looked where Auperson was pointing. A quick calculation told him that a hundred or more Fuzzies were heading toward the burrow that Thirty-fourth FIST's second recon team was in. "Whoa, shit!" He grabbed the orbit-to-surface comm. "Sneaker Two, this is Sky-Eye. Sneaker Two, Sky-Eye. Over. Come in, Sneaker Two."

But Sneaker Two couldn't hear him. The twig-disguised relay worked, but the transmission was blocked by the turns in the burrow's entry tunnel.

An hour's examination revealed that the cavern was a rough circle more than a kilometer in diameter. The side roads they'd seen when they first entered the cavern wrapped all the way around it. Other streets were laid out in an irregular grid. The cavern held more than three hundred of the house structures, and several larger structures that looked like public buildings of one sort or another. Sergeant Saber wanted to say that many of them were government buildings: city hall, police station, courthouse. But they had been firmly admonished not to anthropomorphize the Fuzzies or anything the Marines discovered in the burrows. So, despite the evidence of his own eyes, Saber refrained from assigning the buildings human functions, even though one gave every evidence of being a temple, complete with idols and obvious ritual objects. The possible government buildings and the temple fronted a large square paved with squared-off slabs of sandstone. They'd already seen smaller squares that formed the centers of what the Marines were already thinking of as neighborhoods.

Saber grinned to himself. He and his Marines were imaging everything they saw. When they turned their intelligence over to Commander Daana at FIST intelligence, and he shared it with the anthropologists aboard the *Grandar Bay,* he was certain they'd draw the same conclusions that he had. Then *they* could have the joy of anthropomorphizing the Fuzzies. He hoped they'd suffer consternation, and that Brigadier Sturgeon and Commodore Borland would land an equal amount of consternation on Sharp Edge; after looking at the interior of this burrow, he was convinced that the involuntary servitude of sentient beings was involved here, not animal helpers. Unless Sharp Edge could change its tune and convince someone that the Fuzzies were contract laborers.

"All right, time to get out of here." Saber issued his order at the end of the hour limit he'd put on their recon of the burrow's interior. "Soldatcu, me, Hagen, Sonj. Move out."

He slid his infra into place and watched for the red blob that showed Corporal Sonj was entering the tunnel that led outside, and followed it. He could hear Lance Corporal Hagen and Corporal Soldatcu trailing him.

They'd only gone up a few meters, Sonj barely past the first turn, when the point man whispered into his comm, "Company's coming."

Saber swore to himself. The transceiver relay had failed!

"Back up," he snapped. "Quietly!"

The four recon Marines backpedaled as quietly as they could, barely staying ahead of the Fuzzies coming down the tunnel toward them.

"Third street," Saber ordered. The Marines padded quickly to the third cross street, where they turned and waited. Saber lay on the street with his head around the corner. He used his light-gatherer to watch into the tunnel.

Two Fuzzies cautiously looked around the last corner. Saber couldn't be sure at this distance, but it looked like they were sniffing the air. The two Fuzzies advanced and emerged into the town-cavern, looking all around. Out of the tunnel mouth, they turned onto the perimeter street. They carried old-fashioned-looking rifles, and their noses were twitching—they were sniffing. Shortly after they disappeared into the side streets, one, and then the other, let out a brief squeal. More Fuzzies burst out of the tunnel and raced down the street, ducking by twos and threes into house structures. Some turned onto the first cross street; others came closer to the Marines and turned onto the second. They seemed to be following the orders of a few of their kind who were chittering. All of the Fuzzies were armed with rifles—some with flechette rifles—and all of their noses were twitching. It was obvious to Saber that he and his men had left a scent that the Fuzzies recognized as alien, a sign that an intruder had entered the burrow and might still be there.

The Marines needed to find a way out, and not be discovered getting away. Aside from their instructions to avoid detection, there were far too many Fuzzies for them to expect to win a fight.

"Admin center," Saber said. "Go now."

They all knew where he meant. If anybody got separated, they all knew where to meet. The methodical way the Fuzzies were searching the cavern told the Marines they had a little bit of time to plan what to do before the locals reached the town hall.

"Did anybody see anything that looked like a rear entrance to this place?" Saber asked when they were at the large square in front of the town hall, and in position to watch all approaches. Nobody had. But then, they hadn't completely circumnavigated the perimeter street; there might be another exit that they simply hadn't gone past. But this was no time to look for a back door that might not be there.

He looked up, remembering a situation where his team had been trapped inside a town on St. Katusa. They'd escaped by moving from roof to roof. But that was impossible here, with the structures providing support to the overhead. They couldn't even move from one structure to another via the second levels, because the streets were too wide.

They were going to have to snoop and poop, trying to stick to streets the Fuzzies had already searched. And then hope that nobody was left in the tunnel guarding it, or sitting in ambush outside.

The Fuzzies reached the square sooner than the Marines expected, emerging from the streets alongside the supposed temple and police station. They spread out as they came, and all had their rifles pointed ahead, muzzles moving side to side along with their eyes as they searched for targets. As when they first entered the cavern, some of the Fuzzies chittered, and gestured with short-clawed hands, surely giving orders to the others. The Marines were out in the open, but their chameleons kept them hidden from the Fuzzies. Saber was about to tell his men to leave by the side of the courthouse when Fuzzies approached from that street. The only remaining exit was between the town hall and the courthouse.

"Sonj, check it," Saber ordered.

"More Fuzzies coming," Sonj reported a moment later.

The advancing Fuzzies had spread out to cover the entire square on three sides and were converging on the front of the town hall; there was no way to get around or through their line. Saber thought about the layout of the interior of the town hall.

"Everybody inside," he ordered. Once in, he led the way to the upper level, and to the side where Sonj had reported more Fuzzies approaching. He stuck his head out the window and saw the last of them entering the square.

"This is what we're going to do . . . ," he said on his comm.

Saber slid over the window and lowered himself to the full extent of his arms, leaving his feet only a meter and a half above the street. He pushed back with his toes, let go, and fell far enough from the wall to bend his knees as he hit, reducing the sound of his landing. He took another step back and looked up. His infra showed Lance Corporal Hagen eeling out of the window. At full length, Hagen pushed out the same as Saber had done and let go. Saber caught him, making his landing even more quiet than his own had been. In another minute, all four Marines were on the pavement and moving away from the square, toward a street that led back to the entrance. They went along the street staggered, two on each side. Halfway to the entry tunnel, they saw five Fuzzies coming toward them. All of them were chittering, as though talking back and forth.

"Inside," Saber ordered. He and Hagen ducked into the nearest house structure, Sonj and Soldatcu into the one opposite it. They waited tensely, listening to the approaching footsteps and chittering voices. The voices occasionally dimmed and the footsteps stopped; Saber thought the Fuzzies were checking inside the houses.

He was right. The Fuzzies came closer and the two Marines pressed themselves against the wall on either side of the door opening, waiting. A Fuzzy shot into the center of the room and spun in a circle, pointing his rifle, looking like he expected to see an enemy. When he didn't, he stood erect, chittered to someone outside, got a chitter back, and quickly left the house.

Saber breathed a sigh of relief that sounded loud enough inside his helmet that he thought it should be audible through the air, even though he knew his helmet would totally muffle the sound. He turned and looked outside to see the Fuzzies checking the next pair of houses. He waited until they were another house farther, then ordered his team to move out again. They reached the tunnel without further incident.

They were all past the first turn in the tunnel when Sonj froze and said "Company" into his comm.

Past him, Saber saw a column of Fuzzies making the turn from the entrance.

"Into the alcoves," he ordered. He looked to see that his men did before he stepped into the nearest alcove himself.

A dozen or more Fuzzies filed past, all armed and looking intent. The last was almost completely past when he suddenly stopped and stepped back to look into Saber's alcove. He turned to face it with his nose twitching and pointed his rifle into the space. Through Saber's light-gatherer, the Fuzzy's large eyes looked so dilated he thought the alien could see as well in the dim light of the tunnel as a human could in full daylight. The Fuzzy made some sounds, in a much lower pitch than Saber had heard before. It abruptly lunged, poking the muzzle of its rifle into the alcove, barely missing Saber's arm. It withdrew its rifle, still making the low vocalizations, and plunged its rifle in the alcove again. Saber eased to the side and pressed as tightly as he could against the side of the alcove. The Fuzzy lunged a third time, then lowered its rifle and made a head motion that looked like nothing so much as a human shaking his head after thinking he saw something that wasn't there. The Fuzzy moved on.

Saber waited, listening for anybody else approaching, before getting on his comm and asking if anybody heard anything. None of the recon Marines heard sounds of approaching footsteps.

"Let's go."

There didn't seem to be an ambush set in the heat of the open air. Saber retrieved the camouflaged transceiver and the Marines quickly departed the immediate area of the burrow's entrance.

Once they were at a safe distance, Saber climbed a tree and transmitted a brief report to FIST headquarters. The recon team headed for their extraction point, where a hopper picked them up for transit to the base that Thirty-fourth FIST was setting up some twenty-five hundred kilometers south of Sharp Edge's Base Camp, almost within sight of the main area of mining activities.

CHAPTER FOURTEEN

Mock Turtle lay on her side, in as tight a ball as she could manage. It was tight enough to warm her, loose enough to allow her to sleep, even if only fitfully between bouts of shivering. From crown to root and tip of tail, she wished the Naked Ones had never come to the World. Life had been good before their arrival. Food was easily grubbed from the good ground, and happy clansmen surrounded her, helped to fight off other clans that dared intrude on the Moon Flower Clan's territory. Babies were well raised by many aunts, and even an occasional uncle helped. Their industries were in burrows far enough separated from the living burrows that their stenches and poisons never affected the People.

The living burrows. That was what Mock Turtle missed most of all. The temperatures were even in the burrows. They were cool enough in the day that anyone who felt overheated while grubbing could go home and cool off, warm enough at night that sleeping was a real comfort. On the rare occasions when it was too cold at night for comfortable sleeping, there were blankets to snuggle into in the sleeping chamber. And she could always share body warmth with her mate, unlike here, where the males and females were kept in different enclosures.

Outside was an unnatural place to spend the night, unless you were in a raiding party on the way for a dawn strike on a foe's burrow or grubbing farms. Outside there was no shelter from the cold of night. All the People could do was scoop out shallow hollows in the dirt to huddle in. And the Naked Ones perversely didn't let the People have any of their blankets to snuggle in. Didn't even let them sleep in groups where they could share body warmth, but kept them mostly one by one in small cages, like food animals awaiting slaughter.

It was no wonder that so many of the People were sick most of the time, and that so many had died mining for the Naked Ones.

Mining! The People had proper tools for mining; bronze punches and drills, granite hammers—some hammers were even made from precious iron, which was usually reserved for weapons. But the Naked Ones didn't let the People get their tools and wouldn't give them any, either. Instead they had to dig with their hands and with whatever rocks they could pick up. Mock Turtle's finger still hurt where she had torn a claw slamming a rock into the hard, grainy rock of the mine face two handfuls of days ago.

And for what was all this *mining* effort? Less than a bushel of irregularly shaped, cloudy stones in a handful of days. Yet the Naked Ones thought those baubles were precious. Mock Turtle couldn't understand why. Now, if the Naked Ones wanted to mine the seams of gold, which was worked more easily than bronze but was too soft for tools—that she could understand. The gold was lovely to look at, and even to touch, after it had been cast or worked into beautiful designs.

Mock Turtle sniffed and shivered. She felt like she was getting sick. If only the rumor she had heard the other day was true, that some of the People had risen up and killed the Naked Ones guarding them and driving them in the mines. The rumor also said the People who had risen up were attacking the guards and overseers at other mines, freeing more and more of the People.

But Mock Turtle knew the rumor was only that, not a truth worth the air it was written on. It couldn't be true, because the rumor also said that the first of the People to rise up were from the Bright Sun Clan, and everybody knew that none of the clans in the Brilliant Coalition were bold enough to do such a thing, not like her own Moon Flower Clan, of the Starwarmth Union.

Mock Turtle's waking reveries were rudely interrupted by the shouts of the guards and clanging of alarms; it was the beginning of the morning routine. The guards opened several cages and prodded the People out of them, then harried those chosen ones to rush around opening the rest of the cages.

Mock Turtle had been on the cage-opening detail twice and knew what a simple job it was. Down near the bottom of the cage's door was a hole into which a person would poke a claw to draw out a simple lever. A turn of the lever raised the locking rod on the cage's door, displacing the hooks on it from the eyes protruding from the door frame. A person could reach through the bars of a cage and poke a claw into the hole, unlocking herself. Except that the iron plate the hole was in was large, half the length and width of a person's arm, and bars surrounding the plate were too close together for more than a hand to slip through, making it impossible for a person to reach the hole and stick a claw into it.

Soon enough, all the cages were open and everyone lined up in ranks and files for the morning tail count, except for those too sick to rouse themselves and the overnight dead—and one other. The Naked Ones didn't let the Mother out of her cage. The Mother was kept in her cage all of the time. Unless they let her out while the rest of the People were in the mines working. Mock Turtle didn't know, she'd never been too sick to get up in the morning and go to work. If she had ever been too sick to rise for work, she would probably be dead by now.

After the tails in the ranks and files were counted, and the sick and overnight dead tallied, the People were trooped past the food table. There guards slopped insufficient amounts of barely palatable food, food that had been grubbed long enough in the past to begin to turn bad, into too-small bowls. The People weren't allowed to grub for fresh food, even though there was a rich grubbing farm a short distance from the enclosures. She knew because she'd seen the land in brief glances while going between the food line and the mines.

After a length of time hardly long enough for everyone to eat, the guards began yelling and moving among the People, pushing and striking those who didn't move fast enough to return their small bowls to bins behind the serving table. Then there was more shouting and pushing and striking as the guards chivvied them into line for the short march to the mine.

The mine entrance was in the side of a hill. It was high and wide, dug to allow two of the Naked Ones to walk side by side without having to duck their heads. At the depth of a few loping strides, the tunnel branched, then branched again and again. Here the shafts were only wide enough for two Naked Ones to pass each other if they stood face-to-face, but they were still high enough that the guards did not have to duck their heads, even though they wore metal hats that made them taller than they were. The sides and overheads of the shafts were shored with some exotic metal that seemed as strong as iron, not as soft as gold, and far lighter than either.

Some of the branching shafts went level, others sloped downward. Far enough in, some of the level shafts angled upward while the remainder continued level. Whether they went up, level, or down, all of the shafts through the dirt and rock of the hillside reached a wall of stone that could be broken fairly easily with bronze drills and iron hammers and turned into coarse sand when it was beaten enough. But the People weren't allowed bronze drills and hammers, iron, or even granite. They had to use their claws and whatever loose stones they could find nearby to break through the stone wall. As ready to crumble as the stone wall at the mine face was, it was still almost as hard as most of the stones the People used to hammer at it.

At the stone wall, the mine face, the shafts spread side to side so that more than two people could work chipping away at the same time. Once in a while the overhead of the mine face collapsed because a widening section of the mine face on a higher level was extended over an excavated space, and the shoring wasn't strong enough to hold the overhead in place. Usually, when an overhead collapsed, some people were injured. Sometimes someone was killed.

Too many of the People had died since the Naked Ones came.

The overseers stood outside the mine as the People trudged into it; they didn't enter the mine until all the workers were in. Then they blocked all of the branching shafts with their huge bodies, and their weapons that shot many times without reloading. Their weapons shot needles that smashed flat when they hit the mine face. Unlike the solid bullets fired by the rifles the People's hunters and soldiers used, which would have ricocheted and maybe wounded or even killed the person who had fired it.

The overseers were smart in their choice of weapons. The overseers inside the mines used small weapons that could be held in one hand to be used, unlike the guards who carried needle-shooting rifles. Someday the People would learn how to make rifles that fired needles. Then maybe the People would encage the Naked Ones and force them to work in the mines that yielded gold or iron ore.

But that was too fine a dream for Mock Turtle to dream while she and the rest of the Moon Flower Clan were under the control of the Naked Ones, so she cut off that line of thought.

The light in the mines was harsh and didn't go everywhere like the light in the burrows. Instead of light worms, the overseers carried boxes that cast a harsh bluish light that hurt your eyes if you looked directly at it, and cast hard shadows. The shadows were a cause of injuries to claws, fingers, and hands. If a light moved when someone was beginning to swing a stone at the rock face, or about to jab into a crack with a claw, and cast a hard shadow onto someone's hand, it could cause that person to miss her aim and smash a finger or break a claw.

That was what had happened to Mock Turtle two handfuls of days ago when she broke a claw that still hurt.

In the mine, the females and males worked side by side. It was the only time mates got to see each other, the only time mothers could see their sons, fathers their daughters, sisters their brothers. During the short time they had before the overseers came in after them, wives and husbands, parents and children, sisters and brothers, sought each other out. When they could arrange it, families would work together on the same mine face until the end of the long workday. Then they would be let out, dragging their weary selves, coughing from a day spent breathing in dust and sand from the stone they'd chipped into in search of meaningless baubles.

Outside once more, the guards and overseers shouted and pushed and shoved and struck them in different directions, females this way, males that, heading for their different enclosures.

Oh, if only Mock Turtle could have some private time with her husband! She so missed his touch, the feel of his strong body against hers. But, in addition to the small needle guns, the overseers carried bludgeons, which they used to beat apart wives and husbands who got too close to each other and didn't part immediately when shouted at.

Wives and husbands had been very seriously injured by those beatings, and some had died.

Outside, parted once more in their different enclosures, the People were lined up in ranks and files for another tail count. To that tail count was added the number of people, badly injured or dead, whom the overseers dragged out of the mine. If the tally equaled the number of the morning count, the People were given a brief time to groom one another, to clean the dirt and sand out of their fur.

Mock Turtle didn't know what would happen if the counts didn't match. But she was certain she wouldn't like it.

The grooming helped their diet a little bit. A very little. The People always had mites or lice or other small parasites hidden in their fur. Nimble fingers and claws could catch them, and the groomer would pop the mite or lice or whatever into her mouth. It was never very much, but at least it was fresh food.

After the brief grooming time, the People were once more trooped past the food table, where too little bad food was slopped into the undersized bowls, and the People were given too little time to eat it with their fingers and claws before they were yelled at and pushed and prodded and struck until they put the bowls into the bins behind the food table. Then they were herded back into the cages for the night. People seldom spent two consecutive nights in the same cage; everybody was in too much of a rush to get away from the guards and overseers, who beat anyone too slow to enter a cage. Except for a few who were kept out to lock the cages. Then they were caged themselves. Once all of them were in their cages, the guards and overseers made sure every cage was properly locked for the night.

After that, all anyone could do was scoop out a shallow hollow to curl up in and fall into an exhausted, fitful sleep.

A sleep from which not everyone hoped to wake.

CHAPTER FIFTEEN

Commodore Borland came planetside to meet with Brigadier Sturgeon and his staff. The two recon teams had been thoroughly debriefed—neither had brought back a captive Fuzzy since neither had come across an isolated one. The FIST's staff had studied the recon reports, and the F2 section had written a preliminary analysis. Sturgeon sent Borland a copy of that preliminary analysis to study before his arrival at Thirty-fourth FIST's new base. Borland, being navy rather than Marine, opted to come planetside by the more leisurely three-orbit descent used by everybody except for the Marines, and read the report on his way down. He brought his anthropology officers with him to interview the recon Marines and examine the images they'd collected in the burrows they'd entered.

"Gentlemen," Sturgeon said when his staff, subordinate unit commanders, and their most important people, including the company commanders of the infantry battalion, were assembled in the briefing room, "our mission has just taken a radical change in direction and objective. We've known since we first landed that we aren't going to be fighting Skinks. What we are going to do instead is shut down Sharp Edge's operations, free the Fuzzies, and find out who is behind the operations here so that the Attorney General can commence legal proceedings. I think you will all agree that the situation here is a clear case of involuntary servitude—possibly legally defined slavery. Unless I'm seriously mistaken"—he looked at Borland—"the Confederation laws covering slavery don't make any exception for aliens."

Borland nodded confirmation; he'd had his legal officer check that out as soon as he'd heard what was happening planetside.

"Commodore Borland and I are leaving for the Sharp Edge headquarters to inform Mr. Cukayla of what we are doing, and that he is to stand his people down. During our absence, you will draw up operational plans for securing all of the Sharp Edge mines and freeing the indigenous personnel.

"Colonel Ramadan."

As Sturgeon stepped toward the exit, with Borland following, Colonel Ramadan, the FIST executive officer, shouted, "Attention!" and the assembled officers jumped to their feet and stood at attention until the Brigadier and Commodore were gone.

"Seats," Ramadan said. "Here's what we're going to do . . ."

During the suborbital flight to Base Camp, Commodore Borland contacted Captain Zsuz Maugli, his executive officer, left in command on the *Grandar Bay,* and instructed him to send all of the starship's biological sciences people and the legal officer planetside. There was otherwise nothing to mark the passage from the Marine base and the Sharp Edge facility. The security section of the FIST's headquarters company accompanied them.

Johnny Paska, Louis Cukayla's second in command, stood on the portico of the Base Camp administration building watching as the Marine and navy commanders exited the suborbital and most of the security section took up positions around it.

One fire team accompanied the flag officers when they approached the admin building. The Marines didn't do anything threatening, but they clearly outclassed the two Sharp Edge operatives who flanked Paska. Sturgeon and Borland mounted the stairs and stepped within Paska's personal space. The Sharp Edge number two didn't back up.

"We're here to see Mr. Cukayla," Sturgeon said.

"He's not here," Paska said curtly, with a quick eye flick at the three Marines behind Sturgeon.

"When will he be back?"

Paska shrugged.

"Then where can I find him?"

Paska shook his head. "He's out checking the mines. Could be anywhere."

"He goes off and doesn't tell you where he is? What if you need him?"

Paska shrugged again. "He checks in once in a while. Besides, the boss trusts me to deal with any problem that comes up in his absence."

Sturgeon considered what Paska said, then said, "If that's the way Sharp Edge functions, I've got a major problem for you. We're shutting down your mining operations. When you hear from Mr. Cukayla, tell him to come see me in *my* headquarters."

"You can't do that!" Paska said, shocked. His men started and glared at Sturgeon but made no other move.

"We can, and we are," Borland said, speaking for the first time. "I will have my legal officer supply you with the appropriate sections of Confederation statutes if you need to see them."

"Contact whoever's in charge at every one of your mines and tell them to stand down their operations, and stand by for my Marines to arrive," Sturgeon said.

Sturgeon and Borland turned to leave. The fire team followed.

Paska stood, quietly watching them depart and ignoring the questions the two operatives flanking him threw at him, until the suborbital had lifted off. Then he went inside and radioed Cukayla.

"When is the *Dayzee Mae* due?" Cukayla asked when Paska explained the situation to him.

"Tomorrow morning, local."

"Tell the captain of that scow I want my troops to make a combat assault landing as soon as she's in orbit."

"A combat assault landing? Are you sure? I doubt that any of them have ever made one of them."

"I'm sure. And if they haven't, it's past time they learned. In the meantime, get reinforcements to every mine. Ain't no jarhead and swabbie shutting down *my* operation."

Thirty-fourth FIST's staff had preliminary plans for shutting down the mining operations by the time Brigadier Sturgeon and Commodore Borland returned to the base.

"Sir, we believe that our people should wear garrison utilities when they release the Fuzzies from the mines," Colonel Ramadan said in presenting the preliminary operational plan to Brigadier Sturgeon. Commodore Borland sat in on the briefing.

"Explain."

"So the Fuzzies can see us remove the guards and overseers and take them away under guard. That way they'll know we're releasing them when we open the cages."

Sturgeon nodded. "Continue."

"There are more than fifty known mines, and the *Grandar Bay* is looking for more. We can assemble the Sharp Edge people at their Base Camp and assign one blaster platoon to watch them. One squad from the infantry battalion should be enough to secure each of the mines. If we allow two days each to remove the existing garrisons and release the Fuzzies, we can have all fifty known mines cleared in less than a week, allowing for travel time between mines." There were many more details, but Sturgeon only had one additional question.

"How are the Fuzzies who aren't being held near their home burrows going to return to them?"

"We will have to find a way to communicate with them, sir."

"I can put my linguistics people to work on that as soon as we have a Fuzzy to work with," Borland offered.

Sturgeon agreed with his staff that the infantry battalion should return, company by company, to the *Grandar Bay* to trade in their chameleons for garrison utilities. And, since they had only brought one set per Marine, Borland agreed to have his stores opened to supply each of them with another set.

The change of uniform would take at least a day and a half, more likely two days.

"Chief, I've got an inbound," SRA2 Auperson said.

Surveillance and Radar was dark and quiet, lit only by the displays, the only sounds the *pong*s and *ding*s of equipment calling the attention of the operators to blips on the displays, and the murmurs of crewmen talking to their counterparts in other divisions. Auperson's attention had just been called to the appearance of a blip on the outward radar. As a basic security measure, navy starships routinely kept watch on the approaches to whatever planet they orbited. Approach watch was more important in the Opal-Ishtar system than in most colonized systems not in active conflict because the asteroidal debris orbiting its sun wasn't well mapped.

"What is it?" Chief Nome asked.

"From its size, I'd say either a starship or a planet-buster."

"Shape up, Auperson," Nome snarled. "What do its characteristics say it is?" He rolled the hunk of hemp cable he gnawed in lieu of a cigar while on duty from one side of his mouth to the other.

"Sorry, Chief. Been a long shift. It reads like a starship, probable midsize civilian liner. No IFF up."

"Shoot it to me." Nome's voice was gruff but he wasn't angry, he was as tired as Auperson. The data on the inbound reached Nome's console. He studied it, then got on the talker to the bridge.

"Bridge," said Lieutenant Commander Gullkarl, taking a turn at Officer of the Deck.

"Bridge, Chief Nome, S and R. We have an unidentified starship on approach. No IFF, probable civilian passenger liner." He sent the data on the inbound.

"Thanks, Chief. Bridge out." Gullkarl switched his talker to the radio shack.

"Radio, sir," Chief Petty Officer Obree answered.

"Radio, bridge. Gullkarl. We've got an unidentified inbound. Hail her." He sent the data to the radio shack, and wondered whether he should inform Captain Maugli now or wait until he heard back from the radio shack. After all, the inbound was more than two days out.

"Unidentified starship approaching uncolonized world Ishtar, this is the CNSS *Grandar Bay*," Radioman Third Class Lisa Craven said into the ship-to-ship. "Identify yourself and state your purpose here." She settled back to wait the couple of minutes for the radio waves to reach the inbound and come back.

Time passed: five minutes, then ten with no response from the inbound. Craven turned to look at Chief Obree. "Chief?"

"I can tell the time as well as you can, Craven. I guess you didn't notice the traffic going back and forth between the inbound and Ishtar."

"Traffic, Chief?"

Obree nodded. "My guess is, whoever's driving that inbound wants instructions from someone planetside. And I can guess who." He picked up his talker and signaled the bridge.

"Bridge." Lieutenant Commander Gullkarl answered the call.

"Radio, Chief Obree. Sir, that inbound hasn't replied to our request for identification. But they're sending traffic planetside. Fairly tight beam. I haven't been able to tap into it yet."

"If it's a tight beam, can you tell where planetside it's going?"

"Pretty close, sir. The only known place in the vicinity is that merc base."

"The one they call Base Camp?"

"That's the one."

"Any outgoing traffic?"

"Yes, sir. On an even tighter beam. I was lucky to detect it at all."

"Thanks, Chief. Bridge out." Gullkarl thought for a moment and decided that it was time to inform Captain Maugli.

Captain Zsuz Maugli stepped onto the bridge and took the captain's seat, which Lieutenant Commander Gullkarl had vacated as soon as Maugli said he was on his way. "Tell radio to patch me through to hail the inbound," he ordered, looking at the display that showed the inbound starship. A row of numbers down the side of the display gave data about the unidentified vessel: current location, vector, velocity; the starship's length, width, and mass; projected time to orbit. He toggled to a different view, one that showed Ishtar and the *Grandar Bay*'s orbit. A dotted line showed the likely orbit of the inbound, where it would intercept that orbit, and its position relative to the *Grandar Bay* at the time she achieved orbit. Unfortunately, the unidentified starship would reach orbit at closest approach to Base Camp when the *Grandar Bay* was on the other side of Ishtar.

"Get that to the Commodore," Maugli ordered.

When Gullkarl told him the patch was ready, Maugli picked up the ship-to-ship and said in a firm voice, "Unidentified starship approaching Ishtar, this is Captain Zsuz Maugli, Confederation Navy, on board the Confederation Navy Starship *Grandar Bay*, in orbit around Ishtar. State your name and your purpose."

After a few minutes transit time between the inbound and the *Grandar Bay*, static crackled on the ship-to-ship and a voice came through.

"CNSS *Grandar Bay*, this is the SS *Dayzee Mae*, civilian hauler bringing supplies to the folks on Ishtar."

Maugli signed to Gullkarl to look up the *Dayzee Mae*.

"*Dayzee Mae*, who is your master, and who is your owner?"

This time, the wait for a reply was longer than could be accounted for by just the light-lag distance. Then a new voice came on.

"Captain Maugli of the *Grandar Bay*, this is Captain Herb Trundle, master of the *Dayzee Mae*. On what authority are you questioning my right to be here, and going where I'm going? There's no restrictions around Ishtar that I'm aware of. By my reading of the law, that means I have every right to make my delivery without interference from the navy."

Maugli chose to ignore the challenge. "What kind of supplies are you carrying, and to whom are you to deliver them?" While waiting for the response from Trundle, Maugli read the data on the *Dayzee Mae* that Gullkarl had found. According to *Jane's Commercial Starfleets of the Confederation,* she was owned by Star Tramps, LLC. She was a transport ship, not a freight hauler, and so was used to ferry colonists or immigrants to new worlds. In her most recently recorded configuration, the *Dayzee Mae* had berthing for fifteen hundred people and their personal and household belongings. Considering how much stuff people took with them when they moved to new worlds, Maugli figured the *Dayzee Mae* could carry something on the order of double that number of combat-loaded troops if they didn't have to bring much in the way of ammunition and other supplies.

"Get this to the Commodore." He gave out the order as soon as he had added his estimate to the data.

"Aye aye, sir," Gullkarl said. He sent the data to the radio shack with instructions to send it planetside posthaste.

Trundle's voice came back. "Sorry, Captain, can't tell you. It's a sealed consignment. I don't know what the cargo is. You'll have to ask the consignee."

"That's a blatant lie," Maugli muttered, "and I'm sure Cukayla would lie as well if the Commodore asked him."

"In that case," he said into the ship-to-ship, "I can't allow you to unload your cargo. The Confederation Marines are conducting exercises planetside. Civilian vessels are not allowed to interfere with such exercises. I can provide you with the relevant statutes if you need to check the law."

Again there was a too-long pause before Trundle came back. "Well then, I guess I'll just park in orbit until the exercises are over."

"If you do, I may have to put a security force on board to ensure that you don't release your cargo prematurely."

Trundle's answer to that began with a cut-off bark of laughter. "Always glad to cooperate with the Confederation Navy, Captain. *Dayzee Mae* out."

"Is he, now?" Maugli wondered.

"Captain," Gullkarl said, "I think you'll like to see this as well." He transferred another file to Maugli's console. It was Trundle's entry in *Jane's Starship Owners, Captains, Officers, and Other Notable Crew.*

Maugli read through it, gave out a low whistle, and said, "Thank you, Commander. Kindly see to it that the Commodore gets this."

The entry was only a few lines long, but it spoke volumes about Herb Trundle. He'd never been convicted, or even tried, for misdoings of his own, but his career, from the days of his initial commission into the merchant marine, was filled with voyages undertaken on behalf of known or suspected gun runners, smugglers, and other criminal elements.

"It's a pity we don't know the identities of any of his officers and crew," Gullkarl said.

"It is indeed. If the Commodore authorizes a boarding party to prevent him from landing his 'cargo,' we should find out then."

"Paska did say they had more people coming," Brigadier Sturgeon said after he read the material Captain Maugli had transmitted to Commodore Borland. The two were in the Marine's office, where the Commodore had come as soon as he'd read the material on the *Dayzee Mae* and Herb Trundle.

"Maybe more than twice as many additional men as you have," Borland said, "on top of the couple of thousand he said he already has. That's, what, nearly five times your strength—if they decide to resist?"

Sturgeon shrugged it off and leaned back in his chair, propping his feet on a desk drawer. "My Marines have faced worse odds and come out on top. I'm not overly concerned about being outnumbered by mercenaries."

"What if they join forces with the Fuzzy rebels?"

Sturgeon chuckled. "I hardly think that's likely. The more likely scenario is, the Sharp Edge mercs will stand aside while my Marines deal with whatever Fuzzy rebels want to continue fighting after we shut down the mining operations and free their compatriots."

They were briefly interrupted by Lieutenant Quaticatl delivering a tray with a pot of caff and two mugs.

"Thank you, Lieutenant," Sturgeon said. He waited for his aide to leave before saying, "Sorry about the caff, but the Marines don't provide real coffee to units in the field."

"It'll do," Borland said. But the expression on his face when he took a sip said otherwise.

"I suspect that the Fuzzies will stop their rebellion when they see that we're freeing them from the mines."

Borland considered that briefly before nodding, and said, "I imagine you're right about that." He shifted his posture on the visitor's chair and pushed the mug of caff to the side. "Have you heard anything yet from the first of your platoons to shut down a mine?"

"No, but I expect to within"—Sturgeon checked the time—"the next quarter hour, standard."

Ensign Chimsamy, commander of Mike Company's first platoon, marched erect toward the main gate of Mining Camp No. 8, two hundred kilometers southwest of the Marine base. A fire team from the platoon's first squad accompanied him. The four had their helmets' shields raised to show friendly intent; sweat flowed copiously on their faces. The rest of the platoon remained two hundred meters back, under the command of Staff Sergeant Crain. They stood in full view of the guardhouse, with their weapons held ready. The two guards in the gatehouse stepped outside as the Marines reached them.

"Didn't expect any relief yet," said the first guard, a burly man in a tiger-stripe camouflage uniform with some kind of sergeant's stripes on the sleeves. His helmet had a clear faceplate. The name tag on his shirt said *Neave*. He looked at the Marines with greater curiosity;

their uniforms weren't like his and they carried plasma weapons rather than the flechette shooters that were Sharp Edge's standard issue. "Where are you from, anyway? And who sent you?"

"I guess you haven't gotten the word yet," Chimsamy said. "We're Confederation Marines. We're here to shut this mine down."

"Now see here!" Neave took a step back and put his hand on the flechette pistol he wore holstered on his hip. "I haven't gotten any word about this. And I ain't letting nobody come in here and shut this mine down without instructions from my boss."

Chimsamy made a show of turning his head to look back at his platoon, then back at Neave. "How many men do you have here, Sergeant Neave?"

"What?" Neave said, startled by the question. "Two, three dozen. Why do you want to know?"

"Two, three dozen," Chimsamy repeated. "I have a whole platoon of Confederation Marines with me. Would you care to discuss the question with a platoon of Confederation Marines?"

"Ahh . . ." Neave looked uncertainly past Chimsamy and thought about the thirty Sharp Edge guards and overseers, who weren't ready, against a platoon of Confederation Marines, who looked primed for a fight. "Are you sure about this, ah, Captain?" He didn't recognize the Marine's collar insignia but thought that nobody would send a mere lieutenant to shut down a Sharp Edge operation.

"It's Ensign. And no, I'm not sure—I'm positive. Are you in charge here?"

"N-no, I'm second in command. Captain Bauer is."

"All right then, take me to your Captain Bauer."

Neave nodded curtly. "Come on, Bauer can deal with you. That's why he gets paid the big bucks."

Captain Bauer swore about it—threw a tantrum, actually—but in half an hour, the overseers had brought the Fuzzies out of the mine, and Bauer and all of his men were on Dragons in an Essay, ready to be ferried to Base Camp.

The Fuzzies didn't know what to make of these new Naked Ones who sent them out of the camp and then went away in a metal house that lifted an arm's length above the ground and went away with an earthshaking roar. As soon as the noise died out in the distance, the Fuzzies scurried to a nearby field, where they grubbed for the first good meal they'd had in longer than any of them wanted to think about.

Sated at length, they began discussing how were they ever going to find their way back to their home burrow, since they had no idea where they were.

CHAPTER SIXTEEN

After the experience of Mike Company's first platoon at Mining Camp No. 8, the second platoon of Kilo Company had every expectation of a walkover at Mining Camp No. 3. Ensign Irvin looked at the wire fence enclosing the camp and thought how flimsy it looked at this distance. He left the platoon under Staff Sergeant Jhomin in the waist-high grass two hundred meters from the entrance and began marching toward the gatehouse, accompanied by a fire team.

They had covered half the distance when someone on a loud hailer ordered, "That's far enough. Stop right there."

Irvin broke step at the hailing, but didn't stop. Instead he smiled a crooked grin and adjusted his helmet's speaker to boom his voice out. "No, I'm not stopping," he said loudly enough to be heard in the gatehouse and beyond. "We're coming in. Surely someone told you to expect us."

"Yeah," the loud-hailing voice answered, "someone did." And with that, fire from multiple weapons erupted from the gatehouse. Irvin's chest and belly were shredded by the fire. The three Marines in the accompanying fire team all dove for the ground, untouched—the Sharp Edge guards had all aimed at Irvin.

"Hit the dirt!" Jhomin shouted as soon as the first shots rang out. "Take those bastards *out*!"

Twenty blasters and two guns went into action, their individual CRACK-*sizzles* lost in the combined roar of the weapons. The gatehouse was made of sun-baked brick, sufficient against flechettes but totally unable to withstand the onslaught of so many plasma bolts. The bricks shattered, splintered, and sent overheated shards flying, ripping into the bodies of the already dead and wounded Sharp Edge guards. The building collapsed in a flurry of sparking cinders.

"Cease fire, cease fire!" Jhomin roared into his helmet comm. He silently swore about being in garrison utilities instead of chameleons. But this wasn't supposed to have happened. *What's wrong with these people?* he wondered. *Do they* really *think three dozen mercs can stand up to a Marine platoon?* "How's the ensign?" he asked on the platoon circuit.

"He's dead!" Corporal Wirewych, whose fire team had accompanied Irvin, replied. He sounded more furious than upset. "The rest of us are all right," he added. "Do you want us to come back?"

"No. Change your position so they can't pick out exactly where you are, but stay near where you were for now."

"Roger. Moving."

Jhomin raised himself high enough to see through the top of the grass; he couldn't see grass moving where he knew Wirewych and his men had to be. If he couldn't, probably the bad guys couldn't, either.

Movement inside the wire enclosure drew a few shots from the Marines. Jhomin looked, saw what his men were shooting at, and cried out, "Cease fire! Hold your fire!" Fuzzies, hundreds of them, were moving toward the wire. He'd never seen them in the flesh before, but seeing them through his magnifier screen, they looked reluctant and frightened, wanting to get away. He peered deeper into their mass and swore at what he saw. Armed Sharp Edge guards—many more than the three dozen of them the Marines thought were there—were forcing the Fuzzies forward by swinging cudgels and whips at them.

"Hold your fire!" Jhomin shouted again. "Those sons a bitches are using the Fuzzies as human shields!" he shouted, unconsciously granting the "smart animals" full status as people.

The first Fuzzies reached the wire and were pressed against it by the weight of those behind, forced ahead by the whips and clubs of the guards and overseers. Then the Sharp Edge mercenaries poked their rifles through the mass of Fuzzies and began firing at the Marines. The Fuzzies chittered and screamed in terror and pain.

All the Marines could do was hug the ground and try to find shallow ripples in the soil that would give them some protection from the flechettes buzzing past like manic bees—they weren't even wearing body armor.

Jhomin raised his head just high enough to see though the grass. Even with his magnifier, he could barely make out any of the guards through the mass of Fuzzies shielding them. But he thought they were all behind the native aliens, not mixed in among them.

"Kerstman, take two fire teams around the left and flank them. I think you'll have clear shots."

"Aye aye," Sergeant Kerstman called back. He then addressed his men: "Hungh, Llewellen, you and your people with me!" He slithered backward from the line and low-crawled to his left. Six other Marines began low-crawling with him.

Jhomin hoped the mercenaries wouldn't see the moving grass that marked the Marines crawling to a flanking position.

"Is anybody hit?" he asked into his helmet comm, belatedly remembering to check for casualties. He listened to the fire team leaders' reports. So far, the only casualty was Ensign Irvin. But that couldn't last, and it didn't.

"Wirewych, can you pull back?" Jhomin asked.

"Maybe, but only if we leave the Ensign, and I don't want to leave him behind."

"Then sit tight." *Good Marine, Wirewych,* he thought. *We Marines don't leave our dead behind.*

Flechette fire came fast and hard. Needles zipped past, pocked into the dirt around the Marines, clipped the grass over their heads. Some found marks, and wounded Marines screamed in pain. Other Marines busied themselves patching up the wounded.

After some minutes, the fire from the mining camp slackened and then ended. Someone inside used the loud hailer to call to the Marines.

"Anybody left in charge out there?" the someone asked.

Jhomin adjusted the speaker on his helmet to project his voice and called back, "I am."

"Okay, 'I am,' you ready to surrender yet?"

"You got things mixed up. It's you who needs to surrender before you get seriously hurt."

The man with the loud hailer laughed. "Gotta hand it to you Marines. You got more balls than sense. Can't tell when you're beat."

"Maybe that's why we win so often. People who think they've got us beat stop fighting, and then we kick their asses."

"Yeah? I haven't noticed you shooting back."

"Yeah, well, we're Marines, we're the good guys. Good guys aren't real keen on shooting innocent civilians to get at the bad guys."

"What innocent civilians? All we've got here is a herd of dumb animals. But if you want to think of them as civilians, that's fine with me. We'll just resume fire and keep it up until you're wiped out. How's that sound?"

"We're in position." Kerstman's voice came over the radio.

Jhomin turned off his exterior speaker. "Do you have clear shots?"

"Sure do. Ducks in a barrel."

"That's fish."

"What?"

"Never mind. How many of them do you see?"

"I see about thirty of them. They've got some kind of barrier, something on legs, pressed against the Fuzzies, so only a few of the mercs can keep them against the fence. There are more mercs inside the camp. Maybe twenty, maybe more, I'm not sure."

Jhomin swore. All he had on the flank was seven Marines, facing maybe fifty mercs, maybe more. Awful long odds, even for Marines.

"What's the matter, Marines?" came a taunt over the loud hailer.

"You waiting for relief, reinforcements? I don't think any are coming. So it's up to you, you can surrender or you can die."

"Strange you should say that," Jhomin said after readjusting his speaker to project his voice. "Because that's exactly the choice you're facing. Nah, you had your chance to surrender. Kerstman, kill the fucker."   .

A second later, a lone CRACK-*sizzle* sounded to the left, followed closely by a thud and a piercing squeal as the loud hailer fell to the ground.

"Got him," Kerstman said.

"Take them all out," Jhomin ordered, then said to the rest of the platoon, "Start moving forward."

On hands and knees, not caring that the moving grass would give their positions away, fifteen Marines began moving toward the fence and the terrified Fuzzies pinned against it. Four Marines, too badly wounded to go with them, remained behind. The firefight raged furious beyond the natives.

Sixty meters from the wire, Jhomin shouted, "Up and at 'em!"

The fifteen Marines jumped up and charged. At twenty meters they started roaring out war cries. The terrified Fuzzies grew manic when they saw the Marines jump up out of the grass. When the Marines began yelling, they trebled their efforts to break free from the barriers holding them, and some managed to do it. Most at least got away from the fence.

The fence wasn't as flimsy as it had looked to Ensign Irvin when he first examined it from two hundred meters, but it wasn't so strong that the hundreds of Fuzzies pressed against it didn't warp it; Jhomin thought that if they'd been kept there much longer, they would have brought sections down. A few sections did fall as the Marines clambered over the fence. Many Fuzzies took advantage of that to flee as soon as the Marines got out of the way. They bounded away, tails high in the air, rocking up and down like hobbyhorses.

Nearly half of the Sharp Edge mercenaries who'd had the Fuzzies pinned against the fence were down and out of the fight. The rest of them were down and firing in the direction of Sergeant Kerstman and his two fire teams. Some noticed the commotion to their left and turned to face the new threat bearing down on them. But the Marines with Jhomin were already firing, picking their targets. Most of their bolts hit home. In less than a minute, the survivors threw away their weapons and held their arms up, open palms waving at the Marines.

Deeper in the camp, other mercenaries kept firing at the flanking Marines for a few moments until they received a few bursts from the platoon's guns. They realized that the fence was lost and that the rest of their men were dead or captured. Then they too surrendered.

Staff Sergeant Jhomin sent first squad to bring in the platoon's casualties. Then he put some of his Marines to collecting weapons and had the prisoners collect the dead and wounded—human and Fuzzy both. He had *all* the dead, Sharp Edge and Fuzzy together, laid side by side to drive home a point, even though he wasn't quite sure what the point was that he wanted to make.

"Secure the prisoners," Jhomin told Sergeant Hamas and his gun squad after the dead and badly wounded had been collected. All but two of the able-bodied mercenaries were laying on their bellies in two long lines, with their arms stretched out above their heads; the lightly wounded were lined up with them. The two who weren't facedown were busy tending to the rest of the wounded, Fuzzies included.

Hamas and his men went along the ranks of prisoners, making each man put his hands in the small of his back. They bound their wrists together with self-adhering strips that would hold until they were cut off by something very sharp. Sergeant Kerstman and second squad covered the prisoners while they were being secured.

Only then did Jhomin finally get on the radio to company headquarters to report what had happened.

The thirty Marines of Kilo Company's second platoon had suffered one dead and nine wounded, four badly enough to require evacuation to the *Grandar Bay*'s hospital. The sixty Sharp Edge mercenaries at Mining Camp No. 3 had forty-one men dead or severely wounded. Plasma bolts didn't cause minor wounds.

* * *

As projected two days earlier, the SS *Dayzee Mae* reached orbit around Ishtar when the CNSS *Grandar Bay* was on the opposite side of the planet. But Commodore Borland and Brigadier Sturgeon had no intention of allowing a starship loaded with a couple of thousand reinforcements for the Sharp Edge forces planetside to make orbit and go about her business without intervention. An Essay loaded with the seventeen Marines of one of Thirty-fourth FIST's composite squadron's antiaircraft platoons, not needed for anything else on this operation, was in position to board her as soon as she reached orbit. If necessary, seventeen Marines could hold the lifeboat deck of a tramp liner against three thousand mercenaries indefinitely.

What the Marines and navy hadn't counted on was that the Sharp Edge reinforcements were already loaded into lifeboats and other landing craft and began launching even before the *Dayzee Mae* settled into orbit.

Brigadier Sturgeon was furious. Commodore Borland admired Herb Trundle's imaginative launching of the Sharp Edge reinforcements, and said so.

"Come on, Ted, give the devil his due," Borland said, and took a sip of coffee. He'd had a kilo from his personal supply of Blue Mountain beans brought planetside so that he wouldn't have to suffer with the caff that the Marines were stuck with. "That was a brilliant maneuver, launching everything he had before he even reached orbit."

"We should have stopped him," Sturgeon snapped.

Borland nodded. "And if I'd had any inkling that Trundle was good enough a starship captain to even attempt that maneuver, I'd have found a way to intercept the *Dayzee Mae* before she reached orbit." He shrugged and shook his head. "I could have altered my orbit so that the *Grandar Bay* was waiting for the *Dayzee Mae* when she arrived. My starship isn't a fighter, but she does have weapons. A shot across her bow probably would have given Trundle second thoughts about launching his lifeboats."

Sturgeon grunted. "*Shoulda, coulda, woulda.* The most worthless words in the language." He shook his head. "Now I have to convince Cukayla to hold his mercs back, to stand down, before a lot of people get killed."

"The mercs already had your Marines outnumbered, and their size just more than doubled." He refreshed his coffee mug and checked Sturgeon's, only to find that the Marine had hardly touched his. He moved his head side to side, not quite in a shake; such a waste of good coffee.

Sturgeon abruptly nodded. "I've got one AA platoon aboard the *Dayzee Mae,* holding her," he said. "Sharp Edge has three more starships in orbit. Can you put boarding parties on them?"

A grin slowly spread across Borland's face. "I can indeed. Sharp Edge initiated hostilities, so both Confederation and interstellar law allow me to take their starships. Get your Marines ready to head aloft, and I'll get them on board Sharp Edge's flotilla. Starting with the *Pointy End.* Imagine, an amphibious landing ship force, taking prizes! Including a Bomarc V39!" He reached across the desk to shake hands with Sturgeon. "This is the best idea I've heard since the *Grandar Bay* was released from being 'lost in Beam Space.' "

"All right, Marines," Lieutenant Brewer of the first antiaircraft platoon said, "we're about to perform one of the oldest functions of Marines. Going all the way back to the ancient Egyptians, Marines have conducted ship-to-ship boarding operations, usually against hostile forces." He grinned at the members of his platoon. They were gathered in the passageway just outside the *Grandar Bay*'s well deck, ready to go in and board the Tweed Hull Breacher they would use to cut through the hull of the *Pointy End,* the nominal flagship of the Sharp Edge flotilla. The Marines were visible only through the open faceplates of their helmets; the rest of them were hidden in their chameleoned armored vacuum suits.

"We may be in the squadron, but we aren't wing wipers, we're cannon cockers!" Brewer continued. "Cannon cockers are trigger pullers, just like the grunts. So let's go over to that Bomarc and have some fun!"

"And show the grunts that cannon cockers can fight with blasters, too!" Staff Sergeant del Valley roared out.

The fifteen Marines of the antiaircraft gun teams roared back their readiness for close combat.

Brewer led the platoon at a trot to the Tweed Hull Breacher, which was mounted on top of an Essay for the trip to the *Pointy End.* The lone Dragon inside the Essay was there to hold the crew of the Sharp Edge starship once the Bomarc was secured. The Marines would remain aboard the *Pointy End,* while the crew was returned to the *Grandar Bay* and locked in the brig.

The CNSS *Grandar Bay* floated ten kilometers from the SS *Pointy End,* a brief trip for the Essay carrying the THB. During the Essay's transit, the *Grandar Bay* hailed the *Pointy End,* demanding that the smaller starship open her hatches to receive the boarding party. The *Pointy End* didn't answer the hail. The Marines in the THB laughed with eager delight when the word was passed to them that the Bomarc wasn't going to simply open up and let them take her over.

Two hundred meters from the *Pointy End,* the THB was released from the Essay. Navy crewmen used its jets to maneuver it into position against the target's hull near the bottom end of the conical starship. In moments, the cutting jets sliced a hole in the hull. The Marines held tight for the seconds it took for the air in the hold that the THB cut into to evacuate, then Lieutenant Brewer raced inside, followed closely by the rest of his platoon.

They were met by a single burst from a flechette rifle, which spattered harmlessly into the overhead. The half-dozen Marines who had already spread out to flank him fired their blasters toward the hatch the needles had come from. A rifle came spinning out of the hatch to skid across the hold's deck.

"Don't shoot!" someone shouted from beyond the hatch. "We surrender." A pair of open hands eased through the hatch.

"Cease fire!" Brewer called to his Marines. Two more of the

Marines, who had just reached the line forming on the platoon commander, each fired a single bolt into the hatch's combing.

Brewer waited a few seconds to make sure nobody else was going
to fire, then called out, "Step into the open with your hands above
your head."

A wide-eyed man in a Sharp Edge uniform edged into the hold.
His hands were held open, high above his head. "Cukayla ain't paying me enough to get killed fighting a bunch of Marines who're going
to take his hot rod no matter what I do," he said, nervously looking
around the apparently empty hold.

"Is that so? Then why'd you shoot at us?"

The man looked in the direction the voice had come from and
licked his lips. "I didn't shoot at you. I shot at the overhead. Hell, I
didn't want to piss off the Marines by hitting one of you. That's why I
shot high."

"Are you saying you just put up token resistance?" Brewer asked.

"Yes, sir, that's exactly what I did."

"How many more are aboard?"

"There's just four of us."

"Where are they?"

The man swallowed. "In the passageway, making sure you don't
kill me, before they show themselves."

Brewer raised his voice. "We aren't going to kill anybody who
doesn't try to hurt us. So if you're surrendering, toss your weapons
away and come into the hold with your hands in the air."

Another flechette rifle skittered across the deck, and three more
people entered the hold with their open hands held high above their
heads. They all looked frightened, except for one who looked absolutely terrified. One was a uniformed Sharp Edge mercenary; the
terrified one was a woman in a sleeveless blouse and short skirt. The
third was a middle-aged man in a coverall.

The two mercs were guards. The one in the coverall was an engineer, assigned to keep the *Pointy End* in trim. The woman? "A joy girl.
Cukayla wanted to keep the men taking care of his baby happy," the

engineer explained. The woman's face turned red at hearing that description of her function on the Bomarc.

The ease with which they'd taken the Bomarc V39 was quite a letdown for the AA Marines. But they were very pleasantly distracted by the woman, the first any of them had seen since they left Thorsfinni's World—and likely the last they'd see until they returned.

The Marines put the two guards and the woman on the Essay for transit back to the *Grandar Bay*. The first antiaircraft platoon stayed on the *Pointy End,* along with the engineer. The engineer's first job after the Essay left was to seal the hole the Marines had made in the hull.

CHAPTER SEVENTEEN

The antiaircraft battery's second platoon was picked up by the Essay with the Tweed Hull Breacher mounted on it as soon as the Essay returned to the *Grandar Bay* and debarked its prisoners. The Essay launched into a higher orbit to allow the Interstellar Tramps' freighter the SS *Tidal Surge* to catch up with it. Like the *Pointy End,* the *Tidal Surge* ignored the *Grandar Bay's* hail to open its hatches and surrender to the Marines then en route.

The second AA platoon had also received a rah-rah speech from its commander, Ensign Marston, similar to the one Lieutenant Brewer had given first platoon, with the added proviso that they shouldn't expect as easy a job as first platoon had in taking the *Pointy End.* The proviso was prophetic.

"Go!" Ensign Marston shouted as soon as the cut panel fell inside the tween hulls of the *Tidal Surge.*

"Let's go!" Sergeant Dowling shouted as he charged into the tight space and twisted to move to his left. The other four Marines of his gun team followed, alternating right and left.

The bosuns operating the THB's cutter moved it forward the meter-plus to the inner hull and began cutting another hole. The hold beyond didn't have an atmosphere but was packed bulkhead to bulkhead, deck to overhead with pallets, loaded with supplies needed to support the Sharp Edge operations planetside—needed even more now that they had close to an additional three thousand men. There were aisles every second pallet and a narrow crawl space next to the outer bulkhead, with less than a meter clearance at the top. Unfortunately for the second AA platoon, the crawl space next to the bulkhead was too narrow for a Marine in an armored vacuum suit to squeeze into, and the nearest aisle was more than two meters away from the opening cut by the THB.

The petty officer in charge of the burner detail looked into the hold using the lamp on his vacuum suit's helmet, and swore. He arranged his detail to manhandle the burner and got it moving into position to burn a hole where the aisle was.

Ensign Marston fretted; every extra minute it took his platoon to enter the cargo hold was another minute the *Tidal Surge*'s crew and guards had to prepare for the fight to come. And vibrations he felt in the decking of the tween space told him they were probably readying an unwelcoming party in the hold. In the darkness of the tween hull space, he couldn't even see the faceplates of his men's helmets, much less through them to their faces, not even using his infra screen. He suspected they were as nervous as he was.

The seconds took their time ticking off while the sailors got the burner ring into position, but the cutting went fast and soon a sheet of plate dropped into the hold, its vibrations felt by the feet of the waiting Marines.

"Go!" Marston shouted into his comm as soon as the large disk was out of the way.

Marines shouldered their way past the burner crew, bumping them into the bulkheads. Inside, their infras and light-gatherers allowed them to see faintly. Nothing showed up in the infrared but the plate cut from the bulkhead, and its heat signature blocked out everything else until the Marines were past it.

Corporal Jack Newman led the charge; his gun chief Sergeant Hamsum Dowling was hot on his heels. *Hot* was an appropriate word to use for the first steps into the hold; the sheet of plate cut from the bulkhead was still glowing from the heat it had absorbed during the cutting. The first Marines into the hold had to move across the cut plate fast in order to prevent its heat from demagnetizing the soles of their boots, which would be disastrous if the *Tidal Surge* lost its artificial gravity. The heat rapidly dissipated into the vacuum and was mostly gone by the time the first gun team had passed it.

But by then there was other heat for the Marines to be concerned about.

As soon as the Sharp Edge mercenaries aboard the *Tidal Surge* realized that the starships in orbit were being boarded, they and the crew began preparing hasty ambush positions in the holds. The minute they could tell which hold the Tweed Hull Breacher would cut into, they knew where to concentrate their efforts. The need to cut a second hole through the inner hull gave the mercenaries more time to prepare their positions, designed to conceal the heat signatures of the men hidden in them. Instead of flechettes, which would smack harmlessly into the Marines' armored vacuum suits, the mercenaries were armed with explosive-slug throwers, which could catastrophically penetrate the armor.

Corporal Newman was the first Marine to be hit. He'd barely gotten more than five meters into the hold when a slug slammed into his chest and exploded, blasting a five-centimeter-wide hole through the armor. Tiny fragments from the explosion ripped into Newman's chest, and the air in his suit spurted out, mixed with globules of blood and flecks of meat. He toppled backward, tripping Sergeant Dowling, knocking him down and to his right. That saved Dowling, as the slug that would have hit him in his lower left side continued and exploded on the side of a crate on the opposite side of the aisle, spewing a cloud of wrapping-material fragments and pulverized vacuum-packed foodstuffs.

The Marines behind Newman and Dowling fired down the

length of the aisle. Some of their plasma bolts went the entire length to splatter against the far bulkhead, while others skittered along crates, charring them.

Dowling looked at where Newman was hit and where the next slug had struck the crate and realized that the mercenaries had to be above them.

"Climb!" he shouted into his comm. Putting action to words, he slung his blaster over his shoulder, grabbed handholds on a crate above his head, and began scaling the stack of crates on the right side of the aisle. He wasn't worried about being seen and shot by the mercenaries; even if they had infrared glasses that allowed them to see the Marines' heat signatures, they were on top of the crates he was climbing and so probably couldn't get a good shot at him without exposing themselves.

Behind him, Newman's wound wasn't life threatening in itself, but the venting of air from his vacuum suit would kill him in minutes. His suit automatically sealed off the neck of his helmet so that he could continue to breathe, but capillaries were bursting close to the hole in his chest plate and he was starting to bleed internally.

Corporal Renny Aldridge stopped to slap a seal on the chest of Newman's suit, but Staff Sergeant Fred Knox, the platoon sergeant, grabbed his arm and sent him climbing the pallets with the rest of his gun team. Knox knelt to apply the seal himself, then assigned two Marines to take Newman to the tween hulls for the burner crew to move back to the THB and the Essay for return to the *Grandar Bay*. More explosive slugs erupted into the lower crates on the left side of the aisle, enlarging the cloud of pulverized material and leaving outlines of the chameleoned Marines. It also coated their armored vacuum suits, turning them into ghostlike effigies. Two more vacuum suits were hit, and the Marines in them were quickly evacuated.

Dowling heaved himself to the top of the stack of crates, rolled away from the edge, and unslung his blaster as he did. Looking inboard, he saw a smudge of red near where he thought the slugs had come from, far less than would be given off by a body.

"But just enough to be a reflection," he muttered to himself. He said aloud into his comm, "First gun team, line on me." He felt the slight vibrations that told him his three remaining men were scrabbling across the top of the crates.

"Straight ahead, along the edge. See the glow?" he asked when the vibrations stopped. The three Marines acknowledged. "I think that's where they are. Scoot right and we'll flank them."

The four Marines began edging forward and to their right, pressed close to the tops of the crates because of the closeness of the overhead.

Slugs suddenly tore at them, coming from their left front— the other side of the aisle. There was a groan. Somebody had been hit. Dowling looked for the source of the incoming fire and saw a man-shaped red splotch lying on top of the crates. He snapped a plasma bolt at the form, the first shot his gun team had fired since climbing to the top. He wasn't the only one to fire, and at least one plasma bolt struck the shooter. He stopped firing. But the brief exchange had alerted the nest the Marines were approaching, and weapons were raised above its edge; wild fire came in their general direction. Dowling knew that one of his men had been hit but couldn't take the time to see to the casualty, not when so much fire was coming at them.

"Take them out," Dowling ordered.

The nest was evidently inside a crate; some of the crate's contents had been piled around it like a row of sandbags protecting a trench or fighting hole. The improvised wall around the nest was too high for the mercenaries to look over, so they had to shoot blind. The Marines poured plasma into the flimsy wall. The bolts punched holes straight through the piled-up boxes and containers, too hot to raise debris clouds. Dowling thought the fire from that direction slacked off; maybe they'd hit one of the shooters.

The Marines still below continued to fire down the length of the aisle, although they were shooting higher now, and another gun team was climbing to the top of the crates on the other side of the aisle.

Dowling glanced to the left front again and saw the heat signature of a body slithering into an opened crate. He snapped off three quick bolts at it, and saw it slump, half in and half out of the nest. But more splotches were moving in that direction, and the fire from the front was picking up again.

Suddenly, Dowling heard Lance Corporal Hernan Peasley's voice on the comm. "I've got them flanked."

"Then shoot their asses!" Dowling snapped.

"They're down too low for me to hit them in the ass," Peasley said in reply, "so how about head shots?" A flash of brilliance lanced from his position to the nest, and fire from it stopped for a few seconds. Peasley shot again and again. "I think I got them all," he radioed.

"We'll cover you while you check," Dowling told him. Then he asked his other men how they were; he remembered the groan from the first fire from the other side of the aisle.

"Aldridge is down," Corporal Frank Rushin answered. "I'm fine."

Dowling didn't waste any time swearing. Instead he ordered him to cover Peasley. He and Rushin rapid-fired into the diminishing wall fronting the nest. No more fire was coming from their left front; that nest was fully involved with the gun team that had reached the top of the crates on its side of the aisle.

Peasley scooted forward as fast as he could, firing as he went. There was no return fire.

"Cease fire," Dowling told Rushin when he saw Peasley almost at the nest. He kept his weapon ready to fire at any sign of enemy movement, but his caution wasn't necessary.

"They're all dead," Peasley reported. He sounded like he was about to regurgitate inside his helmet. "They're a mess in there."

"Pull back from them and take a few deep breaths," Dowling

said. He looked around for Corporal Aldridge and spotted him several meters back.

"Corpsman up," he called on his comm as he started crawling toward the injured Marine. "Right-side stacks." He reached Aldridge and quickly found a hole blown through his left chest, under his outstretched arm. Blood dribbled from the wound, visibly evaporating in the vacuum.

"Aldridge, are you with me?" Dowling asked as he worked a patch out of the corporal's repair pouch.

No answer.

"Hang in there, Marine. We'll have you out of here most rickytick." He found the patch and applied it to the opening in Aldridge's armored vacuum suit. "Corpsman's on his way. I'll help him get you out of here."

Rushin came up on Aldridge's other side. "I'll help if you want to move him now."

"Back to where we came up," Dowling said. He called for Peasley to join them. *Shit, have I lost two men?* he wondered.

There were two more nests in the hold the Marines had entered. They were all cleared and the defenders either dead or escaped by the time Dowling saw Aldridge into the Dragon that was supposed to carry prisoners back to the *Grandar Bay.*

Dowling removed Aldridge's helmet while the corpsman checked the vital sensors in their pocket on the chest of the armored vacuum suit.

"Stasis, fast," the corpsman said. He and Dowling quickly stripped off Aldridge's suit and sealed him in a stasis bag.

"Will he make it?"

"The *Grandar Bay* has an outstanding surgery and surgeons." The corpsman shook his head. "But he was exposed to vacuum for so long, and lost so much blood, I don't know."

Newman's suit was properly patched and his chest bandaged; he was ready to return to the fight.

*   *   *

The Marines, less four evacuated casualties, swept through the hold to make sure no mercenaries or crew were still hidden. Then they broke out of the hold. Ensign Marston led them in a sprint to the *Tidal Surge's* bridge.

The bridge's hatch was dogged from the inside.

"If that's the way they want it," Marston said. He was angry enough over the casualties the platoon had suffered that he wasn't going to accept any resistance—and a dogged hatch was resistance. "Burn it." He pointed at the hinges of the hatch.

"Aye aye, sir," Staff Sergeant del Valley said. "Gladly." He used hand signals, signing to the Marines to concentrate fire on each of the three hinges, four blasters firing at the top and middle hinges, three at the bottom one. Once he'd watched long enough to make sure his instructions were being followed, he turned, hand blaster at the ready, to cover the passageway in one direction while Marston covered the passageway in the other. They couldn't assume that other mercenaries or crewmen weren't on their way to engage the platoon.

The fight in the hold had been silent except for voices over the comm units; sound doesn't carry in a vacuum. But in the atmosphere of the passageway outside the bridge, the CRACK-*sizzles* of a baker's dozen blasters combined to mimic the roar heard in the center of a fierce thunderstorm. Only the fact that they were sealed inside their suits kept the Marines from being overwhelmed by the stench of ozone, vaporizing paint, and melting steel.

The paint blistered and peeled from the hinges when the first plasma bolts struck them. The metal turned black, then a ruddy red, grew brighter, turned cherry, and then white. After a hundred rapid bolts struck the hinges they began to sag. The Marines kept shooting, intent on burning the hinges until they had made holes through the surrounding plate. The air turned hazy with vapors from the metal; men breathing that air would be overcome.

"Shit!" del Valley shouted. "Here they come!" He'd seen someone run into the passageway from a side passage and duck back before the shot the Marine snapped off could hit him. "Anybody in sight from your end, Mr. Marston?"

"Negative. How many are there?"

"I only saw one, but that don't mean shit."

Marston turned to look at the progress his Marines were making on the hinges. "Take Dowling's team and clear them out."

"Aye aye. Dowling, with me." Del Valley began trotting away from the bridge, in the direction of the man he'd briefly seen. He stopped meters short of the cross passageway.

"One man with a blaster, put three bolts down there."

"Let me," Corporal Newman said. "Payback." He brushed past del Valley and angled his blaster around the corner. He pressed the firing lever three times and pulled back. There was no sound other than the faint *sizzle* of something scorched by the plasma.

Del Valley groped for Newman's shoulder and pulled him out of his way. He lowered himself to the deck and edged forward to look around the corner. "Gods damn them!" he swore, pulling back and rising to his knees. "The bastards piled some flammables in there. Newman, you started a fire! Get back and finish burning those hinges."

A fire would set off the antifire systems, and the passageways would fill with flame and heat-smothering chemicals that would probably defeat the platoon's attempt to burn through the hinges on the hatch to the bridge.

Back at the entrance to the bridge, the center hinge was almost burned out, and the top hinge wasn't far behind. Dowling and his men resumed firing at the bottom hinge. Although partly slagged, the hinge had turned black and solidified again.

Klaxons began sounding—the fire alarm. Del Valley saw a fog coming from the burning passageway and swore. He looked up, knowing that the heat cast off by the melting metal would soon set off the antifire chemicals, cooling the melting metal front of the hatch.

"Middle hinge through."

Two more blasters added their plasma to the fire raining on the top hinge, and two to the bottom.

"Top hinge burned out."

Now thirteen blasters were firing away at the bottom hinge, which had reached cherry red once more. And vents in the overhead opened and began spewing the chemicals to suppress flame and cool overheated metal.

Del Valley swore again, then yelled in triumph as he saw something he hadn't noticed before—a fire box on the bulkhead a few meters away. He dashed to it and tore it open. It held what he was looking for, an old-fashioned fire ax. He yanked the ax from its tie-downs and raced back to the hatch, holstering his hand blaster as he went.

"Out of the way," he shouted, shouldering the Marines away. "Cease fire! I don't want anybody shooting me, gods damn it!" He didn't wait to make sure everybody had stopped firing at the bottom hinge before he stepped in and swung the ax. Once, twice, three times. His arms vibrated all the way down to his boots with every blow against the hinge, but the hinge buckled a little bit more each time he hit it.

He didn't know if it was the abrupt change in temperature from cherry-red-going-on-white to being cooled by the chemical wash from the overhead, or if it was the blows he hammered with the ax, maybe both, but the hinge suddenly shattered. He jammed the ax head into the gap left by the middle hinge and pushed with everything he had, levering the hatch open.

The hatch budged a few centimeters and stuck. Ensign Marston reached in to help him push on the ax handle and the hatch sprang free, clanging and thudding to the deck, just missing three Marines who managed to jump out of the way in time.

Inside the bridge, the *Tidal Surge's* captain looked awed and frightened as the Marines entered his bridge. He raised his hands and whispered at them. The bridge crew stood at their stations and held their hands up. The two Sharp Edge mercenaries guarding them decided to live to fight another day; they threw down their weapons and raised their hands.

After that it was simply a matter of having the remaining mercenaries assemble in a landing craft bay and loading them into the waiting Essay for transport to the *Grandar Bay*'s brig.

The deaths of ten mercenaries on the *Tidal Surge* and capture of the rest convinced the mercenaries on the *Lady Monika* to surrender without a shot being fired.

CHAPTER EIGHTEEN

While the starships of the Sharp Edge flotilla were being taken by the Marines of Thirty-fourth FIST's antiaircraft company, Brigadier Sturgeon attempted to contact Louis Cukayla, *attempted* being the operative word.

"Sorry, Brigadier," Johnny Paska said, "but the boss is unavailable at this time."

"Unavailable. That could mean that he's not there, or it could mean he doesn't want to talk to me," Sturgeon said. "Which is it?"

"One or the other, it doesn't matter." Paska had the visual turned off on his comm so Sturgeon couldn't see him, but a shrug was virtually audible in the Sharp Edge number two's voice.

Sturgeon let a silence grow for a moment or two before saying, "Deliver a message for me. Your people at Mining Camp Number Three met my Marines with force; they killed one Marine and put four more in the *Grandar Bay*'s hospital. Sharp Edge's losses were forty-one dead or seriously wounded, and the rest taken prisoner. We are going to close every mining camp you have and release every Fuzzy that wants to leave the camp. My Marines will be expecting resistance from your mercenaries the next time we meet. Resistance will be met by even greater violence than in Mining Camp Number Three.

"Sturgeon out." He broke the connection with Sharp Edge's Base

Camp and looked across his desk at the officers crowded into his office; Commodore Borland, Thirty-fourth FIST's chief of staff Colonel Ramadan, Commander Daana of intelligence, Captain Chriss from operations, FIST Sergeant Major Parant, and Commander van Winkle of the infantry battalion.

"You heard the man," he said. "Cukayla doesn't want to talk and doesn't seem willing to surrender anything, even though he must know that the navy has taken control of his starships and"—a smile quirked his face—"all the supplies on them. Which must have his four shop in a tizzy." A "four shop" is logistics; all manner of weapons, ammunition, medical supplies, water, food, clothing, other supplies—in short, everything needed by troops in garrison or in the field. "So we are going to oblige him, meeting force with greater force until Sharp Edge stands down.

"Three," he said, addressing Chriss, "get together with Commander van Winkle and his three, and begin making plans to close every mining camp with as much force as necessary. Coordinate with Four, and with One to deal with the prisoners." "One" was the F1, Captain Shadeh, the personnel officer. "Again, one platoon per installation. Questions?"

"Sir, should we retrieve our chameleons from the *Grandar Bay*?" van Winkle asked.

Sturgeon shook his head. "I want the Fuzzies to see us, to see the Marines are freeing them from the mercenaries. That should pay major dividends later on when we start talking with them."

"Understood," van Winkle said, nodding.

"That is all for now."

Everyone left except Borland and Parant.

When he'd watched the last of the visitors leave, Borland looked at Sturgeon and said with a wry smile, "When *we* start talking with the Fuzzies? Brigadier, I believe it will be *navy* officers attempting to establish communications with these aliens."

Sturgeon smiled back at him. "This is a Marine Corps–navy team, Commodore. So the first-person plural applies."

"I do believe it's commonly stated as 'navy–Marine Corps' team."

"By your leave, sir," Parant said, "but we're planetside now, and the commander of the landing force is in command. So. . ."

Borland had to laugh at that. "That's not exactly how it works, Bernie. But what the hey."

Sturgeon winked at the Sergeant Major, who inclined his head in a brief bow.

"Do you have any platoons going after mining camps now?" Borland asked, turning serious.

Sturgeon nodded. "Yes. And this time, they're wearing body armor."

"Button up, Marine!" Lieutenant Bass snapped at Lance Corporal Schultz. They were on the same hopper, heading to third platoon's landing zone on their way to Mining Camp No. 15.

Schultz's negative head shake was clearly visible—none of the shields on his helmet were closed.

"It's too damn hot out there," Bass said. "I'm not having any of my Marines go down with heatstroke. So button up!"

"I can do it," Schultz snarled.

"No you can't. It's over fifty degrees where we're going. Nobody can take that kind of heat for very long. Now button up." The two men locked eyes for a long moment. Bass could tell that Schultz wasn't going to obey, and he knew he'd have a heat casualty on his hands if the Marine didn't close his faceplate so his climate control could keep his head cool.

"Hammer, if you don't button up, I'm sending you back with the hopper after it drops us off."

Schultz's coppery face darkened at the threat, and he looked like he was about to explode. Instead he jerked his hand up and slapped a clear shield into place.

"That's better," Bass said calmly, and patted the big Marine on the shoulder.

* * *

Third platoon approached its objective much more cautiously than Mike Company's first platoon or Kilo Company's second platoon had approached the earlier mining camps. Hoppers dropped the platoon off five kilometers from their objective; they'd walk the rest of the way. This time the Marines were expecting trouble. The Sharp Edge mercenaries didn't let them down.

"We've got trouble," Corporal Raul Pasquin reported to his squad leader. First squad's second fire team was moving as flankers, a hundred meters to the left of the platoon's main body.

Lieutenant Bass was listening in. "Third platoon, stop in place," he ordered his men on the all-hands circuit. "Defensive posture."

"What do you have?" Sergeant Ratliff asked Pasquin.

"Got an ambush line. The point's already in the killing zone. I can see evidence of thirty men in the ambush. Might be more; I can't tell where the far end is." The vegetation there was sparser than in many other places because the land had been covered by a lava flow recently enough that it hadn't broken into gravel-size rocks and sand, so the colonizing plants had few place to sink roots. Third platoon was on the side of a ten-meter-high lava ridge, staying below the skyline and above the floor of the narrow defile between their ridge and another. The ambushers were on the reverse slope of the ridge opposite third platoon. The lava bed behind the ambushers was rippled. Pasquin and Lance Corporals Quick and Longfellow had taken cover behind one of the ripples.

"Have they seen you?" Ratliff asked.

"I don't think so," Pasquin answered. He whispered, even though his helmet's clear screen was in place. "We're behind them, and they don't seem to have anybody watching their rear. I did see someone using what looks like a periscope to look over the top of the ridge."

"Have they seen us?" Bass asked.

"I do believe so, boss." Pasquin raised his head to look at the ambush line again. "Some of them look like they want to climb to the top so they can open fire. Wait one. Right, someone's signaling them to stay back. So they must have spotted the platoon, and are waiting for you to get moving again, get more into the killing zone."

"Move forward; see if you can find the far end of the ambush." Bass looked forward, along the line of the platoon, and knew that the mercenaries must have seen the Marines. The dull green of their garrison utilities and body armor stood out clearly against the black lava bed; the thin vegetation did little to conceal them from the ridge on the left.

"Aye aye." Pasquin toggled to the fire team circuit. "You stay here and cover me. I'm going forward to find the far end."

"Are you sure you want to go alone?" Quick asked.

"You're a good Marine, Quick; you know how to snoop and poop. But I was recon in Twenty-fifth FIST. I'm better. I go alone. Let me know if anybody starts watching their rear." He considered leaving his blaster behind but decided there was too great a chance he'd be spotted and have to defend himself. He made sure his knife was ready to draw in an instant.

"Good luck," Longfellow whispered at Pasquin's back.

While Pasquin was telling his men what he was going to do, Bass raised second squad's first fire team, which was on the platoon's right flank, a hundred meters beyond the reverse slope of the ridge the platoon was on.

"Negative," Corporal Chan answered when Bass asked if he saw any sign of Sharp Edge, or anybody else.

"Well, stay sharp," Bass said. He wondered why Lance Corporal Schultz, on point, hadn't sensed anything wrong.

Hammer Schultz was wondering the same thing. He'd been shocked when Pasquin had reported that they were walking into an ambush. He looked in the direction of the ridge where Pasquin had said the ambushers were hiding, and couldn't feel *anything* from that direction. Or any other direction. He was shaken by the idea that he almost led the platoon into an ambush. He always took point, or whatever the most exposed position was, because he was *good* at sensing danger before anybody else did. So why hadn't he sensed this ambush before the platoon began walking into it? For the first time in years, Schultz felt uncertain about himself, about his abilities. He began to tremble.

Pasquin went on knuckles and toes, keeping himself as low as possible. It would have been easier to crawl on his belly, but a belly crawl would have increased the chance that he'd make noise that could be heard by the ambushers. His knuckles were sore, his forearms burning, his feet and calves threatening to cramp by the time he eased himself to the lava bed to take a few deep breaths and flex his aching muscles. After a moment he cautiously raised his head high enough to see over the lava ripple that had concealed him. He'd gone a hundred and fifty meters and still wasn't at the far end of the ambush. But he was pretty sure he saw the end, fifty meters farther along.

A two-hundred-meter ambush line. Averaging two meters between men, and allowing close to a meter per man, he calculated there were seventy or seventy-five men in the ambush—more than twice the platoon's strength. He slid his magnifier screen into place and looked closely at a few of the men on the line. He didn't like what he saw. Not all of them were armed with flechette rifles; some had more powerful-looking weapons, maybe weapons that could defeat the Marines' body armor.

"One, One-two," he whispered into his comm. "I have approximately seventy to seventy-five men in the ambush line. And I think some of them have surprise weapons."

"Roger," Ratliff replied. "Stay in place until further orders."

"Aye aye." Pasquin switched to the fire team circuit to tell his men what he'd found. He arranged himself to lie where he could watch the ambush line, and the outline of his helmet would be disguised by one of the few bushes growing on the ripples.

Charlie Bass was in a dilemma. He couldn't move forward, because that would put more of the platoon into the ambush's killing zone. He couldn't back up, because that would confirm to the ambushers what they probably already suspected—that they'd been discovered. Nor could he have the platoon charge into the ambush line, because too few of his men were in position to do that. He could try to have one squad and a gun team flank the ambush, but that would leave most of one squad fully exposed to the ambushers.

So what to do?

The decision was taken out of Bass's hands by an overly anxious mercenary who edged to the top of the ridge without being sent back down by an officer or sergeant. He saw the Marines and couldn't restrain himself, opening fire with his flechette rifle set on automatic. The needles struck harmlessly on the lava, or spattered without effect against the Marines' body armor.

"Second squad, pull back to my position," Bass immediately ordered. "First squad, get on line to flank the ambush. Left flankers, open fire on the back of the ambush. Right flankers, hold position and guard our flank."

"Let's go!" Corporal Claypoole yelled to his men. He twisted around and scooted toward Bass, trailing Lance Corporal MacIlargie, who had begun withdrawing from the killing zone as soon as Bass gave the word. Claypoole glanced back and staggered to a stop—Lance Corporal Schultz was frozen in position, with more and more of the Sharp Edge mercenaries firing at him. Schultz wasn't shooting back.

"Hammer, move!" Claypoole yelled.

Schultz didn't even twitch. Flechette needles were slamming into the lava all around him, splatting on his armor. There was red on his arm where a flechette had hit an unarmored spot.

"*Hammer!*" Claypoole swore to himself. He didn't know what the problem was; had Schultz been wounded badly enough in the opening burst that he couldn't move? He couldn't think of any other reason for Schultz to just be lying there unmoving. Taking a deep breath, he launched himself back to Schultz, to drag him to safety.

"Where are you hit, Hammer?" Claypoole asked during the short sprint. No answer. He thought Schultz must have been knocked unconscious by his wound. He wanted to drop next to the big Marine and check for wounds, but too much fire was coming that way. Instead he reached down, grabbed the back of Schultz's armored collar, and began dragging him, not even taking the time to pick him up in a fireman's carry. Not that he was sure he could lift someone that big over his shoulders anyway.

Claypoole hadn't finished taking his first step when something clamped onto his wrist, feeling tight enough to crush bones. He yelled in shock and pain, and twisted back to see what had caught him. It was Schultz's hand.

"Let go! I'm trying to get you out of here." He looked through Schultz's faceplate and was shaken by what he saw. Schultz's face was beaded with sweat, his mouth opened and closed soundlessly, and his eyes were wide with fear. They seemed to be fixed on something in the far distance—but there was nothing but sky where he was looking.

"What's the matter, Hammer?" Claypoole asked, dropping down so that he didn't present quite as easy a target. "Are you hit bad? Let me get you out of here." His words were punctuated by an explosive round that blew a small crater in the lava centimeters from Schultz's shoulder. "We gotta go, Hammer!" Claypoole shrilled, and gave a sharp tug on Schultz's collar. He gave a grunt of pain as the small bones of his wrist ground together under the pressure of Schultz's grip. Another explosive round hit, this time impacting with a glancing blow on Schultz's hip, digging a crater in the armor but not penetrating the flesh underneath.

Schultz didn't even flinch.

Claypoole tried to stand and take a two-handed grip on Schultz's armor, but Schultz's hand kept his arm too low, and he wasn't able to get his feet under himself.

Suddenly Sergeant Kerr was by Claypoole's side. "What's the problem here?" he demanded harshly. "We've got to get Schultz out of the line of fire."

"I know, but he won't let me pull him."

Kerr looked into Schultz's face. "Oh, hell," he breathed. "Hammer!" he said sharply. "On your feet, Marine! We've got to go. *Now!*"

Schultz finally reacted, turning his head to look at Kerr. His mouth moved as though he was trying to say something, but nothing came out.

"Move, Lance Corporal. Now!" Kerr ordered.

If it hadn't been Hammer Schultz that Claypoole was looking at, he would have sworn that a tear came out of the big man's eye. He shook off the thought and sighed in relief as Schultz's grip loosened. Between them, Kerr and Claypoole got Schultz to his feet, and they ran, half carrying, half dragging the big man. More explosive rounds came at them, but they all missed.

They got back to where the rest of second squad and the gun squad were laying down covering fire for first squad, which was in position to begin moving on the ambush's flank.

"Where's he hit?" Hospitalman Third Class Hough, the platoon corpsman, asked when Kerr and Claypoole got Schultz into a shallow defile. Hough had his med kit ready to give whatever treatment the big man might require.

Kerr shook his head. "He's got a ding on his arm, but that's not the problem." He looked the corpsman in the eye. "If it was anybody but Schultz, I'd say he's suffering from battle shock."

Hough looked at Kerr in disbelief—the *Hammer* suffering from battle shock?—then looked at Schultz's face. "My God, I think you're right." He took a deep breath. "Get back to your squad, I'll deal with him."

"All right, Doc." He clapped Claypoole on the shoulder. "Come on, we need to help with that base of fire."

Corporal Pasquin, still at the far end of the left flank when Lieutenant Bass gave the orders at the beginning of the firefight, ordered Lance Corporals Quick and Longfellow to open up on the rear of the ambush. He himself began picking off the mercenaries with the weapons that looked like they might be able to penetrate the Marines' body armor. But he was only forty meters behind the ambush line, and it took almost no time for the mercenaries to realize someone was to their rear and for several to turn and fire back with everything they had. Even armored, Pasquin had to duck low to keep from getting hit by something powerful enough to seriously hurt—or kill—him. So, after three aimed shots, his fire became ineffective for anything more than keeping the mercenaries down. And it sounded like some of them were starting to maneuver to where they could see him. He began crawling back to his men, who were doing a slightly better job of pinning down the Sharp Edge ambushers. But he had a long way to go before reaching the relative safety of two more Marines. He was almost halfway back when flanking fire began from first squad; the holding fire from second squad started seconds later.

But the first of the maneuvering mercenaries were then in position to see Pasquin, and beyond him the other two Marines. Flechettes impacted on Pasquin's body armor, and explosive rounds started coming at him. The first one to hit tore off the top of his helmet and knocked him flat.

Longfellow heard the fire from the side and turned his head to look. He saw Pasquin get hit. He let out a scream and shifted his fire from the ambush line to his front to the people closing on his fire team leader.

The change in Longfellow's fire caught Sergeant Ratliff's attention. As soon as he looked in that direction, he realized what was happening. "Dorny!" he shouted. "See where Longfellow's shooting?"

The first fire team leader looked. "Yeah," he answered.

"Put your fire team's fire there."

"Roger." Dornhofer told Lance Corporal Zumwald and PFC Gray to add their fire to his and began shooting at the mercenaries maneuvering to flank the flankers. In only a few seconds, all of them were down. Wounded, dead, or simply hiding, Dornhofer didn't care; they were out of the action. He returned his fire team's fire to the flank of the ambushers, who were trying to reorient themselves to answer the threat on their flank.

The gun squad's fire swept across the top of the ambush line, keeping the mercenaries down, forcing them to crawl to change their positions, vastly reducing their ability to return fire.

"I can use some help here, Hound," Ratliff called to Sergeant Kelly.

Kelly looked to Lieutenant Bass. Bass nodded. "Taylor, give first squad some support," Kelly told Corporal Taylor, the second gun team leader.

"With me!" Taylor shouted to his two men. Lance Corporal Dickson, the gunner, picked up the gun and ran with his team leader. "Where do you want us?" Taylor called to Ratliff as he ran.

"Right here," Ratliff said, moving to where he wanted the gun. "You can put enfilading fire on their whole line from here."

Dickson put the gun where Ratliff indicated. Taylor started directing his fire, and PFC Dias dropped down next to the gun, ready to change barrels or reload the gun as needed.

On the left flank, as soon as the additional fire from first squad dealt with the mercenaries who were maneuvering toward Pasquin, Longfellow began scrambling toward his fire team leader. "Cover me!" he yelled back at Quick.

Nobody from the ambush line was maneuvering toward the flankers anymore: Too much enfilading fire was coming at them from their own flank. Because of the volume of incoming fire, they weren't even able to shift their line to meet the new threat. All along their line, without orders, mercenaries began breaking off, scrambling, either crawling or rising to a low crouch, to get away from the deadly fire coming their way.

"Cease fire! Cease fire!" Bass ordered on the all-hands circuit.

"Cease fire!" Staff Sergeant Hyakowa repeated. "Cease fire!"

The squad leaders echoed the orders, and then the fire team leaders. The fire from the Marines quickly died off, and the Marines watched the last of the Sharp Edge survivors running off.

"Casualty report," Bass ordered. It took a few seconds for the reports to filter up from fire team level.

"First squad, Pasquin's down, maybe dead," Ratliff reported. "One walking wounded. We've got him patched up. Doc can take his time getting to him."

"Second squad," Kerr called. "The Hammer's down. Doc's got him. No other casualties."

"Guns, no casualties," Kelly said.

"Doc, as soon as you can, see to Pasquin," Bass said. "First squad, check the enemy casualties. Second squad, guns, cover them." While the squads were moving to obey his orders, Bass contacted the other flanking fire team. "Right flank, how do things look on your side?"

"No one's in sight on the right," Corporal Chan answered.

"Stay sharp. We don't know there're no more bad guys in the area."

"Aye aye," Chan acknowledged.

Of the seventy or seventy-five mercenaries Pasquin had reported were in the ambush line, twenty-seven were still there, dead or too badly wounded to drag themselves away. The plasma bolts from the Marines' blasters usually cauterized the wounds they made, so there were no blood trails to tell the Marines whether other injured Sharp Edge mercs had gotten away.

"Get a hopper in here to medevac the wounded," Bass told his comm man, Lance Corporal Groth. He looked at the wounded mercenaries. "Make that two hoppers; we'll take their wounded, too."

"What about the dead?" Hyakowa asked.

"We'll make sure Sharp Edge knows where to find them."

Corporal Pasquin and Lance Corporal Schultz were evacuated along with the Sharp Edge wounded, and third platoon prepared to move out again. This time, first squad had both the point and the left flank, first and third fire team respectively.

Second squad's first fire team, still on the right flank, stood up for the first time since Bass had ordered them to stay in place when the platoon began walking into the ambush's killing zone. Corporal Chan paused before stepping out to take a good look outward.

"Buddha's blue balls!" he swore. He then toggled on his radio's command circuit. "We've got company coming." He snorted a quick laugh. "Looks like about company size."

"The Virgin's sacred tits!" Bass swore. "Why don't they just stand down?" Then to Chan, "Humans or Fuzzies?"

"Definitely human. They have clear faceplates, so I can see their faces. Human. And not in Marine utilities."

"How far out?"

"A bit more than a klick, maybe a klick and a half."

"Get me Company," Bass told Lance Corporal Groth. In a moment, he was talking to Captain Conorado for the second time in ten minutes. He reported what Chan had described and asked, "Sir, can we get some air support on this? A strike from above will probably discourage them." He listened to Conorado's reply, signed off, then ordered, "Third platoon, move out!"

Ten minutes later, two Raptors from Thirty-fourth FIST's composite squadron dove on the company approaching third platoon from its right rear. Bass joined Chan and his men to watch. Even before the fast flyers finished their first strafing run, the mercenaries were scattering, mostly running back the way they had come.

Third platoon had no more incidents on the way to Mining Camp No. 15, which they found deserted by its Sharp Edge guards and overseers. Hundreds of Fuzzies milled around aimlessly or sat about listlessly. The Marines opened the gates, broke down portions of the perimeter fence, and went through, opening the few cages that still held Fuzzies. They stood aside and watched while the released Fuzzies began wandering toward the open gate and downed sections of fence. Once out in the open, the Fuzzies began to run off in that odd four-legged gait, tails up, bounding rear feet to front in a hobby-horse motion.

CHAPTER NINETEEN

Mercury squatted in his corner of the command post, going over the latest reports from his scouts and raiding parties. The command post wasn't in his own burrow. Indeed, he didn't even know where his home burrow was. When the People were taken by the Naked Ones, they were usually removed from their home territories and taken to distant locations where they didn't know the land or any of the People who lived in them. If there *were* still People living in the strange lands, which there never seemed to be.

He hadn't set out to be a general—no, not *a* general, but *the* general in command of the Fuzzy rebellion against the Naked Ones' taskmasters. But he had led the first of the freedom fights, the one that had released his fellows of Deep Roots burrow from the vile labor in which the Naked Ones held them.

Then, with the blessing of the Mother and the Father, he had led the fighters from Deep Roots burrow to release the people of other Bright Sun Clan burrows. The Clan Mother and Clan Father had then instructed him to find and release the people from Running Water burrow of the Deep Pool Clan and bring their Mother and Father to them. He had done as the Clan Mother and Clan Father had instructed. He was granted the privilege of sitting in when the Clan Mother and Clan Father met with the Mother and the Father of Running Water burrow. The Mother and the Father of Running Water burrow agreed to align themselves with the Bright Sun Clan in their war against the Naked Ones on the condition that the next attack be against the prison where the Clan Mother and Clan Father of the Deep Pool Clan were being held. The Clan Mother and Clan Father agreed that this would be most beneficial to all concerned.

After that successful raid, Bright Sun and Deep Pool were joined to release the rest of the Brilliant Coalition. Thanks to his success, the Clan Mothers and Clan Fathers agreed that Mercury should have command of all of the fighters of both clans, even though high command was reserved for the senior Clan Father of the coalition. The Clan Mothers said, and the Clan Fathers agreed, that neither of the released Clan Fathers was in good enough condition following their release to go afield on fighting missions. They agreed that Mercury had been so successful as leader of the raiding parties so far that he should continue in command.

The subsequent missions had been successful, and all of Deep Pool Clan was released, as were some of the burrows from other clans. But the successes didn't continue.

These latest reports from the scouts and raiding parties told why.

The Naked Ones had reinforced their garrisons with more fighters and given them stronger weapons and other devices that enabled them to fight more effectively during the dark hours, which were the times the raiding parties were most likely to attack. Three raiding parties had recently been beaten off with heavy casualties, and no released people to show for their losses. Several of the scouts had told of new Naked Ones, who went to the places of imprisonment and released the People, even if they had to fight and kill the Naked Ones guards and overseers to do so. These new Naked Ones had horrible weapons that used fire to wound and kill.

Mercury didn't know what to make of the new Naked Ones. He also wasn't sure he could believe everything in the scouts' reports. So he sent out more scouts, to the places where the new Naked Ones had released people. He wanted the scouts to bring people back, if possible a Mother or a Father, to meet with the Clan Mothers and Clan Fathers, to tell them about the new Naked Ones.

As an afterthought, he added that they should attempt to capture one of the new Naked Ones, or one of their weapons. But only if they could do so without being discovered by the Naked Ones. It was far more important that they bring the released people back, and do so without the Naked Ones, the old or the new, being able to follow them to Rock Haven, the burrow that held the Clan Mothers and Clan Fathers as well as his command post.

Henny, of the Deep Pool Clan, was one of the scouts. He led a team of four. The other three were also Deep Pool Clan: Crooked Tail, Red Butt, and Big Nose. Not their true names, or even the names they called one another, but what the Naked Ones had called them when they worked in the mines.

Henny and his teammates were scouts; they weren't supposed to get into fights, but rather to avoid contact with the Naked Ones. So they were armed only with hand weapons: knives and throwing stones. They had not even a bow among them, although Henny carried a thrusting spear with *thikshreep* venom daubed on its point. They set out for the place where the scouts had most recently reported seeing People be released by the new Naked Ones. The hard part, then, would be convincing a Mother or a Father to return to Rock Haven burrow with him and his team. If not, he could bring back anybody who was willing to come along, so long as that person had seen the new Naked Ones release the People from the old Naked Ones.

The journey wouldn't be long, only three days' lope. They would rest during the hottest part of the day, and do much of their traveling at night. Their greatest danger would be from the *granalchits* that could kill a person with one swift bite and swallow an adult whole. Or a sharp-taloned *chirchitt,* whose mighty wings were powerful enough for one to carry off an adult. They were the main reasons Henny carried a *thikshreep*-tipped thrusting spear. One stab with it would throw a *granalchit* into convulsions so violent they would break its bones, and it would soon die, or send a *chirchitt* into screaming flight until its breast muscles froze and it crashed to its death.

Not that Henny or his teammates thought there was any danger of running into a *granalchit* or a *chirchitt*. After all, they were in the highlands and staying out of unoccupied burrows. *Granalchit*s mostly stayed on the lowlands, and they loved unoccupied burrows, leaving them mostly to travel from one to another. *Chirchitt*s were smart enough that most of them recognized thrusting spears and almost never attacked a person who carried one, or anyone near a spear carrier.

A bigger problem would be water. There were no rivers in the area Henny and his team were traversing and few springs and fewer streams. But as long as they could find succulent bulbs and the juicy crawlers that were common just under the surface, they would be fine. None of the area had been extensively foraged recently. Even where the farms had been allowed to go to seed, finding food would not be a problem.

Henny and his team reached the area where there had been recent reports of people who had been released by the new Naked Ones. None of the People were to be seen, but Henny didn't expect to just find them wandering about; they'd have either found and occupied a local burrow or wandered off in a probably fruitless search for their home burrow.

Henny set his team to searching for a trail that would tell them where the people had gone. The four scampered about on their legs, sniffing for the freshest scents of strange people, looking down at the ground for footprints that weren't trodden over. From time to time one would drop to all fours and snuffle at the trunk of a tree or the base of a bush, smelling for a territory marking. Now and again one of them would stop, stare at the ground, and drop down and scrabble at the soil, frequently digging up a subsurface crawler and popping it into his mouth. Food was where food was found; this much food meant people hadn't foraged here in a long time, little food meant they had.

The four began near the center of the area where the scouts had seen the hundreds of lost, released people, it took time to work their way to the outer edges. Red Butt was still many lengths from the edge of the milling area when he suddenly dropped to all fours and took off in an arrow line. He passed the edge and kept going for as many more lengths beyond, then stood erect, looking in the direction he'd run. He looked around for a climbing tree and saw one nearby. After finding a landmark to make sure he'd be looking in the right direction when he climbed the tree, he scampered to it and hunched himself up it as high as he thought it would hold his weight. Four body lengths. That was enough to allow him to see much farther. He looked and peered, shading his eyes with the hand that wasn't holding on to the tree.

There! In the distance he saw three people foraging, far enough away that he wouldn't have been able to see them from ground level. He looked more, farther and closer than the trio, in an arc side to side from them, but didn't see other people foraging. He looked into the few trees near them, and the tops of rock piles, but couldn't detect a watcher. Were the three out on their own, somehow lost and by themselves? Had they gotten separated from a larger foraging group? Were they scouts from another army that Red Butt didn't know about? No, he didn't see any weapons; they couldn't be scouts.

Red Butt turned head down and jumped from the tree, dashing on all fours to where Henny had just noticed him.

"What?" Henny demanded. "Did you find them?"

"I don't know." Red Butt told Henny what he'd seen, and the things he thought about the three foragers. While he chittered, Crooked Tail and Big Nose noticed the excited talking and scampered to join them, to hear what Red Butt had to tell Henny.

"Show me," Henny said when Red Butt was finished.

Red Butt dropped to all fours and raced back to the tree from which he'd seen the trio of foragers. The others sped behind him. At the tree, Red Butt pointed out a landmark before Henny climbed the tree and looked for himself. He did as much looking fore and aft, side to side, into trees and high rocks as Red Butt had, and saw no one but the three strangers. He dropped back to the ground.

Henny was a scout team leader because he was experienced and he was smart. A scout team leader had to be both if his scouting missions were to be successful. He had to be able to find what he was looking for, without anybody finding him or his team. He had to watch out for enemy patrols, *granalchits*, and the other hazards that beset singletons or small groups, and be prepared to deal with whatever dangers his team encountered. When he looked at the three foragers, he'd had all the questions Red Butt had about them. He also wondered if they were a decoy, planted by Naked Ones to lure in more people to be captured and put to work in the unnatural places. They could even be decoys from a clan guarding its borders, set to lure in unsuspecting scouts, or other people from unfriendly clans.

While he was thinking about how to approach the three, he had Crooked Tail and Big Nose climb the tree to see where they were going. When all had seen the foragers, he told them what they were going to do—and how they would avoid walking into a trap, if a trap had been set.

They split into two pairs: Henny and Crooked Tail, and Red Butt and Big Nose. They split in different directions, angling to give the foragers a wide berth. At first they walked upright, then dropped to all fours for a time before lowering themselves to crawl, knees snug against the sides of their bellies, elbows sticking out wide, tails held low to the ground, necks bent so their snouts pointed straight ahead on the same level as their shoulders.

Henny and Crooked Tail at last reached the rock outcropping Henny had picked for their way station. A jagged tower of igneous rock jutted out of the ground, higher than a person standing on the shoulders of another. It was a prime location for a sentry, but no sentry was posted there. Henny stood Crooked Tail on the side of the tower from which they'd come, positioned so he could look around its side at the foragers while showing as little as possible of his own silhouette. He then placed himself at the opposite side. Between them, they could see not only their quarry but a large area around them. And by turning his head, Henny could scan to his rear.

Henny looked hard but could see no sign of Red Butt and Big Nose on the far side. He nodded to himself. Seeing no sign of the other scouts could mean that they weren't in position yet, but he knew his scouts, and knew they were good enough that he shouldn't be able to see them from this distance. He continued to look at the foragers, to peer at the surrounding landscape. He even made an occasional sweep of the sky, just in case a *chirchitt* was lofting on the currents and updrafts.

He was looking at the foragers when one of them, near a clump of bushes, violently hopped up and back, flipping over in mid-arc. The movement that followed the jumper was almost too fast for him to see—a *granalchit*!

Henny shrilled out a warning chitter and burst on all fours from his hiding place, racing as fast as he'd ever run toward the person who had barely managed to jump out of the way of the striking predator. His alarm scream caught everybody's attention, and the foragers, except for the one whose attention was fixed on the sinuous predator, looked at him—even Red Butt and Big Nose stood from their hiding places.

Big Nose was the first of Henny's scouts to spot the *granalchit* their leader was racing toward. He let out a piercing alarm and sprinted on all fours toward the person, who was now standing as though mesmerized by the giant worm. Red Butt instantly followed. Crooked Tail finally saw the predator as well, and began chasing his leader. The two foragers saw the beast and chittered in terror, though neither of them dared approach it.

The *granalchit* ignored the shrill chittering around it, and the thudding vibrations of pounding feet it felt through the ground—its meal was just standing there, trembling, ready to be taken and swallowed. It gathered itself for another strike, one that wouldn't miss. It didn't notice until far too late that one chittering voice and the thudding feet that went with it was upon it, and that voice was letting out a killing shriek.

Henny reached the *granalchit's* tail, and plunged his *thikshreep*-tipped thrusting spear into its barrel-like body. He hopped out of the way of the thrashing tail and bounded to a safe distance to watch the beast's dying convulsions.

Red Butt reached the still-frozen person and pulled her out of the way to safety.

The *granalchit* coiled and uncoiled at dizzying speed and threw itself about. Its venom-dripping fangs slashed at the spear protruding from its tail. It twisted and turned and rolled and looked as if it were trying to tie its long, limbless body into knots. There was a *crack!* as loud as a rifle shot, and the *granalchit* flopped flat to the ground, its spine broken near where the spear still stuck out of it. Then, with its rear portion limply being tossed about, it resumed gyrating with the forward part of its body, the same violent twistings, dizzying coilings and uncoilings as before, until another gunshot-loud *crack* announced the snapping of its neck.

The dying beast struggled vainly, its mouth gaping and snapping shut, burying the tips of its fangs in the ground. Its body merely twitched; the beast couldn't move a muscle beyond a hand's width behind its massive head.

Henny stepped in and wrenched his thrusting spear from the beast's body, being careful to not touch the shaft where it had been scored by the thing's fangs. He stepped back and examined the spear point; he knew he'd have to replace the shaft. Satisfied that the point had been buried deeply enough in the *granalchit's* body that it hadn't been contaminated by the venom, he walked to the beast's head, which now lay almost still, although venom still oozed from its fangs. Still not touching the shaft near the scoring, he raised the spear high and plunged it straight down, driving the point through the center of the *granalchit*'s head, away from the venom sacs, pinning it firmly to the ground.

He chittered at his team and the three foragers and began cutting the beast's pinned head from its body. The seven of them took hold of the body, dragged it away from the head, and rolled it out straight on its back. Henny and Red Butt started in the middle and used their knives to slice though the skin from there to the ends. Two of the foragers followed behind them, deftly peeling the skin from the underlying meat. All of them worked together to butcher the *granalchit,* discarding the portion near the original spear thrust, where venom might have gotten into the meat and contaminated it.

At length, with the butchered meat wrapped in leaves, and the parts of the skin away from the contaminated section rolled up, the seven people, four Deep Pool scouts and three foragers, squatted in a circle facing one another.

Henny identified himself and the members of his team. The three foragers were members of the Sunburst Clan of the Starwarmth Union: Gomez, Thing, and Tuesday—the one the *granalchit* had intended to eat. The Sunburst trio, grateful for the way Henny had saved one of their own, offered to take them in safe passage to the burrow their clan was living in and introduce them to their Mother and their Father, even though the Starwarmth Union and the Brilliant Coalition were long-sworn enemies. They understood that *all* of the People now had a common enemy.

The following day, the scout team from the Deep Pool Clan headed for home. The Sunburst Father went with them. Red Butt stayed behind as hostage.

CHAPTER TWENTY

The day after the Sharp Edge flotilla in orbit had been taken, Commodore Borland visited Brigadier Sturgeon in his command post. He brought some freshly ground Blue Mountain beans with him for Lieutenant Quaticatl to brew a pot of coffee. Master Chief Petty Officer Mbo Bolivar, the *Grandar Bay*'s Chief of Ship, accompanied him.

"Make enough for you to have a cup, too," Borland told Sturgeon's aide.

"Aye aye, sir, thank you, sir," Quaticatl said with a grin. He wasn't very fond of the inferior Marine-issue caff, either.

Sergeant Major Parant joined the flag officers and the Chief of Ship in Sturgeon's office. Sturgeon sat at the side of his desk, Borland and Parant sat at its front, and Bolivar sat behind them—there wasn't room for the four of them to sit in a conversational circle. While they waited for the coffee, Sturgeon told Borland what he needed in additional supplies from the *Grandar Bay*. Parant and Bolivar made notes and exchanged a look that said they'd straighten matters out between themselves after their bosses finished screwing up needed items and quantities.

After Quaticatl brought in the coffee and took his leave, Borland got down to the business that brought him back planetside.

"I've got quite a few prisoners in orbit," Borland said after taking a sip of coffee. "They've filled the brig to overflowing, and I've had to berth more than half of them in the troop compartments." He shook his head thinking about how the Sharp Edge crews might be treating the troop spaces they were billeted in. "Mbo"—he gestured at his senior enlisted man—"agrees with me."

"That's right, Ted," Bolivar said. With only the four of them in the office, the most senior officers and enlisted in the task force, they were on first-name terms. "I want to airlock them, but Roger won't let me."

"Mbo, we simply can't dump excess prisoners into the vacuum. Aside from issues of inhumane treatment, we'd get court-martialed once word got out. Crimes against humanity, you know?"

Bolivar shrugged as though a court-martial for such a minor offense was of no consequence and took a deep swig of the coffee. He made a face; the coffee was a bit weak for his taste, it wasn't grow-hair-on-your-chest strong like proper navy coffee.

"I don't want them down here," Sturgeon said.

"I didn't think so. I have another idea of what to do with them."

Sturgeon's eyebrows raised slightly, and he nodded for Borland to continue.

"Prime Minister Foxtable and his cabinet all claim they know nothing about what's happening here. I don't believe them any more than you do, Ted. And I want to check out those permits Cukayla gave us."

Sturgeon nodded. He took a sip of coffee to hide the smile that was beginning to crease his face behind his mug.

"So I want to take the prisoners to Opal and rub the government's faces in it."

"Roger, I think that's a great idea." He held out his mug in a toast. The four clinked mugs.

Prime Minister Duane Foxtable and his cabinet stood on the same beachside flagstone terrace where they'd greeted Commodore Borland and Brigadier Sturgeon on their first meeting.

Commodore Borland didn't bring any Marines on that trip planetside, but he instructed the coxswains of the two Essays to make the descent in combat assault mode—a straight-down dive—anyway. He wanted to give the prisoners a good shaking up. The only difference in the landing this time was the Essays didn't come across the beach, the Essays landed in the middle of the plaza. After Borland and Lieutenant (jg) Flynn, the *Grandar Bay's* legal officer, who was also the officer in charge of the Small Arms Department, exited the first Essay, Chief Petty Officer Ault, the *Grandar Bay's* Master at Arms, led the sailors of the Small Arms Department out of the Essays. The sailors weren't in dress uniforms; they wore working coveralls and carried weapons at the ready. The sailors formed two ranks in front of each Essay, through which the crews of the three Sharp Edge starships exited. The crewmen were shackled at the wrists and ankles, and a chain led from one to the next. The clothing on many of them testified as to how their digestive and excretory systems had responded to the combat assault dive. Borland and Flynn weren't dressed in their whites; they wore their workaday khakis—this was no social occasion for them.

While the navy personnel were forming up, Prime Minister Foxtable and his cabinet scampered to turn so they were facing the plaza rather than the beach, and the police and lesser functionaries who attended them hastily repositioned themselves behind their reoriented masters.

Borland came to a halt in front of the Prime Minister.

"Commodore Borland, what an unexpected sur—" Foxtable began, but Borland cut him off.

"Mr. Prime Minister, members of the cabinet," Borland said harshly, "the last time I was here, not only did all of you deny any knowledge of mining activities on Ishtar, you stated clearly that there were no activities of *any* sort on your sister world.

"You see before you men in chains. These prisoners are the crews of the SS *Pointy End,* the SS *Tidal Surge,* and the SS *Lady Monika.* Starships we found in orbit around Ishtar. They were there in support of the ground operations of a mercenary force running slave-labor mining camps. You will notice"—he leaned in at Foxtable—"that there are no Marines with us today. That is because the Marines are all planetside on Ishtar, engaged in hostilities with the comrades of these mercenaries." He stood erect and looked from one end of the cabinet line to the other. "In case you are wondering, the mercenaries initiated the hostilities by shooting and killing a Marine officer!"

"Bu-bu-but—" Foxtable objected.

Up and down the line of cabinet members, the ministers were also objecting. Some looked honestly surprised by Borland's statement, others horrified, as though they'd been caught out doing something they really shouldn't have done.

"Your system scanning must be the worst among settled human worlds," Borland snarled, "if not one but *three* starships could enter your system and take up orbit around your sister world without you noticing!

"Or *did* you know?" he demanded accusingly.

Borland turned to look at the prisoners, obviously not listening to anything the Prime Minister might have to say in response. "These *sailors*," he said derisively, "are not worthy of being on a starship, much less a Confederation Navy starship." He turned back to Foxtable. "So I am handing them over to you for safekeeping. You *will* secure them until I can arrange for their removal to a proper venue to be tried for piracy, slave running, and other crimes as may be determined."

There was no reaction to that announcement from the prisoners; they were all still recovering from the planetfall.

Foxtable paled. "Bu-but, Commodore, Opal doesn't have proper facil—"

Borland rounded on the Prime Minister. "Then you will *make* proper facilities," he snapped. He leaned so close that Foxtable took an involuntary step back. "I cannot yet determine that *you* or your ministers are responsible for what is happening on Ishtar, but if *any* of these prisoners are not immediately available for pick up and transport when they are come for, *you* and your ministers will be held *personally* responsible and may face criminal charges yourselves! Do I make myself clear, Mr. Prime Minister?"

Foxtable swallowed several times and ran a finger around the inside of his collar. Down the line, the Minister of Security and one or two other cabinet members looked distinctly ill.

"Y-yes," the prime minister croaked. "Yes, sir."

Borland gestured toward the prisoners. "Now these are yours. Deal with them."

"Deal with them, yes." Foxtable craned his neck to look along the line of cabinet ministers. "M-mister Rondow," he said, "kindly see to the prisoners."

Minister of Security Rondow flinched, but turned to the Berrican police chief, who stood behind him, and said, "Lock those people up, Chief Madlow."

Chief Madlow blanched and mouthed "Where?" but ordered his policemen to take control of the prisoners from the sailors guarding them. Master at Arms Ault, in turn, had to take control of the policemen to straighten out the ensuing confusion.

"Now, Mr. Prime Minister," Borland said once the policemen had the prisoners marching off to the city jail, "shall we retire to your office?" He phrased it as a request but it came across as a command.

"B-by all means, Commodore." Foxtable led Borland to his land car and ushered him into it. He tried not to be taken aback when Lieutenant (jg) Flynn and Master at Arms Ault joined them. Foxtable made a couple of attempts to make polite conversation during the short ride to the Prime Minister's palace, but the navy men didn't respond, didn't even look at him, so he stopped trying and sat in uncomfortable silence until he was finally able to scramble out of the vehicle.

The four of them, along with Minister of Security Rondow, met in Foxtable's office at Borland's demand—he had phrased it as a request, said the office would be more comfortable and conducive to open and honest conversation.

As soon as he entered his office, Foxtable scurried to the perceived safety of his desk. Borland and Flynn took visitor's chairs facing the desk, virtually forcing Rondow to sit between them. Chief Petty Officer Ault closed the office door behind them and stood in front of it at parade rest. When he casually patted the hand blaster holstered at his hip, it became obvious that he was going to let *no* one get past in either direction.

"Mr. Prime Minister," Borland began, "we have a serious situation here. There are numerous violations of Confederation law involved, enough to send people to prison for the rest of their natural lives—not to mention a possible threat to the security of the Confederation of Human Worlds, and, just incidentally, the security of Opal. I want to make sure you are aware of that."

Foxtable nodded dumbly.

"You heard what I said about slave labor being used by the mercenaries on Ishtar. Do you have any idea *who* those slave laborers are?" He watched Foxtable's face closely as he spoke. Flynn watched Rondow just as closely.

"N-no. I didn't even know s-slavery or anything else was happening on Ishtar. How could I know who is being kept in such dire circumstance?"

Borland gave him a sharklike grin. "Aliens, Mr. Prime Minister. The mercenaries have enslaved an alien sentience indigenous to Ishtar."

"No!" Foxtable shouted. "That's not possible! When the Bureau of Human Habitability Exploration and Investigation explored Ishtar before we colonized Opal, they didn't find any sign of a sentience. Our own explorations didn't find anything, either. It's not possible!"

Borland shook his head. "It's not only possible, it's true. Behind"—the derisive colloquial name for BHHEI—"didn't look in the right places, and neither did Opal's explorers. The indigenous sentience lives in burrows—its villages are all underground. We've been inside them. We have collected and examined samples of the artifacts of the sentience. Technologically, they're at a level roughly analogous to our own early Industrial Age."

Foxtable looked aghast at Rondow. "Do you know anything about this?"

Rondow shook his head. Borland wondered if the Minister of Security was unable to speak out of fear that his voice would give him away.

"I noticed a similarity between your name and the name of the chief of police," Flynn said conversationally. "Are you related?"

Off balance at the unexpected and off-topic question, Rondow stared at the officer for a moment. "No, no," he said at last. "Just a coincidence of sounds. That's all."

Flynn looked over his shoulder at Ault, who nodded, got out his comp, and took a note.

Rondow saw the byplay, as he was supposed to. "A distant cousin, that's all. Not a close relative. No, not at all close. Anyway, nepotism isn't illegal on Opal." He looked to Foxtable for confirmation.

"That's right," Foxtable said quickly. "Everything he said is true."

"I see," Flynn said in a calm voice that implied he didn't believe a word of what either man said.

"Mr. Prime Minister," Borland said in a friendlier tone than he'd used so far, "I believe, and Brigadier Sturgeon concurs, that these mercenaries could not have established their slave-labor mining operations on Ishtar without the connivance of some of Opal's industrialists and, possibly, some ranking members of your government. I would like to have your assistance in ferreting out the guilty parties. Bear in mind, please, that the discovery of an alien sentience is a matter of great security interest to the Confederation of Human Worlds."

Foxtable was taken aback by the sudden and unexpected change in Borland's tone, and by the request for assistance. It took several seconds for him to collect himself. When he did, he said slowly and with relief, "Commodore, my office will give you every assistance we can in coming to a proper and successful conclusion to this matter. An alien sentience indigenous to Ishtar is indeed, as you said, a matter of great security interest. Not only to the Confederation, but to Opal itself!"

"I'm very happy to hear you say that," Borland said. He produced several sheets of flimsiplast from his jacket pocket. "I have here copies of permits signed by your Ministers of Commercial Enterprise, Space Operations, and Mines and Resources, granting Galactic Enterprises, Ltd., permission to develop and exploit the resources of Ishtar. Galactic Enterprises is—"

Foxtable cut him off. "Let me see those!" he snapped, yanking the sheets out of Borland's hands. His eyes widened as he skimmed the copies. Aghast, he looked up at Borland after reading the permits. "Minister of Mines and Resources Bijuterie died in an accident seven months ago. Minister of Space Operations Kugis resigned and went off world nearly a year ago—I don't know where she is now. And Minister of Commercial Enterprise Shouhou retired to his estate on Minisan last year." He looked at the permits again, and said slowly, "The dates on these permits suggests that signing them was just about the last thing each of those ministers did in his or her ministerial capacity." He rolled his head from side to side and murmured, "None of them said anything to me about these permits."

"What about their successors? Do they know about?"

"I'll damn well find out!" Foxtable shouted, banging his hand on his desktop. He turned to Rondow, who looked distinctly uncomfortable. "Get those three ministers in here, *right now*! I want to see each of them individually, and I don't want them to know what I want to see them for. Understand?"

"Yes, Prime Minister, I fully understand," Rondow said as he jumped to his feet and rushed out of the office.

"And get Shouhou in here!" Foxtable shouted after his Minister of Security.

Minister of Commercial Enterprise Perkara was the first of the summoned ministers to arrive. She was dressed in a business suit a decade out of style in the older worlds of Human Space, but she wore it like the latest fashion, which on Opal it probably was. Commodore Borland and his people sat in a row off to the side of Prime Minister Foxtable's desk. No other chairs were available, so Perkara stood directly in front of the desk.

"What's going on here?" she demanded after casting a harsh glare at Borland. She made a show of looking at the absence of seating for herself. "Is this the way you receive your ministers now, Duane? Like misbehaving students brought in to the headmaster's office?"

Foxtable didn't answer her, just handed over the permit signed by her predecessor. "What do you know about this?"

She looked at it and shrugged. "Before my time," she said. "I've never seen it before. For all I know it's been revoked."

"Well, find out. I expect a full report on this permit and its current status by the end of the afternoon."

Perkara sniffed, spun on her heel, and marched out of the office without a word.

Minister of Mines and Resources Khaan was next. He was flushed, sweaty, and in gym clothes.

"What's the meaning of this, Duane?" he demanded, not seeming to notice that he wasn't offered a seat. "You know I work out every day at this time."

Again, Foxtable ignored his minister's protests and handed over a permit. "Explain this to me," he ordered.

"What?" Khaan took the permit and looked it over. "It seems to be in order. What's the problem?"

"What the problem is, is I don't know anything about it. But evidently you do. Explain it to me."

Khaan shrugged. "It's a permit for a mining operation on Ishtar. Everything seems to be in order."

"Galactic Enterprises, Ltd., to whom the permit was issued, is a holding company. For whose benefit are they holding it?"

"I don't know. You'll have to ask Bijuterie. He signed it, not me."

"Minister Bijuterie is dead, as you well know. Since I can't ask him, I'm asking you. Explain it, if you please."

Khaan looked at the permit again, and waved it at Foxtable. "Everything I know about it is right here."

Foxtable simply stared at Khaan.

"Well, I guess I can find out," Khaan admitted.

"I expect a full report on my desk by the end of the afternoon. Now get back to the gym and clean yourself up. You look a mess, and you smell."

Looking offended, Khaan left.

Minister of Security Rondow returned. "I haven't been able to find Avaruus," he reported. "He's not in his office or any of his usual haunts. Nobody seems to know where he's at."

"Keep looking. What about Shouhou?"

"I've sent an atmospheric flyer to Minisan to bring him to you."

"Did you talk to him, tell him why you're sending the flyer?"

"No, I didn't speak directly to him. I told his major domo that you wanted to see him, that was all."

"All right. Keep looking for Avaruus." Foxtable waved Rondow away. When the security chief was gone, he turned to Borland with a questioning expression on his face.

"Thank you, Mr. Prime Minister. I would like to see those reports once you've read them."

"I'm happy to cooperate, Commodore. I think we've got a serious situation on our hands. Now, you said you wanted to see some industrialists as well?"

"Yes I do."

In short order, Commodore Borland had meetings scheduled with Navio Acalli, the owner of the starship yard; Smaragdna Boja, the owner of Opal's primary gem mining fields; Beimat Sawder, the owner of the principal private security firm; and Relv Arma, Opal's sole weapons manufacturer. There was subterfuge involved; the meetings weren't set directly with the industrialists—they weren't even told in advance that they would be meeting with Borland. Instead the four were invited to an impromptu luncheon at the Prime Minister's palace, and the meetings would take place before they were allowed to leave. Foxtable carried enough weight that all four showed up promptly, even though Boja tried to beg off, citing a major new find on an arctic island that he was preparing to visit. If the industrialists were surprised by the presence of two Confederation Navy Dragons standing outside the entrance of the Prime Minister's palace, or the armed Confederation sailors dressed in work coveralls standing at parade rest outside the entrance to the conference room where the luncheon was being held, they didn't give voice to it. Nor were they surprised at the absence of the cabinet ministers. Conversation over the hastily thrown together yet elaborate five-course meal was perfunctory; basically how are your families, how's business, and what help might you need from the government?

Commodore Borland, Lieutenant (jg) Flynn, and Chief Ault weren't present for the meal. Instead the three navy men were in a nearby office preparing to interview the four luncheon guests.

While the luncheon dishes were being cleared away, an aide to the Prime Minister entered the room and leaned over Navio Acalli's shoulder. After a few whispered words, Acalli followed the aide from the room. He didn't return. Smaragdna Boja was the next to be summoned. Beimat Sawder and Relv Arma, both of whom were in a hurry to get back to their businesses but were prevented from leaving by armed Confederation sailors who had entered the room immediately after Boja left, demanded to know what was going on.

"Please, please, gentlemen," Foxtable said, patting the air. "Nothing is wrong, I assure you. Mr. Acalli has already returned to his shipyard, and Mr. Boja will soon return to his office to continue preparing to visit his new arctic gem field. You will shortly be allowed to leave and attend to your businesses."

"Duane, I'm in the security business," Sawder said. "I can tell what's going on here. You dragged the four of us in here so that fancy sailor from the Confederation can interrogate us without our being able to talk about it until everybody's been questioned. You think I don't know he's here? With his sailors carrying weapons in the Prime Minister's palace? Now what the hell are they so curious about? Talk about violations of sovereignty!"

"All right, all right, Beimat," Foxtable said, again patting the air. "You're partly right about what's happening—that Commodore Borland is interviewing each of you independently. But that's not because he suspects any of you of wrongdoing, no, not at all. Someone *else* is violating Confederation law in a way that involves the navy, and he's looking for assistance from the four of you to find out who."

Sawder snorted. "Right. 'Interviewing' each of us in such a manner that we can't communicate among ourselves until we've all been questioned. That sure sounds to me like none of us are under suspicion!" His voice dripped sarcasm. "Isn't that right, Relv?"

Arma looked at the holstered hand blaster at the hip of one of the sailors. "You know, Beimat, I'd feel complimented if the Confederation military thought I had cloned those blasters of theirs and was manufacturing them. And I'd be a rich man if I was." He looked at Sawder and shook his head. "I have no idea what they're looking for, but whatever it is, I didn't do it." He looked back at Foxtable. "As long as we're waiting, I'd like another dessert."

After interviewing the last of the four, Commodore Borland asked Chief Ault what he thought.

"Well, sir," Ault said, measuring his words, "that weapons man, Arma, is hiding something for sure, but I don't think it has anything to do with Ishtar. Acalli's shipyard can't do anything more than repair starships well enough to make it to the nearest Class-A yard, so I rule him out as being involved, at least in the beginning. I've got to say, though, he stands to profit hugely if he's given any kind of backing to the operation. Sawder throws out so much garbage in his overstated outrage that I can only say he bears watching. On the surface of it, Boja seems the most likely to be involved. But he seems too involved in his own operations here on Opal. My sources tell me he's got everything tied up in that arctic field his geologists recently discovered, and he's liable to go bust if it doesn't pan out as big as he hopes. I couldn't help but notice that not one of them said anything useful."

Lieutenant (jg) Flynn raised an eyebrow at Ault's mention of "my sources," but he'd been in the navy long enough to know that chief petty officers often have ways of finding things out that officers aren't privy to.

Borland turned to Flynn to ask his opinion, but Ault said, "One more thing, sir." He got out his comp and referred to it. "That distant cousin of Security Minister Rondow, the Chief of Police? He really is remotely related, third or fourth cousin several times removed, something like that. But he's married to Rondow's sister-in-law." He looked at Borland. "That man stinks, sir. And you'll note, his ministry is responsible for keeping tabs on every starship that enters the system."

"Thank you, Chief. Very good thinking—and your sources are to be commended. Now, Mr. Flynn, what do you think?"

"Sir, I didn't see anything about Arma to make me suspect him, I think he's in the clear—even if he is hiding something, the way the Chief thinks he is. But I'd really like to get a look at Boja's books. Now *that's* a man who bears looking at. According to *my* sources"—he nodded at Ault—"he's been suspected of illegal trafficking on several occasions, but nobody has tried very hard to prove or disprove the allegations. Sawder's bluster strikes me as an attempt to cover something, probably illegal. And if anybody outside the government is able to subvert the space security system, it's him. As for Acalli, I'm in agreement with the Chief." He smiled. "And I agree that Rondow stinks."

"Thank you, gentlemen," Borland said. "Now I think it's time we thanked Prime Minister Foxtable for his assistance." He grinned the kind of grin the captain of a warship might have when his starship is about to deliver the coup de grâce to an enemy. "And see what happens when we let him think we learned a great deal more than we did." He stood and led the way to the conference room where the luncheon had been held.

* * *

Prime Minister Foxtable was waiting for them. Servants started bringing in food as soon as they entered the room. Having already eaten, Foxtable contented himself with tea.

Borland began as tea was being poured. "Well, sir, I must compliment Opal on its industrial and business leaders. That fine group of gentlemen was *most* cooperative, and provided us with a *great* deal of information that I'm sure will quickly lead to the identification of the parties responsible for the illegal activities on Ishtar."

"Really? That's wonderful news," Foxtable said with evident relief. "Especially in light of the fact that one of my ministers seems to have vanished off the face of Opal. And a retired minister is likewise absent."

"Avaruus and Shouhou?" Borland asked.

Foxtable grimaced and nodded. "The current Minister of Space Operations, and the retired Minister of Commercial Enterprise, yes."

Borland looked thoughtfully into a distance that only he could see. After a moment, he said, "That certainly suggests that there is more illegality here than simply Sharp Edge initiating hostilities with Confederation Marines."

"I'm afraid it does, Commodore." He snorted a rueful laugh. "I don't believe any of the permit fees or royalties from those mines has been paid into Opal's treasury. If that is indeed the case, I suspect that there are considerable violations of Opal law, as well as of Confederation law."

"Mr. Prime Minister, I and my legal people will do everything in our power to work with you to investigate the matter and bring the guilty to justice."

"You can do that? I mean, the navy has that kind of jurisdiction here? Remember, Opal is an independent world."

"On violations of Confederation law and matters of security? Absolutely. On longer-settled worlds, even independent ones, the Confederation often has a stronger presence, and the Ministry of Justice has resident agents who would conduct such arrests. Similarly, on worlds with a Confederation military presence, one could expect the resident military to make the arrests. But on worlds such as Opal, where the Confederation doesn't have a strong presence or a military garrison, visiting navy starships *do* have that jurisdiction where there are demonstrable violations of Confederation law or potential security threats. And there seems to be several such violations here, as well as a possible threat." Borland smiled the smile of a righteous man about to deal harshly with evildoers.

Borland, Flynn, and Ault dug into their meals with gusto. Prime Minister Foxtable looked like he wished he hadn't joined Relv Arma in that second dessert.

While Commodore Borland and Lieutenant (jg) Flynn rode one Dragon back to the waiting Essays, Chief Ault took the other one to Berrican's police center, where the prisoners from the starships were being held until a better secure location could be found. Chief of Police Madlow greeted him with something less than warmth, and showed him the cells into which the prisoners were crowded.

"We can't hold them here for long; you'll have to get them off world soon," Madlow insisted. "This is unhygienic. If one of them is sick, I could have an epidemic on my hands."

Ault looked at the cells. "They've got more space here than they did in the *Grandar Bay's* brig," he said blandly. "Of course, Confederation Navy starships have strongly enforced stringent cleanliness standards. I guess if the sanitation of your jail leaves something to be desired, you might have a problem."

Madlow was deeply offended by Ault's remark but held in his anger. Ault was confident that, for a while at least, the prisoners were secure.

Back on the *Grandar Bay,* the three discussed their trip to Opal. They agreed on one major point that they hadn't previously voiced: The *Grandar Bay* didn't have the necessary resources to conduct the kind of in-depth investigation needed to learn who was behind the operations on Ishtar. Commodore Borland composed a message to send to the Chief of Naval Operations on Earth via drone. The message requested that the Attorney General send an investigative team to Opal and find out on whose behalf Galactic Enterprises, Ltd. was operating.

CHAPTER TWENTY-ONE

"Look alive, people," Lieutenant Bass said on the platoon all-hands circuit. Again, third platoon had been dropped off five kilometers from its objective, Mining Camp No. 57, so the Sharp Edge people there wouldn't have advance notice of their approach. Not that the five-klick walk on their approach to Mining Camp No. 15 had helped any. The terrain the platoon was moving though was similar to where they'd previously been ambushed. But the lava flow here was older and broken into smaller chunks so that more vegetation grew on it, sometimes enough to completely block Bass's view of the flankers. He didn't know if the Sharp Edge mercenaries had learned their lesson about firing on Marines, but he wasn't about to bet they had. He'd encountered beaten forces in the past that kept going as though they were winning.

Sounds like Marines, he thought. *But Marines never suffer such lopsided losses.*

Corporal Dornhofer's first fire team, first squad, had the point. Corporal Dean's third fire team, first squad, had the platoon's left flank, and Corporal Doyle's third fire team, second squad, held the right flank.

"I think he can handle it, and it's time his men got the experience," Bass had said when Staff Sergeant Hyakowa looked like he was going to question Bass's choice of Doyle to lead the flankers.

Hyakowa had let it go at that.

Damn! Bass wished he understood what had caused the Hammer to freeze the way he had. Did extended combat, always being in the most exposed position, finally catch up with him? That was why most commanders routinely rotated the Marines in the most exposed positions, so that stress wouldn't build up until it incapacitated them.

But Schultz *wanted* to be in the most exposed position; he was *supposed* to be immune to that kind of stress. Had it finally made a casualty of him?

Corporal Doyle was very nervous on the flank, but nervousness was his normal state in any situation that might result in combat. He did his best to hide his nervousness and fear, the way Sergeant Kerr kept telling him. "Pay attention to your men," Kerr always said. "They look to you and take their clues from how you act. If you come across as confident, they feel confident. If you look like you're scared shitless, you better believe they are, too. When Marines are scared shitless, they make mistakes, and mistakes kill Marines."

So Doyle hid his nervousness as best he could. He used his light-gatherer screen when he looked into shadowy areas and his magnifier when he looked into the middle and far distance. He didn't bother with his infra, because the heat radiating from the ground would give false readings everywhere and mask the heat signatures of actual people. He took frequent sips of water and sucked on a pebble to keep his mouth and throat lubricated, so that when he spoke to his men, as he often did, his voice wouldn't come out as a croak. He moved slowly and deliberately so he wouldn't trip or wander off in a wrong direction; that helped him look to his men as if he knew what he was doing, and they imitated him. He looked all around constantly, out of fear of someone sneaking up or lying in ambush, which his men understood as being alert, so they were alert as well. He frequently checked where he was relative to the main body of the platoon, and where his men were, redirecting them if they were out of place, because he didn't want to become lost and be alone, which his men understood as lessons on maintaining proper contact, and they did the same. He kept his ears turned up all the way so he could hear any sound that might indicate an enemy was creeping up on him or lying in wait.

So it was that Corporal Doyle, doing his best to hide his fear and nervousness from his men, was the first to hear the distant sounds of combat.

"Two, Two One," he radioed much more formally than was necessary.

"What do you have, Doyle," Kerr came back.

"Gunfire up ahead."

"Hold where you are. I'm joining you," Kerr told him, then made sure Lieutenant Bass knew. Bass halted the platoon, and Kerr trotted the hundred and fifty meters to where Doyle and his men waited, on the far side of a nearby low ridge of broken lava. The ridge wasn't high enough to hide the flankers from the main body, but the vegetation on it hid the flankers from easy view.

"Where?" Kerr asked as he reached Doyle and knelt next to him.

Doyle pointed. Kerr swiveled his head side to side, listening with one ear and then the other.

"I don't hear anything."

"Turn up your ears."

Kerr made the adjustment to his helmet's audio pickups and listened again. This time he heard what Doyle did, and in the direction the fire team leader had pointed. He called up his HUD map, and oriented it in the direction of the distant firefight.

"Six, Two," Kerr radioed. "It sounds like a firefight at our objective."

"Stand by," Bass ordered. No other Marine unit was supposed to be in this area, so who was fighting? "Get a string-of-pearls view of the objective," he told Lance Corporal Groth.

Groth got out his UPUD Mark II and called up the signal from the string of observation satellites orbiting high above. In seconds, he had real-time imaging of the objective and handed the device to Bass.

"Can't you get better resolution on this thing?" Bass asked after peering at the image.

"I can ask, sir."

"Do it." Bass waited impatiently while Groth talked to the *Grandar Bay*'s Surveillance and Radar section.

"Sir, that's the best resolution we can get on the UPUD, but the *Grandar Bay*'s SRAs are taking a look with their equipment. They'll tell us what they see."

In a couple of minutes the word came down: People they tentatively identified as Fuzzies were attacking Mining Camp No. 57, third platoon's objective. It looked to the SRAs in orbit like the Fuzzies were winning.

Bass took the UPUD's comm from Groth. "This is Lima Three Actual. Say again your last," he demanded.

"Lima Three Actual," a gruff voice said, "we can't tell positively, but it looks like Fuzzies are attacking Mining Camp Number Fifty-seven. Whoever the attackers are, it looks from here like they're winning, like they're about to overrun the camp."

"That you, Chief?"

"Yeah, this is Nome. That you, Charlie?"

"That's me. Listen, Chief, I gotta check with my boss, but I've got something I want you to do, so don't go away."

"I'll wait for you, Charlie."

"Son of a bitch," Bass murmured as he handed the comm back to Groth. "Tell them to hang on. I might have something else for them. And get me the Skipper." He toggled on his all-hands circuit.

"Listen up, people. Got some real-time intelligence from the eyes in the sky. Someone, possibly Fuzzies, has our objective under attack.

Stand by for new orders." He toggled his helmet comm off as Groth handed him the comm.

"I've got Company, sir."

"Lima Three Actual," Bass said into the comm.

"Lima Three Actual, Lima Six. Stand by for Lima Six Actual."

"Roger," Bass said.

"Three Actual, this is Six Actual," Captain Conorado's voice said. "What do you have, Charlie?" Bass told him what he'd just learned from the *Grandar Bay,* and Conorado asked, "What's your recommendation?"

"Sir, I want the eyes in the sky to clear the path for us, and us to pick up our pace, get to our objective as quickly as possible."

"What will you do when you get there?"

"That depends on the situation."

"Give me the situation at the objective before you take action."

"Aye aye, sir."

"Lima Six Actual out."

"Get me the *Grandar Bay* again," Bass told Groth. In a few seconds, he was talking to Chief Nome again.

"Chief, I've got to move fast. Can your people keep a path cleared for me, let me know if I'm walking into anything?" •

"Piece of cake, Charlie. I've got one of my best people on duty. I think you know the other one, a second-class by the name of Hummfree."

Bass thought for a second. "Used to be on the *Fairfax County,* when it took my platoon to Society 437?"

"The very one."

"Good man, Hummfree. I know he can clear for us."

"He's off duty now, but I'll get Auperson in here, too. You liked the support he gave you on Kingdom."

"Thanks, Chief. I know I can count on you and your people. Let me know as soon as they've cleared the way for us."

"Will do. Golf Bravo out."

Bass handed the comm back to Groth and toggled his all-hands back on. "Everybody, listen up. Change of plans. We're going to move out at speed. The *Grandar Bay*'s best SRAs are going to lead us, so there's no sweat that we'll run into an ambush. We won't do anything at the objective until I get the go-ahead from the Skipper. Right now we'll continue as we were until I say to pick it up. And don't nobody complain about the pace; we only have three more klicks to go."

The landscape around Mining Camp No. 57 was desolate. The vegetation had been cleared and the ripples in the ground filled in with tailings from the mine. By the time third platoon reached it, the firefight was over and the last of the imprisoned Fuzzies were disappearing into the thin woods a kilometer and a half to the north. Even at that distance the Marines could see that most of the Fuzzies seemed sluggish, although several of them were armed and looked alert. The only movement visible through the broken fence surrounding the camp was debris wafting in air currents, and occasional dust devils spinning. All of the cages visible appeared to be vacant. The Marines moved into a defensive position several hundred meters from the fence, with most of them facing the camp.

Lieutenant Bass reported what he saw to Captain Conorado.

"All right, Charlie, check it out," Conorado said. "But be careful, and stay out of the mine shaft—we know that the Fuzzies booby-trap the tunnels. I'll ask the *Grandar Bay* to track the northbound Fuzzies."

"Roger," Bass said. "We'll be careful, and we'll stay out of the mine shaft." *I lost a good Marine to a booby trap in a tunnel on Haulover,* he thought. *That's not an experience I want to repeat.*

"Listen up," he said into his all-hands after the company commander signed off. "We're going in. We're staying out of the mine shaft, but watch for booby traps anyway. First squad first, on a staggered line. Second squad follows fifty meters behind. Guns, provide cover, and watch our rear. I'm with first squad. Staff Sergeant Hyakowa stays with guns. Move out."

"All right, first squad," Sergeant Ratliff said. "You heard the man. Up and at 'em. On line, fifteen-meter intervals—and stagger that line!" Ratliff rose to his feet and began advancing toward the camp. He looked to his sides to make sure his men were with him and that the line was staggered. "Spread it out, first squad!" he ordered when he didn't like their intervals.

The ten Marines of first squad advanced at a walk, but they slowed when they crossed the areas filled with trailings; the footing was treacherous on the loose rock and dirt. When they'd gone fifty meters, Sergeant Kerr had second squad follow. Sergeant Kelly set his guns where they could give covering fire to the advancing Marines and fire to the flanks and rear if danger came from those directions.

"Looks like they used some kind of explosives here," Corporal Dean said as he and his men entered the compound over a downed section of fence to the right of the gate. He stretched to step across a small crater; whatever had made the crater had also torn the fence apart for several meters to either side.

"Same thing here," Corporal Dornhofer said. "The gate's been knocked off its hinges. What's this? I see fragments of metal embedded in the wood of the gatehouse." He paused to look inside. "Got a body."

"Are you sure it's dead?"

"Affirmative. Half the head's been blown away by something with a hell of a punch."

"Leave it and keep moving," Ratliff said. "What do you see, Quick?"

Lance Corporal Quick, acting as fire team leader since Corporal Pasquin had been evacuated, said, "The fence here was just knocked down. I don't see any signs of explosives. Got a lot of blood, though. Looks like the trails are going out, not coming in."

"Explain that."

"More than one casualty, walking or being carried out of the camp, not into it."

"All right. Keep moving," Ratliff said. He went through the fence to the left of the gatehouse. "Anybody else see bodies or blood?"

"Not on the right," Dean answered.

"There's something up ahead," Dornhofer said, "but I can't tell what it is yet. Could be a couple of bodies."

"I've got a lot of blood on the ground," Quick reported. "The ground's scuffed up, like there was some heavy hand-to-hand here."

"Dorny, Dean, keep moving. Quick, stay where you are, I'm joining you."

Ratliff trotted to where Quick and his men waited. Quick and PFC Sturges, filling in from Whiskey Company, were examining the scuffed, blood-soaked ground while Lance Corporal Longfellow watched their surroundings.

The red dirt was hard packed, baked by the sun and heat. It didn't take marks easily but it held any marks that it did take. An area more than twenty meters by ten was scuffed with boot prints and other marks that the Marines guessed were Fuzzy footprints, and the shallowest of indentations that looked like bodies that had been slammed hard to the ground. There were lines that could only be drag marks. Scorch marks suggested weapons had been fired next to the ground; small gouges had to be bullet impacts; smaller gouges were likely from flechettes. And there was blood. Spatters here, splashes there. Ratliff had neither the time nor inclination to sort out the details just then, but he guessed more than a score of entities, human and Fuzzy, had collided there. He couldn't guess at which side won—except that they'd seen the Fuzzies leaving, and the only Sharp Edge mercenaries they'd seen so far were dead. Blood trails led toward the fence and toward a nearby building.

Ratliff looked at the building the blood trails led to. "Check it out," he told Quick. "And check for booby traps."

"Right," Quick said, then said to his men, "Let's take a look."

On the other side of the compound, third fire team approached another building. There was a sign next to its door:

SHARP EDGE, Ltd.
Ishtar Mining Camp No. 57
Administration

The door had been battered in and the windows were broken. There was blood on the ground outside the door. A length of tree trunk nearby must have been used as a ram. Corporal Dean cautiously approached the entrance and peered in over the sights of his blaster. There was a room with doors on both sides and a railing separating most of the room from the entrance. Two bodies lay sprawled in the middle of the room behind the railing; blood pooled around them. Motionless legs jutted from behind a desk. Just inside the door was a large smear of blood, as though someone— or something—had lain there and been carried away after bleeding out. Insectoids buzzed about in the room, lighting on the pools of blood, and on the bodies' wounds. There was no other movement.

Dean looked to his right. "Triple John, look through the windows on the right. Tell me what you see." To his left. "Ymenez, take a look inside the window on your side."

"I've got bodies," PFC John Three McGinty said. "Four of them. Looks like they put up quite a fight. I don't believe all the blood in here came from them."

Lance Corporal Ymenez reported, "This is the head. Looks like one man was taking a shower when the fighting started." He stopped and swallowed. "It looks like he was unarmed."

Dean sighed. "I don't see any weapons here, either. How about you, Triple John?"

"No weapons. But I'll bet they had them."

"Keep moving," Ratliff ordered his men on the squad circuit.

First squad's second and third fire teams moved out to keep pace with first fire team. "Did any of you see weapons?" he asked. Dornhofer and Quick both said they hadn't. He shook his head. It looked like the Fuzzies were taking all the firearms and knives from the mercenaries.

First fire team reached the area of cages and spread out to prowl through them. The gates of several were open. All were empty. Second and third fire teams came to more buildings. Their doors had been battered open and their windows were broken. The Marines looked into them without entering. There were bodies and blood inside each building, but no visible weapons.

First squad eventually reached the far end of the enclosure without finding anybody alive, just dead bodies—and no weapons.

When second squad reached the fence, the Marines went around the perimeter, checking the trenches and bunkers. They found more bodies and a lot of blood. Despite the lack of weapons, it looked like there had been fierce fighting on the perimeter; there was a lot of blood that wasn't near any of the bodies, with no blood trails leading to the bodies.

"It looks like the Fuzzies took their dead and wounded with them," Sergeant Kerr observed.

Lieutenant Bass was listening. "That's another sign of sentience," he said. "As if we needed more proof."

Second squad's second fire team had almost reached the rear of the compound when Corporal Claypoole heard a groan.

"I think I found a live one," he shouted.

"Where?" Sergeant Kerr asked as he trotted toward Claypoole. Bass also headed over.

A short stretch of narrow trench was dug twenty meters behind the perimeter trench, with a zigzag trench leading to but not joining it. A ten-centimeter-square beam with rounded edges was fixed across uprights almost forty centimeters high over the trench. An unpleasant smell wafted from the narrow stretch of trench. Claypoole circled to the end of what was obviously a slit trench for the use of sentries on the perimeter. The bar aboveground indicated it wasn't meant to be used during a firefight.

"Who's there?" Claypoole asked. He held his blaster on the short trench, ready to fire if someone—or something—popped up with a weapon.

"Don't shoot, don't shoot!" came a weak voice from the trench. "Are you people? Real people?"

"I'm human, if that's what you mean." Claypoole stopped three meters from the slit trench. From there he could see into the far end; it had obviously been used for its intended purpose. "Raise your hands to where I can see them."

"Okay, here they are." There were some scraping and squishing noises, as of a body moving about in muck, and a pair of filthy hands appeared above the edge.

"Stand up."

"I—I'm not sure I can. Hit in the hip." There were more noises, and a grunt, followed by a cry of pain. "I—I don't think I can stand without help."

By this time, Lance Corporal MacIlargie had circled around to the rear of the trench and stepped close enough to look into the end where the man was.

"There's one man in there," MacIlargie said. "He's not holding a weapon."

"Cover me, Wolfman." Claypoole slung his blaster and stepped to the end of the trench. This close, it stank. He looked in and saw a man struggling to stand. Claypoole dropped to a knee and reached down. "Give me your hand," he said. The man reached up and grabbed Claypoole's outstretched hand with both of his. Claypoole tugged and stood, pulling the man out of the slit trench. "Hell of a place to take cover," he said.

The man lay on his back, gasping. "I, I was relieving myself when they attacked," he said. "I got hit right away and f-fell in."

MacIlargie kept his weapon on the man as he walked around to stand by Claypoole. "Damn, honcho, but we got to sluice you down, you smell like shit!" he said.

"Very funny, Wolfman."

The injured man groaned. Blood was still oozing from his hip. He feebly put a hand on it to stop the slow flow.

"Corpsman up," Claypoole said into his comm.

His call wasn't necessary. Doc Hough arrived with Lieutenant Bass and immediately saw what needed to be done. "Get water," he said.

"Wolfman, you and—I'm sorry, what's your name again?" Claypoole asked the Whiskey Company replacement for Lance Corporal Schultz.

"Me? PFC Berry."

"Berry. Right. Go with Wolfman and get water for the doc." Claypoole shook his head. He'd always been edgy around Lance Corporal Schultz and didn't really want him in his fire team. But now that the big man was gone, he missed him badly. He knew it was wrong, but he took it out on the temporary replacement from Whiskey Company by not remembering his name.

Hough pulled on disposable gloves and pulled the man's hand away from his wound. "What's your name?" he asked.

"W-Wasman," the wounded man said through clenched teeth. "Soda Wasman."

"Well, Soda Wasman, you did a pretty good job of packing your wound," Hough said as he cut away the man's trousers and began probing the wound. "But you picked a real shitty packing agent." He looked up. "Where's that water?"

Bass knelt next to Wasman, opposite Hough. "How many of you were there?" he asked.

Wasman looked at him blankly.

"Your garrison, how many?"

"I—I don't know." He was gasping for air, and his eyes wandered.

MacIlargie and Berry arrived with buckets of water. Hough took one and began pouring it around the wound to clean off the worst of the offal smeared on and in it. He looked up and snapped, "Couldn't you get hot?"

MacIlargie looked offended. "You didn't say you wanted *hot* water."

Hough bent back to his work, muttering "Dumbass."

"How many were in the attacking party?" Bass asked.

"I—I don't know." Wasman's voice was weaker than before and his eyelids slid over his eyes.

"Hold your questions for later, sir," Hough said, then slapped Wasman's cheek. "Don't go to sleep, man. Stay with me." With the worst sluiced away from the wound, he began gently daubing muck out of the hole. "Where are you from, Wasman. Wasman? Answer me, dammit!" But Wasman had faded into unconsciousness. Hough swore and pulled a stasis bag out of his med kit. "Give me a hand getting him in here," he said as an order, and swore. "He's probably suffering from heat as well as blood loss."

Bass stood and stepped back while Claypoole and MacIlargie helped the corpsman seal the wounded mercenary in the stasis bag that would hold him until he reached the hospital aboard the *Grandar Bay* when it returned from Opal.

Bass called Company to ask for an explosive ordnance disposal team and medical evacuation for the wounded man. The same hopper that brought in the EOD team took the wounded man in his stasis bag.

Third platoon didn't find any more survivors among the approximately seventy bodies they retrieved. Bass wasn't concerned with a more exact count. He thought Brigadier Sturgeon would agree with him that Sharp Edge should be made to deal with their own dead. He was, however, concerned that they didn't find any weapons or ammunition. He wasn't as sure as the Brigadier that the Fuzzies would see the Marines as liberators; he thought they might see the Marines as being rivals of Sharp Edge, mostly interested in taking over the operation once they'd gotten rid of the competition.

The EOD team found and disarmed three booby traps: one in the administration building attached to one of the corpses, and two more inside the mine shaft. They obtained samples of the liquid the booby traps would have sprayed had they gone off, and took it back for shipment to the *Grandar Bay* for analysis. They also took back a basket of freshly mined gems.

"When the *Grandar Bay* gets back, I'll check to make sure they reach her safe," Bass told the EOD team after he counted the gems.

CHAPTER TWENTY-TWO

Mercury wasn't happy. He'd lost too many fighters in the last attack on a Naked Ones mine. Yes, his fighters had killed all of the Naked Ones. Yes, they'd freed all of the people held in the mine. But his force of two hundred fighters had lost more than a third of its strength, killed or badly wounded, and that was too many. The Naked Ones had reinforced the garrison and had almost managed to drive off the attackers. The only reason the attack succeeded in the end was that the People being held in that camp were High Trees Clan, and a few of the fighters were High Trees who had been away when the Naked Ones raided their village to take them away. Those High Trees fighters weren't going to stop fighting until they freed their clan mates—or died in the attempt.

Mercury now knew that his scouts needed to learn more about the strength of the garrisons before he made his attack plans. And he had to come up with new tactics to defeat the reinforcements if he expected to win without losing so many fighters. If he continued to lose fighters at that rate, his force would stop growing, and many fighters would desert. At least many of his fighters were now better armed, with the Naked Ones weapons that didn't have to be reloaded after each shot and didn't get fouled as quickly as those of the People.

Then there was the question of the other Naked Ones. Had they been on their way to that camp to reinforce or assist it? Or had they been going there to attack? His scouts had reported seeing the two different groups of Naked Ones fighting each other. There weren't enough of the new Naked Ones to defeat the garrison that had caused such severe casualties among Mercury's fighters, even though his scouts had seen the new ones defeat garrisons larger than themselves. The new Naked Ones *must* have been going to assist those Naked Ones. He didn't understand why they had made no attempt to harry Mercury's fighters and the freed people on their withdrawal. But how had they responded to the attack so quickly? Surely they must have been on their way to further reinforce the garrison. It was good that they didn't arrive earlier, for they would have tipped the battle the other way.

Mercury sent scouts to reconnoiter the base of the new Naked Ones. It would take them two hands or more of days to get there and back, but their base was much closer than that of the Naked Ones who had first enslaved the People.

"I've got this real funny feeling, honcho," PFC McGinty said.

"Yeah, Triple John? What kind of funny feeling?" Corporal Dean asked his junior man.

"Like somebody's eyeballing me real hard," McGinty said. He rotated through his screens as he nervously looked around.

The fire team was on a security patrol around the advance position third platoon had established after returning from Mining Camp No. 57. This new camp, which they named Camp Godenov in honor of the Marine they'd lost on Haulover, was less than half the distance from the mines to Thirty-fourth FIST's base of operations. From there they could head quickly toward any mining camp they were sent to. Camp Godenov was closer in a straight line to where the *Grandar Bay*'s Surveillance and Radar section had seen the Fuzzies from Mining Camp No. 57 go to ground. There was also, so the command thinking went, a greater possibility for a small unit to make contact with the Fuzzies and establish some form of communication with them. That was why Brigadier Sturgeon had sent Lieutenant Prang, the *Grandar Bay*'s xeno-zoologist, along with third platoon.

"Yes, I know, the Fuzzies are obviously sentient, and Prang isn't a linguist or anthropologist," Brigadier Sturgeon had said in explaining his selection. "But the *Grandar Bay* only has one officer in each of those disciplines, and I want them at my headquarters for when one of my units brings a Fuzzy in. Prang is, however, a zoologist, so he can surely figure out *something* about how to deal with the Fuzzies, so he's going."

For his part, Prang was both frightened and delighted at the prospect of being the first human being to establish communications with an alien sentience.

And for *his* part, Lieutenant Bass wasn't in the least bit cowed by having an officer attached to his unit who technically outranked him. As far as Bass was concerned, Prang was just another squid underfoot who needed to be kept out of trouble.

"Where?" Dean asked McGinty. He looked around himself, using his magnifier screen. He also checked in all directions with his motion detector.

"I'm not sure," McGinty said hesitantly. "But the feeling's stronger in—"

"Don't point!" Dean snapped. "If you're right, that'll tell whoever it is that they've been detected. Just tell me what direction."

"Oh, good idea, honcho."

"That's why I get paid the big creds. Now what direction?"

McGinty thought for a moment about how to say it and get the direction right. "Stop," he said, and stepped in front of Dean and off to the side a bit. "From where you are, the strongest feeling is past me."

Dean nodded approvingly. "Not bad. Now start moving again." Dean followed McGinty's movement with his head but kept his eyes pointed in the direction the other had indicated.

Third platoon's advance position was near the bottom of a sheltered valley in the lower foothills. The sun didn't beat down in the valley as harshly as many other places, making for slightly cooler temperatures, and thin ribbons of water dribbled down from the highlands. Those things combined to grow lusher vegetation— although *lush* was a relative term. The valley would have been called a scrub desert on Earth. The trees were thin and crooked, spiky with thorns, and less than seven or eight meters high. Bushes were scraggly and seldom grew even waist high. There were numerous patches of bare, red ground among the growth.

But it *was* cooler here than on the flat; not so cool, though, that they weren't buttoned up using their cooling systems to keep themselves from overheating.

Dean slid his infra screen into place and tried again. He couldn't be positive but he thought a few spots showed up warmer than their surroundings. He examined the landscape to the front and on the floor of the valley. The patrol route called for them to go three kilometers up the north side of the valley and cross to the south side on the return. Each of them had a HUD map with the route and rally points marked in case anybody got separated. They kept going until their movement took them perpendicular to the location and they could no longer see it without turning their heads. They continued on their route while Claypoole considered what to do.

"Change of plans," Dean said into his helmet comm. "Triple John thinks someone is watching us. I think he's right. We're going to find a place where we can cross to the south side without being seen, and double back." He then notified the platoon of what he had planned.

"Don't cross over yet," Lieutenant Bass told him. "I'll check with the sky-eyes, see if they can spot anybody. Where are they relative to your current position?"

"I'd say about three-quarters of a klick, maybe more," Dean answered. "I don't want to do something obvious to alert them, so I won't shoot an azimuth on them. But they're more than ninety degrees to my left, maybe a hundred, hundred and ten."

"That should be close enough," Bass said. "Keep moving. I'll get back to you."

"Roger." Dean toggled on the fire team circuit. "Did both of you hear that?" They had. The patrol continued while Dean waited to hear from Bass.

Lieutenant Bass quickly got the SRA department on the radio. "Chief Nome? Charlie Bass here."

"Hi ya, Charlie. How's it hanging down there?"

"It's about the hottest place I've ever served," Bass answered. "How're things on the high ground? And don't give me any kwang-duk droppings about the comfortable temperature you're suffering through."

Chief Nome laughed. "Nah, I wouldn't tell you that, Charlie. But it is a nuisance, what with the temperature going back and forth from one degree too warm to one degree too cool, and never hitting that sweet spot right between the two." Before Bass could say anything about that, Nome went on: "Listen, I've got one of my aces on duty, and he needs a workout to keep in trim. You have a job for us? A tricky one, I hope?"

"Yeah, I do. I've got a security patrol out . . ." As Bass gave Nome directions to the patrol's position, the chief passed them on to SRA2 Auperson, his "duty ace."

"Got 'em," Nome said. "I thought you said this was a tricky one?"

"You haven't heard the rest of it yet. Can your ace see the direction my patrol is heading?" He waited a moment before Nome came back with an affirmative. "All right. Roughly a hundred, hundred and ten degrees to the left of their line of movement, maybe three-quarters of a klick away, maybe more. My patrol leader thinks he saw some spots in infrared that were a tad bit warmer than their surroundings. Could be hot rocks, could be grazing animals. Could be bad guys of some sort watching them."

"Couldn't get anything in the visual?"

"Negative."

"All right, that's better. Now let's see young Auperson earn his keep."

It took three minutes, but Auperson found them.

"You got five Fuzzies," Nome reported. "Four of them are hidden well enough that almost nobody could find them from orbit, but I've got two aces who *can* find them. I'll download their position to you."

"Four of them are hidden? What about the fifth?"

"He's hightailing it out of there. And I do mean hightailing. I couldn't make it out, but Auperson assures me his data show that Fuzzy's tail is sticking straight up. Hell, I couldn't even tell positive that the beastie was galloping on all fours!"

Bass chuckled, then said, "Do me a favor. Can you let me know if those four Fuzzies move? I want my patrol to check them out. Maybe attempt friendly contact."

"You don't sound like you really mean the friendly-contact bit," Nome said.

Bass shrugged, even though Nome couldn't see the movement. "I'm not convinced they want to be friendly. My Marines have already run into three different alien sentiences. Two of them wanted to fight, and the third was willing to ally with us against the Skinks but didn't seem to want anything to do with us once the fighting was over."

"I hear you, Charlie. I'll have Auperson keep an eye on them. You tell your people to be careful out there. You have that download yet?"

Bass checked the UPUD. "Got it, thanks. I tell my people to be careful all the time, Chief. Bass ou—"

"Oh, one more thing. Do you want to know where that fifth Fuzzy is going?"

"Yeah, that sounds like a damn good idea."

"All right, I'll bring my other ace in and have him track the beastie. Hell, he's been off duty for three hours now. That's enough sleep for anybody."

Bass laughed. "Are you sure you've never been a Marine gunnery sergeant?"

"Nah, never. I'm a navy chief petty officer. We got gunnies beat, hands down."

"Must have been in a past·life, then."

"Nope. I'm navy through eternity! Nome out."

Bass shook his head, chuckling as he put the UPUD down and toggled his radio to the patrol's circuit.

"Three Two Two, this is Three Six Actual. Over."

"Six Actual, Three Two Two. Go," Corporal Dean answered immediately.

"You were right, there's four Fuzzies over there. Stand by. I'm sending their exact coordinates to you. The sky-eye's going to keep a watch on them, so you'll know if they change position."

"Thanks, Six." Dean got out his comp and checked it. The data came in. "Got it," he said.

"Let me know when you begin to cross the valley. Three Six Actual out."

They weren't able to cross right away, even though the vegetation was thicker than in most other areas, and more than thick enough if the Marines had been in their chameleons; most of it was still too thin to be good for hidden movement for men wearing dull green garrison utilities.

"Angle upslope slightly," Corporal Dean told Lance Corporal Ymenez, who was on point. "See that knot of trees?"

"I see them," Ymenez replied.

"Head for them. I think I see a place beyond there where we can duck out of sight."

"Aye aye, honcho."

"Triple John, do you still feel like we're being watched?" Dean asked McGinty.

"Yeah, but not as strong as before." He shrugged. "That could just be because we're farther from them." He felt vindicated since the report that the *Grandar Bay* had spotted four Fuzzies about where he thought observers might be. He was also not afraid, exactly—concerned, say—about the Fuzzies watching them. Brigadier Sturgeon thought the Fuzzies would turn out to be friendly, which was why the Marines weren't wearing their chameleons, but nobody

was sure of that. Those Fuzzies could be an ambush. And just because the *Grandar Bay* had seen four of them didn't mean there wasn't
a whole platoon of them, better hidden, in ambush. Really bad odds
for a single fire team.

They reached the knot of trees—too thin to be called a copse—
and Dean called a brief break. Even though they were sealed inside
their uniforms, there was just enough shade that it *felt* cooler among
the trees, even if the feeling was all in the mind. After a few minutes
Dean left his men in place and scouted ahead. He'd been right about
what he'd thought he saw: A small gully led down to the valley floor.
It looked like a similar gully ran on the opposite side of the valley. He
returned to his men.

Dean radioed in for an update on the Fuzzies and told Bass what
he'd found, and that that was where they were going to cross. Bass
said the Fuzzies were still in place and to be careful crossing the
valley.

"Got that right, boss," Dean said. He looked back to where his
HUD map showed the Fuzzies were. They were more than a klick
and a half distant now.

"Listen up," he told his men. "Unless the Fuzzies have much better eyesight than humans, I'm pretty sure they can't see us through
this knot of trees. So when we move, we're going low and keeping
these trees between us and them. Fifty meters up, there's a shallow
gully. We'll crawl down it to the valley floor and then stay low while
we climb to the other side of the west wall. When we get perpendicular to them, we'll come back over the top and come down from
above them. That way they won't see us coming. Questions?"

"What do we do if they change position, or move out?" McGinty
asked.

Dean shook his head. "I won't be able to answer that question
until they move or move out. Now, if there's nothing else, let's do it."

They went fast and low, keeping the knot of scraggly trees between them and the Fuzzies, and dropped into the gully. At first the
Marines had to low-crawl on their bellies, very carefully so they

didn't raise a dust cloud that would give them away. After fifty meters the gully was deep enough that they were able to go on hands and knees, which was a lot easier. Near the bottom they had to low-crawl again. The valley floor, thanks to the water that threaded down it, was more thickly vegetated than the slopes, and they were able to walk, though usually in a low crouch.

Dean called a halt along one of the waterways and checked in. The Fuzzies still hadn't moved. Now Dean really wondered what they were doing. Had the Fuzzies had third platoon under observation long enough to know that a patrol went out on one side of the valley and back on the other, and were waiting for his fire team to come back? If so, why? Did they plan to make friendly contact? Were they an ambush? Or did they have something else in mind altogether, something unguessable to a human? Dean had no idea, and neither did Bass.

"Be careful," Bass said. "I've got the rest of the platoon ready to move out if you run into something you can't handle."

"Thanks, boss."

"Three Six Actual out."

"All right, you know where we're going," Dean told his men. "Let's move out. Ymenez, you've got the point."

They headed toward the other gully Dean had spotted and crawled to the top of the valley wall and over it.

The climb up the south wall of the valley was easier than the climb down the north wall. The sun didn't beat as harshly on the south wall as on the north, so more vegetation grew there. The Marines took advantage of that vegetation to crawl on hands and knees, or climb in a crouch; the few times they had to snake on their bellies, the movement was easier because their heads were higher than their feet and they didn't have to struggle as hard not to raise dust clouds. They reached the top of the wall and went over it to the reverse slope in less than half the time it had taken them to descend the north wall, even though it was a longer climb. No longer concerned with being spotted by the hidden Fuzzies, the Marines went fast on the reverse slope.

Sporadic reports from the *Grandar Bay* told them the four Fuzzies still hadn't moved. But the surface radar analysts in orbit had to keep many areas under observation and were only occasionally able to check on the quartet of Fuzzies, and even less frequently look at the surrounding area.

The three Marines were descending the south wall of the valley and had the Fuzzies in sight when they got a call from Lieutenant Bass.

"The sky-eyes see a large group of people coming from the west," Bass told Corporal Dean.

"People? You mean human?" Dean asked.

"That's what the squids say they look like," Bass said. "It's got to be Sharp Edge. They look to be two platoons, maybe a few more They're two klicks to your west. Current movement indicates they'll be parallel to you in about twenty-five, thirty minutes."

"As long as they stay on the reverse slope, they'll pass behind us. What do you want us to do?"

"They're still a couple of klicks away. Can you head back without alerting the Fuzzies?" Before Dean could answer he heard an excited voice in the background, then Bass said, "Wait one."

Dean told his men about the Sharp Edge troops while he waited for Bass to get back to him.

Bass came back on. "The sky-eye has more information," he said. "There's another unit trailing the first one, and it looks just as big as the first one. But more important, there's a squad-size flanking element on your side of the ridge. You have to get out of there, *now*! Do not engage."

Dean looked at the four Fuzzies. From here, he and his men could take them out easily—they weren't watching their rear and didn't seem to have any idea the Marines were less than a hundred meters upslope from them. They could take them out and still have plenty of time to get away, even if the mercenaries heard the firing.

But the Marines weren't fighting the Fuzzies, the Sharp Edge mercenaries were, and Sharp Edge was fighting the Marines. Dean thought he could call to the Fuzzies and signal them to come with him and his men as they withdrew. But contact hadn't been established yet and he didn't know how the aliens would respond if he called to them.

He snorted. *Aliens!* On Ishtar the humans were the aliens, just as they had been on Avionia and Society 419, both of which worlds had indigenous sentient species.

Here the indigenes were enslaved by mercenaries, and that was a violation of Confederation law. More than that, Dean found slavery morally repugnant.

If the Marines simply withdrew, would the Fuzzies see the flankers in time to make their own withdrawal? Or would the mercenaries see them in time to kill them?

Dean didn't like any of the choices he had, but his orders were to withdraw *now.*

"Lots of bad guys coming," he told his men. "Lieutenant Bass wants us to pull back to the rest of the platoon." He looked downslope.

"What about them?" Ymenez asked, also looking at the Fuzzies. "We're supposed to make friends with them. If we just go, the mercs will kill them."

"I'll think of something. Let's go now, quietly."

Again, Ymenez took the point.

As they crept along the valley wall, Dean decided that once they were another hundred meters away, he'd turn and yell to alert the Fuzzies that they'd been seen. With any luck they'd take off and get away before the mercenaries were close enough to kill them.

As it turned out, he didn't have the chance to warn the Fuzzies.

CHAPTER TWENTY-THREE

Captain Sepahi Fassbender, commandant of Mining Camp No. 26, heard the racket of landing aircraft and got up from his desk to investigate. Nobody had told him to expect visitors from headquarters, and it wasn't time for resupply or troop rotation. From his command center's veranda he saw a MicMac C46 braking down the runway outside the compound fence, the same kind of aircraft that had brought him and his men to the camp, as well as the reinforcements that brought the camp's strength up to seventy men after the Fuzzies started to rampage; smaller aircraft were used for resupply and to rotate the men out of this hellhole to the relative coolness of Base Camp. Another C46 was on final approach.

What the deuce? he wondered.

Sergeant Vodnik was already there, arms folded across his chest, looking sternly at the aircraft.

"Do you have any idea what this is about?" Fassbender asked.

Vodnik shook his head.

The first aircraft turned off the runway and rolled toward the main gate. The second aircraft was braking on the runway when the first stopped seventy-five meters outside the fence. The Mic-Mac's hatches opened and soldiers in new-looking uniforms piled out, more than thirty of them. If Fassbender had to guess, he'd guess that their weapons were as new as their uniforms looked. Aircrew busied themselves chucking duffels out of the cargo compartment.

Fassbender waited patiently. He'd find out soon enough if he and his men were unexpectedly being relieved. The second aircraft taxied behind the first and disgorged its passengers as well as pallets that likely contained supplies for the newcomers.

Two men, one from each aircraft, got together, exchanged some words, and headed for the gate, leaving the others to get into formations handled by sergeants. The gate admitted the two, who marched straight toward Fassbender.

"Sir," one said, saluting, "I'm Lieutenant Crabler. This is Lieutenant Zamenik. We're here with two platoons to reinforce your garrison."

Fassbender cocked an eyebrow at the two officers. "Really? This is the first I've heard of more reinforcements."

Crabler nodded. "We were told you might not expect us. I have orders." He got out his comp.

"Come on inside."

Fassbender led the two through the large room with its clerks, comps, and files and into his private office. He waved them to seats. Vodnik came in with them and closed the door behind himself.

"Let me see." Fassbender held out his hand for Crabler's comp and sat behind his desk to read the orders. He gave the two a sharp look when he finished, then read the orders again and grimaced.

"This is wrong," he said. "Wrong, wrong, wrong." He shoved the comp to the front end of his desk for Crabler to retrieve, and toggled his intercom. "Get Cukayla for me." A moment later, his clerk signaled and he picked up his satcomm.

"Hi, Johnny," he said. "This is Sep Fassbender at twenty-six. I need to speak to Louis. . . . What do you mean, he can't talk to me? Where is he? . . . Busy? So big fucking deal, we're *all* busy. I need to talk to him. . . . Oh, all right. I'll talk to you now, and him later. Listen, two MicMacs just landed here with"—he looked at Crabler and gestured for a number—"sixty-five reinforcements. Why the hell do I need sixty-five additional men, and why wasn't I told they were coming?"

He listened for a few moments while Johnny Paska explained about the reinforcements. His expression grew grimmer as the explanation went on.

"*What!* This is kwangduk shit, Johnny, and you know it," he said when Paska was through, then listened to what Paska had to say next. "The Fuzzies have been taking *what?* Why wasn't I told about this before? . . . What do you mean, we've got troops fighting Confederation Marines? Has Louis lost his ever-loving mind? Why isn't he standing everybody down? I didn't sign up to fight a war, and I sure as Hades didn't sign up to fight Confederation Marines! I've got two MicMacs here. I'm putting these 'reinforcements' back on them, and me and my troops, too, and we're getting out of here. Mining Camp No. 26 is hereby shut down! . . ." He started to put the satcomm down, but Paska said something that made him squawk, "What do you mean, it's too late?"

At the sound of aircraft engines starting up, he jumped from his desk and ran to the window. One of the C46s was already speeding down the runway to lift off, and the other was turning onto the runway. He poked his head into the outer office and shouted at his chief clerk: "Contact those aircraft and order them to turn around. They aren't leaving here yet!"

The chief clerk got on the radio to contact the two C46s. Neither responded to his calls. Fassbender watched them disappear into the distance.

His shoulders slumped. "That fucker, that absolute fucker," he whispered. His shoulders straightened and steel glinted in his eyes.

"Contact the mine," he ordered the chief clerk. "Lock down. Put the Fuzzies back in their cages. Then I want everyone in formation in front of the admin building. On the double! Make sure all your bubble storage is up-to-date and destroy your hard copies." He strode back into his office and began going through his desk and files, updating his electronic storage and stacking his hard copies for the clerks to destroy.

"We're getting out of here," he told Crabler and Zamenik. "There's no way I'm sitting here, waiting to be attacked by Fuzzies armed with flechette rifles. Ah, you didn't know that, did you? Well, that's the latest word. They've been taking all the weapons from the mining camps they've overrun." He shuddered. "And now some fool decided to fight Confederation Marines. No way in hell am I fighting Marines!"

"But, sir, that's why we're here," Zamenik said. "To strengthen the garrison so we can properly defend the mine."

Fassbender looked at them. "You're new on Ishtar, aren't you?"

"Yes, sir. We came in on the *Dayzee Mae*."

"Well, now, 'Came in on the *Dayzee Mae*,' there's only a hundred and thirty-five of us, including you and your reinforcements. Just how much combat experience do your troops have?" He paused to give them a chance to answer. When all they did was look at each other uncertainly, he said, "That's what I suspected. How well do you think we'll do if five hundred Fuzzies armed with flechette rifles attack us?" He glared at the two lieutenants. "Or worse, just how do you think green troops will do *if* a platoon of Confederation Marines shows up and starts blasting away? Have you ever seen the Marines in action? Well, I have. I was with the Tenth Light Infantry Division on the Diamunde campaign. Ever hear of it? The Marines, infantrymen with their own air support and damn little artillery, went up against the first armored army anybody had fielded in centuries. And those infantrymen beat whole divisions of tanks. No way I'm going up against them. *Nossir!*"

"What do you plan to do, sir, if I may ask?" Crabler asked.

"I'm no fool. I'm taking my men to the Marine base and surrendering."

Crabler shook his head. "Well, sir," he said hesitantly, "we've got our orders." He took a deep breath, knowing that what he was about to say could be considered insubordination. "I guess if you want to desert, we can't stop you. But we've got two platoons, we'll run the camp ourselves, with any of your troops who want to stay and do their duty."

Fassbender paused in his sorting. "Oh really? Do you know how to run a mine? Do you know how to handle Fuzzies? You might *think* you do, but I guarantee you *don't*. If you stay here, not knowing what you're doing, the Fuzzies will turn on you before you can learn how to deal with them. And then you'll all be dead. Unless the Marines show up and kill you first." He returned to his preparations for leaving.

Crabler and Zamenik put their heads together and talked quietly while Fassbender continued what he was doing.

Finally, just as Fassbender finished, Crabler said, "Sir, we'll go with you. I'm not sure we'll surrender to the Marines, but we'll go with you as far as their base."

"Fine. Get your troops in formation with mine." He headed outside. On his way he checked with the chief clerk to see if the C46s had taken the week's gem supply. They hadn't.

It only took a few minutes for everybody, the existing garrison and the reinforcements alike, to line up in formation in front of the administration building.

"Listen up," Fassbender said from the veranda. "As you know, the Fuzzies are in full rebellion throughout the entire mining fields. That's why all the mining camps were reinforced in recent weeks, and why we"—he glanced at the two new lieutenants standing nearby—"just got some more reinforcements. What you don't know, and I just found out, is the Fuzzies have been taking all the weapons from the mining camps they've overrun." His face twisted in a sour expression. "It seems that has been going on for some time now, but nobody saw fit to tell Mining Camp Number Twenty-six. They've overrun maybe a dozen mine garrisons, including some that were tripled in strength by reinforcements, and killed all the Sharp Edge personnel. And that ain't all. Some damn fool killed a Confederation Marine lieutenant, so the Marines are attacking mine installations as well. Sharp Edge wants us to stay here and fight to the death whenever the Fuzzies or the Marines attack. But I'm not going to die for Sharp Edge, and I'm not going to sacrifice your lives, either. Sharp Edge won't provide us with transportation out of here, so we're going to *walk* to the Marine base and surrender. If any of you are fool enough to stay, well, that's on you. As for the rest, all of you who are part of Mining Camp Number Twenty-six's garrison get a full share of the gems we have on hand. The men who arrived today each get a quarter share. No difference in size of share for different ranks—the lowest private who's been here for more than a day gets the same share I do. The lowest private among the reinforcements gets the same share the reinforcement lieutenants do." He paused and looked over the formation. "Only the men who leave get a share. Anybody who wants to stay and die, can collect whatever they want from the mine.

"Now pack up whatever you're going to take and let's get ready to move out. Just remember, we've got a long way to go, and food and water—particularly water—will be a problem and we'll have to carry as much as we can, so leave everything you don't absolutely need behind. Sergeant Vodnik, see to the division of the gems.

"Dismissed!"

The next morning, scouts from the Brilliant Coalition, reconnoitering the camp in preparation for an attack, watched the Naked Ones march out in a long line. When the Naked Ones were out of sight, they went into the camp and freed the captured people of the Rock Flower Clan from the cages in which they'd been abandoned, and led them to safety.

Three days after leaving Mining Camp No. 26, by pushing hard the garrison and reinforcements had gone nearly a hundred kilometers, their route marked by discarded personal belongings that men burdened with food and water had dropped along the way. They were tired and hungry and thirsty—mostly thirsty. Their morale was low, and discipline was deteriorating. The column was in a narrow but shallow valley leading out of the foothills. A small rivulet that ran down the middle of the valley allowed them to refill most of their canteens and other water containers, but the rivulet was thin enough that they couldn't fill them all, and nobody was able to drink his fill.

Having been together longer, the garrison's two platoons were somewhat better disciplined, and their single file was relatively tight. The reinforcements had lower morale and trailed several hundred meters behind; their file was far more strung out. A small squad acted as flankers on the reverse slopes of the valley sides; the right flank was covered by men from the garrison, the left by men from the re-inforcement unit.

The left flankers kept radioing in that the valley they were in looked like it had more water in its bottom, and the column should move into it. Captain Fassbender refused and ordered those flankers to stay out of the bottom of that valley, that they'd be too far away for the main body to come to their assistance if they ran into trouble.

Fassbender had once again ordered the flankers to stay on the slope of the valley side when shouting and the sound of gunfire came over the radio, followed quickly by the distinctive CRACK-*sizzle* of blaster fire.

"What's happening over there?" Fassbender demanded.

"We've got wild Fuzzies up ahead, and they're with Confedera-tion Marines!"

He heard the distant whine of a hopper.

Henny was the leader of the scouts Mercury sent to investigate the base camp of the new Naked Ones. He had Crooked Tail and Big Nose with him just as before. Red Butt was still a hostage at the bur-row of the Sunburst Clan, the Sunburst's Father still being in negoti-ations with the Clan Mothers and Clan Fathers of the Brilliant Coalition. For this patrol, Henny also had Lester and Spot. For reasons known only to him, Mercury thought a larger patrol was in order. And a more strongly armed patrol. While three of the patrol members carried only knives and throwing stones as was usual, Mercury had given Henny and Big Nose each one of the Naked Ones' weapons, the rifles that fired needles instead of bullets, and didn't have to be reloaded after every shot. Henny liked being entrusted with a Naked Ones rifle but wasn't happy about his scouting patrol carrying *two* rifles instead of the customary one. That made it more likely, he thought, that they would be tempted to take offensive action instead of evading detection, and escaping in the event that they *were* detected.

Two days' walk out from Mercury's command center, the scouts came upon something unexpected: a small camp of the new Naked Ones. There were few more than three tens of Naked Ones in the camp. Henny remembered one of the standing instructions for the patrols: "If it is possible to do so without alerting the Naked Ones, capture one of them and bring him back." Henny thought it would be easier to capture a Naked One from this small camp than from the large camp he was supposed to scout. And it would be far faster to bring a Naked One back from here than from the large camp, which was still several days' march away.

Henny withdrew his patrol into a nearby valley, where he and his team could keep an eye on the Naked Ones' camp without being seen from it. He discussed the situation with his fighters. While he listened to everything they had to say, the final decision was his. What he decided was to send Lester back to Mercury's command post with word of this unexpected small camp and to tell Mercury that they were going to attempt to capture and bring back one of the new Naked Ones.

Lester hadn't been gone very long when Henny saw three Naked Ones enter the valley from the camp. They were on the opposite side of the valley, too far away to make out details that would allow him to tell one from the other—not that he could tell them apart anyway, but he *could* see that the cloths the Naked Ones wrapped themselves in and the weapons they carried were different from the wrappings and weapons of the Naked Ones who had enslaved the People. These were new Naked Ones, and it seemed likely that they were walking up the valley for the same reason he and his team had come down it—they were scouts. But were they going someplace, or were they merely patrolling the area?

Henny's eyes enlarged and his heart raced. If they were a security patrol, he and his fighters had an excellent chance of capturing one of them. Maybe even all three! All they had to do was wait until the Naked Ones came back—surely if they went out on one side of the valley they would come back on the other side, that's what he would do in their place—and jump on them when they were close enough. Henny knew from the freeing of the mining camp where he'd been enslaved that even though the Naked Ones were bigger than the People, one-on-one his fighters were stronger than the Naked Ones. His four against their three should make for an easy fight. Even if his fighters had to use their knives and the thrusting spear that Spot carried to kill two of the Naked Ones, they would still have one captive to take back to Mercury.

Henny watched as the Naked Ones slowly angled up the far side of the valley until they disappeared into a small wood. He kept watching but didn't see them reappear on the far side. At first he thought it was because they were taking a rest in the shade of the trees. But when they didn't reemerge after a more than reasonable time, he wondered if they were lazy patrollers, the kind who would go out until they were beyond the sight of their camp and then hole up until it was time to return, instead of following their entire patrol route. He blew air through his lips, sounding a disgusted buzz. Yes, it would be easy to capture one or even all three of these Naked Ones; they wouldn't be very alert on their return.

Knowing that they might be there for a while, Henny set a watch rotation. One of them would watch the wood for the Naked Ones to emerge, one would watch the camp for other Naked Ones to come out, and the other two would rest. They'd eaten when they withdrew into this hiding place, so it would be some time before they needed to dig in the ground for tubers or crawlers to eat.

Henny settled in for a long wait. He was dozing when he heard a panicky shout and a CR-CRACK-*sizz-zzle*.

First squad's third fire team had gone less than fifty meters when Lance Corporal Ymenez suddenly froze.

"What in all the hells is *that*?" he whispered, slowly shifting his blaster's muzzle to point at a large clump of bushes.

Corporal Dean looked where Ymenez's blaster pointed and let out an almost inaudible whistle. Behind him he heard PFC McGinty whisper an awed "Sweet Mother of God."

A snakelike creature was under the bushes, slowly drawing itself into tight S coils—its massive body was as big around as a big man's thigh. The way it was coiled, he couldn't tell how long it was, but surely it was more than ten meters from head to tail. And what a head! The head, as wide as the body and nearly a meter long, was pointed straight at Ymenez.

"Start moving back. Easy. One short step at a time," Dean told Ymenez. He pointed his blaster at the thing and took a backward step himself. Behind him, he heard McGinty also backstepping.

The thing raised its head and its huge mouth sagged open; venom dripped from the fangs that popped into view.

"Run!" Dean screamed. He fired a bolt into the beast. He felt the heat of the bolt McGinty fired as it *sizzled* past him.

The two plasma bolts struck the snake-thing and it buckled in its strike, not quite reaching Ymenez, who staggered backward and fell, then scrabbled backward, trying to get away from the thing, which seemed to shake off the effects of two hits and slithered toward him. Its jaws unhinged, opening its mouth wider than its body, and then it coiled to lunge forward. Dean fired a bolt into the gaping maw, and McGinty fired more plasma into the head above the opening mouth. The two new hits threw the creature's head and upper body flopping back. Dean dashed to Ymenez and reached down to grab his arm. He yanked him to his feet and backpedaled as fast as he could, dragging the other man with him. McGinty continued firing into the snake-beast as it writhed, thrashing its heavy body about.

"Are you all right?" Dean asked Ymenez.

"I-I— Yeah, I'm okay." Ymenez patted himself, then looked down. "Where's my blaster?"

"Oh shit," Dean swore.

"There it is," McGinty said. He sped toward the dying creature and grabbed hold of Ymenez's blaster where it stuck out from under a coil of the beast. He yanked it out and turned to run with Dean and Ymenez but only got a few paces before he let out a scream and tumbled to the ground.

"Triple John, what's wrong?" Dean shouted, running back to pick him up. Ymenez went with him.

McGinty could only whimper. His left glove, where he'd grabbed Ymenez's blaster, was eaten away. The hand visible through it was an angry red and purple and was beginning to swell. Something glistened on his palm and fingers.

Dean glanced at the blaster lying where McGinty had tossed it when his hand began to burn. It was wet with something, obviously whatever it was that had burned through McGinty's glove.

"Destroy that," he ordered Ymenez.

Ymenez picked up McGinty's blaster and put a bolt into the trigger and receiver section of his own blaster. While he was doing that, Dean tore off McGinty's left glove, careful not to touch any wet portion of it. He scooped up some loose dirt and poured it onto McGinty's hand, hoping it would absorb some of the toxin. While he was doing that, he called for a medevac; he was afraid that McGinty would die before he and Ymenez could carry the Marine back.

Something clanged off the side of his helmet, and he looked up to see the four forgotten Fuzzies racing toward him and his men. Two of them carried flechette rifles, one had a spear, and the fourth had his arm cocked to throw another stone.

"We all need to be evacuated!" he shouted into his comm.

* * *

Henny spun toward the scream and the strange, loud noises. There were the three Naked Ones! How did they get there? A *granalchit* was readying itself to strike at one of them. These Naked Ones wouldn't know how to fight the beast, and it might kill all of them before he and his fighters could capture one of them!

"Let's go!" he shouted, leaping to his feet to race to the Naked Ones and the *granalchit*. They had only gone a few paces when fire lanced from the weapons of two of the Naked Ones; Henny and his fighters staggered to a stop, shocked by the flashes. The *granalchit* gathered itself to strike again, and two more lightning bolts flashed at it, throwing it into death throes.

That was a mighty weapon, that fire rifle. The People needed it!

"Move!" he shouted, and the four raced again, to reach the Naked Ones while they were distracted by the *granalchit,* and the Naked One who looked like he'd been stung by the venom.

They were still a few paces away when Spot threw a rock at the head of the Naked One bent over the poisoned one. In those few paces, the Naked Ones swung their weapons around and fired. Spot and Big Nose fell, shot through by the fire bolts; they died so fast they couldn't even scream.

Henny smashed the butt of his needle rifle into the chest of one of the Naked Ones, and Crooked Tail swung the staff of his thrusting spear at the head of the other.

The Naked One that Henny hit surprised him; when the force of the blow knocked the Naked One back, he grabbed the stock of the needle rifle and pulled, bringing Henny with him. The Naked One rolled on his back so his legs kicked into the air, into Henny's gut, knocking the wind out of him, and threw him in a high arc so that he landed hard on his back past the Naked One's head. Before Henny could even wheeze a breath, the Naked One had him flipped onto his stomach and bound his hands behind his back.

Henny didn't see what happened to Crooked Tail, but he was

equally quickly dispatched. Instead of taking prisoners, Henny and one of his scouts were *taken* prisoner!

Henny didn't know if these Naked Ones were as strong as the People's fighters, but they certainly knew things about fighting that he didn't.

CHAPTER TWENTY-FOUR

Lester looked like he was on the thin edge of collapse when he was escorted into Mercury's command post in the Safe Nights burrow. Mercury sat the scout on a comfortable ledge and offered him water to gulp down. After a few minutes to catch his breath, Lester told his tale. A small new Naked Ones camp was much closer than they had realized. A large party of Naked Ones was marching to join them. Here, Mercury asked a question, and Lester's answer told him the large party was of the Naked Ones who had abandoned the People of the Rock Flower Clan, locked in cages.

That abandonment angered him even more than the fact that this new Naked Ones camp was entirely too close to his command burrow, and amplified it. His anger brought about his decision.

There were more than three hundred fighters in the burrow, and almost another two hundred within a hard day's run. Mercury sent runners to the outlying burrows with instructions to bring back every available fighter for a major battle against the Naked Ones.

"Hang in there, Triple John," Corporal Dean said to PFC McGinty, giving his shoulder a reassuring squeeze. "The hopper's on its way. I can see it coming."

McGinty groaned. Through the screen in the PFC's helmet, Dean could see unseeing eyes staring out of a sweat-drenched face.

"Hang in there; the hopper will be here in a minute."

The hopper's whine grew and pitched higher as it came in for a landing. Dean glanced at Lance Corporal Ymenez and saw that he already had the two captured Fuzzies standing out of the way of the landing hopper; he was ready to hustle them aboard the second it touched down. But just before the hopper landed, one of the Fuzzies pitched forward, and blood spurted from its back. A second later, Dean heard several reports of flechette fire. He spun toward the sound of the fire and triggered off a plasma bolt before he even saw where the flechettes came from. Ymenez was also down, returning fire. The remaining Fuzzy still stood, looking aghast up the valley.

"Knock him down before he gets shot!" Dean yelled at Ymenez.

Ymenez twisted to see where the Fuzzy was and saw it standing near his feet. He kicked at the Fuzzy's ankles and the creature flopped to the ground.

"Stay down!" the Marine yelled, not caring that the Fuzzy probably couldn't understand his words.

Dean had seen where the fire was coming from and began placing bolts in front of the target area, breaking and skittering the plasma balls along the ground, increasing their chances of hitting a target.

"See where I'm shooting?" he shouted at Ymenez. "Do the same— and move your bolts around."

"Roger." Ymenez added his shattering, skittering bolts to Dean's. Small flames started licking up in the area where the two Marines were firing, but the vegetation was too thin for the fires to spread.

Suddenly, Doc Hough's voice crackled in Dean's helmet. "Come on, you two. We've got your casualties aboard. Stay low and bring your prisoner. The crew chief will cover you with his gun."

"Right, Doc," Dean said as a stream of plasma bolts began sizzling over his head. "Ymenez, grab the Fuzzy and get him into the hopper. I'll cover you."

"We're in," Ymenez shouted a moment later.

Dean twisted around and rapidly crawled to the hopper. It lifted before he was all the way through the hatch; Ymenez grabbed him and pulled him in the rest of the way as the crew chief kept pouring fire at the enemy position until the hopper's nose was pointed toward Camp Godenov.

Captain Fassbender ran toward where the fire had come from even before he heard the hopper lift off. On the reverse slope, where he thought the flechette fire had come from, he found five corpses. Three men were running down the valley, firing pointlessly at the withdrawing hopper. He chased them, yelling at them to stop, to cease fire. He finally got through to them and they turned back.

"What the hell happened here?" he yelled as he ran up to the three.

"There was Fuzzies," one of them gasped. "They were with Marines."

"So?" Fassbender screamed.

"We got one!" one of them shouted triumphantly.

"We figured the Marines and the Fuzzies were a patrol, looking for us. So we took them out before they spotted us," said another.

"What ever made you think they were working together against us?" Fassbender shrilled. "Come with me!" He grabbed one of them and shoved him, hard, toward the bodies. He pushed and shoved at all of them, forcing them back to where they'd begun shooting. He forced them to look at the corpses of their companions.

"Back at the mining camp, you said the Marines were fighting us," the third said. He shrugged, then looked at the bodies, and bent over to throw up.

"Had they seen you?" Fassbender screeched. "Or did you shoot first?"

"Wanted to take 'em out before they saw us," the first one said. He looked distinctly ill.

"Why didn't you ask for instructions before you opened fire? You got five men killed, and for what?" Fassbender's voice rose even higher.

"We thought . . . ," the second said, and waved a hand uncertainly.

"No, you didn't!" Fassbender's voice dropped. "You didn't think at all. And because you didn't think, you might have just gotten all of us killed."

The three looked at him, stricken. They didn't necessarily understand *how* they might have gotten them all killed, but they thought that maybe the captain knew what he was talking about.

While Fassbender was yelling at the surviving flankers, the garrison platoons came over the top and gathered behind him. Some of the men looked at the bodies; others looked everywhere *but* at the bodies.

Fassbender ignored the platoon while he got out his comp and marked their position on his map.

"Bury the men you got killed," he told the trio. He moved off and got on his radio to call for the rest of the column to join up in this valley. He wanted to see the two lieutenants as soon as they reached him. Sergeant Vodnik set about arranging the platoon in a defensive position without waiting to be told to—he might be a fighter for money now, but he had once been a platoon sergeant in a regular army and knew how to do his job. He called the right flank squad in to set an observation post on the reverse slope of the valley they were now in.

This wasn't a combined Marine-Fuzzy patrol out looking for the garrison from Mining Camp No. 26. Fassbender knew that perfectly well. If it had been, there wouldn't have been a hopper so close that it was able to extract them almost as soon as the shooting started. The extraction came too soon, which meant the hopper must have already been on its way when the flankers opened fire. Were they closer to the Marine base than he'd been told? Or did the Marines have an outpost nearby? And why was the hopper already on its way? Had the Marines spotted his company and were on their way back to report?

No, that didn't make sense. The Marines would have reported

by radio and probably have shadowed the Sharp Edge company so they could continue reporting. And what were they doing with the Fuzzies? He shook his head; too many questions. And not a good answer for any of them.

Whatever, now that his men had fired on the Marines—and shot one of them, if the flankers could be believed—surrendering was going to be much more difficult. The Marine commander might issue a shoot-on-sight order. Captain Fassbender needed to come up with a way to approach the Marines that wouldn't get him and all of his men killed.

"I think I've got the Fuzzy patched up all right," HM3 Hough said to Lieutenant Bass. "I don't know where his internal organs are, but if they're arranged anything like ours, nothing vital got hit. But McGinty, I don't have any idea how to treat that swelling. I've cut off circulation in case the venom travels through the blood system, but . . ." His voice trailed off. "We've got to get him to a hospital fast. As it is, he'll probably lose that hand—if not worse."

"Get him ready to medevac to FIST HQ," Bass said.

They were in Bass's headquarters bunker, which for the moment doubled as sickbay. It wasn't much of a bunker, merely a meter-and-a-half-deep hole in the ground covered by a tent, because they didn't have the materials for a proper overhead. Bass's cot had been commandeered for use as a surgical bed, and the wounded Fuzzy was resting on Staff Sergeant Hyakowa's cot.

Henny had watched as Hough extracted the flechette from Crooked Tail's back and bandaged his wound; Hough had been gentle with him. That wasn't treatment Henny expected from the Naked Ones. The Naked Ones he knew would have left Crooked Tail in the valley to bleed to death. Maybe Mercury was wrong; maybe he had been wrong himself. Maybe these new Naked Ones weren't like the ones who had enslaved the People.

Bass looked at the Fuzzy, watched it swivel its body, push its bound wrists away from its back and wiggle its fingers. The Fuzzy chittered more, poking its snout at McGinty, closing and opening the fingers of one hand. The Fuzzy looked at his wounded comrade and nodded vigorously, then back at McGinty and nodded just as vigorously, chittering all the while.

"If he was human," Bass said reflectively, "I'd say he was trying to tell us he's friendly, and he knows a cure for that."

Hough nodded. "Could be. Until now, there hasn't been any fighting between us and them."

Corporal Dean was keeping out of the way, watching McGinty with concern. Now he spoke up for the first time since telling what had happened out there.

"When they attacked us, they could have killed us. They had two rifles but didn't shoot. That one"—he nodded at the sitting Fuzzy— "gave me a butt stroke instead of shooting. The other one whapped Ymenez upside the head with the butt of his spear instead of sticking him. I think they were trying to capture us instead of killing us."

Bass thought about that for a moment, watching the Fuzzy. The Fuzzy carefully rose to his feet and turned his back to Bass, offering its bonds to be cut.

"Cover him, Dean." Bass drew his knife and sliced through the tie.

The Fuzzy took a few seconds to rub his wrists, then made a curious gesture, hand held below shoulder level and flopping. He ducked out of the tent and looked around. With a glance and a stream of chitter back at Bass, he started trotting toward the surrounding brush, flopping his hand below his shoulder as he went. Bass and Dean followed; Dean kept his blaster aimed at the Fuzzy.

The Fuzzy reached the scrub and slowed down, peering intently at the bushes. He abruptly stood erect and chittered excitedly, pointing at one of the bushes. To the Marines, it didn't look much different from the other bushes, but the Fuzzy certainly seemed to think it was. He squatted next to the bush and pulled leaves from it. When he had an overflowing handful, he stood and began trotting back to the tent. Bass and Dean followed.

Inside, the Fuzzy gestured for Hough to stop sealing the stasis bag the Corpsman was putting McGinty into. Hough looked to Bass, who nodded.

"I want to see what he's got planned," Bass said. "We can knock him away and seal McGinty fast if he tries anything funny."

"Whatever you say, boss." Hough slid out of the way and let the Fuzzy approach.

The Fuzzy held his hands over McGinty's swollen red hand and crushed the leaves between his hands. He rolled the crushed leaves and the thin liquid that oozed from them between his palms, and let the liquid drip onto McGinty's hand. McGinty moaned, and his hand twitched, but he didn't seem to be in any greater pain. The Fuzzy kept rolling and squeezing, dripping liquid on McGinty's hand and up onto his wrist. When no more liquid dripped, the Fuzzy flicked the bits of leaf away, and briskly rubbed McGinty's hand and wrist for a couple of minutes, then settled back on his haunches to wait.

"So what's supposed to be happening?" Hough asked the Fuzzy.

The Fuzzy looked up at him and chittered, made odd patting motions with its hands.

"It looks like he's trying to tell you to be patient and let the medicine do its work," Dean said.

Bass merely grunted.

Hough leaned forward to look through McGinty's helmet screen. "It's doing something," he said reverently. He looked up at Bass. "He's not sweating as much as before, and he looks like he's resting quietly."

"Let me see," Bass said. He moved close. So did Dean, momentarily leaving the Fuzzy unguarded. They agreed with Hough: McGinty looked better.

The Fuzzy was still squatting when they looked back at him; he calmly returned their gaze. Then the Fuzzy nodded toward McGinty and raised a hand to flash his fingers twice.

"What are you telling me?" Hough asked. "It's going to take ten days for him to heal and recuperate?"

"Maybe ten hours," Bass said, looking at the Fuzzy. Among humans, the handshake was an almost universal gesture of friendship; most humans saw the shoulder clasp as a gesture of comradeship. But the Fuzzies weren't human, and for all the Marine knew an offered hand or a pat on the shoulder was an invitation to a fight. But a nod seemed to be a positive gesture. He motioned at McGinty, and nodded at the Fuzzy. He didn't smile; to nearly all Earth mammals, bared teeth was a threat and given that the Fuzzies had muzzles rather than faces, it might be the same with them.

The Fuzzy nodded back.

"I still want to put him in stasis and send him to a hospital," Hough said.

"I think that's a good idea," Bass agreed.

Hough finished sealing the stasis bag, then he and Dean carried it to the waiting hopper.

Finally allowed to examine the alien up close, the *Grandar Bay*'s xenozoologist Lieutenant Prang was beside himself with excitement. He was anxious to attempt to communicate with the Fuzzy. He got out his canteen and went to take a drink. But a glance at the Fuzzy's face told him the creature probably wouldn't be able to drink like a man. Instead he poured water into a canteen cup and took a drink, then offered the cup to the Fuzzy.

The Fuzzy took the cup in both hands and looked into it curiously. He sniffed at the water and his face wrinkled, just like a human asking, *What is this?*

Prang took the cup back and took another drink before returning it to the Fuzzy. The Fuzzy had watched Prang's face with interest. He took the cup, stuck his face into it, and began lapping at the water.

Henny decided these Naked Ones weren't at all like the other Naked Ones.

"What's he chittering about?" Hough asked, looking at the Fuzzy seated on the ground, facing Lieutenant Prang.

* * *

Captain Fassbender sent Sergeant Vodnik in command of a point unit half a kilometer ahead of the company's main body. The point and flankers were all from his own garrison platoon this time; he wasn't about to trust the new men or their officers, not after what had just happened. When the main body set out, he positioned himself between the two new platoons. The remaining men from his own platoons, those who weren't on point or the flanks, brought up the rear, with strict orders to prevent stragglers. That was a job they accepted with relish. They were as unhappy as their captain was about the flankers from the reinforcing platoons opening fire on the Confederation Marines and looked forward to an excuse to beat on the newcomers.

A couple of kilometers farther down the valley, Sergeant Vodnik radioed Fassbender.

"I see a tent and a wall up ahead," he said. "It looks like there are some bunkers, or other defensive positions, and I can see what I think are a few Confederation Marines moving about."

"How far ahead?" Fassbender asked.

"About another klick."

"Have they seen you yet?"

"Negative. I don't think their infrared sensors can pick people out in this heat. And nobody looks all that alert except for one guy in a sentry tower, and he doesn't act like he's seen anybody."

"How big is the camp?"

"Looks like platoon size. Hey, that hopper that picked up the patrol, I don't see it anywhere."

"All right, hold your position." Fassbender contacted the flankers and the reinforcement lieutenants, telling them to halt in place and take defensive positions, and for the lieutenants to join him.

Fassbender gave Lieutenants Crabler and Zamenik a hard look when they joined him. The lieutenants looked surly.

"There's a Confederation outpost up ahead. I should send you two in with a white flag, you know. It was your men who fired first and told the Marines we're hostile, so if the Marines have a fire-on-sight order, they should be shooting at you and yours, not at me and mine." He took a deep breath. "But that would be abrogating my responsibility as commander. I'm going in under a white flag, and I expect you to keep your men under control. No firing unless I order it. Do you understand?"

"What if they kill you before you give the order to open fire?" Crabler asked defiantly.

"Well then, I won't have given the order to open fire, will I? Keep your men in place *here*. Do *not* move forward until I tell you to. Do you understand?"

"Yes," Zamenik said reluctantly.

"Yes what?"

Zamenik shot him an angry look. "Yes, *sir!*"

He looked at Crabler.

"I understand, *sir.*"

"I hope you do. I'm taking those three trigger-happy people of yours. They can all carry white flags. Now return to your platoons—and remember my orders. And obey them!"

Captain Fassbender had the three men going with him leave their weapons with Sergeant Vodnik and the point element. He left his sidearm as well. Each of them carried a piece of white cloth. They stepped into the open and began walking toward the Marine outpost, holding their open hands out and to the side.

"Somebody's coming!" PFC Gray shouted from his perch on the sentry tower.

"Where? How many?" Sergeant Ratliff shouted back.

Gray examined the distant men through his helmet's magnifier screen. "Looks like four. I can't see any weapons. They're waving something white."

Ratliff clambered up the tower to take a look himself. After verifying what Gray had reported, he looked farther up the valley. His magnifier didn't enlarge anything enough for him to tell whether there were more people hiding out there. He tried his infra shield but it only showed a blur. Even the four men coming toward him were hard to make out against the hot background.

"Talk to me, Rabbit," Lieutenant Bass said; he'd heard Gray's shout and came to find out what was happening.

"Four men, white flags, sir," Ratliff reported. "I can't make out any weapons."

"Can you tell if anybody else is out there?"

"Negative. Infra can barely pick up those four, and I can't make out anything that looks remotely like a human beyond them."

Bass climbed partway up the tower and took a look for himself. He estimated it would take the four men less than ten minutes to reach Camp Godenov. He dropped off the tower and called out, "Squad leaders up! Gray, keep a sharp eye out, let me know if anything changes."

In little more than a minute, Sergeants Ratliff, Kerr, and Kelly, along with Staff Sergeant Hyakowa, joined him in a circle.

"Looks like somebody wants to surrender," he said. "I don't want to let them just walk into the camp, so I'll go out to meet them, find out who they are and what they're doing."

"Sir," Hyakowa said, "let me go instead. If it's a trap, the platoon can't afford to lose you."

"Are you saying I can't take care of myself, Staff Sergeant?"

"Not at all, sir. Just being realistic."

Kelly cut off a snicker.

"I'm going, no argument. I'll have them demonstrate that they're not a suicide mission, that they aren't packed with explosives, before I let them get close. I want one fire team to go with me, and the rest of the platoon on alert. Wang, make sure our rear and flanks are covered. Now do it."

"Who do you want to take with you?" Hyakowa asked.

Bass thought for a few seconds before saying, "Give me Doyle."

The others looked at him as though he'd asked for a team of army recruits. He looked back blandly.

"All right, people," Hyakowa said after a few seconds, "you heard the man. Kerr, get Doyle and his men for the boss. Put the rest of your squad in positions to cover our rear and flanks. Rabbit, put your people up front. Hound, you know where to put your guns."

Minutes later, Bass stepped outside Camp Godenov, accompanied by Corporal Doyle and his two men. Bass kept his sidearm holstered but the three enlisted men had their blasters pointed in the general direction of the four men approaching them.

Bass and his escort marched a hundred meters from the edge of the camp and halted. He turned his helmet's speaker to full volume and waited.

When the four were fifty meters away, he shouted for them to halt. His magnified voice was loud enough to carry to well beyond where they were.

"I'm Lieutenant Charlie Bass, Confederation Marine Corps," he said when the four had halted. "State your name and business here."

"Sir," the man standing slightly forward of the others shouted, "I'm Captain Sephai Fassbender, commandant of Sharp Edge's Mining Camp Number Twenty-six. When I heard that hostilities had broken out between Sharp Edge and Confederation Marines, I refused to participate. I'm here with my garrison to surrender."

Bass cocked his head, hiding his surprise. "Your garrison is three men?"

"No, sir. I have a hundred and thirty more men waiting in the valley."

"And they all want to surrender?"

"Most of them do, yes, sir."

"And what about you and these men? I don't see any weapons."

"That's right. We came unarmed to show peaceful intent."

"How do I know you don't have explosives strapped to your bodies, that you aren't on a suicide mission?"

Fassbender looked at Bass for a moment, then turned and said something to his men that the Marines couldn't hear. He started stripping off his uniform, exposing himself to Ishtar's heat. He snapped at his men, and they reluctantly did the same. When the four men were naked, they moved away from their piles of clothing.

"Doyle, take one man and check their clothes for weapons or explosives."

"Ah, aye aye, sir. Summers, come with me." The two Marines headed for the discarded uniforms.

"Shoup, keep them covered," Bass ordered.

At the clothing, Doyle and Summers picked up each item and patted it down for weapons or other foreign objects. They didn't find anything other than personal possessions. Doyle reported that to Bass, who told him to return.

When Doyle and Summers were halfway back, Bass boomed out, "Get dressed before you roast out here."

Fassbender and the three men with him gratefully hustled into their uniforms and set the cooling systems to eat off some of their body heat. When they were dressed again, Bass signaled them to come to him.

"Do you have comm with the rest of your people?" Bass asked. When Fassbender said he had a radio, Bass told him, "Have the rest of your people approach to five hundred meters and stack their weapons, then approach to one hundred meters, unarmed."

Fassbender grinned wryly. "I'm not sure that all of them know how to stack arms."

The way it worked out, the Sharp Edge mercenaries who didn't know how to stack arms simply piled their rifles on the dirt. When they reached a hundred-meter distance, Bass had them spread out and sent first squad to search them for hidden weapons.

After searching the mercenaries and reporting that they were unarmed except for their cartridge belts and knives, first squad went out to collect their weapons.

That was when things got exciting.

CHAPTER TWENTY-FIVE

"Ah, sir? Someone's coming down the valley. Sir?"

PFC Fisher was on the tower and Lieutenant Bass stood near the tower's base, watching as the Sharp Edge troops formed up just outside Camp Godenov.

Bass was wondering what to do with more than a hundred prisoners until battalion or FIST sent transportation to take them away, and didn't hear Fisher at first.

"What's that, Fisher?"

"Someone's coming down the valley, sir. It looks like a lot of Fuzzies."

"Fuzzies?" Bass asked. He climbed the tower and looked up the valley through his magnifier shield. He saw Fuzzies, hundreds of them. He couldn't tell at this distance, but it looked like they were all armed males. He looked down for Sergeant Kerr.

"Kerr, get your people out there to help first squad collect the weapons. And all of you, get back here most ricky-tick." He looked around and found Sergeant Kelly. "Hound, guns alert on the prisoners." He slid down the tower ladder and ran to where Captain Fassbender stood facing his troops.

"Captain," he said softly, "a lot of Fuzzies are approaching along the same route you came by. I don't know what their intentions are, but they might be hostile. Just in case they are, I want you to march your people around to the rear of my camp and keep them quiet and in formation."

Fassbender looked like he'd been punched in the gut. "They're probably coming after us," he said. "They've been attacking the Sharp Edge mining camps. That's why I've got so many men; reinforcements came in right before I decided to surrender to you Marines."

"If they see you're our prisoners, maybe they won't attack."

"But what if they do?"

"We'll cross that desert when we come to it," Bass said, but he was already considering what to do if the Fuzzies did attack—and remembering the attack on the patrol he'd had up that valley only a couple of hours earlier.

Mercury sent scouts to locate the column of Naked Ones who had abandoned the Rock Flower Clan locked in the cages at the mining camp, and to report back on where they were going.

On the second day of his march, a scout reported that the Naked Ones were only a day ahead of Mercury's war party and that their paths were converging. Mercury's heart leaped in his chest; did that mean those Naked Ones were on their way to link up with the camp of the new Naked Ones? He ordered his fighters to pick up the pace; they would be much better off in the coming fight if they caught the marching Naked Ones first and killed them before they linked up with the new Naked Ones.

The third day, scouts reported that the marching Naked Ones were mere hours ahead. Mercury thought it likely that he could close the gap before nightfall and have time to give his fighters a short rest before attacking. The Naked Ones had smaller eyes than the People, and he suspected their night vision wasn't as sharp as that of the People. If that turned out to be true, the next night they could attack the camp of the new Naked Ones.

But that wasn't to be. The camp of the new Naked Ones was closer than Mercury had realized and the marching Naked Ones were going to reach it before he and his fighters caught up with them. Then his scouts reported finding where Henny and his scouts had fought the Naked Ones. Two were dead, and Henny and one other were not to be found.

Mercury was furious. His anger was so great that thoughts of the advantages that better night vision would give his fighters in a night attack were driven from his mind, and he resolved to attack the Naked Ones as soon as his fighters were in position in front of the Naked Ones' camp.

"Everybody, take as many rifles as you can carry," Sergeant Ratliff ordered as soon as his men reached the stacked and piled weapons left behind by the mercenaries. He began gathering rifles and slinging them over his shoulders. He managed eight in addition to his own blaster.

Damn! he swore. The nine Marines of first squad wouldn't be able to carry all of them at one time.

"Get the piled rifles," he told his men. "The stacked ones will be easier to spot for whoever comes out to get them."

"Three One, this is Six Actual," Lieutenant Bass's voice said into his helmet comm. "Fuzzies are coming your way. Gather as many weapons as you can, and get back here on the double. Second squad is on its way to help you."

"Roger, Six." Then he said on his squad circuit, "Pick up as many rifles as you can double-time with. Second squad's on their way, leave the rest for them. Move it!" He shrugged his shoulders, wondering if he'd be able to double-time five hundred meters with the load he had on his shoulders. He decided he could. He looked at his men. Each looked to have at least five rifles, and some of them were already running back to the camp. "All right, that's enough," he told the rest. "Let's go. On the double!" He looked up the valley and swore again; Fuzzies, a *lot* of Fuzzies were running in his direction—and they didn't look like they were making a social call. He gave another look around to make sure all of his men were headed back, then followed them, keeping an eye out for anybody who couldn't keep up. Two hundred meters from the remaining weapons, he passed second squad on its way out.

Second squad was starting back with most of the remaining flechette rifles when first squad, panting heavily, finally reached Camp Godenov's perimeter, where Staff Sergeant Hyakowa directed them in piling the rifles and hustled them into defensive positions.

"Secure the Fuzzies!" Bass ordered.

Doc Hough hustled to bind both of the Fuzzy prisoners. When he got there, he found the wounded Fuzzy sleeping quietly, and Lieutenant Prang intently speaking and making signs with the Fuzzy who had gotten the leaves that seemed to ease PFC McGinty's suffering. It looked like they might be making some progress, so Hough simply told Prang to be ready to take cover.

"They're shooting at us!" Corporal Claypoole squawked, sounding deeply offended. He had five rifles slung on his shoulders and was looking around to make sure no others were lying about when the first flechettes zinged past. He looked west and saw the closest Fuzzies were no more than five hundred meters away.

"We're loaded, honcho," he radioed to Sergeant Kerr.

"Then what're you doing standing there? Get back to the perimeter. *Now!*"

Claypoole didn't need to be told twice, and neither did his men. They sprinted.

Kerr saw that not all the rifles had been picked up. "Move, move, *move!*" he shouted, and the rest of second squad raced back toward the perimeter. The zings of flechette fire zipping past sped them on their way. The Marines hadn't been able to carry all of the weapons, so Sergeant Kerr fired a few plasma bolts into the ones they had to leave behind, hoping to destroy them so the oncoming Fuzzies couldn't use them.

*   *   *

"Lieutenant Bass, sir," Captain Fassbender said, nervously looking at the hundreds of Fuzzies chasing second squad, "I request that you rearm my men and let us join in the fight. It looks like there are more Fuzzies than your command can defeat."

"You've never seen Marines fight, have you?" Bass asked, without taking his eyes off the oncoming Fuzzies.

"Yes, I have, on Diamunde."

Bass cocked an eye at him. "What was your unit?"

Fassbender chuckled. "We were on the same side, sir. Tenth Light Infantry. I saw you Marines take on those tanks. I wouldn't go up against a Marine platoon with the hundred and thirty-five men I have, not even if I was in a strong defensive position and the Marines were in the open. But it looks like a whole battalion of Fuzzies charging your position, and your defenses aren't all that strong. No offense intended, but I don't think a single Marine platoon can stand up against an entire battalion. Particularly not a Fuzzy battalion armed with modern weapons."

"I'll take that under advisement, sir. Now if you would be so good as to attend to your people and keep them under control."

"You're a fool, Bass!" Fassbender snorted, but turned and headed back to where his troops waited. The mercenaries were nervous; many of them looked panicky, like they were ready to break and run.

Fassbender was right, though. Camp Godenov didn't have good defenses. Third platoon had only been there for three days. On the second day, a light earthmover from the *Grandar Bay* had come for a few hours to dig some defenses. It dug a meter-deep trench around the perimeter and piled the excavated dirt on the outside to make a low wall in front of the trench. It had also dug two larger holes on the front side of the camp and piled dirt around them to form bunkers, and dug the meter-and-a-half-deep hole for the command bunker. Unlike the command bunker, the two on the perimeter had plasteel overheads. There were no bunkers on the sides or rear of the perimeter.

Bass watched second squad as the Marines ran toward the perimeter, staggering under their loads. A couple of them stumbled, but nobody fell. The NCOs kept everybody moving as fast as they could go. They were spread out, making them harder targets for the Fuzzies to hit. But that same spread put them before the platoon's entire front, which meant the Marines in position couldn't fire at the rapidly approaching Fuzzies because of the danger of hitting their own men.

"Hound, put one of your guns way out on the left flank; try to give second squad some covering fire."

"Aye aye," Sergeant Kelly replied. He moved one of his guns fifty meters to the left, where it was able to fire past second squad and hit one side of the Fuzzies' charging line. He shouted for joy when he saw that side of the assault line drop.

Bass thought while he watched the rapidly approaching Marines and the Fuzzies pursuing them. He remembered Fiesta de Santiago, when the rump element of his company met a couple of hundred bandits armed with stolen Marine-issue blasters and chameleons. The rump company, one platoon reinforced with half of the company's assault platoon, beat off part of the assault by putting concentrated fire on the limestone some of them were firing from, and melting the rock into lava. But that rump element had the assault guns, which put out heavy streams of much more powerful plasma bolts than Kelly's gun squad had. And he remembered on Elneal, where a single squad had fought off charging horsemen using the same tactic. But again, the horsemen were crossing a barren stretch of limestone and attacking on a very narrow front.

He wondered if he could use the same tactic here. But here the Fuzzies were attacking across dirt, studded with low-lying vegetation, not bare limestone. Could concentrated blaster fire make the dirt run like lava?

He might have to bet his life—and the lives of his Marines—on it.

Then second squad burst through the perimeter. Staff Sergeant

Hyakowa had them dump the flechette rifles they carried, and hustled them into line on the trenches and bunkers. Even before they were all in place, someone called out, "Corpsman up!" Doc Hough grabbed his med kit and dashed to tend to the wounded Marine.

"Volley fire, four hundred!" Bass shouted. *"Fire! Fire! Fire!"*

Holes appeared in the mass of Fuzzies, but there were too many of them for the thin fire from the Marines to make serious numbers of casualties.

"Put your bolts into the dirt in front of them," Bass yelled. *"Fire! Fire! Fire!"*

The bolts hit the dirt and brush in a staggered line, skittering forward along the ground, snagging on bushes and igniting them, splitting into multiple bits of star stuff, bouncing high and into or over the rear ranks of Fuzzies. More of the aliens fell, but still they came on, their excited chittering coming clear through the air, along with more and more flechette needles, and bullets from single-shot rifles.

"Kelly, see if you can get a fire line going. Wang, take over running the volleying."

Bass crawled to Kelly while the gun squad leader was directing his guns to put their fire into bushes in front of the charging Fuzzies, to see if they'd ignite.

Hyakowa took up the rhythmic cry of *"Fire! Fire! Fire!"*

"Listen, Hound," Bass said when he reached Kelly, "do you think concentrated fire can melt the dirt here? Turn it into something like lava?"

"I don't know," Kelly answered, watching his guns' fire slowly igniting bushes. "The dirt's got a head start, as hot as it is here. But those bushes don't want to burn easily, so maybe not."

Bass looked at the Fuzzies again. They were 350 meters away and coming fast. It was too late to try to melt the ground in front of them. "Pour your fire into the mass; kill enough of them that we can beat them man-to-man when they breach our perimeter."

"Right," Kelly said. He gulped. *When,* Bass had said, not *if.* Bass wouldn't say *when* unless he thought the situation was really dire.

Bass got up and ran doubled over to the rear of the perimeter, where Fassbender barely had his men under control, so he didn't see the Fuzzies drop to their bellies and begin to crawl toward the Marines' perimeter, firing as they advanced.

"Captain, move your people forward and arm them," Bass said.

"Thank you, sir," Fassbender said, jumping to his feet. "You heard the man," he shouted at his company. "On your feet and get your weapons. We have a battle to win!"

Most of the mercenaries dashed to where their flechette rifles lay. Nobody tried to locate his own; they just grabbed the first they came to and began blasting away at the Fuzzies. But there weren't enough weapons to go around.

Fassbender looked at the score of men who didn't obey his order. "Cowards!" he snarled. "If you don't fight, you don't have a chance, and you'll just die right where you are." He turned to the fight and looked for a rifle so he could join in.

"We weren't able to get all of your weapons," Bass told him. "See those men?" He pointed at a group of unarmed Sharp Edge troops, huddled behind the firing line. "Organize them into stretcher teams. If any of your people get hit, you can use your stretcher bearers as replacements on the line."

"Yes, sir," Fassbender said, and shouted at his unarmed men to join him. About then, a few of the men he'd called cowards dashed toward the weapons and joined their captain and the other unarmed mercenaries.

The Fuzzies didn't crawl well; crawling was a submissive, awkward movement, made by an inferior before a superior. Their shoulders hunched, forcing their arms forward, and their legs turned outward at the hip. They pushed their flechette rifles ahead of themselves and fired randomly. Many of their needles went high; others spent themselves in the dirt or the stems of bushes before reaching the perimeter. But enough got through to force the defenders to stay down.

The mercenaries fired equally randomly into the brush, unable to see exactly where the Fuzzies were, except when one had to cross a patch of bare ground. All they had to go on to locate the attackers was the Fuzzies' constant chittering, and the chittering came from too many directions and was too muffled for them to get an accurate fix on any one Fuzzy. Hardly more than a hundred flechette rifles firing into the brush that hid hundreds of Fuzzies weren't enough to stop the advance.

The Marines hardly fared better with their fire. They didn't see the Fuzzies any clearer than the Sharp Edge troops did. Their main advantage was that they were trying to fire into the dirt in front of the advance, trying to skitter the plasma bolts along the ground, trying to fragment the bolts so that bits of plasma would spread out, covering more ground per shot. But many bolts and fragments ricocheted high, and some stuck in the bushes and smoldered, igniting small fires that didn't spread. And there were fewer than thirty Marines throwing plasma at the hundreds of Fuzzies.

"Medic, over here!" came the call from the mercenaries, again and again, "Medic, medic!" Along with occasional cries of "Corpsman up!" from the Marines.

It was a full minute before anybody noticed that the chittering and fire from the Fuzzies had stopped.

"Cease fire!" Lieutenant Bass shouted.

"Cease fire!" the squad leaders repeated.

"Cease fire!" the fire team leaders echoed.

"Cease fire!" Captain Fassbender yelled, and his lieutenants and sergeants shouted in turn.

"I said stop shooting, goddammit!" Fassbender roared when some of the mercenaries kept firing.

The fire from Camp Godenov slowed and stopped.

"Did we get them all?" one of the mercenaries shouted.

"No," Bass said softly. Then loud enough for everybody to hear, he said, "No, we didn't get them all. They're still out there, waiting for us to make a mistake. Everybody, maintain your positions. Squad leaders report."

The reports filtered in. None of the Marines was in full body armor, and some weren't wearing *any* body armor, so there were casualties among them. Corporal Doyle and Lance Corporal Little had been wounded while they were running back to the perimeter with the Sharp Edge rifles, but their injuries had already been tended to and were minor enough that they could continue fighting. During the fight, Sergeant Ratliff and Sergeant Kerr were both wounded, as were Corporal Kindred from the gun squad, and PFC Shoup. All of them had been patched up and were able to continue.

PFC Sturges, the Marine brought in from Whiskey Company after Corporal Pasquin was wounded, was hit the worst. He'd been shot several times and lost a lot of blood. Doc Hough had him in a stasis bag.

The casualty situation for Sharp Edge was worse, even though the mercenaries hadn't been in the fight for as long. None of them had body armor, and they weren't behind cover as good as the Marines had—many were altogether out in the open. Captain Fassbender's report came in slow; his company wasn't as well organized as third platoon. He finally reported three dead and eighteen wounded. When Doc Hough finished with the injured Marines, he helped the Sharp Edge medic in tending their wounded.

Bass called for a medevac—and gunships to protect it. He was told it might take awhile; all the hoppers were out on other missions.

Mercury's force was close to the Naked Ones. Even though they greatly outnumbered the defenders, he realized he was taking too many casualties. If they continued the assault, even when they won the battle and killed all the Naked Ones, there would be far too many dead among the People's fighters. Perhaps two hundred had already been killed or wounded, and the closer they got to the Naked Ones, the heavier their casualties became. He knew his fighters had caused casualties among the Naked Ones, but not enough to severely reduce their rate of fire—especially not of the horrible fireball weapons.

He chittered a series of orders, and his fighters stopped firing and reversed their direction, crawling back far enough to increase their distance from the Naked Ones by half. There they would wait until nightfall, or until the Naked Ones made a mistake, a mistake that the fighters would take advantage of in order to kill them all.

Lieutenant Bass and Staff Sergeant Hyakowa huddled together in the command bunker; its tent cover was badly shredded by flechettes.

"They're still out there," Bass said. "We killed or wounded a lot of them, but most of them are still there."

Hyakowa nodded. "I agree. The question is, what are they waiting for? If they'd kept coming, they would have overrun us with their numbers."

"They could be waiting for reinforcements, or they might be moving to hit us from a different direction, or even moving to surround us. We need to get a look at where they are, what they're doing."

"The sky-eye."

Bass nodded. "If one of Chief Nome's aces is on duty. If he can pick the Fuzzies out from the background heat. It might be impossible if the Fuzzies are under the brush." Bass looked in the direction the Fuzzies had come from. "It's worth a try. Where's Groth?"

"I've got another idea, sir," Captain Fassbender said. He'd come up to them while they were talking, and now hunkered down.

"Tell me," Bass said.

"Somebody should climb the tower and take a look. I haven't been up there but I know that in this kind of landscape you get a much better view of the ground from an elevation."

Bass stared at him. "I already thought of that," he said, "and rejected the idea. It would be suicide."

"I've got six cowards back there." Fassbender hooked a thumb over his shoulder. "Men who refused to join in the fight. If one of them goes up the tower and gets killed, it won't be a loss. Especially if he can tell us anything about the Fuzzies' deployment before he dies."

Bass shook his head. "Marines sometimes send men into situations where they're probably going to get killed, but we always have the hope that they might survive. We *don't* send men into situations where they *will* get killed."

Fassbender shrugged. "All right. You've got body armor. Dress up one of those cowards in the body armor, and he's got a chance."

Bass stared at the Sharp Edge officer for a long moment. "How are you going to pick someone to go up?" he finally asked.

"Draw straws."

"And if the loser refuses?"

Fassbender shook his head. "Summary justice." Summary justice for someone disobeying a direct order in combat was often summary execution. But a commander who ordered it better be prepared to defend his actions before a court-martial.

Bass looked deeply into Fassbender's eyes. "Pick your man," he said.

CHAPTER TWENTY-SIX

Both of the *Grandar Bay*'s best Surface Radar Analysis techs were beginning to study the area a kilometer around Camp Godenov when Captain Fassbender returned with a terrified looking Sharp Edge soldier.

"He's one of the new ones off the *Dayzee Mae*," Fassbender said.

Bass signed for the man to sit and sent Staff Sergeant Hyakowa to get body armor. "Two sets," Bass said. He didn't speak to the mercenary or even look at him after the first glance.

Hyakowa was back in a couple of minutes. He tossed a set of body armor at the seated merc and said, "Put these on." He had to help the man get into the unfamiliar protective gear. Once the mercenary was in the body armor, Hyakowa wrapped additional sections of armor to the man's arms and other parts of his body that weren't covered by the main set and secured them with the same ties the Marines used to secure prisoners. "That'll give you extra protection," he told the frightened man. "Now you don't have to worry about anything worse than an arm or leg wound that'll put you on light duty for a week or two, and probably not even that." He squeezed his shoulder through the armor and gave him a reassuring smile.

"You might have a lot of Fuzzies shooting at you," Bass said. "All this should protect you from penetrating shots, although you might have a lot of bruises tomorrow."

Last, Hyakowa put a helmet on the man's head. "The comm is already set to the platoon command circuit, so all you have to do is talk, and we'll hear you. Any voices you hear will be either me or the lieutenant."

Bass looked at the extra set of body armor, and then at Hyakowa.

"Sturges's," the platoon sergeant said.

Bass nodded. Right, the new man. He was in a stasis bag and wouldn't be needing his helmet. He looked at the mercenary, who was looking ill.

"You throw up in that helmet, you clean it." He turned to Fassbender. "He's your man. Get him up the tower."

"You've got your orders," Fassbender said. "Climb."

The man stepped close and raised a trembling hand to the ladder.

"If I don't have to worry about anything worse than light duty, why don't one of you do it?" the man muttered, but he started up the ladder without further complaint.

Individual Fuzzies started shooting at him before he reached the perch at the top of the tower. Most of the shots missed, but the flechettes that splatted against the armor, and a couple of bullets that thudded into it, made him flinch. He didn't climb all the way onto the perch, but stood clutching the ladder, just high enough to see over the small platform at the top.

"You're going to have a few bruises," Bass called up to him. "That's all. Now look around and tell us what you see."

The man peered outward. "It's hard to tell," he finally said. "It looks like most of them are under bushes, maybe three hundred meters out. I can't see any of them closer than that."

"What about the flanks? Are any of them moving to flank us?"

The man looked carefully to his right. "I don't see anyone, or any movement there," he said in a quaking voice. He turned his head to the left and looked long and hard. "Nobody the—" He lost his grip on the ladder to fall groundward.

Bass and Hyakowa managed to catch him enough to break his fall without getting injured themselves.

"Why'd you let go?" Bass demanded. Through his faceplate, Bass saw the man's lips moving, but no sounds came out.

"Oh, shit, he's hit," Hyakowa said. "Corpsman! By the tower." The platoon sergeant unfastened the body armor around the man's neck and blood spurted out. Hyakowa pressed his thumb on the man's throat. "Looks like a flechette got through and nipped his carotid," he said when Doc Hough arrived.

"Keep the pressure on," Hough said as he dropped to his knees next to the mercenary's shoulder and opened his med kit. In seconds he had what he needed positioned above the wound. "Move your hand," he told Hyakowa. Bright red blood spurted as soon as the platoon sergeant's thumb lifted. Hough suctioned blood out of the wound so he could see what he was doing.

"Shit!" he swore. "That flechette really ripped in there." Blood spurted again, once more filling the gaping hole, but Hough had seen enough. He clamped the artery below the wound to stop the blood, then used a tweezer to extract the flechette. Working swiftly, but with a delicate touch, he cleaned the torn edges of the carotid and tacked them together. Then he brought the lips of the wound together and applied a synthskin patch. Only then did he look at the man's face. He swore again at how pale his face was. He looked beyond at the ground and swore once more.

"He's lost a lot of blood, and is in danger of exsanguination, if my patch doesn't hold. He should be in a stasis bag." He looked up at Bass. "But both of ours are in use." He turned his head to Fassbender. "Do you have any stasis bags?"

The Sharp Edge officer shook his head. "We had to concentrate on carrying water and food, so I had my men leave everything not absolutely essential. I didn't think we'd need heavy-duty medical equipment." He looked away. "I was wrong."

"I have some blood plasma," Hough said. "Someone give me a hand here. I have to bare his arms." Staff Sergeant Hyakowa was still kneeling on the man's other side. Working together, the two of them removed the armor tied onto the soldier's arms, broke the seals on his sleeve cuffs, and rolled them back to expose the inner sides of his elbows.

Hough went back into his med kit and drew out two flat containers, each of which held half a liter of blood plasma. He stripped a protective backing off one container and pressed the newly exposed surface to the man's inner elbow, then did something to the container's top surface.

When the corpsman went to work on the other container and elbow, Fassbender asked, "What about tubes and drips?"

Hough kept working as he answered, "Confederation milspec. The bags have integral needles that inject when I do this. . . ." He did the something to the top of the second bag, which he'd already affixed to the mercenary's inner elbow. "The needles find the vein and insert themselves into it. No need for tubes or drips." He and Hyakowa rolled the man's sleeves back down and resealed the cuffs.

"That should hold him until he gets to a surgeon," Hough said, standing up. "As long as the seal on the artery holds." He shook his head, wishing he had another stasis bag. He looked around unhappily. "That's a big tear. It's not safe to move him. We're going to have to leave him right here until he gets medevaced." Then he said to Fassbender, "Have some of your men make a barrier of some sort between him and the Fuzzies, to give him some protection from their fire."

"Right," Fassbender said, somewhat taken aback. Sharp Edge medics didn't give orders to officers, they made suggestions. Evidently it was different with Marines and their navy corpsmen. Or maybe it was because the corpsman didn't acknowledge a private army officer as a real officer. *Well,* Fassbender thought, *not only am I not in his chain of command, I'm technically a prisoner.* He asked Lieutenant Bass what he could use to make a protective barrier for his wounded man, whom he'd stopped thinking of as a coward.

* * *

The right side of the Fuzzies' line was held by fighters from the Crawling Vines Clan of the Starwarmth Union. Their leader was Junior. Junior contemplated the high casualties his fighters had suffered in the failed frontal assault against the Naked Ones camp and seethed. When the representatives of the Brilliant Coalition had first come to the Crawling Vines Clan to request alliance against the common foe, Junior had argued against it in private council among the leaders of the Crawling Vines Clan. Junior was not a Clan Father, or even a Burrow Father. But he was a bold and daring fighter, so he was brought into the discussions because his opinion on matters of warfare was valued.

The Brilliant Coalition cannot be trusted, Junior had argued. They'll send our fighters into battle first, to fight and die before they join in. And then, after we've driven off the Naked Ones, they'll attack and destroy us.

But the Clan Mother and Clan Father had not agreed with Junior. The Clan Father had led the fighters of Crawling Vines Clan against the clan fighters of the Brilliant Coalition many times in the past. In both victory and the occasional defeat, he knew the fighters of the Brilliant Coalition to be honorable. He did not believe they would do such a thing as Junior said they would. Then let the major battle leaders be from the Starwarmth Union, Junior argued.

No, the Clan Mother had said. It was fighters from the Brilliant Coalition who first fought the Naked Ones and defeated them. It was the Brilliant Coalition that sought to make peace with the Starwarmth Union. And other clans of the Starwarmth Union had already joined in alliance with the Brilliant Coalition, and their fighters had fought alongside the fighters of the former enemy. Never had the Clan Fathers of the Brilliant Coalition sent the fighters of the Starwarmth Union ahead to fight and die before engaging their own fighters.

Indeed, said the Clan Father, the Clan Fathers of the Brilliant Coalition were more likely to send their own fighters ahead and bring in the fighters of the Starwarmth Union after battle had been joined. Junior was wrong, the Clan Father insisted.

Even though Junior had argued forcefully against an alliance with the Brilliant Coalition, he was still a renowned fighter, and a war subleader under the Crawling Vines Clan Father, so he was given a command of his own in the allied army. And so it happened that Junior was the leader of the more than one hundred fighters of the Crawling Vines Clan that waited in the Safe Nights burrow for the call to action when Lester brought in his report of a new Naked Ones camp, much closer than the large camp that had been known.

On the second day of the march to the new Naked Ones camp, when scouts reported that the Naked Ones who had abandoned the People of the Rock Flower Clan were on a path that would lead them to the new camp, he'd urged Mercury to change direction and attack those Naked Ones while they were in the open. He'd been on attacks against two Naked Ones camps and believed that it was only their defensive works that made them so strong and so hard to defeat, that they would be easily defeated if caught in the open. But Mercury had refused to do so; he wanted to take the new camp before the other Naked Ones reached it. Then, Mercury had said, *we* will have the defenses and be even more easily able to defeat the larger force of Naked Ones, who would be in the open.

Junior gritted his teeth, but he was sworn by his Clan Mother and Clan Father to obey the orders of the Brilliant Coalition war leader.

But Mercury had been wrong, and the large force of Naked Ones reached the small camp before the army of the People did and had the advantage of the defensive works. And too many fighters had died in Mercury's ill-advised frontal assault.

Junior was tired of obeying the orders of this Brilliant Coalition war leader, who threw away too many lives. Now he was going to fight this battle the way *he* knew it should be fought.

Lieutenant Charlie Bass stood behind the trench and wall, facing the scrub to the west. Out there, even though he couldn't see them, he knew there were hundreds of Fuzzies waiting for the Marines to make a mistake. Well, Charlie Bass wasn't about to accommodate them.

But, dammit, he had to know what they were doing. In their place, he wouldn't simply be lying there, waiting for his enemy to make a mistake, or waiting until dark when he might have an advantage, or waiting for reinforcements. Especially not if he knew his foe might have reinforcements on their way, and knew his opponent could call in fire from the sky.

But he couldn't tell what the Fuzzies were doing from where he was.

He turned and looked at the tower. It was high enough to give him the information he needed, but the one time he'd sent somebody up after the battle had begun, that man had been severely wounded, and might yet die. Still, he needed to know. But he wasn't about to expose somebody else to the kind of fire that had almost killed the mercenary.

"Wang," Bass said on the command circuit, "come to me. Bring Captain Fassbender." He kept watching outward while he waited.

"What's up, boss," Hyakowa said when he reached Bass.

"Radios off, screens up," Bass said, putting his words to action. "I don't want anybody overhearing what I'm about to say." The three men stood close, face to bare face. Sweat began beading and then flowed in the heat.

"I have to know what's happening out there," Bass said. "So I'm going up the watchtower. No argument," he said, holding up a hand to stop what Hyakowa was about to say. "After the last one, I can't send somebody else. I have to do it myself. But I'll take a little extra precaution."

He looked at Fassbender. "If anything happens to me, Staff Sergeant Hyakowa is in command. Do you understand?"

Fassbender hesitated, but finally said, "Yes, sir. Your platoon sergeant will be in command if you are incapacitated."

"Good. Here's how I'm going to do it. . . ."

* * *

Little more than fifteen minutes later, Lieutenant Bass stood at the base of the tower. Like the Sharp Edge trooper, whose name he still didn't know, he had extra armor wrapped around his arms and legs to protect them. Beyond that, he and Hyakowa had disassembled another set of armor so it made narrower strips than a full jacket or pants. Hyakowa affixed them around all the places where two pieces of armor came together and might allow a flechette or bullet through if Bass turned the wrong way.

Bass bent his arms and legs to make sure he had sufficient movement to be able to climb the tower, turned his head, and twisted his body to make sure he wasn't limited to looking straight ahead.

"Loosen this one, Wang," he told Hyakowa, lifting his left arm and showing that the elbow only bent halfway. Hyakowa did, and Bass went through his bends and twists again. He ignored the Marines and mercenaries who were watching.

"All right, here I go," he finally said.

"Sir!" came Sergeant Kerr's voice over the radio. "Wait a minute."

Bass looked and saw the squad leader trotting toward him. He waited.

"Listen, boss," Kerr said when he reached Bass, "you shouldn't do that. We can't afford to lose you. Let me do it."

"Sorry, Tim," Bass said, shaking his head. "You're too damn big a target. It would take too damn long to get me out of this and you into it. Besides, you almost got killed once, no need to tempt fate. But thanks for the offer."

"Just being in the Marines has me tempting fate."

But Bass ignored him and, without another word, started climbing. Flechettes and bullets from the Fuzzies started hitting him before he was halfway to the perch.

It was an awkward climb; the extra armor around Bass's shoulders, elbows, and knees cut into their range of motion. He climbed high enough that he could lean the backs of his thighs against the front of the perch, and looked out over the scrub. It was as the man off the *Dayzee Mae* had said; Bass could see Fuzzies lying prone under and behind bushes. Through his magnifier screen, he could make out some of them aiming their weapons at him. He controlled his flinches when the occasional bullet smacked into his armor; he barely felt the impact of the flechettes. He turned to his right to look over the scrub in that direction, but overbalanced and had to grab hold of the perch to keep from falling off. He tried again: This time he held the perch with his right hand and swung his left foot out from the ladder. The landscape to the right was the same as to the front—scraggly bushes dotting red dirt. This time his examination didn't show any Fuzzies. Still moving cautiously, he brought his left foot back onto the ladder, gripped the perch with his left hand, and swung his right leg out so he could twist to his left.

The brush-speckled red dirt to the left of Camp Godenov looked the same as the landscape to the front and the right. Unlike the ground to the right, and very much like the ground to the front, there were Fuzzies on the left. They were crawling through the scrub, far enough out and too low to the ground to be seen from ground level. The Fuzzies farthest to the left had already stopped moving and were facing the Marine defenses. He couldn't tell with any certainty, but it looked like nearly a hundred Fuzzies were flanking the position.

Bass toggled his all-hands circuit. "Third platoon, pivot left! Fuzzies are flanking us. Five, have the Sharp Edge officer move all of his troops to replace us on the front line. I'll stay up here to direct."

Mercury had smiled with relief when he saw the Naked Ones' lookout topple from the watchtower. He wondered why it had taken so many shots to kill the Naked One. Were his fighters so excited at the prospect of shooting such an easy target that they forgot to aim? Maybe he needed to increase marksmanship training. But that would have to wait until they returned to Safe Nights burrow. First, they had to kill these Naked Ones, and get their weapons—especially the fire weapons.

After a short while passed, Mercury watched as another Naked One clumsily climbed the watchtower. Again, fighters shot at him, but fewer than had shot at the first lookout. Their bullets and projectiles seemed to be missing, just as when they shot at the first lookout. Soon Mercury would have to order them to stop shooting lest they use up too much ammunition before he ordered the next assault on the Naked Ones' camp.

It was then that he realized that none of the fighters to his right were shooting at the lookout. They were the Crawling Vines fighters, under the command of Junior. Mercury needed to know what was happening with the Crawling Vines fighters. Keeping low, he scrabbled to his right.

Junior and his Crawling Vines fighters weren't there.

Where were they? Had they run away? Mercury crawled back to the last fighter in the line and asked him what he knew. The fighter told him they had gone off to the right; he thought they were going to encircle the Naked Ones' camp. Wasn't that what Mercury had ordered them to do?

Mercury was furious at Junior for going off on his own, without even informing the war leader. He started to scrabble in the direction the fighter said they had gone, but sudden increased fire both from his own fighters and the Naked Ones' camp made him stop and rise up high enough to see over the brush. He saw Naked Ones running to the right and firing their fire weapons into the brush on that side. He heard bullet and flechette fire from the right of the Naked Ones' camp.

That fool! Mercury swore. Now the main force had to support the flanking attack, or it would fail, and Mercury would have to break off and take his fighters back to Safe Nights burrow.

First gun team was on the far left flank of the defensive line. Corporal Kindrachuck's head snapped to the left when he heard Bass's all-hands.

"Tischler, gun left!" he shouted, and raised his blaster to his shoulder to fire at the mass of Fuzzies who were erupting through the scrub little more than a hundred meters to his side.

In seconds, Lance Corporal Tischler had shifted his gun and was spraying plasma in an arc at the oncoming Fuzzies. PFC Yi, the assistant gunner, readied to load a fresh battery into the gun and would switch in a fresh barrel when the one on the gun glowed too brightly. Flechettes splatted into their body armor; bullets slapped almost hard enough to knock them backward.

Second squad pounded up to form a line alongside the gun team, but they had to run through a hail of bullets and flechettes to get there.

A flechette found its way through the seam between Corporal Chan's armor jacket and pants, but Chan barely felt it—until he'd taken a prone position and was firing at the onrushing Fuzzies. The blood loss made him light-headed.

A flurry of bullets and flechettes hit low on PFC Summers's helmet, knocking it loose enough for a bullet to tear along the side of his neck. He fell before he reached the new line.

Lance Corporal MacIlargie flopped to the ground when a ground-hugging bullet hit his boot and tore through his ankle. He crawled the rest of the way, swearing at the pain.

The other seven Marines reached the line and dropped into firing positions in the trench without injury. They added their fire to that from the gun.

The Fuzzies' charge staggered, and shuddered to a stop as they fell to the ground and fired from whatever cover they could find. Many of them had been killed or wounded, because the Marines had opened fire on them earlier than they had expected—they'd neglected to consider that Lieutenant Bass, from his vantage on the watchtower, would see them and alert his Marines.

Bass was still up high and began directing the fire of the gun, to inflict the greatest possible damage on the flanking element. The rate of flechettes and bullets striking him increased dramatically as the Fuzzies to the front began pouring supporting fire at the camp. A bullet hit the ladder rung he was standing on, splintering it. He was shifting his weight, moving his feet to a different rung, when another bullet slammed into the wrist of the hand with which he was holding on to the perch, with numbing force even through the armor wrapped around it. His grip loosened and he fell off the ladder. He landed on his shoulder and rolled, but his landing was hard enough that he cried out in pain as he struggled to his knees.

"Keep your fire low," Captain Fassbender yelled to his men. "Watch where they hop up, and shoot where they drop back down!"

Even before third platoon's first squad reached the defensive trench on the left, the Fuzzies to the front had begun advancing, firing as they came. They didn't stand up and charge the way they had originally; instead they advanced in something that resembled fire and maneuver. Individually, they rose to all fours and hopped forward a meter or two before dropping back down to fire their weapons. They were never up long enough for a man to see and aim before they were back down again. The air between the men and the Fuzzies began to fog with leaf and twig fragments hit and thrown skyward by flying flechettes and bullets. Few of the flechettes fired by either side made it far enough through the scrub to reach the opposing line, but bullets from the Fuzzies' single-shot rifles did, and the Sharp Edge medic was soon busy rushing along the defensive line, patching up wounds.

Doc Hough found Summers, who was struggling to make his damaged helmet fit right, and bandaged his neck. Then he slithered forward where he found MacIlargie and his bleeding ankle. Hough bandaged him, then went in search of more casualties. Chan was unconscious and going into shock by the time he reached him.

"Is anyone else wounded?" he asked on the platoon circuit. When nobody acknowledged an injury, he began dragging Chan back from the line. He needed to get the corporal to the command bunker to treat him for shock and to stop the bleeding. He wished he had another stasis bag to put him into. Before Hough and his seriously injured patient reached the bunker, he got a call from the platoon sergeant.

"The boss is down, Doc," Staff Sergeant Hyakowa said. "I think he's got a broken shoulder."

"I'm on my way to the CP bunker with Chan," Hough said. "He's pretty bad off and I can't leave him. Is the boss able to move on his own?"

"I think so, yeah."

"Then get him to me. I'll deal with his shoulder as soon as I've got Chan stabilized."

First squad reached the line without suffering any casualties. Few flechettes were making it through the scrub, and the bullets were all fired blind, so many went high. The Marines couldn't see where the Fuzzies were firing from.

"Tim," Sergeant Ratliff called on the squad leaders' circuit, "how far out are they?"

"They were about a hundred meters out when they went to cover, Rabbit," Sergeant Kerr answered. "They might have crawled closer, I don't know."

"I'm going for volley fire," Ratliff said.

"Good idea. I'll stagger volley fire with you."

"First squad," Ratliff said on his squad circuit, "the Fuzzies are no more than a hundred meters out. Maybe closer. Volley fire, skimming the ground. Shift your aiming points between volleys. *Fire!*"

First squad sent a volley of ten plasma bolts downrange, sizzling through the brush.

"*Fire!*" Kerr shouted right after first squad fired its first volley.

"*Fire!*" Ratliff ordered first squad.

"*Fire!*" Second squad shot another volley.

Some bolts glanced off woody stems and bounced high over the scrub. Other bolts fragmented when they hit stems, sending a shotgun spray of bits into the dirt, into the air, off on odd angles to the front. More blasted through foliage, burning narrow tunnels until they hit something that deflected their forward motion. Here and there a shrill scream told that a bolt or fragment struck home on a Fuzzy.

"Fire!"

"Fire!"

"Fire!"

"Fire!"

But the Marines' fire cleared enough of the brush that more flechettes began making their way through to impact on the Marines' helmets, arms, and shoulders.

CHAPTER TWENTY-SEVEN

Mercury was still angry at Junior, but he admitted to himself that the maneuver had been a good idea. The Naked Ones were distracted by the maneuver, and the most fearsome of their weapons were firing at Junior and his Crawling Vines fighters. Little loss if Junior was killed in his assault. The distraction allowed Mercury to advance his fighters against the weaker weapons. Hop forward a body length, then crawl a body length. When he saw that the flechettes often did not reach through the brush, he ordered his fighters with Naked Ones' weapons not to fire until he told them to. So let the Naked Ones waste their ammunition in a vain attempt to strike at the fighters. The fighters with bullet rifles were to fire one round when they crawled forward between hops; their bullets could get through the scrub. Mercury wished he had used that maneuver at the beginning of the battle. His force could have reached the Naked Ones' camp with fewer casualties along the way and saved ammunition. This was an important lesson for him to remember for future battles. Soon the main force would be close enough to rise up and charge the short remaining distance to the Naked Ones. Then, greatly outnumbering the defenders, they would be victorious!

* * *

Captain Fassbender heard the fierce fighting on the left flank and the screams of Fuzzies struck by the Marines' blaster fire. The firing on his front was just as fierce, but only bullets seemed to be coming his way—then he realized that there were no screams of the wounded from the Fuzzies advancing toward his position.

Damn! The brush must be blocking the flechettes from getting through! He crawled to Sergeant Vodnik.

"I don't think our flechettes are making it through the scrub," he said. "What do you think?"

Vodnik thought for a moment, listening to the sound of fire from the scrub to their front. "I think you're right," he said. "And the Fuzzies already figured it out—they're only firing their bullet rifles."

"Then we're just wasting ammo."

Vodnik looked sick when he nodded.

"Cease fire!" Fassbender shouted to his troops. "Cease fire! You're wasting ammunition. The flechettes can't cut through the scrub to reach the Fuzzies!"

Only half of the Sharp Edge troops stopped shooting. And many of them continued to fire even after Fassbender screamed his cease-fire order again. Keeping low in the trench to avoid the bullets, he scrambled along the line, yelling at the men still shooting, punching shoulders to get their attention, yanking weapons away from those who just wouldn't stop firing. Vodnik ran along the line in the oppo-site direction, doing the same. Between them, they got everybody to stop shooting.

"We've got to keep them steady," Fassbender said to Vodnik when the two got back to the center of the line.

"We can split up, each of us behind half the line," Vodnik offered.

Before Fassbender could say anything else, Lieutenants Crabler and Zamenik joined them.

"Why did you call a cease-fire?" Crabler demanded. "We're under attack! We need to beat them off. We have to pour fire at them!"

"I called a cease-fire because our flechettes aren't doing any good," Fassbender snarled. "All we're doing is wasting ammo. When the Fuzzies get closer, then we can fire on them again."

"The Marines are still firing," Crabler shouted, and swung an arm to point at the left flank, where the steady CRACK-*sizzles* came in volleys that drowned out individual shots.

"The Marines have blasters, dammit. Their bolts burn right through the scrub. Our flechettes can't get through that much growth. Listen to the fire from the Fuzzies. They knew that before I figured it out. They aren't firing their flechette rifles, only bullets from their own rifles!"

Fassbender glared at the two lieutenants. "We need to keep everybody steady. When the Fuzzies get close enough, we'll open up with everything we've got."

"And when will that be?" Zamenik shrilled. "When they come over the wall?"

"We'll know soon enough to do some damage to them before their final charge," Fassbender snapped. He looked at the tower and muttered, "We need somebody up there, to let us know how close they are."

Sergeant Vodnik heard. He looked at the tower, swallowed, and whispered, "I'll go, sir."

Fassbender shook his head. "No, I can't afford to lose you."

"I'll armor up, just like the Marine officer did. All I'll have to do is watch to the front. They won't knock me off like they did him."

Fassbender looked at Vodnik. The sergeant was right on both counts. "All right, do it. Let me know when you're armored." Vodnik scrambled to the rear to find Lieutenant Bass and get his armor.

Fassbender turned to the two lieutenants. "You're officers. You have to help me keep the troops steady. Now get behind your platoons and get them calmed down. Tell them we'll open fire when we can do some damage to the Fuzzies, and then we'll stop their advance, drive them back. Do you understand?"

"Yes, sir," they said in grudging agreement. They went. Not

sharply, not as though they were doing the right thing; they went because soldiers obey orders.

On the left flank, the two blaster squads continued volley fire while both guns swept the scrub brush side to side. Even though much of the brush in front of the Marines had been burned away by the fire, they still couldn't see the Fuzzies because the burning foliage was giving off a lot of smoke.

"How the hell can they breathe in there?" Lance Corporal MacIlargie asked on the fire team circuit.

"How the hell do I know?" Corporal Claypoole shouted back. "Damn, but they just keep coming!" He flinched as another flechette splatted against his faceplate. *A few more hits like that and it could crack,* he thought. *Then I'm cooked,* he thought, unconscious of the pun. More flechettes zipped close by; one or two pinged off Claypoole's armor; many plunged into the dirt wall in front of the trench. Then he saw something he hadn't noticed before.

"Hey, honcho," he called on the squad circuit. "Have you seen, there's a clear space between the ground and the bottom of the smoke."

Several meters to Claypoole's right, Sergeant Kerr stuck his head over the wall and then ducked low.

"I think you're right, Rock," Kerr replied. "*Fire!* That's how come they're still able to come at us; they stay below the smoke. *Fire!* Let's try to make our bolts stay below the smoke."

"H-how can we do that?" Corporal Doyle asked.

"*Fire!* You're smart," Kerr answered. "Figure it out for yourself. *Fire!* *That's a good question,* he thought. *How* can *we make our bolts stay below the smoke?*

The Marines kept volley firing, and the smoke kept thickening.

In the CP bunker, Sergeant Vodnik explained to Lieutenant Bass what he wanted to do.

"Good man, Sergeant," Bass said dreamily. Doc Hough had given him a sedative. "I'd help you, but the Doc has me bandaged up too tight for me to move much." Bass's right arm was tightly bound to his torso to keep the edges of broken bone from shifting about and causing more damage.

"I'll help you," Hough said. He began putting Bass's armor on the Sharp Edge noncom.

Bass was clearheaded enough to be able to give the corpsman some direction on applying the supplementary armor for additional protection. After only a few minutes, Vodnik vaulted out of the dugout and sprinted to the tower. Bass went back to watching Lieutenant Prang and the Fuzzy in their animated attempts to communicate. Prang was obviously excited at trying to talk with a previously unknown sentience. The Fuzzy looked agitated.

Sergeant Vodnik didn't have to climb all the way to the top to see where the Fuzzies were.

"Captain Fassbender!" Vodnik shouted. "They're only thirty meters away!"

Staff Sergeant Hyakowa, in overall command of the defense of Camp Godenov, had been concentrating almost all of his attention to the south wall, where the camp's flank was still under attack. Vodnik's shout and Fassbender's immediate call for his men to open fire brought his attention back to the front.

"Hound!" Hyakowa shouted. "Get a gun turned around to sweep the front. The Fuzzies are close!"

Sergeant Kelly snapped orders, and Corporal Kindrachuck quickly reoriented his team so that Lance Corporal Tischler was firing across the front of the Sharp Edge troops.

"Marine gun," Sergeant Vodnik shouted from his perch clutching the watchtower ladder, "left ten meters! You're shooting in front of the Fuzzies."

Kelly didn't think that the Fuzzies were suicidal enough to jump up and try to charge through the enfilading fire, but it might have been possible for them to crawl under the stream of plasma bolts and then appear in the trench with the defenders before the gun could do any damage to them.

"Gun one," Kelly ordered, "left ten. Pound the ground!"

Kindrachuck directed Tischler in adjusting his fire until the plasma bolts were striking among the Fuzzies closing on the front of the perimeter.

"You're getting them!" Sergeant Vodnik cried exultantly.

Mercury watched as another Naked One climbed the watchtower and ordered the fighters with needle rifles nearest himself to fire on the exposed Naked One, but their fire seemed to have no effect. Mercury was close enough to see that the Naked One was indeed being hit, so what magic was this? How was it possible for a Naked One to be hit so many times and not be injured? Mercury knew how devastating the needles were to flesh; he had been in enough battles and seen the effects with his own eyes.

He looked more closely at the Naked One; something was wrong with his shape. Yes! He was thickened; he must be covered with something that was impervious to the needles. But bullets had been fired at the Naked One as well, and Mercury couldn't believe that all of them had missed. Whatever the covering was that the Naked One was wearing, after the battle he would have his fighters strip it from the corpse so that they could use it in future battles.

Then all thought of the body covering was driven from his mind by a stream of fire that shot across his front. He shrieked in surprise and shock. Instantly, he realized that the Naked One on the watchtower had the fire-stream gunner adjust his aim so the stream of fire blazed along the line of fighters. He leaped to his feet and shrilled the command to charge—just as the fire-stream gunner adjusted his aim and balls of fire began blasting into the prone fighters.

"Here they come!" Captain Fassbender shouted at the top of his lungs. "Blow them away!"

A hundred and then some flechette rifles opened up at the charging Fuzzies. But the Fuzzies were close and outnumbered the defenders more than two to one. The gun took down a few more but most of them reached the trench and jumped into it.

Staff Sergeant Hyakowa saw that the incoming fire from the left flank was slackening; either the Fuzzies there were backing off because of the increasing smoke or the platoon was killing more of them. The hundred Sharp Edge troops were in danger of being overwhelmed by the Fuzzies who were leaping into their trench.

"Hound," Hyakowa yelled, "get both guns firing on the flank. Rabbit, move first squad to help the mercs!"

In seconds, Corporal Kindrachuck had Lance Corporal Tischler firing into the burning, smoking scrub on the left flank again, and Sergeant Ratliff had first squad pounding toward the melee in the front trench. When they had clear shots, a few of the Marines fired single shots at Fuzzies that were in the trench or jumping into and over it.

In seconds the nine Marines of first squad were barreling into the flank of the Fuzzies.

Lance Corporal Zumwald jumped into the trench, landing hard with both boots on the lower back of a Fuzzy who was grappling with a Sharp Edge soldier. The three went down in a pile. The merc had his breath knocked out, then was stunned when his head struck the hard bottom of the trench. The Fuzzy, stunned by the sudden agony in his back, collapsed, his full weight falling on the soldier when Zumwald raised himself to his knees and slammed the butt of his blaster into the back of the Fuzzy's head. Blood splashed from the blow, and bone cracked and splintered.

Just past where Zumwald had killed a Fuzzy, Corporal Dornhofer jammed the muzzle of his blaster into the side of a Fuzzy. A bolt of plasma burned a hole through the Fuzzy's torso and shattered against the outer wall of the trench; bits of star stuff splashed back, striking that Fuzzy, the soldier he'd been grappling with, and the Fuzzy next in line up the trench, wounding all three. Dornhofer jumped into the trench, past the soldier, and hammered the butt of his blaster into the next two Fuzzies, whom he'd just wounded.

PFC Gray, running alongside Dornhofer, held his blaster cross-body and slammed it into two Fuzzies who had just jumped over the trench, bowling them over. He stuttered his step just enough to bring one foot pounding onto the neck of one of them, breaking it. The other Fuzzy scrambled to all fours and dove at Gray, tumbling him to the ground. The Fuzzy clawed at him with hands and feet, but Gray's body armor protected him from the knifelike claws. Gray whipped his fighting knife from its scabbard and plunged the blade into the Fuzzy's shoulder where it met his neck. The Fuzzy reared back and screamed, blood gushing from the wound. Gray viciously twisted the knife, then jerked it out. He jumped to his feet and looked for his dropped blaster.

Corporal Dean led his men past first fire team. He saw a knot of Fuzzies who had leaped the trench and were headed for the watchtower and Sergeant Vodnik. Dean skidded to a halt and threw his blaster to his shoulder to start pressing off bolts at them. He got three before the others realized they were being attacked from the rear and turned to charge the new threat. But Lance Corporal Ymenez shot them down.

Sergeant Vodnik waved his thanks to the three Marines.

Lance Corporal Quick and his men bolted past third fire team while they were dealing with the Fuzzies charging the watchtower and ran into more Fuzzies who had jumped the trench. As soon as they were clear of their fellow Marines, they began firing straight ahead, boring instantly cauterized holes through many of the Fuzzies.

A Fuzzy who had just killed an unarmored Sharp Edge soldier leaped out of the trench and slashed at Quick, with claws gory from disemboweling the man. The blow staggered Quick. Before the Marine could regain his balance, the Fuzzy was on him, bloody claws slashing and ripping at his armored neck and shoulders. One claw got stuck in Quick's neck seam and broke off—but not before breaking the seal, baring Quick's neck. The Fuzzy chittered a cry of victory as he drew his hand back to plunge it down in a death blow. But he couldn't strike the blow; Dean and his men had caught up, and the corporal slammed the Fuzzy's head with the butt of his blaster.

Ymenez speared a charging Fuzzy with the muzzle of his blaster, and then pressed the firing lever. With the muzzle pressed against the Fuzzy's flesh, the plasma bolt spread wide and burned out his middle, almost cutting him in half.

The Marines of first squad were making short work of the Fuzzies at the south end of the trench, but a hundred meters away, at the center and far end of the trench, the Fuzzies were overwhelming the defenders.

In the nearer bunker, four Sharp Edge soldiers fought fiercely against the Fuzzies who were trying to break in to get at them. The Fuzzies had already killed two of the mercenaries in the bunker with rifle fire but the others jammed themselves into the corners next to the entrance and were stabbing and slashing with knives to keep the Fuzzies at bay. The bodies of three Fuzzies were clogging the entrance. So far, none of the Fuzzies had thought to go around to the front and fire their rifles through the aperture—but it would only be a matter of time.

Farther along, the mercenaries were doing their best, beating at the Fuzzies with rifle butts and spearing with muzzles. Some fought with knives. Most of the Fuzzies dropped their rifles in favor of using their claws. The knives were no match against the claws, and most of those fights saw the men go down with blood flowing out of their rent climate-control uniforms. The men's sole advantage was that their arms and shoulders had evolved from tree-dwelling ancestors and had greater upward reach and striking power than the arms and shoulders of the Fuzzies, which had evolved from ground-walking legs. If only they'd had bayonets to turn their rifles into spears.

*   *   *

Lieutenant Prang and the Fuzzy who had gotten the leaves to ease the pain in McGinty's hand were still intent on their attempts to communicate, but the Fuzzy was struggling against the bonds that held his hands behind his back and hobbled his feet. Lieutenant Bass was barely conscious and crooning a tuneless song. Doc Hough, busy tending to the wounded who had been brought to the topless bunker before the final assault, was the only person who could hear the raging battle and do anything defensive—but he was too engrossed in his ministrations to pay any attention to what was happening outside.

Until he heard the *crack* of bullets just overhead.

Then he looked up, over the edge of the bunker, and saw Fuzzies coming in his direction, chittering and firing as they moved. He dove for a blaster.

The agitated Fuzzy trying to get a point across to Prang saw Hough go for the blaster and looked up to see the oncoming Fuzzies. He sprang to his feet and shrilled out rapid chittering, waddling to stand between the humans in the bunker hole and the attacking Fuzzies.

At an order from one of the Fuzzies, they all dropped to the ground and pointed their rifles at the bunker, but they stopped shooting. There was a rapid exchange of chitters between the one who'd evidently given an order to drop and cease fire, and the Fuzzy prisoner. Then the leader snapped another order, and the rest of the Fuzzies, looking confused, pointed their rifles away from the bunker. The prisoner turned his head around to look at Prang. He chittered at the officer and wiggled his hands. Prang looked uncertainly among him and the Fuzzies outside the bunker.

"I think he wants me to cut him loose," Prang said to Hough. "What do you think?"

The corpsman nodded. "I think that's what he's asking," he agreed. "Why not? If they want to kill us, we can't beat them off. And it does look like he got them to stop shooting at us."

"All right," Prang said slowly. He stood and walked over to the prisoner, careful not to make any sudden movements. He slowly and openly drew his knife and reached for the bonds holding the prisoner's hands behind his back. He stopped when several of the Fuzzies suddenly aimed their rifles at him. He held the knife up and reached for the bonds with his other hand. The prisoner presented his wrists to Prang and bent over to give him easier access. None of the muzzles wavered as the officer reached the knife to the bonds and cut them loose. Then he crouched and cut the bonds on the prisoner's ankles.

"Now we'll see what happens next," Prang said. He handed the knife to the Fuzzy.

The Fuzzy, no longer a prisoner, held the knife up. He pointed at Prang, pointed at Doc Hough, pointed at the wounded Fuzzy whom the corpsman had patched up before the arrival of the Sharp Edge company, chittering all the while. The other Fuzzies listened intently, then their leader chittered something. The Fuzzy cocked his head for a moment, looking like a man lost in thought, then looked at the leader, at Prang, tossed the knife out of the bunker, and stood with his hands spread wide, facing the human. Prang considered for a few seconds, then mirrored the posture.

The Fuzzies outside the bunker chittered among themselves, but it was more muted than before and didn't sound hostile. The leader cut off the others, put his rifle down, and got up on all fours to hop the few remaining meters to the bunker. He dropped into it and stood in front of Prang, hands open and arms spread. Prang faced him and did the same. Hough also stood erect and mimicked the posture.

"Shake my hand," Prang suddenly said.

Hough stepped to him and held out his hand. The two men shook. Prang faced the Fuzzies and held out his hand. They had watched the humans with interest and now looked curiously at Prang's hand. Then the leader reached out and, careful not to poke his claws into the officer's glove, shook hands with him. He pulled Prang to the side of the bunker facing the ongoing fighting at the perimeter and gestured toward it, chittering excitedly. He gestured at the former prisoner, at Hough, and at the Fuzzies who had come with him.

"Sir, I think he wants us all to go out there together and stop the fighting."

"I think you're right, Doc. Let's give it a try. If we're wrong, hey, they can kill us right now if they want to."

Together, the four climbed out of the bunker and started walking toward the fighting. The leader chittered something at his squad, and they stayed in place.

Prang and Hough turned up the volume on their helmet speakers and shouted, "Cease fire, cease fire! Everybody, stop fighting!" They waved their arms above their heads.

The two Fuzzies chittered loudly, waving their arms side to side.

Slowly, the men and Fuzzies at the trench stopped fighting and looked at the four walking toward them.

"We've started communicating!" Prang called out. "We've agreed to stop hostilities!"

The chittering from the two Fuzzies probably meant the same.

CHAPTER TWENTY-EIGHT

The toll had been horrendous. Seventy-six of the Sharp Edge troops were dead or wounded. All but one of the nine Marines who hit the Fuzzies from the flank were wounded, as well as three more from second and gun squads who had fought on the Marine flank.

Mercury had his fighters gather their dead and wounded and get them out of the compound as quickly as possible so the Naked Ones wouldn't know how many of them had been killed in the battle. But the number was very high; everybody knew that. On Henny's urging, he allowed the more seriously wounded to stay long enough for Doc Hough and the Sharp Edge medic to bandage them before he had them carried away. Mercury hadn't heard from Junior, and the scouts he sent to find him in the slowly clearing smoke from the fight in the diversionary attack reported that Junior was nowhere to be found; he wasn't one of the dead or wounded still lying between the smoldering bushes.

Brigadier Sturgeon arrived in a hopper an hour after the battle ended. He brought Lieutenant Yethador, the *Grandar Bay*'s linguist, with him, along with the FIST's assistant surgeon, Lieutenant Haku, and two of the corpsmen from the FIST medical platoon. Haku and his corpsmen put together a field expedient surgery and treated the wounded humans, preparing them for transport to Camp Usner for further treatment—or direct transit to the *Grandar Bay* for the more seriously injured. The surgeon and his corpsmen made no distinction between the Marines and the mercenaries in deciding the order in which to care for their patients.

"Sir," Lieutenant Bass asked Brigadier Sturgeon after he and Lieutenant Prang had been debriefed on the action and the beginning of communications with the Fuzzies, "do you have any word on my other casualties?"

Sturgeon nodded. "In brief only, Charlie. You'll have to wait until later to get more complete reports. Corporal Pasquin will survive, but he'll never rejoin the platoon; the brain damage was too severe. Young McGinty is not only going to survive, he should be back with you by the time we get back to Camp Ellis. The *Grandar Bay*'s scientists are fascinated by the venom that afflicted him, and the herbal medicine the Fuzzy used to treat him." He looked into nowhere for a moment before turning back to Bass and continuing.

"As for the Hammer, the *Grandar Bay*'s psychiatrist is treating him. It looks like a case of battle fatigue—at the same time it doesn't look anything at all like battle fatigue. Basically, he seems to have suddenly lost his self-confidence. I'm sure he'll get it back, though."

"Thank you, sir." Bass looked around at the damage wreaked on Camp Godenov, and the blood making darker stains on the red dirt. "What's next?"

A corner of Sturgeon's mouth quirked in a repressed smile. "Commodore Borland is at Base Camp right now, arresting Louis Cukayla and his top people."

A suborbital off the *Grandar Bay* led two Essays to a landing at Base Camp. They didn't land on the airstrip; the suborbital and one Essay landed on the quad outside the administration building. The second Essay splashed down on the lake, then sped ashore to join the other two vessels. The water-lander dropped its ramp, and three Dragons roared out. They dropped their ramps and sixty armored and heavily armed Marines from the FIST headquarters company boiled out to take positions surrounding the quad and administration building. Half of the Marines around the administration building faced it; the rest faced outward.

The suborbital opened and Commodore Borland stepped out. He was accompanied by an officer and a chief petty officer. All three had sidearms belted around their waists. The three marched onto the portico, where Louis Cukayla and Johnny Paska stood. They were not in climate-control uniforms. They hadn't been given warning of the Commodore's visit and didn't have time to change into them before Borland and his companions exited the suborbital. They were already sweating in the heat. In the background, the other Essay opened up and disgorged three more Dragons. Thirty armed sailors in working coveralls exited the Dragons and stood in formation, facing the administration building. The six Dragons moved to form a ring around the quad.

"Well, Commodore," Cukayla said, cocking an eyebrow when he saw that Borland was armed, "to what do I owe the honor of a visit from the Confederation's senior officer in this system?"

"Mr. Cukayla," Borland said brusquely, "let us dispense with the pleasantries. The officer standing to my left is Lieutenant (jg) Flynn, the *Grandar Bay*'s legal officer. On my right is Chief Petty Officer Ault, the *Grandar Bay*'s Master at Arms. They are here to place you, John Paska, and your other top people under arrest."

As Borland made his announcement, Flynn and Ault stepped forward and manacled the two men's hands behind their backs. They didn't use lightweight ties such as the Marines used when they took prisoners, but old-fashioned iron manacles that needed a key to unlock.

That done, Ault signaled to the sailors in the quad. Six of them broke formation and trotted onto the portico, where they followed Ault into the building.

"What is the meaning of this outrage!" Cukayla shouted. The sudden redness in his face was due to more than just the heat.

"The meaning is," Borland said, "Sharp Edge and its officers stand in violation of several Confederation laws regarding sentient species and slavery. Sharp Edge and its officers are also suspected of violating a number of Confederation laws and regulations regarding smuggling, contraband, and interplanetary trade. You will be informed of the specifics on board the *Grandar Bay*."

Flynn signaled the sailors and four burly petty officers broke ranks to mount the portico. They took Cukayla and Paska firmly by the arms and marched them to one of the Dragons the sailors had ridden from orbit. When they were safely aboard and the Dragon's ramp closed, Borland turned his head to Flynn.

"Well, Mr. Flynn, I must say that went easier than I feared."

"It must have been the element of surprise, sir."

"Indeed. Let's go inside and see how well in hand Chief Ault has matters."

"Knowing the Chief, sir, I'd say very well."

And Chief Ault did have matters very well in hand. The clerks and other office workers stood lined up against one wall, holding their hands on top of their heads. A few sidearms and knives were laid out on a desk well out of reach of the workers. The sailors Ault had led in were busily collecting every bit of data, digital and hard copy, in the offices and packing them for transport to the *Grandar Bay*.

"Sir, I think we'll be finished here in a few minutes," Ault said. He didn't bother to come to attention when the Commodore entered the office.

"That's fine, Chief," Borland said. "Which one of them is the comm chief?" He indicated the office staff.

"This one, sir." Ault stepped over to the clerks and pulled one out of the line.

"Fine, fine," Borland said with a nod. "What's your name?"

"S-Stubbins, sir," the man stammered. "M-Mark Stubbins."

"Well, Mark Stubbins, are you aware of what just happened outside?"

"Y-yes, sir."

"You don't want to be arrested, do you?"

"N-no, sir!" Stubbins blanched.

"Very good. Then you will assist me in contacting all Sharp Edge installations on Ishtar, won't you?"

"Absolutely, sir! Whatever the admiral wants, sir!"

"It's commodore, not admiral, but that's all right. Now, is there a way you can let me communicate with all the Sharp Edge personnel here at Base Camp? I mean, at the same time?"

"Yes, sir. There's a PA system."

"Excellent! Lead me to it, if you please."

"Right this way, sir." Stubbins scurried to Cukayla's inner office. Borland followed on his heels but seemed to move at a much more leisurely pace. Inside, Stubbins handed Borland a microphone and asked, "Do you want me to turn it on now, sir?"

"If you please, Mr. Stubbins."

Stubbins put a finger to a touch point on a console, and an indicator light turned from red to yellow to green. "There's a—"

"I know how to use a microphone, Mr. Stubbins. Thank you anyway." Borland flicked the toggle that turned the microphone on and began speaking.

"Attention everybody at Base Camp. This is Commodore Roger Borland, Confederation Navy. I am the senior military officer currently present in the Opal-Ishtar system and, by default, the senior representative of the Confederation of Human Worlds in the Opal-Ishtar system. By my orders, all Sharp Edge operations on Ishtar are to cease as of this moment. All human beings on Ishtar are, as of this moment, under the authority and control of the Confederation military. All personnel present at Base Camp are to assemble in front of the administration building, *now*! In fifteen minutes, Confederation military personnel will commence a search of Base Camp. Anyone found in any of the buildings, or anywhere else other than assembled in front of the administration building, will be placed under arrest.

"That is all."

Borland handed the microphone back to Stubbins, who put it on its cradle next to the console.

"Thank you, Mr. Stubbins. You've been very helpful. Now to contact the mines and any other Sharp Edge facilities on Ishtar . . ."

"The comm room's over here, sir." Stubbins led Borland out of the inner office to another side room.

"Will the setup allow me to talk to all of them at the same time?"

"Yes, sir. Just give me a couple of minutes to set it up, sir." Borland nodded, and three minutes later watched as Stubbins brought all the mines online.

As soon as they were all on, with either the commander or second in command at each facility listening, Borland announced to them that Cukayla and Paska were under arrest, their operations were over, that they were to stand down, release all the Fuzzies, and prepare to receive transportation to Base Camp. He finished with a warning that any facility that failed to do as instructed would be forcibly shut down by all the resources available to a Confederation Marine Corps Fleet Initial Strike Team.

Stubbins swallowed when he heard that.

"Yes, Mr. Stubbins?" Borland said.

"Sir, I was on Ravenette. With the Ruspina forces. I know what the resources available to a FIST are—from the receiving end. I hope everybody does exactly what you said."

"You're a good man, Mr. Stubbins."

Evidently everybody else in Base Camp also knew what a FIST could do. The Marines and sailors who searched the camp didn't find anyone trying to hide.

The Marines went in company strength from mining camp to mining camp to make sure the operations were shut down and the Fuzzies freed. The navy transported the Sharp Edge personnel back to Base Camp. There was only one holdout: a camp commander who saw continued mining after Sharp Edge was shut down as his avenue to personal wealth. His troops mutinied when they were confronted by the company of Marines—and a division of four Raptors that flew low overhead. The mutineers promptly surrendered to the Marines. The whole operation took a month. On receipt at Base Camp, the navy transported the Sharp Edge personnel to the four starships owned or leased by Sharp Edge, which were still in orbit. There they were held under guard by sailors off the *Grandar Bay* and the Marines of the FIST's artillery battery, which hadn't had anything else to do on the deployment.

Finally, Thirty-fourth FIST boarded Dragons that drove onto Essays and lifted to orbit, where they reboarded the *Grandar Bay* to return to Thorsfinni's World.

The day after the *Grandar Bay* broke orbit, Lieutenant Bass visited first squad in their compartment. Along the way, he stopped at the squad leaders' compartment to get Sergeant Ratliff.

"I've got news on Corporal Pasquin," Bass said when he had everybody's attention. "As you know, he suffered a very bad head wound."

"Is he going to make it?" Lance Corporal Quick asked.

Bass paused before answering. When he spoke again, his voice was heavy. "I'm about to tell you. Please, no more interruptions until I finish." He looked at the men of first squad and waited until each of them nodded agreement. "All right, then. As I was saying, Corporal Pasquin suffered a very serious head wound. He's going to live, but . . ." His voice trailed off for a moment, then he began more briskly. "The bullet and helmet fragments blew away some of his brain matter. Unlike bone and muscle, brain matter can't be regenerated. Raoul is going to be in rehab for a long time, and the rehab won't begin for some time yet, not until his bones reknit and missing pieces of bone regenerate. It's going to be some time before he's able to talk again, and walk unaided. It's probable that he'll never be able to return to duty, so he's going to be medically discharged." He waved off any questions that statement might have raised. "He'll be given the best care and treatment the Confederation Veterans Authority can give him. But he's no longer with third platoon, and he won't be returning.

"Now, does anybody have any questions?"

"Can we see him?" Ratliff asked.

Bass shook his head. "The surgeons here did everything they could for him. He's in stasis until he reaches a hospital where any remaining work can be done and he can start rehab. Next question."

There was a moment of silence before Ratliff asked, "What happened to his helmet? They're supposed to be able to stop bullets. Other Marines got shot in the head and nothing happened. His helmet got hit and broke."

Bass spread his hands helplessly. "His helmet has been thoroughly examined. Evidently a manufacturing flaw somehow got past quality control. Now," he said very firmly, "that doesn't mean you can't trust your helmets to keep your brain boxes safe. It was a fluke, one in a million. *More* than one in a million."

Someone murmured, "Shit happens." Several of the Marines nodded.

"I've got some good news, too," Bass said. "PFC McGinty will be rejoining the squad before jump point."

Nobody asked who was going to replace Pasquin as fire team leader. It was too soon for the Marines of first squad to worry about that.

At his own request, Lance Corporal Schultz remained in sickbay rather than rejoin his squad for the duration of the return to Thorsfinni's World.

EPILOGUE

Lieutenant 'Prang stayed on Ishtar until the last possible moment, continuing his attempts to communicate with the Fuzzies. The entire science department of the *Grandar Bay* tried to convince Commodore Borland to stay for several more weeks—months would be better, they said—so that they could study the Fuzzies, their language, their culture, and their herbal medicines. Borland refused, saying that other scientists were already on their way. He suspected that wasn't true; he'd only sent a drone to Earth requesting a scientific party be assembled and dispatched little more than a week before. For all he knew, the message hadn't even been received yet. But he was certain a team *would* be assembled and dispatched.

The same sailors and Marines who'd acted as guards on the SS *Pointy End*, the SS *Lady Monika*, the SS *Tidal Surge*, and the SS *Dayzee Mae* remained on them as guards during the starships' journey to Fourth Fleet Marines headquarters at MCB Camp Basilone on Halfway, where the Sharp Edge personnel were to be held until the Attorney General's office decided what to do with them. The four starships would be impounded there while awaiting final disposition. The sailors and Marines would be transported back to Thorsfinni's World via the first available military vessels.

Louis Cukayla, Johnny Paska, and the commander of the mining camp that hadn't stood down when Commodore Borland gave the order were held in the *Grandar Bay*'s brig as far as Thorsfinni's World. There they were handed off to another navy starship for the next leg of their trip to Earth, where they likely faced numerous charges from the Attorney General's office.

The Ministry of Interplanetary Affairs sent delegates to Opal to establish diplomatic relations, a necessary step before beginning the investigation to discover who on Opal was behind the secret operations on Ishtar, and possible subsequent criminal charges.

The *Grandar Bay* reached Thorsfinni's World in due time, and Brigadier Sturgeon granted the FIST a week's planetary leave.

Lance Corporal Schultz reluctantly rejoined third platoon. He didn't speak to anybody, or in any way acknowledge anything said to him.

Third platoon didn't waste any time getting to Big Barb's and causing instant pandemonium. Shrieks and screams of joy reverberated off the walls as soon as the girls saw the Marines come through the door. If any of them had attempted to walk to the Marine she liked the most, she would have been trampled by the rest, who ran so fast their feet barely touched the floor.

"Tim, Tim!" shouted two voices in point and counterpoint. Big Sergeant Kerr braced himself well enough that he barely staggered when blond Frida and dark Gotta threw themselves into his arms.

Skinny-almost-to-the-point-of-painfulness Carlala shrieked and threw herself at Corporal Dean, wrapping her arms and legs around him and kissing him as though trying to suck the air out of his lungs. Either that or blow his lungs full.

Young Stulka, too excited to emit a proper shriek, squealed as she ran to PFC McGinty and peppered his face with tiny kisses.

Vinnie was more restrained in greeting Corporal Doyle. It was as if she knew he'd be embarrassed if she simply jumped on him at first sight.

The other women exuberantly greeted their men, except for

Hildegard, who hadn't paired off with anybody since Godenov was killed on Haulover—she hadn't paired off with anybody in particular before him, and then only the one time, right before Thirty-fourth FIST deployed to fight the Skinks. And for Erika.

Not all the Marines were there. Corporal Claypoole had headed straight for Brystholde and Jente's farm, where, to the extent they could, they were "living in sin."

Sergeant Ratliff wasn't there, either. He'd decided to go to the village of Hryggurandlit and pay a surprise visit to Kona, the widow who'd taken up with him at a FIST party. This was the first time he'd been to Kona's village, and at first she wasn't exactly happy to see him. After all, she was a respectable widow woman, and it was unseemly for her to be having an affair with one of those ruffians from Thirty-fourth FIST. On the other hand, she *was* a widow, and her neighbors should grant her a certain leeway. Ratliff was quite an acceptable man to come courting, if that's what he was doing. And if it wasn't exactly what he was doing, well that was just too bad, and her straitlaced neighbors could go and suck eggs if they didn't like it.

Einna Orafem heard the commotion and burst out of the kitchen, almost bowling Big Barb over in her haste to get to Lance Corporal Schultz. After ascertaining that he was alive and well and in the barracks, she retired to the kitchen and called him on his personal comm. She ordered him in no uncertain terms to meet her at her home. The FIST had a week's leave, and she was taking a week off to spend with him. If Big Barb didn't like it, tough. Just go ahead and try to fire the best chef her establishment had ever had.

There was one other. Erika rampaged through the mass of bodies tangling inside the entrance to Big Barb's, pushing people out of her way in her search for Corporal Pasquin. She finally pried Dean and Carlala apart and demanded to know where her Raoul was. She wailed when he turned a stricken face on her.

"He's not dead," Claypoole said. "But he's bad off—"

That was all Erika waited to hear. She broke through the rest of the crowd to the door and headed for Camp Ellis. She made such a fuss at the main gate that the Sergeant of the Guard assigned an MP to take her to the base dispensary—and bring her back once she found out what had happened to her man.

Lieutenant Haku, the FIST's assistant surgeon, was still at the dispensary, making sure the base medical team had the information it needed to treat the few wounded who still needed hospitalization.

"Where is he?" Erika demanded when she broke in on a conference he was having with a general practitioner and two nurses. "Where is Raoul?"

"Raoul? Who's Raoul? And who let you in here?" Haku asked, taken aback.

Erika gathered herself and said more calmly, "Corporal Pasquin, Company L. He was wounded. Where is he, I need to see him."

"Oh, my." Haku turned to the other doctor and the nurses. "Will you excuse us, please?" He guided Erika into an unoccupied examination room and closed the door.

"Please sit, Miss . . . What's your name?"

"Erika. Raoul's my man. Where is he? Why haven't you taken me to see him?"

Haku sighed, and guided her to a chair. "Please sit, Miss Erika." He waited until she was seated, and squatted down in front of her. "I'm afraid Corporal Pasquin, Raoul, was very badly wounded. He's in stasis, waiting for transshipment to a proper hospital."

"In stasis?"

"Yes. To keep him stable. We did everything we could for him on Ishtar, and then on the *Grandar Bay,* but he needs more surgery and more care."

"Where are they going to take him? I'm going with him."

"I'm sorry, but that's not possible."

"Then how long is he going to be gone? How long will I have to wait?"

Haku hung his head for a moment. This felt worse than telling someone her husband had been killed—something he mercifully seldom had to do; the Marines usually took care of informing the next of kin.

"He's not coming back."

"Then I'll go to him."

"Miss, you won't know him. He suffered very severe brain damage. He's going to undergo years of therapy and rehabilitation before he'll even be able to talk normally and walk without assistance."

"I don't care. I'll nurse him."

Haku shook his head again. "Erika, he lost a big chunk of his prefrontal cortex. That's the part of the brain that controls decision making, social behavior—and personality. The Raoul you knew doesn't exist anymore."

After a few more minutes, Lieutenant Haku escorted Erika back to the entrance of the dispensary and handed her over to the waiting MP, who took her back to the main gate. She cried softly the entire way. The Sergeant of the Guard took pity on her and had the MP drive her all the way home. She never stopped crying.

Erika disappeared into her apartment and wasn't seen for several days. When her friends came to see her, she sent them away without even opening the door.

When Erika finally emerged, she wore black.

DAVID SHERMAN is a former U.S. Marine and the author of eight novels about Marines in Vietnam, where he served as an infantryman and as a member of a Combined Action Platoon. He is also the author of the military fantasy series Demontech.

www.novelier.com

DAN CRAGG enlisted in the U.S. Army in 1958 and retired with the rank of sergeant major twenty-two years later. He is the author of *Inside the VC and the NVA* (with Michael Lee Lanning), *Top Sergeant* (with William G. Bainbridge), and a Vietnam War novel, *The Soldier's Prize*. He recently retired from his work as an analyst for the Department of Defense.

ABOUT THE TYPE

This book was set in ITC Berkeley Oldstyle, designed in 1983 by Tony Stan. It is a variation of the University of California Old Style, which was created by Frederick Goudy. While capturing the feel and traits of its predecessor, ITC Berkeley Oldstyle shows influences from Kennerly, Goudy Old Style, Deepdene, and Booklet Oldstyle, all of which were also designed by Goudy. It is characterized by its calligraphic weight stress, and its x-height, now described as classic, is smaller than most other ITC designs of the day. The generous ascenders and descenders provide variations in text color, easy legibility, and an overall inviting appearance.